Mountain Shadows

An Adirondack Novel
of Courage, Danger, and Love

by
Patricia Reiss Brooks

Pinto  Press

Mt. Kisco, NY

Printed in the United States of America.

For information address Pinto Press, 35 Stewart Place, Ste. 503, Mt. Kisco, NY 10549

Publisher's Cataloging-in-Publication
(Provided by Quality Books, Inc.)

Brooks, Patricia Reiss.
   Mountain shadows : an Adirondack novel of courage, danger, and love / by Patricia Reiss Brooks.
      p. cm.
   LCCN 2004107333
   ISBN 0-9755677-0-5

   1. Tuberculosis—Fiction. 2. Prohibition—Fiction. 3. Adirondack Mountains Region (N.Y.)—Fiction. I. Title.

PS3602.R6446M68 2004   813'.6
                              QB133-2056

10 9 8 7 6 5 4 3 2 1

Mountain Shadows

Dedication

Mountain Shadows is dedicated to two brave women who began their lives in New York City and came to the mountains as very young women seeking "the Cure": one for herself, the other for her husband.

Evelyn Bellak was 16 years old when she arrived at the Ray Brook Sanatorium to take the cure. I came to know her very well through her faithful entries in a 1918 daily diary. Although I read many biographies and autobiographies of those sent to the mountains in hopes of curing, for me the process came to life when I met Evelyn. Her diary stopped before the end of the year and I always wondered why. Did she return home to New York City a healthy woman? Or did tuberculosis claim her?

Daisy Reiss, my mother, traveled to the Adirondacks in 1925 with her year-old son and a husband stricken with tuberculosis. Only after poring over Evelyn's diary did I come to understand my mother's life as a young parent caring for a tubercular husband. My mother's fortitude made it possible to raise a family of six healthy children, and to help her husband successfully recover, all in the days before antibiotics.

Acknowledgments

It took four years to thoroughly research the many facets of *Mountain Shadows*. I never could have written knowledgeably if it weren't for the advice generously given by many wonderful people. I want to thank:

The helpful people at Historic Saranac Lake for locating several former TB patients who read an early draft of the book, making sure it was authentic.

The Franklin County Historical and Museum Society for locating needed information on Captain Broadfield and the Black Horse Brigade, including Sgt. Henry Schermerhorn.

Troop B of the New York State Troopers for allowing me access to their museum and archives in Ray Brook.

The Saranac Lake Free Library for allowing me access to Evelyn Bellak's diary and dozens of other items.

The Lake Placid Library for pointing out many biographies and autobiographies of TB patients.

Irma McLoud, who shared with me her firsthand knowledge of what it was like to work at the Lake Placid Club as a single woman in the twenties.

David Morton and his antique car club for steering me in the right direction in choosing the right car for the job and instructing me in its operation.

My big brother, Tom Reiss, for his firsthand tales of life in the Adirondacks in those bygone years, particularly how the snow was "rolled," not plowed.

My brother, Peter Reiss, and his wife, Agnes, who, in addition to supplying backup information on cars of the twenties, gave me a main character for this novel: Agnes's father is the prototype of the book's Joe Devlin.

My sister, Mary Watson. Time and again during the years of researching and writing, I asked Mary how I might find out about something. Time and again she came up with the right answer.

My brother, Paul Reiss, and his wife, Rosemary, and my brother, Bob Reiss, and his wife, Joan, for putting me up when I had to be in the Adirondacks to conduct research.

Although all the people mentioned above were necessary for my research, this novel never would have been written if it weren't for Bob Brooks, my husband, who relentlessly insisted I learn how to use a computer, and asked almost daily, "How's the book coming?"

1

November 1925

"How did you heft him in the sleigh?" Emma puffed with the effort of carrying the unconscious man into her house.

"Drug him through the snow. Got a rope under his arms and winched him up. Had a devil of a time of it with Gus as skittish as a colt."

It took the two of them to settle the man in the spare room off Emma's kitchen. She shook the snow off the man's raccoon coat and buried her face in its softness before draping it over the rocking chair.

"Don't like the sound of that coughing one bit." She watched her husband remove the young man's trousers and union suit.

"Look at that now. Soaked through to the skin. What's that chain in his hand?" Emma stepped up to the bed and worked a small chain out of the man's clenched fist. "Why it's one of them prayer beads," she said, eyeing the cross before placing the beads on the nightstand. The kettle started to whistle and she hurried off to fill hot water bottles.

"The boy's feet are frostbitten," Clarence said, when his wife returned with a hot water bottle in each hand. Making mother hen noises, Emma tucked a rubber bottle on either side of his legs and studied her patient's toes. Already they were the telltale blue-black and swollen.

"Do you think you can save them?"

"Depends how long they've been this way. Doesn't look good. How are his fingers?"

"Seem fine."

"You start working a little kerosene into his feet and I'll fry up onions for the poultice. Mind you now, keep him warm."

Emma stepped out on the kitchen porch and selected an armful of limb wood. After stoking the cookstove, she opened the draft to the bake position before hurrying down to the root cellar for an apron full of onions.

Eyes watering, she sliced onion after onion into a cast iron skillet. She dipped her hand in a container of water and sent the droplets dancing on the stove top. Adding a sizeable dollop of lard to the onions, she set the mixture to cooking.

While the onions sizzled, sending their pungent aroma through the farmhouse, Emma pulled a chair to the counter and climbed up. Glancing quickly over her shoulder, she opened a cupboard and groped along the back of a top shelf. Soon she emerged with a milk bottle filled with an amber liquid. Emma clutched it to her and went back to stirring her onions. She located an empty sugar bag in her pantry and stuffed it with the cooked onions. Picking up a spoon and the milk bottle she hurried to the sick room with the sugar bag of steaming onions.

Clarence looked up from his task of gently massaging kerosene into the boy's black toes. "Thought we was out of moonshine," he said, eyeing the milk bottle.

"And wouldn't this boy would be in a fine fix if I let you help yourself to it?"

Clarence moved away to let Emma place her sugar bag poultice on their patient's chest. She covered him with several blankets and, pulling up a chair, settled down to work spoonfuls of moonshine down his throat. After a time she set the moonshine aside and sat quietly observing her patient. Satisfied, she stood and turned down the light, preparing to leave.

Clarence stood in the door while Emma pulled the third blanket up around the man's shoulders.

"What's he mumbling?" he asked.

"Can't rightly make it out, except for 'Saranac'. Seems like he wants to get there real bad." Suddenly she jerked her hands away from the covers like she had touched a hot pot on her stove. "You don't suppose he's one of them lungers on his way to cure? Listen to him cough! Lord God, get him out of here, Clarence, before we both catch it." Emma pushed by her husband to the safety of the kitchen, her apron held protectively over her nose.

"Aw, Em. We dasn't turn him out in a snowstorm. He'd surely die. I'll call Doc Bixler."

"Are you out of your senses? Doc can't get through on a night like this."

"He could surely tell us what to do." Clarence cranked the phone on the kitchen wall.

"Doc says he'll come by in the morning," he reported to Emma, who cowered like a cornered mouse as far as possible from the sickroom. Every time she heard coughing, she covered her face with her apron.

"He says to wash our hands after tending him and keep his dishes separate. Boil them. Same goes for the bedding."

"I'm glad you listened so good, because any tending that man gets is going to come from you. And till he's out of here, you're not welcome upstairs."

"Take a deep breath." The young man obeyed the doctor, flinching at the cold stethoscope. Clarence stood at his post in the door and Emma drank coffee at her scrubbed kitchen table.

"Lungs are clear," Doc pronounced. He stuffed the stethoscope into his black bag. "Another one of Emma's onion poultices wouldn't hurt. Helps keep them clear."

"What about them frostbit feet?" Clarence asked. "I rubbed kerosene on them."

"Main thing is to keep them warm. Soak them once or twice a day in warm water. Mind you, not hot water. A kerosene rub for another day or two wouldn't hurt." Turning to the patient, the doctor continued, "The best thing you can do is stay put and rest, young man."

"Must get to Saranac Lake." He attempted to sit up, found it too difficult, and sank back on the plump pillows. Determined dark eyes burned in his fevered face.

"If you'd like to arrive in Saranac in something other than a pine box, you best stay put. I'll be back the end of the week. I expect to find you right here."

"No money, can't pay."

"Don't worry about that." Doc Bixler closed his bag and left the room.

"Any more coffee, Emma?" The doctor sat down at the table.

"Shouldn't you be washing your hands?" Emma poured coffee from an enameled pot and set out sugar and the thick cream she had separated yesterday.

"It's all right, Emma. His lungs are clear. Doesn't have consumption. Just needs rest and your good cooking."

"How can you be sure? Don't you need that machine to take pictures?"

"X-rays? That's the big city way. 'Round here, you learn to cultivate a certain sense for a consumptive-like character. There's no gurgling in his lungs."

Emma nodded.

"You wouldn't like me to finish off that pie so you could wash the plate, would you?"

"I'm sorry, Doc. Don't know where my manners went. It scared me silly thinking Clarence brought home a lunger." Emma slid the pie onto a plate and cut a big chunk of cheddar cheese to go with it.

"More coffee?"

Doc nodded, his mouth full of pie.

"Suppose we ought to talk about paying you," Clarence said, sitting down at the table. "'Spect we could dress out a couple of chickens."

"Not necessary. You know, that fur coat of his is the kind I've seen on bootleggers tearing down to New York City from the Canadian border." He forked the last of the pie into his mouth. "Likely as not," he continued, talking around the pie, "this young fellow was the loser in a run-in with a competitive bootlegger. This fella, did he tell you his name?"

"Joe Devlin."

"The way I figure it," the doctor waved his fork at Clarence," Joe was probably on his way to the city with a load of booze and got highjacked. Once Joe is back in business, and believe me, these rum runners have their ways of getting fast cars, he could show his gratefulness by lightening his load a little as he passes my house."

It took several days of Emma plying Joe with her chicken soup and egg-rich custards before he had the strength to sit up. Although Emma piled blankets on his bed, Joe's tortured feet stuck out in the open, propped on pillows. Blisters sprouted on his feet and toes; Doc had instructed Emma to keep the blankets from touching them. He warned about infection.

Morning and night Clarence's big calloused hands soaked Joe's feet in soapy lukewarm water and gently dried each toe before placing small wads of soft flannel between them. The second day after Doc's visit, Joe Devlin's head cleared enough to ask about his car.

"There weren't no car," Clarence said.

"Got to find my car. Hundred miles left to go."

"What kind of car?"

"Model T. . .open roadster. . .Alice waiting. . ." Joe drifted off.

"Where you driving to?" Clarence nudged Joe's shoulder and cocked his ear to hear his mumblings.

"Alice. . .Saranac. . ."

"Who's Alice?"

"Quit pestering that boy," Emma said, entering the room with a hot water bottle.

Clarence stood up and hooked his thumbs in his overall straps. "Says he has a car."

"Hadn't you best go look for it?" Emma groped under the blankets and slid out the cooled water bottle.

"'Spect I could ask around."

That night, Joe was able to sit up and eat supper, pausing to rest after each mouthful. "Thank you," he said. "For everything."

"Found your car," Clarence said. "A good stretch back from where I found you. Don't seem a likely car to take into the mountains, what with winter commencing."

"Couldn't afford anything better."

The farm couple listened as Joe told his story of placing his wife, Alice, on the train in New York City for the twelve hour trip to Saranac Lake. Emma caressed the thick luxurious fur of Joe's coat as she listened to his story. Her rocker creaked comfortingly on the bare floor.

"She has tuberculosis," Joe said. "Any chance of getting better will be by taking the cure up in those mountains. They say she'll have to stay a year or more."

"How come you didn't drive her in your car?" Emma wanted to know.

"It's only twelve hours by train. Days by car." Joe stopped to catch his breath and reached for the hot tea Emma kept on the nightstand.

"The doctor was really worried because she coughed up blood," Joe continued. "In my open roadster Alice wouldn't have any protection from the weather. Her doctor said she wasn't strong enough to handle the trip. 'Specially seeing the car isn't big enough for her to lie down."

"Seems it would have been a mite wiser for you to take the train with your wife. Seeing winter's setting in," Clarence said. He pulled a checked handkerchief from a pocket and blew his nose noisily.

"No money for two tickets." Joe's long fingers gripped the covers.

"Seems likely a coat like yours would bring the price of a ticket or two," Clarence challenged.

"Not my coat. Mr. Bingham's," he loaned it to me." Joe pressed his fingers against his closed eyes.

Emma jumped to her feet. "See what you've done to Joe with all your gabbing?" She took a piece of toweling and dipped it in the water jug and pressed it about Joe's face. "He'll tell us his story when he's good and ready."

"Didn't mean no harm," Clarence said, and turned to leave.

"Wait," Joe said. "I'd like to finish."

Emma helped him sip more of her tea. Then he started again:

"I set out a few days later in my car. Not the best car I ever worked on, but I thought I could keep it going. I was making such good time till it started to snow." Joe passed a hand down his face. "Then I had a devil of a time keeping the car from going off the road. Constantly changing from high to low. Probably was the last straw for the bands. Just gave out. Pushed it off the road and started to walk. My feet got so wet and cold I couldn't feel them."

He remembered walking along and fingering the metal rosary he kept in a pocket of the fur coat. When he found he couldn't concentrate, he began saying the Hail Marys out loud, turning his face up against the wet snow.

"When the wind came up I couldn't take any more," Joe recalled, prodding himself along by bringing to mind Alice as he last saw her through the train window, coughing into a handkerchief. He promised her he'd see her through this thing.

"Never saw a soul after that. Snow was so heavy, couldn't make out any houses either. I kept thinking if I could just rest out of the wind, down in one of the snowdrifts, I'd get warm." He remembered rebuking himself for being such a Milquetoast about the cold when Alice would be expected to sit out in it every day.

"Tried to find a house where they might let me spend the night in the barn, but the snow was so blinding I could hardly follow the road." Joe swallowed hard, recalling how the snow had overpowered him. He was drained of the last remnant of the will to go on.

"I remember burrowing into a drift." He paused, his heavy brows almost meeting in a frown. "Don't remember anything after that till I woke up in this bed."

"Clarence brung you home," Emma said. "You've been here eight days."

"Eight days! I thought to be in Saranac Lake by now."

"You've got some mending yet to do," Emma said, getting up to fetch more of the tea she'd left steeping on the back of the stove. She had doctored it with honey and whiskey.

"Here." She offered it to Joe. "You keep working at this."

Joe sipped the strong brew, then wrapped his hands around the cup.

"So, you're really not a bootlegger?" Emma asked, after hearing how Joe had acquired the coon coat from Jake Bingham, a man who brought his Pierce-Arrow to Joe to maintain. The coat was loaned to Joe for the trip.

"No, Ma'am. If I had the money some of those bootleggers flash around, I'd had driven Alice to Saranac Lake in a fancy closed car." Joe paused to catch his breath, allowing himself to get caught up in the daydream of having a booze runner's wealth. He looked out the window, imagining different circumstances. "I would have bought both of us fur coats for the trip. Paid to have her cure in the best cure cottage in town, too." And tell my father-in-law what he could do with his three hundred dollars. He kept that to himself.

It still rankled Joe that Mr. Lattimer wouldn't have anything to do with his daughter after she married Joe. Somehow his father-in-law learned about Alice's need to take the cure at Saranac and sent the required down payment directly to Alice's doctor. As if Joe couldn't take care of Alice! Joe closed his eyes on the memory and turned to face the farm couple who had rescued him.

"It's all behind you now," Clarence said. "You might try walking some on those feet in the morning."

"Don't go rushing things," Emma scolded. "He's going to take a lot of building up before he can leave here. Come on out of here now so he can settle down for the night." Clarence followed Emma out to the kitchen.

"Such a good-looking young man," Emma said to her husband as she poked at the fire in the stove. "Sure am glad he's no bootlegger. Course he could use some filling out.

"It's not right for one so young to have such burdens," she continued. "He should be out driving around in some fancy roadster, wearing his raccoon coat." Emma adjusted the draft on the stovepipe. "And not taking a hike in the middle of winter. And such sadness in the dark eyes of his. Looks like all the misery of the world has settled on those thin shoulders."

"Seems to me," Clarence said, "any woman who can get a man to walk hundreds of miles into the mountains must be some looker." He wrapped a gray wool scarf about his neck and sat down to pull on his barn boots. "Why else would a good-looking fellow damn near get himself killed to get to some lunger up in those mountains?"

"I declare, you can be dense at times." Emma turned to look at her husband. "Ever cross your mind Joe just might love that poor girl?"

A week later, Joe, dressed in a pair of Clarence's coveralls, looked up from where he was tinkering under the hood of Clarence's big tractor when he heard Doc's Chevrolet backfiring as it came down the road.

"I don't recall saying you could get out of bed," Doc said.

"All cured," Joe grinned.

"I thought that was my decision to make."

"I'm a darn sight better than that Chevrolet you're driving. Let me have a look." Joe walked gingerly toward the car on his frostbitten feet. "Sounds like the timing could use some adjustment."

"It's all right, Doc," Clarence said. "Joe here's a mechanic. Got himself a job up at that Lake Placid Club working on all them fancy touring cars."

"If that's the case, I might as well see what Emma has cooking." Doc rubbed his hands together and headed for the house.

Before Doc left, his belly full of Emma's stew and homemade bread, he made a big to-do about thumping on Joe's chest and carefully checking each toe.

"I'm leaving tomorrow morning," Joe said.

"Got the Model T running, have you?"

"Not a chance. Just me and my two feet from here on."

"I can't stop you, young man. At least try to set yourself a reasonable pace. Get a good night's rest." Doc stuffed his stethoscope back in the worn black bag.

"Your way with automobiles should earn you a hot meal and a warm bed just about anywhere." Doc reached in his pocket and retrieved a rumpled scrap of paper. A search through another pocket produced the stub of a pencil. The doctor scribbled a few words on the paper.

"Keene is the last village you'll come to before climbing on up through the Cascade pass," Doc said. "I want you to look up Dr. Decker. He has a Chevy a year older than mine. Tell him you'll go over it in exchange for a checkup." Doc handed Joe the paper, looking him straight in the eye.

"The pass isn't something to fool around with in winter even if you're in the best of health. Could be the snows have already closed it." Doc wrapped a plaid scarf around his neck and, securing it with his chin, pulled on his coat. "That little woman of yours might find herself waiting a lifetime for you if you try to tackle it before Dr. Decker says you're ready for it."

"Thanks, Doc." Joe carefully folded the paper before placing it in his shirt pocket. "I'll look him up."

As soon as Doc's Chevrolet purred out of the farmyard, Joe asked Emma's permission to use the telephone.

"Go right ahead. You may have to wait some for Nell Simon to hang up. Of all the people in Warrensburg I sure wish we didn't have Nell on our party line. Makes me wonder how she gets her work done with all the gabbing she does."

Some minutes went by before all the connections were made and the telephone rang in Dr. Hayes's house in Saranac Lake. The doctor was out on calls, his wife said. Would Mr. Devlin care to leave a message?

"Dr. Hayes was supposed to meet my wife at the Riverside Inn. I was hoping the doctor could tell me how she made the trip. Do you know my wife? She has wavy black hair and. . ."

"I'm sorry, Mr. Devlin, but I don't get involved with my husband's patients."

"Oh, it's just that she was so sick and she never made a trip all by herself. Could the doctor tell her I've been held up and will be there in another week?"

"Certainly. And the doctor's patient is Mrs. Devlin, then?"

"Yes, Ma'am. Alice Devlin. I know she'll be worrying something happened to me. Please tell her I'm fine, and I'll be with her just as soon as I can."

"I'll see the doctor gets your message, Mr. Devlin. Goodbye, now."

"Goodbye." Joe stood looking at the phone, not wanting to break contact. He wanted to say so much more, like how was Alice's cough and please tell her I love her.

Clarence and Emma had been good to him, he thought, but he had wasted so much time here. A hundred miles to go and winter getting snowier and colder by the day. He had to give up on the Ford and leave it behind the barn where Clarence and his horse had towed it.

On top of everything there were his frostbitten toes to contend with. Daily he practiced various ways of stepping on his feet to alleviate the pain. He experimented with layering his socks to insulate his toes against the misery of putting pressure on them. Nothing worked. He might as well accept the pain as his constant companion.

"House is going to seem kind of empty without Joe," Emma said, as she and Clarence prepared for bed the night before Joe planned to leave. "Sure wish he'd stay another week or two so I could get him filled out a bit."

"What do you say if I come up with some reason for taking the sleigh up to Chestertown tomorrow? It's only ten miles but every ten miles that boy doesn't have to walk on those feet should ease his burden a bit."

"Good thinking!" Emma smiled and pulled the goose down comforter up to her chin.

Old Gus's steamy breath billowed out on the frosty dawn. Joe pulled himself up onto the seat beside Clarence and wrapped the coon coat about his thin legs. Emma handed up her bundle of pork sandwiches and a big block of cheese.

"Care for your toes now, hear?" Emma said.

"Yes, Ma'am."

"Got your extra socks pinned to your union suit like I showed you?"

"Sure do. No more wet feet for me!"

Emma had shown Joe how to pin his extra wool socks to the inside of his union suit, to keep warm with his body heat. Whenever his frostbitten toes got wet, he was to change socks, putting the cold wet ones next to his skin to dry and warm up. Joe shivered at the thought.

"You two have been swell. When Alice is cured, we'll stop here on our way home. I want her to meet the folks that saved her husband's life." Joe smiled down at Emma.

"You do that. I'm sure she's a lovely girl."

"Oh, she is, Ma'am. You know when she was well, her blue eyes would sparkle just like sunlight dancing off the water." Joe's expressive mouth hardened into a grim line of determination. "I'm going to do whatever it takes to get that sparkle back in my Alice's eyes."

2

"*G*uten morgen!" Hilda strode into Alice's room and set the breakfast tray on the dresser."Ach, such a face. TB feeds less willingly on cheerful tissues than upon the gloomy." Hilda's voice boomed out like a tuba as she went about closing the windows.

Rule number one, Alice thought, recalling yesterday when the woman had opened the rules pamphlet and jabbed at a sentence on the first page. "Rest," she'd quoted from the printed page, "is the basic treatment of all tuberculosis. This means physical as well as emotional rest. Emotional excitement or unrest frequently causes more harm than physical exercise. You will erase all unhappy thoughts from your mind." Hilda's uncompromising bearing left no doubt that Alice would find herself in a snowbank if she didn't conform.

Hilda was a tall, powerfully built brunette of some indeterminable age. It appeared the Almighty had chosen an ax to hew her large coarse face. While He was at it, He fashioned a perpetual smile on her wide mouth. Thick eyebrows nearly obscured her lively hazel eyes. Her broad shouldered, six foot frame and immense strength made it possible for her to move patients about with ease.

Yesterday, when Dr. Hayes brought Alice to Conifer Cottage in his Franklin, Hilda had been standing on the porch. Alice was intimidated by the woman's size and thought she looked like a prison matron. She introduced herself as Hilda Guenther, who owned and operated Conifer Cottage with her sister, Ursula.

"You'll feel better after a proper Conifer Cottage breakfast." Hilda set the tray on the bed. Alice's stomach rebelled at the sight of a bowl of steaming oatmeal and pitcher of cream plus soft boiled eggs and a mound of buttered toast.

"I couldn't begin to eat. . ."

"Nonsense. Poor nutrition increases susceptibility. Dr. Hayes believes fat is insurance. Look at me!" Hilda postured her ample body. "I've helped dozens of consumptives to cure, and there's nothing wrong with my lungs. My sister Ursula will be along to get you prettied up before rolling you out on the porch for your morning cure. Don't dally over breakfast."

Alice resolutely picked up her spoon. "I will do whatever it takes to go home."

"Have you studied the rules?" Hilda asked. She picked up a pamphlet from the nightstand.

"Yes, Ma'am."

"Then you know there is a statement to be signed." Hilda opened the pamphlet to the last page and placed it on Alice's tray, then turned and left the room. Alice read the statement: "I have read and agree to the foregoing rules."

Dozing with the spoon in her hand while her half eaten oatmeal cooled into sticky lumps, Alice opened her eyes to see Ursula smiling down at her.

"*Guten morgen*, Alice. How was your first night at Conifer Cottage?"

Her tight bands of loneliness loosened slightly at the woman's caring manner. Unlike her sister, whom Alice heard trumpeting the prescribed cheer through the halls and rooms of Conifer Cottage yesterday, Ursula quietly appeared at Alice's bedside several times, offering a clean hankie for a cough and a willing ear when she found Alice weeping out her loneliness.

"It was so quiet I found it hard to sleep," Alice found herself confiding to Ursula. "I don't believe I coughed once all night."

"It's the air. When you do feel the need to cough something up, use this sputum cup," Ursula said, indicating a small metal jar fitted with a cardboard liner on the nightstand. "The lab will test it for bacteria."

"Every day?"

"Yes. If they find bacteria it means you're positive. Positive patients are very contagious. We'll collect the cup every day to wash it with carbolic solution." Ursula bustled about gathering washcloth, soap and toothbrush.

"You've probably already read it in the rules, but expectorating in handkerchiefs or in the washbowl is strictly forbidden. My, but we're talking the morning away! My sister will be upset if I don't have you outside curing."

Hard to believe she's Hilda's sister, Alice thought. Ursula was at least a foot shorter than Hilda. Her faded yellow hair was drawn tightly off her face and secured in a knot on the top of her head. And she didn't speak with her sister's harsh German accent. A perpetual smile appeared to be the only physical characteristic the sisters shared.

"Such lovely curls. And as soft as down," Ursula said, gently brushing the snarls out of Alice's black hair. "So nice to see long hair instead of those silly bobs."

"Joe wants it long. He took over brushing it since I've been sick. I think he's afraid I might cut it all off. It's such an effort to care for now."

"Let's get you bundled up and out on the porch. What a glorious day to cure, the air so crisp and still." Ursula piled on heavy blankets, plumped pillows and offered Alice woolen mittens for her hands. She tucked her in so tightly that Alice felt like a letter in a sealed envelope.

She was amazed at the ease with which Ursula rolled her iron bed through the French doors onto a tiny open air curing porch. The second floor porch was part of the roof of the expansive first floor porch, which wrapped around two sides of the house. The porch was surrounded by a solid waist-high railing.

It's true, Alice thought, as she watched Ursula slide open the glass windows that ran across the entire length of the porch from the top of the railing to the roof. I'm going to lay outside in the cold all day!

"Two nice young ladies, Charlotte and Lilly, share this porch with you," Ursula said. "Can you smell our balsam tree?" Ursula smoothed Alice's blankets again. Exhausted from the morning routine, she could barely manage a nod. She hoped she wasn't expected to talk to the other patients.

"Balsam has special medicine in its aroma. Get it into your poor lungs and it'll chase the germs away in no time. But no deep breaths."

She waved her index finger. "You must let your lungs sip at the air, like a cup of hot tea."

Sipping balsam-spiced air, she drifted into sleep.

Downstairs, Ursula joined her sister and the day girl in cleaning up the kitchen after serving breakfast to their eight patients, all young women.

"Dr. Hayes called," Hilda said. She was up to her red elbows in hot soapy dishwater. "He read the new girl's X-rays. She may deteriorate very quickly."

"Oh, no! Are they so very terrible?" Ursula pursed her lips.

"Ja, not good. Her right lung is three-quarters covered with speckles." Hilda pulled her arms out of the dishwater. "And that's the good one. The left has a heavy black area on top with a hole in the center."

"We've cured worse, Sister."

"Ja. But it will years take. Dr. Hayes didn't think her family has money for a private cure. Prepare yourself. She may go to the State Hospital."

Laughter nudged Alice toward wakefulness. "Sssh, Lilly," a voice admonished. "You'll wake the new girl."

Alice turned in the direction of the voices and saw her porch-mates.

"Oh, don't worry so. I hear Miss Twinkle-Toes coming up the stairs for midday temps." Lilly, the young woman closest to Alice, applied blood red lipstick to her cupid's bow mouth. Finishing, she peered into a hand mirror and patted her gold marcelled hair.

"Hi," said Lilly. She lay on a white lounge chair, its gracefully curved back supported by delicately carved spokes. One wide arm rest held a magazine.

"Hope we didn't wake you, but we're dying to meet you." She pulled on blue mittens and then tugged a fur robe up to cover her chest. "I'm Lilly, and if you look real hard, you can see Charlotte under that fur robe."

Alice looked past Lilly at the other woman, snuggled up to her shoulders under a rusty brown bear robe. The woman's straight hair looked just like the robe. She smiled feebly at Alice, her dark eyes huge in a pasty white face. Her brown chair was built on much simpler lines than Lilly's. The back was slats of straight wood and the whole chair was supported on six sturdy legs.

These must be what the rulebook calls cure chairs, Alice thought. She recalled reading that once she was allowed to sit up, she could rent one of these for two dollars a week.

"Dr. Hayes, he's our doctor, too, told us your name is Alice Lattimer and you're from New York City. Gosh, I'd give anything to go to New York. Everything exciting happens there. Have you been to the speakeasies?"

"Lilly! New patients must keep talking to a minimum." Charlotte chided.

"It's okay," Alice said. "It's nice to have someone to talk to." She paused to rest her lungs, as the rule book instructed. "But Lattimer is my maiden name. I've been married three years, and my last name is Devlin. And no, I've never been to a speakeasy."

"Oh, another married lady! Charlotte's married. Can you believe she has three little girls? Do you have children?"

"No. But we want to as soon as I'm cured."

"Tell us about your husband," Charlotte said.

"Well, his name is Joseph Devlin. He's a very good mechanic. He fought in France during the war."

"What does he look like?" Lilly asked.

"I think I fell in love with his brown eyes first. They say so much without Joe ever speaking one word."

"And you liked what they said?"

"So much. From the beginning he was so attentive to everything I said. And he delights in the simplest of things. It all shines in his eyes. They're as sweet and warm as a cup of hot chocolate."

Hilda strode onto the porch, thrusting thermometers into the other girls' mouths.

"Again?" Alice asked when presented with a thermometer.

"Ja. Three times a day," Hilda said, sliding shut large sections of the porch's glass windows. "Dinner's up in a minute."

"Well, ladies, I'm off to dine in downstairs." Lilly tugged at her covers the second Hilda retrieved her thermometer.

Alice was surprised to see she was fully dressed. The fine wool jacket hung straight from Lilly's thin shoulders almost to her shiny red fingertips. The pleated plaid skirt swung about her legs as she hurried off to dinner.

"Getting dressed up means so much to Lilly," Charlotte said. "I'm glad she's well enough to go down to dinner." They watched Lilly sashay off the porch.

"Do we go back in our rooms to eat?" Alice asked.

"Goodness, no. Be thankful Hilda shut the windows. Eight hours of air a day, you know. Hilda will open the windows again after we eat."

"I suppose that's another rule."

"Actually, it's half a rule. The other half decrees all of Saranac will nap between two and four o'clock. They're strict about it, too. Drivers who honk their horns during nap time get fines. Even up patients like Lilly must nap."

The two porchmates fell silent while they concentrated on their dinners. Alice found her mouth watering at the good smells coming from her tray. One had to eat quickly before meals cooled in the frosty air.

Alice yearned to talk to Charlotte about this disease that had forced them both to leave their homes. It wasn't necessary for her to hide this terrible thing from those around her anymore, and Alice so hoped to have long satisfying talks with her porchmates. Unfortunately, the ten pages of rules decreed it wasn't to be.

She put down her fork and turned to the page in the rules. There it was in bold capital letters: "Conversation between patients as to their disease, their symptoms or any subject relating to illness is discouraged."

"Don't let the rules get you down," Charlotte said. "I felt the same way when I first came. Before long they simply become a way of life."

3

Sure feels good to be on my way again, Joe thought, after leaving Clarence in Chestertown. The sun was as high in the brilliant sky as it would get on a December day. Fortunately it stayed cold enough so the snow squeaked under his feet, making a soft, dry cushion for his toes. Joe tried not to dwell on the pain of each step, but there wasn't much to take his mind off it on this stretch of road.

Clarence and Emma said he should be able to make Olmstedville by night. They told him how to find the place Clarence's cousins farmed. Emma was sure Betty and Stanley Yungman would take him in.

The road followed Schroon Lake for a time. Snow-covered cottages dotted the western bank. As he rounded a bend, the forest stopped before a windswept clearing leading toward the lake. On a rise above the lake stood a rambling white inn with boarded up cabins huddled at the edge of the forest.

Joe approached cobblestone pillars with a sign arched between them announcing the entrance to Lake Edge Lodge. He stopped, trying to visualize it with sharp scented petunias and geraniums nodding in a summer breeze off the lake. The sweet smelling lawns would be neatly shorn. And there'd be laughter, he thought, as he resumed his painful, short-strided journey.

It was laughter that had first drawn Joe to Alice, and it was at a summer lake resort, much like the boarded-up inn, where he first heard it.

Joe had taken a job at the inn doing everything from busboy to yard work. He was on a ladder washing the windows for a fussy guest who complained the view of the lake was spoiled by her dirty windows. A girl's laughter, lighthearted and merry, came to him from somewhere on the lake.

Joe took a few quick swipes at the glass and hastily came down off the ladder, ignoring the guest's indignant tapping on the window.

"Young man!" The woman hung her pigeon-like bosom out the window, calling down to Joe. "This is not a satisfactory job."

"I know, Mrs. Ainsworth," Joe said, annoyed that the woman's voice cut roughly into the laughter. "I need more rags."

He stuck his ladder behind the hydrangea bushes and hurried down to the boathouse to investigate the source of such glee. It came skipping across the water again, alluring and so full of good spirits. Joe took a rag from his pocket and pretended to wipe the windshield of a power launch while he located the laughter coming from a canoe zig-zagging toward shore.

A small dark-haired girl sat in the bow of the inn's canoe. She lightly swiped at the surface of the lake with her paddle. Her companion thrust his paddle deeply into the lake, alternating sides, causing the canoe to stagger toward shore. Joe stood at the water's edge until the canoe nudged the shore.

"Hello," the girl said, looking up at Joe with the merriest round blue eyes he had ever seen.

Joe couldn't think of anything to say, but he did think of helping her out of the boat. The girl before him was hatless and smelled of sunshine. He lifted her onto the shore. Her black hair formed a cloud of curls about a delicate oval face dominated by the marvelous blue eyes.

"Come on, Alice," her companion said. Left by himself to clamber out of the canoe, he scowled at Joe, who still held the girl's hand.

"Thank you." The girl's small rosy lips parted in a smile over even white teeth. Lightly, as fleeting as the stroke of a butterfly's wing, she pressed Joe's hand and turned to join the impatient boy. Joe's heart slammed against his chest when she squeezed his hand. He watched her climb the rise to the inn. Her hair, held in a floppy blue ribbon at the nape of her neck, almost touched her waist.

"Alice." Joe softly tested the name and turned to pull the canoe farther up on the shore. It was the summer he fell in love.

Emerging from his daydream, Joe looked about him. Another couple of hours before dark, he judged. Clarence didn't think Joe would have any difficulty making it to his cousin's farm by night. He hoped Clarence was right. This first day back on the road was tiring. He was beginning to sweat with fatigue under Bingham's heavy coon coat.

Occasionally a new Packard or Marmon came speeding out of the north, swirling snow in Joe's face. He had given up trying to get a ride from the bootleggers on their return trips to Canada. Some slowed, studying him with stern faces, but always raced on without stopping.

Joe heard a voice in the woods to the left. Scanning the forest, he saw a team of work horses plodding out of the woods, their driver walking behind, leaning his weight against the lines. At the forest's edge, the driver turned and halted his team, then proceeded to back them into place behind a long bobsled. By the time Joe caught up, the man had the pole through the ring on the horses' neck yoke.

"Hello," Joe called. The man bent over behind his team, hooking the off horse's tugs to the whippletree. He stared at Joe over the horse's big rump, taking in Joe's coat and stiff-legged gait. He bent to hook the near horse then came around to meet Joe.

"Problems with your car?" the man asked. His greasy brown hair curled around a black knit cap. Unkempt whiskers covered his swarthy face.

"Car? Wish I had a car to have problems with," Joe said. "I'm afraid my transportation is just these two tired feet." Joe shifted uncomfortably from one foot to the other. "Hoped I might get a ride if you're headed toward Olmstedville."

"How come a fella like you doesn't have a car? Trooper take it?"

Joe laughed. "I'm not a bootlegger. Just trying to make it to Yungman's farm tonight. Know where that is?" Around these parts it seemed a coon coat was a badge of a successful bootlegger.

"Yup. Going right by Stanley's." The man pulled himself up to the high seat. "Climb aboard." The team lurched forward, throwing Joe roughly onto the bare board seat.

The man laughed. "They want to get home as bad as me after a week in the woods." Steam rose from the horses' backs. Icicles hung from the long hair on their flanks.

"Looks like Stanley's in the barn," the lumberjack said, as he pulled his team up next to a white farmhouse. The horses protested the unaccustomed stop and began tossing their big heads, sending specks of foam into the cold twilight.

"Thanks for the lift," Joe said, easing off the seat, trying to not land on his toes. He stood for a moment looking at Yungman's farm, deciding what to do. Lights burned in the house and in the big unpainted barn quite a distance behind the house.

Guess I should see if Yungman needs help with chores, he reasoned, before I go asking for a place to stay. He shouldered his pack and headed toward the barn.

"Hello?" Joe called out as he opened the squeaky door to the steamy barn smelling of ammonia and silage. He looked in at the bony rumps of a long row of cows. A few, chewing contentedly, turned their heads within the confines of their stanchions to look at Joe.

A tall, thin man dressed in stained coveralls and knee high rubber boots walked toward Joe. He carried a stainless steel pail of foamy milk in each hand.

"You must be the fella walking to Saranac," he said. "Been 'specting you." He walked right past Joe and continued down the aisle.

"I'm Joe Devlin," Joe said to the man's back. "Emma said . . . "

"Know all about you," Stanley said over his shoulder. "We'll go to the house directly."

Joe followed Stanley to the brightly lit milk room and stood by while the farmer went through his routine. "Something I could do to help?"

"There's a broom alongside that door you came through."

Joe had swept down to the back of the barn when Stanley came out of the milk room turning lights off behind him.

"That'll do," he said, reaching for Joe's broom. He hung the broom next to the door and waited for Joe to go through before him.

A thin crescent moon hung in a starry sky. Snow crunched under Stanley's boots as he took long heavy strides toward the house.

"I disremember winter setting in so fierce in December."

Joe followed him as he clumped up the steps to the wood porch off the kitchen. He sat on the woodpile and started to tug off his boots.

"Wife don't take kindly to messing up her kitchen."

Joe dropped his pack and took off his boots as Stanley suggested. He followed the farmer into the kitchen. A small plump woman stood at the stove sipping from a long-handled wooden spoon. Her white hair was pulled into a neat knot on top of her head.

She turned as the men entered, bringing the cold night air with them. A smile lit her round face when she saw Joe standing in his stocking feet behind her husband.

"You made it," she said. "Emma thought you'd be here before dark. Come set and warm yourself."

"Thank you, Ma'am,." Joe said, moving toward the rocking chair the woman indicated. "Sure nice to get in out of the cold."

"Call me Betty," she said, standing before him. "Emma said to check your frostbite first thing, said they could probably use a warm soak and clean flannels."

It pleased and embarrassed Joe to have this kindly stranger tending his frostbite. Betty let his toes soak in a bowl of warm soapy water while she tore a piece of flannel into tiny bits. Sitting on a stool in front of him, she held first one foot and then the other on her lap, gently drying each toe, then placing a piece of clean flannel between each. Several toes on both feet, where there were blisters, had developed a hard black carapace, like the shells of beetles.

"Do you think I'll lose those black toes?"

"Not if you keep them warm and dry. The black will fall off in bits over the next couple of months." Betty pulled a clean pair of heavy wool socks over his feet. "There," she smiled up at Joe." Go sit in the front room. Put those feet up on the footrest." She went to the stove and gave the pot another stir. "We'll eat soon as the biscuits brown up."

Stanley never looked up from his paper when Joe came in and settled in a chair. Joe picked up a picture of a young man in a uniform that stood on the table next to him. The picture showed the same big-eared, long face as Stanley's, but the young soldier had a wide grin showing a mouthful of uneven teeth. Had to be the Yungmans' son, Joe thought.

"That's my boy," Stanley said from across the room. "Gassed at St. Mihiel. Never lived to see his twentieth birthday."

"I'm sorry," Joe said, not able to think of anything else to say. It wouldn't seem right to mention he was in the war, too. And made it back.

Back to Alice. Waiting for him when he came off the ship. Waving and jumping up and down. He remembered wanting to tell everyone to be quiet so he could hear her laughter again.

He knew he would ask her to marry him as soon as he got a job and put some money aside.

But that was when his love for Alice was uncomplicated, before his parents knew he was serious about a Protestant girl. Before Alice's parents prohibited her from seeing an Irish papist who wanted to be a mechanic.

Joe and Alice eloped. What else could they do with both sets of parents so pig-headed? Even so, Joe ended up with a black eye on his wedding day. He never for a minute thought that the Lattimers would hold on so long to their hate. Especially when Alice's cough was called tuberculosis. He could live without his parents and the Lattimers talking to him. But a daughter was different.

The letter took the cake. He came home one noon to find an opened envelope addressed to Alice Lattimer on the table and Alice crying in the bedroom. When he couldn't get Alice to talk rationally, he picked up the letter.

A Dr. Hayes in Saranac Lake, Joe read, acknowledged receipt of funds from Mr. Lattimer to be used for expenses relating to curing Alice's tuberculosis. Dr. Hayes advised Alice to use "all due haste" and depart to the mountains immediately. He would choose the cure cottage best suited for her after his initial examination.

"Just like your father to assume I can't provide for you!" Joe fumed, pacing the tiny flat. His bitter words were lost on Alice as she sobbed in the next room. Eventually he controlled his rage and joined her.

"Look, Alice," he said, "I don't like your father's interference after completely ignoring us since our marriage." He ran his hand through his hair. "But it does mean you won't have to go to the Ray Brook Sanatorium." Joe lay beside her on their bed. He held her close till her sobs quieted.

"You're no different than my father. You both want me away from here so no one knows you're related to a tubercular."

"Alice! That's not true. I hate your father for what's he's doing to you, but I do believe we both want the best for you." Joe turned on his side so he could look at his wife.

"You have to do what it takes to cure your lungs. I don't want you worrying about anything else." He reached out and pulled her on top of him.

"The doctor said we're not suppose to do this," Alice protested.

"Sssh. I'm doing my job to make sure we have a happy patient." His fingers worked the tiny buttons down the back of her shirtwaist. "Because, you see, everyone knows happy patients have happy lungs." Joe grinned when Alice giggled. "And happy lungs cure faster."

"You'll be late for work," Alice whispered huskily.

"Would you be quiet, woman!"

Their lovemaking reached a higher plane that noon with reassurances sought and lovingly given. They touched and stroked with a new awareness springing from a need to store up memories for the terrifying separation ahead.

4

"You're spilling water on me," Bruce whined.

"Quit yer bellyaching," Earl retorted, struggling to keep his balance on the snow-packed embankment while carrying two pails of water. "I figure this'll be the last bootlegger we hijack before winter sets in. We'll have money to hole up in Lake Placid in style."

"Yeah," Bruce said. "Three squares and something to keep us warm at night, right?" He nudged the other man, setting the water to sloshing. They trudged up the remainder of the steep bank from the stream in silence.

"Real smart of you, Earl, making this hill a regular chutey-chute just by dumping a few pails of water on it." Bruce watched Earl tip his buckets, one at a time. Water spilled out and froze into ice within seconds of touching the snow-packed road. Bruce picked his way down the hill aways before emptying his pails across the road. "What do you think? One more trip for water will do it?"

"Yup. Best part of this whole setup is the suckers never know what's happening till it's all over and their fancy cars shoot off the cliff."

"It'd be more fun if you'd let me finish them off." Bruce pouted like a little boy denied a promised candy.

Finished with icing the hill, the pair retreated off the road to wait for their prey. "You gotta make some sacrifices," Earl said, rolling a cigarette. "This way keeps the troopers off our backs with the accidents looking all natural-like."

"Tell me again what'll it be like in Placid." Bruce pleaded for his favorite story while they waited.

Earl leaned back against the broad trunk of a hundred-foot pine. He exhaled smoke through his nose, watching it rise into the branches. "First, we're gonna take some of the money we get off these bootleggers and spend it on a little hooch, just like they was planning on doing. I figure there's plenty left to get a snug cabin with real beds . . . and real womens, too. Do you hear that?" Earl dropped his cigarette in the snow. They climbed the hill for a closer look.

"Just some guy walking," Bruce said.

"Look at the fur coat he's wearing. Bet he's a bootlegger. Car must of broke down and he's heading into Keene for help. Let's jump him. His pockets got to be filled with green stuff."

The pair crept to the crest of the bank. From behind the trunks of white pines they watched a man trudge past in a slow, stiff-legged gait. At a signal from Earl, Bruce bounded forward, slamming the butt of his rifle against the back of the man's head. Without a sound, their victim slumped in the road. Bruce smiled as tobacco-stained saliva dribbled on his grizzled beard.

"I did good, huh?"

"You did good," Earl said. "Help me turn him over and let's see what he's carrying." They turned the man face up and Earl unbuttoned the coat. Bruce picked him up and shook the man from the coat like he was emptying a sack of potatoes.

"Two lousy dollars." Earl searched the coat and bed roll. He dumped the contents of their victim's pack in the snow and dropped to his knees to sort through the tools and clothes. "Leastways we can take the coat."

"Yeah, we can dress like rich folks when we get to Placid." He stooped to pick up a dull metal chain with a large cross dangling from it. "What's this?"

"Prayer beads," Earl said. "There's them that say a prayer at each little bump on the chain. Keep it. Might bring you good luck or something."

"Can I finish this one off, please?" Bruce tugged the chain over his head.

"He ain't worth a bullet for two dollars of loot. Just drag him off the road. He'll be froze before anyone finds him." The pair quickly strapped on their snowshoes and disappeared into the pines.

From the opposite side of the road, a gray wolf appeared at the edge of the forest. Ears pricked, he raised his nose, testing the air before silently crossing the road to where Joe lay.

"Come, Louie." A small black-haired man emerged from the woods in the same place as the wolf. He knelt in the road and removed his snowshoes. The wolf came obediently to the man's side, whining and pushing his big head under his hand. "So, what have you found?" The man followed the wolf across the road.

"Holy *Mere*," Jean-Paul exclaimed, blessing himself. The little trapper dropped to his knees beside Joe, throwing off the animal hides he had strapped to his back.

"*Comment ça va?*" Jean-Paul slapped Joe's face. Joe moaned and attempted to stop the man. He felt like a dozen bowling balls were smashing around his head. "Ah, *bien*, you have not left us."

Joe opened his eyes and a bolt of pain flashed through his head. Bile rose in his throat. He moaned and tried to shut out the world.

"You cannot rest now, my friend, or very quickly you'll freeze like ice." Joe opened his eyes again and tried to focus on the man kneeling over him. He saw friendly black eyes in a small-boned weathered face. A red toque was pulled down over his ears. There was frost on his neatly trimmed black beard.

"Not a day for a walk without a coat, no?"

Joe looked down. "I must have been robbed. I don't remember anything." He paused, feeling sick every time he shifted his gaze. "Someone stole Mr. Bingham's coat," he groaned. "The letter! Mr. Bingham's letter!" Joe tried to sit up, but the ground swirled around him. "The letter was in the coat."

"I'm afraid your letter is with the coat," the trapper said. "You should be thankful they left you your life, *mon ami*. Where is it you travel?"

"I was hoping to walk as far as Keene before dark." The cold gripped Joe and he shook uncontrollably.

"You don't have far, my friend." Jean-Paul undid the antler buttons on his fur parka and took it off. "Put this on and sit against a tree," he said, helping Joe into the still warm parka and propping him against a tree trunk.

"Move your hands and feet about. I cut a walking stick for you."
Gradually Joe's belly convulsed less with each movement. He risked
opening his eyes again. A cry froze in his throat at his first sight of
the wolf looking down at him with eerie yellow eyes.

"You've met Louie?" Jean-Paul returned just then with a stout
walking stick for Joe.

"He's yours?" Joe relaxed. "Looks like a wolf."

"He is. I shot his mother when she stole bait from my traps. The
she wolf left Louie, a half grown pup, in the forest. I couldn't leave
him there with winter coming on. Like I can't leave you here."

With the help of the walking stick on one side and Jean-Paul's
hand at his other elbow, Joe rose unsteadily to his feet. The forest
swayed before him. Jean-Paul stayed at his elbow, helping him to the
firmer footing of the road.

"You stand still, there. I'll harness Louie." Joe leaned heavily on
his stick and watched Jean-Paul slip a soft deer hide collar about the
wolf's neck and shoulders. With a few practiced motions, he turned
his snowshoes into a travois for the wolf to pull. He stuffed Joe's
meager belongings back in his pack and strapped it and Joe's bedroll
onto the snowshoe travois. The trio moved slowly up the road as a
cold, colorless sun fell below the mountains.

"I think something more than your head is hurting, my friend,
no?"

"My toes are a little frostbitten." Joe's head throbbed and his toes
burned. Every painful step sent jolts of pure agony through his head.
His belly churned. *I've lost Mr. Bingham's coat and the last two dollars I had on earth,* he thought.

Joe's misery was tempered by not having more hills to climb for
now. The road followed the Ausable River that cut through the valley
connecting Keene Valley and Keene.

Before he was ambushed, Joe had enjoyed the river's company,
finding it a kindred spirit as they both hurried to their destinations.
Though it was neither deep nor wide, Joe came to think of the
Ausable as a serious river, its cold black water relentlessly working
around every rock in its path. It seemed as determined to get to
wherever it was heading as he was to reach Alice, no matter how
many rocks got thrown in his path.

"A little of my woman's stew and a warm place to sleep and you'll feel like new man." Jean-Paul led Joe off the road, following a path through a grove of white birch. The thought of being warm all over sounded good.

There, at the edge of a small stream skipping on its way to join the Ausable, stood a tin-roofed log cabin. Joe saw smoke rising straight up from its river-stone chimney. A warm yellow light spilled from the lone window.

"Marie," Jean-Paul called. "We have a hungry guest." The door flung open and Joe saw a small slim woman silhouetted against the cabin's light.

"Evening, Ma'am," was the last thing Joe remembered saying before blacking out.

He woke to the murmur of voices. Cautiously, he opened his eyes and saw shadows from the hearth fire flickering on the ceiling. He flexed his toes and was conscious of being warm all over. Louie padded over and lay his head on Joe's chest.

"So, you wake?" Jean-Paul asked. "Marie, get my friend some food." The room swayed before Joe's eyes as Jean-Paul helped him up from the pallet. But not nearly as badly as before, he noted.

Joe sat at the rough board table and supported his head in his hands. Trying not to appear nosy, he looked around the cabin. The chinks between the yellow logs had been painted white, as had the plank ceiling. As far as he could see from his place at the table, the cabin consisted of just one large room. To Joe's right, he saw two rocking chairs resting on a braided rug. The chairs, draped with furs, hugged the fireplace. A large recess on the left looked to be a baking oven.

In a similar niche on the other side Joe recognized a statue of the Blessed Virgin in her long blue robes, her arms reaching out. It looked like the same one his mother kept on a little table in the hall back in New York. And, like his mother's statue, this one had a votive candle in a red glass holder flickering at the Virgin's feet.

It brought back boyhood memories of the after supper routine when the Devlin family gathered in front of the Virgin to say the rosary. Surely God would hear his constant prayers and make Alice well. She was, after all, one of His incredibly sweet creations. Any God that didn't love Alice enough to release her from the disease was—Joe quickly banished the disrespectful thoughts from his head.

Marie placed a steaming bowl with chunks of meat, potatoes and carrots in front of him. Joe's belly cheered loudly.

Jean-Paul laughed at the sound. "*Mange, mange,*" he encouraged. Marie set out bread and cheese and a mug of strong tea.

Jean-Paul grimaced at the sight of the tea. "That's no drink fit for a man. Let him have a drink from the jug."

"The tea will quiet his head pains," Marie said.

"Ah, well, so be it."

Joe slowly made his way through the stew while the couple silently looked on. Jean-Paul worked on a piece of antler with a small knife. Sopping up the last of the juices with bread, Joe looked up. "Thank you," he said.

"Now your belly is full, you'll tell us where you walk to." Jean-Paul continued to scrape away at the antler. Marie poured another mug of her herb tea and set it in front of Joe. He stared into the fire and told the French-Canadian couple his story, starting with the night he put Alice on the train and Mr. Bingham gave him the prized raccoon coat.

"That's a good tale for a winter night," Jean-Paul said when Joe finished. "One you'll tell your grandchildren." He yawned and scratched his beard with the tip of his carving knife.

"Do you know where I can find Dr. Decker? I'm supposed to get my frostbite checked and give his Chevy a good going over."

"The doctor lives near Hulls Falls. A couple of miles from here. We'll go over in the morning."

Marie rose from the table and poked at the fire. "We need more wood," she said. Jean-Paul got up. He took his knit toque off a peg and went out, Louie at his heels.

"The tea will help you rest well," she said to Joe. "Your head will feel much better if you lay quietly and don't toss about."

"I could sleep for days," Joe said, easing himself down on the narrow pallet. The door opened. Louie bounded in like a pup, bringing with him a flurry of snow. Jean-Paul followed with an armful of wood.

"Snowing hard with a sharp wind, too," Jean-Paul said. He dropped the wood on the hearth and threw a log on the fire. The fire spit and sputtered at the snow then attacked the log with long tongues of orange flame. Marie extinguished the two kerosene lamps. The couple disappeared to their sleeping alcove and within minutes the only sounds in the cabin were frequent crackles from the fire.

"Jean-Paul," Marie whispered, reaching out a hand to stroke the back of her husband's neck. He turned over and pulled Marie into the crook of his arm.

"You must do something to help Joe," she continued. "He knows nothing of survival in the mountains. When he leaves there's nothing but wilderness till he reaches Placid."

"You think I don't know that, woman? I could teach him respect for the winter if he would stay a few days with us."

"You know he'll leave the minute his head clears. I saw his toes. They're black. He'll lose them if they get cold and wet."

"I'll do what I can. Then we place him in God's hands."

Outside the wind picked up, hurtling snow at the cabin. The little glass window shivered. Louie pricked an ear. He whined softly, turning his great head to look at each of the three humans.

5

Joe's belly woke him the next morning, growling hungrily at the good smells of Marie's cooking. He opened his eyes and looked about the cabin, avoiding moving his head. So far, so good. He tried sitting up, propping his head on a hand. No dizziness. He gingerly explored the crusty lump on the back of his head.

"Good morning," Marie said. "How's your head?"

"Much better." Joe sat up and cautiously moved his legs over the side of the pallet. "What did you put in that tea?"

"The mountains are full of healing plants. Even so, I don't know of a plant to heal your aching heart."

"My heart will heal when Alice's lungs heal. I came close to giving up when I had to abandon the Ford. Then I had this notion that fighting the winter might knock out the. . .the bitterness I feel over Alice's disease."

"Church history is full of pain and sacrifice endured for loved ones," Marie said.

Joe took a deep breath and blurted the truth that constantly burned at the back of his throat: "Alice isn't Catholic. We weren't married in the Church. I get to wondering if God sent the TB as punishment." He buried his face in his hands. "But damn it, it should be my pain, not Alice's. If God is so good," Joe challenged Marie, "how can He be so harsh to one of His gentlest creatures?"

"It's not for us to question His ways," Marie said softly. "You may not come to understand even in this lifetime."

"You believe we should follow our Shepherd like dumb sheep?"

Jean-Paul came in, brushing snow from his clothes. "There's at least a foot of new snow and it's still coming down hard." He threw an armload of wood on the hearth and turned to look first at Joe and then Marie. "Something I should know about?"

"No," Marie said. "Breakfast is ready."

"Do you think the road is passable? I'd sure like to knock off a few miles today." Joe was grateful Marie ended the discussion and took her cue to change the subject. He cringed at the ugly accusations he had flung about.

The two men sat at the table and Marie brought them tin plates heaped with potatoes, applesauce and a thick slice of ham. Jean-Paul attacked his breakfast. Eventually he put his fork down, backhanded his mouth and looked at Joe.

"I think you do not understand. The last fifteen miles of your journey is through the pass. The snow rollers have not got through for two, three weeks and won't till spring. After this storm, the pass will have knee-deep snow."

Joe studied the trapper's face, not believing what he heard. "But how do they move supplies into Lake Placid and Saranac Lake all winter if the road is closed?"

"The train, she run all year from Utica to Saranac. The same train your woman took. And, there's a road running north from Keene to Champlain. Those rum runners, they make sure that road stays open." Jean-Paul smiled at Joe and bobbed his head. "Champlain, you see, is at the Canadian border. You go as far as Plattsburgh on this road, then take south fork to Saranac."

"If those roads are passable, isn't that the way I should go?" Joe warmed his hands around his tin mug.

"You can do that," Jean-Paul said. "Getting to Saranac Lake by going through Plattsburgh is a hundred miles."

"That would take a week or more if I have any luck hitchhiking. And those bootleggers are so suspicious I haven't been able to get a ride since I left New York." Joe's shoulders slumped. "I could be with Alice by now if just one of those bootleggers picked me up."

"Do not be sad, *mon ami*. There is a way to get through the pass before spring. Then you'll be with your woman in three, four days."

"What do you mean? You just told me the pass is snowed in!" Face it, he told himself, I'm not going to make it before Christmas. If only I'd insisted Alice leave months ago when the doctor first said she should go. I'd have missed all these winter storms.

"Why do you think we have the snowshoes? It lets us walk on top of the snow, like Christ on the water."

Joe sighed and shook his head. "I don't have money for snowshoes. Even if I did, I don't know how to walk in them."

"While you rested your head, I fixed up an old pair of snowshoes. A city fellow like you can learn when the teacher is Jean-Paul, no?"

Joe attempted to smile, but defeat ate away at the last of his strength. He stared into the fire, lost in his thoughts as Jean-Paul talked on. His toes still burned if they got cold or wet and that was just about all the time. Ever since he left Clarence and Emma's he had to concentrate on taking one painful footstep after another. The snow got deeper daily. Dry feet weren't possible, even using Emma's spare sock method.

And now, the frosting on the cake, as Emma would have said, was he didn't even have a coat or the means of obtaining one for the last leg of his trip. According to what everyone told him, this last leg was going to be a real doozy if he tried the pass.

I'll have to spend at least one night in the woods, maybe two to cover fifteen miles of unrolled roads. Jean-Paul said there are no more houses after I leave Keene. That means I have to carry food. What kind of animals are in those mountains? Do I need a gun? No use even thinking about a gun, Joe sighed. I can't buy one.

"Why do you look so sad, *mon ami*? You were not listening, no, about how Jean-Paul would teach you to snowshoe to your woman?"

Joe held his head in his hands and massaged his temples with his thumbs. "This whole trip is too much to think about. I don't see any way I can get to Saranac before the first of the year."

"Sure." Jean-Paul shrugged his shoulders. "You can go back to New York and wait till spring. Of course it'll take longer to walk back to the city than to walk the last leg on snowshoes." Jean-Paul took out his knife and scratched away at the antler piece. "It's not for the weak of heart to spend a night or two in the pass on the way to Placid. Your woman, she probably not want her husband to risk his life."

Joe pushed away from the table and went to the window. There was nothing but snow and snow-covered trees as far as he could see.

"I promised Alice I would be there to see her through this thing." Joe spoke softly. "I can't let her down."

Jean-Paul exchanged glances with Marie. He nodded and smiled, rose from his chair and placed the antler and whittling knife on the mantel.

"Then it's time we try the snowshoes. We'll get them strapped on then go to Dr. Decker. By the time we get back, you be an expert. Marie, find that old wool jacket for *mon ami*, here."

"I was hoping to start up the pass after I finish with Dr. Decker's car."

The little trapper shook his head vigorously. "You cannot start until the storm finishes her work. The pass is no place to be in a snowstorm. No, *mon ami*, you stay here tonight and by morning the sky and your head will be clear."

Jean-Paul took his fur jacket off a peg. Marie returned from the sleeping alcove and held out a worn buffalo plaid jacket. Joe tugged it on over his flannel shirt. The sleeves didn't quite reach his wrists. Obviously meant for a smaller man like Jean-Paul, the jacket stopped at his waist. When Joe buttoned up, it was uncomfortably tight across his shoulders.

"You better not grow before you get to Saranac, no?" Jean-Paul laughed heartily.

"It's a darn sight better than no coat at all," Joe said.

Marie offered him a pair of deerskin mittens. As he put them on, Joe discovered the fur had been left on the inside. "These are wonderful, Marie."

The trapper had Joe sit on the edge of the porch and introduced him to the snowshoes. Joe was taken with how delicate they looked. The rims were large ovals of a springy curved wood held in place by two flat braces and an intricate network of rawhide thongs. The ends of the wood were clamped together at the back. These tails extended another foot beyond the oval.

In the middle of the ovals were harnesses made of deer hide to fasten his feet to the snowshoes. Long rawhide thongs hung from the harness. Jean-Paul instructed Joe to tie these about his legs.

"Now are you ready? Use these poles until you learn balance." Within three steps, Joe banged his legs with the snowshoes and fell flat on his face. Louie barked and stuck his cold nose in Joe's face.

"First we learn to get up," Jean-Paul laughed. He instructed Joe to roll on his side and untangled the snowshoes. The trapper showed him how to dig one pole in the snow and pull himself upright.

Cautiously planning the flight of each foot and the corresponding diagonal pole, Joe picked up the rhythm. He concentrated so hard in putting one foot in front of the other, he lost all sense of time and distance. Jean-Paul cautioned him to avoid snowshoeing near trees. "Wood on wood is slippery like ice. And the webbing gets snagged in the brush."

Soon they emerged from the woods and there, at the far end of a clearing, Joe saw a three-story rambling white house with a steeply pitched red tin roof.

"This is where the doctor lives," Jean-Paul said.

Feeling lucky to find Dr. Decker at home, Joe introduced himself and arranged to give the Chevy a tune-up in return for having his frostbite treated. The doctor sent him to the barn to work on the car.

Finally he closed the hood and wiped his greasy hands on a grain sack. He set the throttle, pulled the choke out and cranked the Chevy to life. It caught on the third turn and purred like a barn cat offered a bowl of cream. Joe switched off the key, patted the Chevy on the hood, and went to find Dr. Decker.

The doctor took a great deal of time examining each of Joe's frostbitten toes. Gratefully Joe accepted the dollar Dr. Decker gave him for the work on the Chevy. He folded it several times and placed it in the breast pocket of his flannel shirt.

The two strapped on their snowshoes and started back to Jean-Paul's cabin. The snow had stopped. The temperature had dropped twenty degrees since morning. Joe shielded his eyes and stared at the intensely blue sky.

"That's the direction you'll head tomorrow morning." Jean-Paul pointed to the north. Joe turned and studied the purple mountains rising from the valley floor. A pale yellow winter sun was about to slide behind the snow-covered peaks. Somehow he must find his way through fifteen miles of those formidable mountains. Jean-Paul said these clumsy snowshoes would get him through. He wanted so badly to make it before Christmas; he'd try anything for Alice.

"An Indian I came across when I checked the traps on the south side of Seward Mountain called these mountains the 'Couchsachraga'. I figure it means 'dismal wilderness.'"

A north wind picked up, whipping down from the mountains and gathering force as it funneled through the valley. Joe tried to pull his jacket down to cover the top of his pants. He yearned for Mr. Bingham's coat to see him through the next few days.

"No Indian ever lived in these mountains," the trapper continued. "Iroquois, Algonquins, they all say the same thing. The hunting is great, but no tribe is so foolish to set up the tepees. The young bucks, they prove their manhood by spending three weeks alone with just a knife in the Adirondacks."

Joe shivered as the wind slipped under his jacket and blew up his back. He wondered how many Indians survived the three weeks. Would he have what it took to survive the couple of nights Jean-Paul told him it would take to get to Placid? The two men struck a rhythm. When they came to a short hill, Jean-Paul showed Joe how to climb with his toes pointed out, creating a herringbone design in the fresh snow. He watched from the hilltop as Joe perfected the new step.

"That works pretty good for the short hill. Most of what you find in the pass will be long hills. You climb those hills at an angle."

"That'll take twice as long," Joe said, leaning on his poles to take the weight off his feet.

"But you'll not tire so quick. It makes short the steepness. You still breath hard from the little climb, no?"

"My feet are beginning to sting," Joe admitted. "It sure is getting cold." He looked back at the mountains. "I have to confess I'm a little. . .uneasy about being on my own up there."

"A good respect for the winter is the best provision to keep you alive." The two men fell into the snowshoe gait. "Marie, she'll make sure your pack has plenty to eat. Think you can make a fire in the snow?"

Joe stopped and turned toward the tracker. "I was going to say 'of course'. But where do you find small stuff to start the fire with all this snow? And the wind, will it blow the fire out before it really starts?"

"*Bien!* You begin to think like a woodsman, *mon ami*. Jean-Paul will show you how to start the fire." The trapper set out toward the edge of the forest where a stand of young beech trees grew. When Joe caught up, the trapper pointed to the trees. Shriveled brown leaves clung to the branches, crackling in the north wind.

"Look for the beech tree. It keeps some leaves all winter. When the snow gets deep, you'll find the deer standing on their hind legs to reach the leaves. The leaves are good to start the fire, no? When you find the beech, you find the venison and make the fire to cook it. All in one spot!" Joe began to tear the dried leaves from the tree only to have the wind grab them from his deerskin mittens.

Jean-Paul laughed. "I think you not make too many fires in the city streets. Break off small branches with leaves." Joe snapped off an armload of branches. Every time he raised his arm, the wind snuck under his short jacket, stealing precious heat.

"Where do you think to lay the fire?"

Joe looked around. Could he start a fire on top of the snow? If the fire caught, wouldn't it melt the snow and then the water put the fire out? He looked toward the pine forest. The early winter snow had not entirely penetrated the thick branches. There were some bare patches under the densest pines. And the pine needles on the ground would be fuel along with dried grasses and weeds not covered by snow. "There's hardly any snow under the pine trees, the fire should catch good there."

"You can try," the trapper nodded. "What do you think will happen when the fire heats up the air and melts the snow in branches over your newborn fire?" Joe's shoulders slumped. He got the picture and chose a spot in the open, laying some big base wood on top of the snow, as Jean-Paul directed.

"Keep your back to the wind, *mon ami*. The new fire is as tender as a baby's ass." Joe struck a match, but the wind extinguished the tiny flame. He tried again, keeping it close to his body.

Crouched over the leaves and dried grass, he began to shiver, finding it hard to keep his bare hands steady. The tiny flame tasted the dried grass and wanted more. The wind worried about Joe's back and found its way up the jacket. Joe hunched closer to his new fire. The leaves began to burn.

"Your fire is hungry. Feed her some twigs." Joe seemed to get colder even while his fire grew. He offered the flame twig after twig. He found it difficult to clasp his cold fingers about the twigs.

"I thought this would be easier."

"Nothing about winter in the Adirondack is easy, *mon ami*. She demands respect, the winter. Then she will allow you to live." Under Jean-Paul's watchful eye Joe fed the fire bigger pieces of wood until it crackled pleasantly. The men silently soaked up the fire's warmth.

"I am thinking," Jean-Paul said as they strapped on their snow-shoes and resumed their walk home. "I could start out with you in the morning. I have traps to check a couple of miles up the pass. Would you like Louie's and my company?"

"That'd be swell."

Joe had second helpings of everything that night, including the warm bread pudding topped with maple syrup. He couldn't help but wonder where he'd be spending the next night. Could he gather enough wood in the deep snow to keep a fire going all night?

Jean-Paul belched contentedly and leaned back in his chair. "We'll check your pack."

"I'd like that," Joe said, and went to get his pack. "Sure am glad whoever took my coat left me this." He emptied the contents on the table.

Jean-Paul pushed aside a sweater and a change of clothes. He shook his head at what was left. "You tell me how you use these?" He pointed to a small pocket knife, a wrench, pliers and two screw drivers.

"I need those to work on cars. It often pays for my dinner."

"What you need now, *mon ami*, are things to keep you alive. Marie," he said as he headed for the door, "bring us the jug. I'll get supplies for Joe."

Joe pulled his carefully folded dollar from his shirt pocket and offered it to Marie as she placed the moonshine on the table.

"You have been so good to me. Food and a jacket and a warm place to sleep. I wish I had more to give you."

"I won't take your money." Marie shook her head. "Jean-Paul makes sure we never want. It would be best if you held on to your money. Your journey is not over yet."

"I'd feel much better if you'd take it." Joe took her hand and closed the small fingers around the folded bill.

"You're a good man, Joseph Devlin." Marie smiled and put the money in her apron pocket. "Remember, the Lord never sends a trial you can't endure."

Jean-Paul opened the door. The fire snapped at the rush of frigid air he brought with him. "Holy *Mere*, it's cold out there!"

"At least it's not snowing." Joe looked out the window. A million stars pierced the black velvet night.

The trapper placed a small hatchet, several lengths of rawhide, a small tin pan and a tin box of matches on the table. Pointing to each one, he explained their functions. "I wish, me, you had a gun, but a good fire will keep the varmints away."

Marie joined them with several brown paper wrapped packages of food. Jean-Paul nodded his approval.

By the time they finished, the pack was stuffed. After Marie extinguished the kerosene lamps, Joe lay on his cot, his hands laced behind his head, just above the tender lump.

Today was an eye-opener, all right. Even though he'd been walking for weeks now, his legs ached. Mastering the snowshoe gait used muscles he never knew he had. Would he be able to keep at it for three more days?

Marie sure tried to make me comfortable, he thought. Wasn't it something how she went out of her way to be hospitable. Just like Emma. He realized his journey would be quite different without the kind mountain people who took him in.

He would tell Alice how the women had seen him through tough times. Wouldn't it be nice to name our first daughter after them? "Emma Marie." He tested the name quietly and smiled at the pleasant sound.

His eyes began to close as he watched the shadow of the flames dancing on the ceiling. "Thank you, God, for sending good people to help me. Just when I figure I'm a goner, someone comes out of the snow to help. I hope I'll be able to return all those kindnesses someday. And I apologize for my ugly outburst, but Your ways are hard to figure at times. I hope You find a way to help me through the pass. But most of all, please watch over Alice till I get there."

6

The sun crested the eastern mountains as the two men on snowshoes struck out from the cabin. Joe tried not to dwell on the wall of mountains that rose before him. They merged with a cold morning sky only lightly touched by blue. Jean-Paul, a good twenty feet in front, broke track in the fresh snow. Joe marveled at how fast the little trapper moved in that odd duck-like snowshoe gait while carrying a full pack and a rifle.

He led Joe across a clearing. Then the climb began and the dense evergreen forest closed in. Within a mile, Joe's muscles loosened up and his heart thudded. The arctic air, creating tiny icicles on the hair in his nose, made it impossible to fill his lungs. When he opened his mouth to gulp air, his teeth ached at the cold.

He lost his rhythm. The toe of his left snowshoe sank in a deep drift. Instinctively he thrust out his arms as he fell, plunging shoulder deep in the snow. The short sleeves of the old jacket exposed his wrists and snow found its way into his mittens and up his sleeves.

Louie barked, alerting Jean-Paul to the problem behind him. "I don't know how this boy will make it," he said to the wolf.

Joe extracted his upper body from the drift, but his snowshoes kept his legs captive. He lost the pole in his fall.

"Don't sit there, the snow will rob the heat from your body."

"Got to catch my breath." Joe's chest heaved in an effort to get air to his starved lungs.

"You let the cold bewitch you into lying down. Get up!"

"How?"

"Untie the snowshoes, find your pole."

That meant taking off Marie's deerskin mittens. A half hour out and I'm freezing, he thought. With his bare fingers, he picked ice off the rawhide thongs. The last time he sat in the snow for a rest he ended up with frostbite and he still paid for it with each painful step. What would he do after Jean-Paul left him?

Freed from the clumsy snowshoes, Joe stood up, picked up the snowshoes and poles and waded to a rock. Sitting down, he strapped them back on.

"Come, *mon ami*, the days are short."

The two men fell in line behind the wolf.

The sun poked through the evergreens, sending shards of light glancing off the snow. Joe, blinded by the glare, narrowed his eyes to slits and concentrated on following Jean-Paul. He wasn't cold anymore, but his head ached from squinting. The lump on the back of his head throbbed.

Up ahead Louie stopped. Standing as silent as one of the mountains, he looked to the left. Joe saw the hair rise on the back of the wolf's neck.

Jean-Paul gestured to stop. The men froze. The silence was unsettling. Finally Jean-Paul motioned for Joe to move up to where he stood next to Louie.

"Smell the smoke?" Jean-Paul whispered. Joe sniffed the air. "Comes from that direction." The trapper pointed to a ravine. "I have my traps there. There's a lean-to I use to gut my catch."

Joe looked down the ravine. He couldn't hear or see a thing. Jean-Paul took the rifle off his shoulder.

"I think someone is stealing from my traps. Louie and I will go in for a closer look. Stay here."

"You don't know how many are there. You might need my help. Don't look at me like that," Joe said. "I don't know much about these mountains, but I did fight in the war."

"You can come, but you must do as Jean-Paul says. Take off the snowshoes. Too many rocks."

They stuck the pointed ends of the snowshoes in the snow and picked their way down the ravine, the wary wolf in the lead. A crow's raucous cry cut through the silence. Jean-Paul touched Louie's back. When the wolf turned, he pointed toward a boulder the size of a small cabin. Louie changed direction and the three gathered behind the protection of the rock.

Now Joe smelled the smoke and heard the mumble of voices. Or was it just the murmur of the cold black brook tumbling by the lean-to?

"There's two." Jean-Paul turned to Joe. Joe gripped the boulder, inching around its bulk till he could see. Two men huddled near a small campfire in front of the log lean-to. Each held a stick with something on it over the flames. Just then the smaller man stood. Joe gasped. Jean-Paul yanked him back behind the rock.

"My coat!" Joe whispered hoarsely. "He's got my fur coat!"

"Calm yourself, *mon ami*, or they'll have us, too." The little trapper peered around the boulder. Eventually he turned back to Joe.

"I see two rifles. If we can get to them while they're still at the fire, we'll have the upper hand. I'll send Louie around to their backs." The trapper crouched in the snow and took the wolf's big head in his hands. He made a sweeping motion with one hand and said, "Around, Louie. Guard!" Louie took off, weaving silently through the trees.

"We'll give him time to guard their backs, then we move in. I go first. Soon as we have them standing with their hands up, you get the rifles." Jean-Paul looked at Joe. "Jean-Paul will get your coat back, *mon ami*. You see the rifles?"

Joe stole another look. One rifle was propped against the outside edge of the lean-to. The other lay on a split log bench at the back of it.

"Never get between them and me," Jean-Paul cautioned. "Bring the rifles back to me. Then we take the coat, no?" The trapper checked his rifle and stepped out from behind the boulder. With the snow muffling their steps, they walked to within twenty feet of where the unsuspecting men picked the last of their meal off the charred sticks.

Jean-Paul stopped and raised his rifle. "Good morning, gentlemen!"

The surprised men jumped up, embers sparking about their feet.

"Stand where you are. Hands over your heads."

"Kinda unfriendly, aren't you, mister?" The smaller one smiled like a weasel. His whiskey-colored eyes darted from Jean-Paul to Joe.

47

"You're a little late for breakfast, but we'll make more coffee." He made a move toward the coffeepot.

"Stand where you are," Jean-Paul repeated, cocking his rifle. Joe kept his distance from the two and headed for the rifle on the bench, turning his back on the men as he entered the lean-to.

"Don't I know you?" Jean-Paul narrowed his eyes. He glanced briefly at the bigger man. "Of course! I think you are the pair caught breaking into Le Blanc's store down in the valley."

"Don't know what you're talking about," the weasel muttered.

"Sure! You're Earl Tierney and that's your dim-witted brother, Bruce."

The weasel called Earl had inched his way behind the bigger man's bulk, just three steps from the rifle propped on the outside of the lean-to. He made a dive for it.

Joe, about to pick up the rifle in the lean-to, heard Jean-Paul shout and then a menacing snarl. Wheeling with rifle in hand he saw Louie leap on Earl's back, knocking him to the ground. The man rolled over and Louie pounced on him. Earl threw up his hands against the wolf's attack, but Louie seized an arm and sank his teeth into the man's hand, snapping the small bones like twigs. Earl screamed.

"Joe!" Jean-Paul shouted.

Out of the corner of his eye, Joe saw the flash of sunlight off metal. It was a pistol Bruce had aimed straight at him. In one fluid movement, Joe raised the rifle, reeled and shot Bruce. The force of the rifle shot sent the man stumbling backwards into the fire, his head slamming onto a stone. Joe heard the sickening sound of his skull cracking open. Blood and brains trickled onto the snow.

Joe slumped, dropping the rifle to the ground. "I've killed him."

"Good thing you did, *mon ami.*" Jean-Paul made his way to Earl. He raised his rifle, pointing it at the man's head. "Guard, Louie," he said to the wolf. The wolf backed off, growling deep in his throat.

"On your feet, you." Jean-Paul kept his rifle pointed at Earl.

"Keep that crazy beast away." Earl got to his feet, cradling his injured right hand close to his chest. Several small white bones protruded through the skin and blood dripped from the puncture in his palm. Both hands were coated with gore.

"You've killed my brother," Earl said, his narrow face pinched in anguish. "You had no right, Bruce was hardly more than a baby."

The unexpected show of compassion took Joe and Jean-Paul by surprise.

"Your baby brother was ready to kill my friend," Jean-Paul said quickly. "Take that coat off and be careful about messing it with your dirty blood."

"Are you loco? I'll freeze."

"I don't think that bothered you when you take the coat from my friend here and left him for dead."

Earl looked at Joe. His face turned a dirty yellow. "I should've let Bruce finish you off." Earl shrugged the raccoon coat from his narrow shoulders and let it drop at his feet.

"Walk away." Jean-Paul motioned with his rifle. Earl took a few steps. "Louie, guard." The wolf growled.

"Come, get your coat, *mon ami*."

Joe came forward, making sure he didn't get between the trapper's rifle and Earl. He picked up Mr. Bingham's coat and backed off.

"You tell me how you happen to be here?"

"We was going to Placid for the winter." Earl shivered. "When the storm hit, we holed up here."

"I think we send you back the way you came. Joe! Search this rounder. Make sure, you, he does not have hidden surprises."

"Don't touch my arm," Earl protested, protecting his injured hand from Joe's search. A low growl rumbled from the wolf's throat. Earl froze, submitting to Joe's probe. Joe pulled a little skinning knife from Earl's left boot and brought it over to where the trapper stood, his rifle still trained on Earl. The two men watched the highwayman shake in the cold.

"We can't leave him in just a shirt," Joe said.

"Holy *Mere*! And they worried how they left you?"

"He can't hurt us now." Joe unbuttoned the old jacket he bought from Marie and threw it at Earl. "Put this on." Earl grabbed at it, crying and cursing as he worked his mutilated hand through the narrow sleeve.

Joe picked up Mr. Bingham's coat from where it lay in the snow. Scooping up handfuls of snow, he rubbed Earl's blood from the fur.

"What do you say to *mon ami* here who worries about your worthless body?"

"Thanks," Earl mumbled.

Joe shook Mr. Bingham's coat, amazed and grateful to find it all in one piece. He put it on, pleased to be wrapped in its bulky warmth once more.

"On your way." Jean-Paul motioned with his rifle down the mountain toward Keene.

"What about my pack and snowshoes?"

"No!"

"You're crazy! Let me have my snowshoes."

"You wish to stay here with your brother?" Jean-Paul raised his rifle to his shoulder and took aim.

"All right, I'll go."

"Wise choice. I'll send Louie with you, so you don't forget the way." The trapper lowered his rifle. "Louie! Follow. . .home." The big wolf fell in step behind Earl.

Joe and Jean-Paul watched the highwayman's labored steps through the deep snow. "You ain't seen the last of me, you bastards! I'll find you and take care of my brother's murderer." His curses carried clearly on the still mountain air.

Now that the danger was over, Joe walked around Bruce's body and sat down. "I didn't mean to kill him." Elbows on knees, he rested his head in his hands.

"They left you for dead, *mon ami*." The trapper watched Earl and Louie fade into the forest as he talked. "And that big one had his heart set on killing you. From where I stood, me, I could not risk a shot. I don't miss often, but if I did, you would have received my bullet, no?"

Splinters of pain stabbed Joe's head. He found it hard to justify killing a man, and an idiot to boot. But the throbbing lump the dead man had inflicted painfully reminded him of Bruce's murderous nature.

It certainly wasn't the first time Joe had killed. In France he had thrown grenades and watched Fritz after Fritz fall before his gun when his troop made advances. Sure he had problems sinking his bayonet through flesh and bones. But he never let himself dwell on those he killed as being. . .people. It was a job. Wipe out the enemy or be wiped out.

"Come," Jean-Paul called. "Help me move him away from camp."

"We have to bury him."

"Bury him! Holy *Mere*! Where do you get these thoughts? Do you also know how to dig through two feet of snow and frozen ground?"

"I didn't think." Joe got up, walking to where the body lay. "What do we do?"

"Carry him away from camp." The two struggled with the body and dumped it on the south side of a boulder. Something metallic on the dead man's neck flashed in the snow-bright sun.

Joe stooped for a closer look and recognized his rosary around Bruce's neck. He began working the rosary up over Bruce's ears. Suddenly he changed his mind.

I can't give him much of a burial, he thought. Not even a marker for the grave. Guess the least I can do is leave him with a cross. Joe repositioned the rosary around Bruce's neck and gently centered the cross. Taking his hatchet, he cut evergreen boughs to cover the body. The little trapper stood by, shaking his head.

Joe pulled off his knit toque and bowed his head. "I'm sorry, God," he prayed. "I didn't mean to kill Bruce and I feel badly we can't bury him. Please be merciful to Bruce and all us sinners." He blessed himself and pulled his toque back on.

He looked up to see Jean-Paul pull a whistle from inside his parka and put it to his mouth. Joe couldn't hear a sound.

"What are you doing?"

"Calling Louie back. The whistle talks just to Louie."

"How do you know Louie won't lead Earl back to us?"

"Louie will slip away. He will not let himself be followed. I think it's time you move on, no? But first let us see what gifts our friends left for you." Jean-Paul insisted Joe add Bruce's pistol and Earl's skinning knife to his pack.

Joe rummaged around in Bruce's pack and found a pair of heavy woolen socks. He sat down to exchange them for his wet ones, suddenly growing apprehensive about continuing on his own. But then he gave himself a pep talk. Hell, what's fifteen miles after almost three hundred!

"I wish I could do more than just thank you." Joe strapped his pack in place.

"It will be your turn to offer help next. It's the way of the mountains, *mon ami.*"

"I've had a great teacher." They shook hands and Joe trudged back up the ravine to retrieve his snowshoes. Jean-Paul walked away toward his traps.

Joe found the going slow. Lonely, too. Early afternoon and already the sun had inched below the western mountains, casting long blue-black shadows on the snow. The sky remained clear and Joe felt the temperature drop steadily. He savored the warmth of the fur coat even though its length hindered his progress.

He was hungry, but knew if he stopped now it would make for a long, cold night. Best keep at it till dark, he thought, his snowshoes making muffled plopping sounds through the new snow.

An almost full moon had risen by the time he stopped. He chose a spot where the road crested a ridge. Dropping his pack at the base of a towering white pine, he went off the road with his hatchet in search of wood.

Back at his camp he resisted the urge to take shortcuts. He used a snowshoe to scoop away snow in the middle of the road, beyond the snow-laden branches of the pine. He layered the wood as Jean-Paul instructed. Finally he was ready to light a match to the handful of dried grass he pulled from under the pine. Crouched over the fire, he painstakingly fed it grass and leaves till it grew strong enough for the bigger limb wood.

Only when the fire crackled pleasantly did he dare leave to retrieve his pack and bedroll from under the tree. His hunger demanded attention, but after placing his pan of snow on the fire to heat for tea, he took the time to tend his feet.

First he lay the socks he carried under his union suit on a log near the fire. He placed the liniment next to them. Removing his cold, clammy socks, he examined his feet.

His throat went dry when he couldn't feel his warm hands on the cold toes. Dr. Decker had cautioned that loss of feeling was an early symptom of new frostbite! Fortunately, Joe also remembered Emma saying not to use dry heat, but to warm his toes in lukewarm water.

He could do that! The pan of melted snow would work, he thought. He wrapped a sock around the handle and removed it from the fire. After testing the temperature, he set the pan on his bedroll, stood and dipped his foot, almost up to the heel, into the water. Within moments stinging set in, indicating renewed circulation.

Much relieved, Joe sat down, refilled the pan with snow and set it to heat while he dried and dressed his warmed foot. By morning I would have lost those toes for sure, he thought as he repeated the whole process on his other foot.

Huddled over the fire, Joe was seized by loneliness. Never in his life had he been so far from a single sound of humanity. The realization made him feel tiny. Not even as significant as one of the billions of evergreens surrounding him, he thought. He felt he was inching his way across the universe, completely at the mercy of the silent mountains.

A vision of the man he killed, skimpily covered with pine boughs, accosted him. Jean-Paul was right, these mountains weren't very forgiving. If you wanted to trespass, you had to follow their rules to survive.

He dug into his pack for one of Marie's venison sandwiches and a wedge of cheese. His third pan of water held some of her tea. Sitting cross-legged before the fire, he slowly chewed each mouthful, trying to keep at bay the oppressive fear of a night in the wilderness.

The cold creeping inside his bedroll forced him awake. He reached out to his supply of wood and tossed several logs on the dying fire.

He lay back, looking up at the white moon. It cast so much light, he debated breaking camp and heading out, but the heat from the fire made him drowsy again. His thoughts turned to this vast wilderness. I've never gone so long without talking to someone, he thought, straining to hear some sound of life. From down the mountain, he heard the faint gurgling of a brook.

He remembered Alice's doctor back in New York mentioning that cure cottages encouraged patients to stay out on the curing porches all night. Now that he was experiencing the formidable cold of his first Adirondack night outdoors, he wondered how it could be true.

Could Alice be right about all those things that went on in the cure cottages? Was the torture worth a possible cure? How could his frail wife endure a night like this? He fell into a troubled sleep. His dreams churned with pictures of Alice being left on a snow-covered porch, calling for help while inside nurses sat around a fire.

A rifle report cracked the stillness of the bitterly cold dawn. Instantly awake, Joe reached for his pistol and scanned the woods for movement. The hair rose on the back of his neck when he heard two more shots behind him. What the hell? Shots rang out randomly. Had the weasel they let go yesterday come back with reinforcements to avenge his brother's death? What chance did he have against so many? He tugged on his boots and crept toward the area where he heard the most shots.

Pistol held ready, Joe huddled beside a maple tree, alert for any movement. A loud crack reverberated at his ear. He swung, firing wildly as he dropped to the ground behind the tree.

His heart pounded in his throat. For long moments he stayed crouched in the snow without his coat, sweat trickling down his back. He neither saw nor heard anything.

Suddenly another crack resounded not two feet away. Slowly Joe lowered his gun and stood. An embarrassed smile split his face. He chuckled. Softly at first, then throwing his head back, he laughed deep from within his soul. The mountains returned the laughter as if understanding the grand joke they had played on him.

It all came back to him. Jean-Paul said it got so cold in the mountains the trees cracked as loudly as rifle shots as the sap expanded.

Anxious to be on his way, he broke camp quickly after a hasty breakfast of Marie's ham biscuits and strong, hot tea. I could be in Placid tonight, he thought.

Pleased he could start off downhill, he prepared for the descent by snugging up the thongs on his snowshoes to keep the toes of his boots from slipping under the crosspiece. He studied the hill for a moment, deciding the incline looked steep enough to try one of the more advanced snowshoe techniques Jean-Paul had shown him.

Placing one foot in front of the other, Joe used his pole to push off from the hillcrest, then crouched down over the rear shoe. He sailed down the hill, the bitter air making his eyes tear. At the bottom he paused to loosen the thongs. Dr. Decker had cautioned him not to restrict the circulation to his damaged toes or he would increase his chances of additional frostbite.

This is going to be a great day, he thought, striding off.

7

From the length of the shadows, Joe judged the time to be about three. The ache in his head grew worse and he found himself stopping to catch his breath more frequently.

Guess it's another night in the woods, he thought, giving up hope of reaching Lake Placid before dark. At every bend in the road he kept looking for the forest to give way to the vast level plateau. Jean-Paul said once he reached the plains there'd be just six miles to go.

Ever since he prayed over Bruce's body and walked away, Joe hadn't seen the slightest indication of a cleared field. Trees crowded the road he traveled closer than buildings on a city street.

As he rounded the next curve, the road climbed again. I'll make camp at the top, he thought, sizing up the incline. Definitely a diagonal hill, he decided. His thighs ached with the effort of maneuvering one snowshoe around the other.

His progress was agonizingly slow as he zigzagged up. He sweated and shivered and wondered where he'd find the strength to build a fire. Pausing near the top, Joe leaned heavily on his pole, his chest heaving in exhaustion.

His head was ringing. No. . .no! It's bells. . .sleigh bells. He struggled to the crest. There, the omnipresent forest stopped abruptly at the edge of an ocean of snow.

Coming out of the dark woods, the glare of the setting sun stabbed at his eyes. He scanned the plain for the source of the sleigh bells. Movement! Silhouetted on the horizon, a team of draft horses hitched to a big work sleigh plodded along.

People! Joe cupped his hands and yelled, "Hello! Hello!" The horses kept moving. They can't hear me, Joe realized. In a panic, he started after the sleigh. Pumping arctic air, his lungs ached with the effort.

Again and again he called. It felt like a nightmare. How can I make them hear me? His weary muscles refused to obey. The gun. Frantically, he pulled the pack from his back and dug out the pistol. He fired three quick shots in the air. Immediately the horses stopped and the people turned toward him.

Joe shouted and waved both arms wildly about his head. After a few moments one of them waved back. They saw him! He dropped his hands and watched the horses turn toward him. Picking up his pack from where he had flung it in the snow, he walked to meet them. As they neared, he saw a man and woman perched on the high wagon seat, a blanket around their legs. The man held the reins lightly in one hand. The other held a rifle.

Suddenly Joe realized he must be a strange sight, emerging from the woods, shooting a gun and yelling like a madman, and dressed in a full-length fur coat. A wonder they didn't keep going, he thought. Hastily he put the pistol back in his pack.

"Hello," he called, keeping his hands away from his sides to assure them he wasn't hiding a weapon. The round-faced young woman looked down from her sleigh seat, warming Joe with a dimpled smile. The cold and utter loneliness that had pervaded his long journey melted ever so slightly.

"Quite a ways from the village," the man at her side said. "Where you headed?" Joe heard the man's uneasiness at finding a stranger snowshoeing out of the woods.

"The Lake Placid Club. . ."

"The Club?" The man snorted. "You can't just walk in there." His eyes narrowed. "It's members only. . .wealthy members."

"Oh, Pa!" The young woman took a mittened hand from under the robe and squeezed her father's arm. "Why don't you let him tell us?"

"I'm not a guest. I'm on my way to report for a job in the garage. Supposed to see Tom Madden. My name's Joe Devlin."

The horses tossed their big heads, setting the bells to jingling. The man checked them with a jerk on the lines. He returned his attention to Joe. "Where're you coming from?"

"I left Keene yesterday morning." And killed a man, Joe's conscience reminded him.

"You walked all the way up from Keene?" The woman raised her neatly arched brows. "And spent a night in the woods? You must be exhausted. Get those snowshoes off, hear? We'll deliver you right to Tom Madden's door. Won't we, Pa?" She nudged her father.

"Throw your gear in the back. We've a ways to go."

Joe bent down to remove the snowshoes. He heard the man speak in a voice not intended for him: "You got to stop picking up strays, Kate. This man has a gun." Joe smiled. Sure glad this Kate did pick up strays. He threw his pack in the back and placed the snowshoes on top.

"Climb on up here." The woman's smile more than made up for her father's sourness. She reached out a hand to Joe and pulled him up to the seat. "I'm Kate Thurber," she said, "and this old grouch is my father, Emmett Thurber. Wrap the blanket around your legs."

The woman, squeezed between the two men, tugged the blanket from her father's side. Once again Joe was taken with the way these north country people lent a helping hand to him, an absolute stranger. During the entire ordeal, someone always appeared in the nick of time. Marie was right. The Lord never sends tribulations beyond endurance.

"That's sure a swell coat." She stroked a sleeve. "I've never seen such an unusual arrangement of the pelts."

"Belongs to the same man who got me the job at the Club." Joe looked down into lively cinnamon eyes. "He loaned it to me for my trip from New York."

"New York City?" She looked at Joe, her eyes huge with wonder.

"That's three hundred miles!" Thurber said, disbelief clear in his voice.

Once again Joe told the tale of how his Ford broke down and he came to walk into the Adirondacks with winter coming on. For a moment he worried Thurber might kick him out of the sleigh when he learned his wife was a tubercular. But Kate and her father never interrupted.

He came to the part where Jean-Paul and Louie had found him with a baseball-size lump on his head and Mr. Bingham's fur coat stolen. The tale of how the trapper and his wolf helped him get the coat back brought a smirk to Thurber's face that clearly indicated he felt Joe was spinning a pretty good yarn.

Joe never spoke of killing Bruce.

"Crazy risking your life that way," Thurber mumbled, urging the team on with a slap of the lines on their big rounded rumps.

"You must love your wife very much," Kate said softly.

"Yes."

"So," she changed the subject, "what do you know about the Club?"

"Only that it's a big hotel for really rich people. And they're fussy about who's a member."

"They are that! Fussy about the help, too. I'm a waitress there. Don't go on till breakfast, but rules say I have to be in tonight."

"You live there, too?" Joe asked, conscious of a pleasant warmth at the prospect.

"Sure do." Kate went on to explain how she went home for her day off. Her father, she said, was farm supervisor of Marcy Meadows, one of the Club's eight dairy farms, located about a mile from where they had picked up Joe.

"I can always catch a ride on one of his milk runs." She flashed her dimples at Joe. "The Club's a good place to work. All you can eat and it's the same food they serve the guests. But, oh my, the rules!" Kate rolled her eyes. "They're awfully strict about tuberculars, Joe," she said, suddenly serious.

"What do you mean? I don't have TB."

"Won't make any difference if they even think you're visiting your wife in Saranac Lake. Best keep it to yourself. Tom Madden can recite the Club rules by heart. About the only thing in his heart."

"You've got no call to bad mouth Madden, daughter. He does his job. . .well, too."

Kate's look clearly said she didn't agree with her father's opinion of Tom Madden. To Joe she said, "I have it on good authority that Mr. Madden drinks vinegar for breakfast."

Joe laughed.

The team strained against their collars. Heads lowered, their calk-shod hooves bit into the packed snow of Mill Hill. Chimney smoke rose from the handful of small wooden buildings clinging to the side of the steep incline.

"Almost there," Kate said, pointing out some local landmarks. Soon they came to Mirror Lake, snug under its blanket of snow, separating the village on its west side from the Club on the east. In the moonlight, Joe could make out several groups of people traversing between the two sides.

"Club workers taking the shortcut," Kate said, answering Joe's unspoken question. "The local people take the shortcut across the lake, but the guests like to walk the three miles around. . .for exercise. Taking long walks in the snow is what they come for."

Thurber pulled the team up in front of a large brown-shingled building. "This here's the garage. You're in luck. I see the light on in Madden's office."

Joe lowered himself from the sleigh, wincing as he put weight on his frostbitten toes. "Appreciate the ride, Mr. Thurber. If it wasn't for you, I'd be camping out another night."

Thurber grunted.

"Look for me when you come in for breakfast, hear? I'll see you meet some of the gang." Kate waved as her father drove off.

Joe dug Mr. Bingham's rumpled letter of introduction out of the coat's secret pocket and knocked on the door.

"Come in," a deep voice barked. A burly man with a full head of hair the color of frost shuffled papers on an oak desk. Joe stood quietly until the man raised his head and looked at Joe with pale eyes nearly hidden in the folds of a beefy face. Something about the man made Joe stand at attention until invited to speak.

Holding Joe prisoner with his eyes, Madden drummed the desk with sausage-like fingers.

"The Club garage is for members only." His voice rattled harshly like someone long used to giving commands.

"Yes, sir. I know, sir." Joe was surprised at his words. *I haven't spoken like that since my army days,* he thought.

"Well?"

"My name's Joe Devlin. I'm looking for Mr. Madden. . .sir."

"Why would you be looking for me?" Not once did the man's ice blue eyes leave Joe's face. What made the man so unfriendly? Realization hit Joe like a snowball in the neck. He knows, he thought. Somehow he knows I killed Bruce. Joe broke out in a cold sweat.

"Hey, buddy. Care to tell me what you're doing here?"

Joe pulled himself together and attempted to hand the man the letter. "It's from Mr. Bingham," Joe managed to say. "Told me he spoke to you about a mechanic's job." Madden made no move to take the letter from Joe's hand, so he placed it on the desk.

Keeping Joe locked in his glare, Madden picked up the letter, popped the seal and ripped it open. He pulled the letter from the envelope with a flourish and began to read.

"So you're the whiz from the city? Took your good sweet time getting here." Madden folded the letter and proceeded to tear it into tiny bits, dumping them in an ashtray.

Joe stood quietly at parade rest. The fear of being discovered as a murderer abated, but his feet begged to be released from his wet socks.

Madden struck a match on the side of his chair and lit the pieces of the letter. "You think you're pretty good?"

"I know my cars. . .sir." What's this, Joe fretted, some kind of test? Isn't he going to give me the job? Why is he burning Mr. Bingham's letter?

"Take your gear up the outside stairs. Your room's the third door on the left. You'll be on your own up there till summer." The springs groaned loudly as he leaned back in his chair and looked up at Joe. "So if anything is missing we'll know where to look. Shower's at the end of the hall."

"Do I have the job?"

"For the time being. Pay's nine-fifteen a week with room and board. I'll warn you up front, with wages like that the Club won't put up with second-rate work." Madden opened a drawer and pulled out a small booklet. "These are the Club rules for employees." He tossed it toward Joe. From another drawer he took out a paper and began writing on it. Finished, he handed it to Joe.

"This will get you in Finches where the help eat. Breakfast is from five to six every morning." Madden dropped his pencil in a cracked ceramic mug.

"There's no big call for cars this time of year. Guests go more for sleighs." He rested his elbows on the chair's arms and studied Joe from beneath the thick forest of black brows. "I'll give you tomorrow to settle in and we close the shop on Saturdays and Sundays in the winter. I'll expect you on the job seven sharp Monday morning." Joe picked up the Club rules pamphlet and his dining room pass and turned to leave.

"By the way," Madden shot the question at Joe's retreating back. "How'd you get here?"

"Walked after my Model T broke down," Joe turned around to face his boss. "Walked to Keene, snowshoed the rest."

"And Bingham's star mechanic couldn't put a Model T back on the road? I doubt you'll keep your head above water with the Club's fleet."

After Joe left, Madden planted his elbows on the desk and supported his head in his hands. A toothpick bobbed from one side of his mouth to the other. Suddenly it snapped. He spat it out and reached for the telephone. "Edna," he said in the mouthpiece, "get me a village line." Then after several moments, "Plattsburgh 73." Madden's pale eyes were in constant motion while he waited for the connections. "Yeah, Madden here. Thought I'd drive up on Monday. You going to be around? Quit worrying, don't I always have the money?"

The rumblings of steam coming up the pipes woke him. He didn't remember much after leaving Madden. I must of taken care of my feet, he reasoned, wriggling his toes in the blissful dry warmth of a real bed in a heated room. He felt the wads of dry flannel separating each toe and drifted off to sleep.

Some time later Joe came awake and lay quietly with his hands laced behind his head. Never in his life had he been so lonely or cold or so close to quitting as this past month. Never would have made it, he thought, without the good people I met along the way.

He dared to hope the worst was over. What could possibly be worse than killing Bruce? Damn it! He didn't set out to kill the man. . .only wing him in the shoulder. Self-defense. Who could blame him for shooting at the hijackers? That pair sure as hell had no problem walking off and leaving him to freeze to death. But it was obvious Bruce wasn't much more than a kid in the head.

Outside his room's one window, stars shone in the black sky. Sure was nice to be looking at it from a warm room.

As he lay trying to guess the time, the bells of a church across Mirror Lake solemnly rang five times. Morning. Joe threw off the covers and let his feet test the bare wood floor. He looked forward to a real breakfast. By then it should be getting light and he'd head out to Saranac Lake.

"Today," he said, "I'll see Alice!" What good fortune not to have to work before Monday. Three whole days to see his wife and take care of any problems. He emptied his pack on the bed and picked out his clean change of clothes. Picking up his straight-edge razor and bar of Ivory from the jumble on the bed, he headed for the bathroom. Hope there's hot water, he thought.

There was. And in minutes the bathroom was steaming. Joe couldn't get enough of the hot stream kneading his shoulders and sluicing down his hard lean body. It seemed a lifetime since he last enjoyed a real shower the night before he left Clarence and Emma's. He wiped steam from the mirror and worked up a lather for shaving.

Wish I had money for a haircut, he thought, noticing how his brown hair capped his ears. It'll have to wait till my first payday.

Back in his room, he put his belongings in the dresser and his tools in a corner of the closet. Running his hands over the snowshoes, he sat on the bed, acknowledging the major role the delicately curved wood had played in getting him to Lake Placid before Christmas. He decided he would get a hammer and nails from the shop on Monday to hang them on the wall behind his bed.

Sitting on his bed, rubbing ointment on his toes, Joe planned his day. He knew ten miles separated Lake Placid and Saranac Lake, but it would be ten easy miles. Kate told him the villages used horse-drawn snow rollers that kept new snowfalls packed down, so he wouldn't need his snowshoes. And she thought his chances of hitching a ride were good.

Quietly, he closed the door to his room and headed down the stairs as quickly as his toes allowed. He took a deep breath of the cold, dry air and, smiling, decided the mountain air was different. . .better. To the right, the famous rambling hotel loomed darkly against the white mountains. Smoke rose from numerous chimneys. Pulling the coat's collar up around his freshly shaved face, he started for the building, his feet crunching in the snow.

As he neared, Joe saw people headed toward a rear entrance with a big overhead hooded light. Reasoning it could only be Club employees on their way to breakfast at this early hour, he hurried along, looking forward to a sit-down meal with real dishes and hot food.

He couldn't see through the steamy kitchen windows, but even before he opened the door he smelled the bacon. Inside, to his left, the vast kitchen was alive with clanging pots, billows of steam and good cooking aromas. On the right people ate breakfast at a dozen long tables. Joe hung his coat with a collection of woolen jackets and colorful scarves and hats on pegs along the wall.

The outside door opened and Kate came in, talking animatedly to a tall, thin girl wearing wire-rimmed glasses.

"Joe." A smile dimpled her rosy round cheeks. "Come eat with us. This is my roommate, Louise." Kate stuffed green mittens in her coat pocket.

"Hi. You're the fella who walked from New York City?" Louise took off her hat and ran long scarlet-tipped fingers through her cropped brown hair.

"Yes." Joe smiled. The girls' cheerfulness was infectious. He waited while they straightened their starched gray uniforms, his eyes lingering over the way Kate's rounded figure filled out the simple outfit. They waited while Louise wiped the steam from her glasses and then the three picked up trays.

"I don't have to report to work till Monday," Joe said, setting a plate piled with eggs and sausage on an empty table. "So I'm going to Saranac Lake and see. . ." Across the table, Kate crossed her lips with a finger. He stopped mid-sentence, sat down and forked scrambled eggs in his mouth.

"See what?" Louise asked. "Saranac Lake gives me the heebie-jeebies with all those consumptives." Louise shivered and sipped her coffee.

"Oh, would you look at the time?" Kate pushed back her chair. "I have to be at my station in two minutes. Come on, Joe, I'll show you where to take your dishes."

Joe took a last gulp of coffee and followed Kate. "Hey," he called over his shoulder to Louise, "sorry to run off on you. See you around." He caught up to Kate at the kitchen door.

"Thanks for taking my foot out of my mouth."

"You must learn to be more closemouthed, Joe," Kate chided. "The Club doesn't want any of Saranac Lake's germs creeping over here. Read the rulebook. I'm sure it was the first thing Tom Madden gave you."

"It was."

"Let's see if we can get someone to pack you a lunch." Kate flashed her dimples at a cook who immediately stopped flipping pancakes and made sandwiches for Joe.

She walked to the door with him, explaining how to find Saranac Avenue.

"Someone's sure to give you a ride," she said, watching Joe pull on his deerskin mittens. "Maybe you'll come across my brother, Al. He drives the village snow roller. He'll let you hitch a ride."

The sky began to lighten as he started out across Mirror Lake. In spite of the early hour, he passed a number of solitary figures hunched against the cold, headed for their jobs at the Club. He found Saranac Avenue, the main road rising steeply from the lakeshore. At the crest of the hill a white frame church stood, a small cross on its modest steeple.

Joe hesitated, noting people climbing the steps, removing their caps before disappearing inside. Only a Catholic church would hold an early weekday service. Obviously morning Mass was about to start.

He didn't want another delay in his journey to Alice. But to deliberately pass by when he knew Mass was starting? He hadn't been inside a church since he left New York. Joe sighed and crossed the street. Sure enough, the sign out front said it was St. Agnes Roman Catholic Church. He opened the door and saw the priest in the purple robes of Advent praying before a white steepled altar. Suddenly he realized he needed this as much as the hot breakfast he just consumed. He pulled his toque from his head and slipped into a back pew.

Quietly he lowered the kneeler and blessed himself. Thank you God for getting me here, he prayed. And forgive me for taking a life to save mine.

8

"I certainly sleep the days away!" Alice commented to her friends one morning as she woke from an after-breakfast nap.

"It's the air," Charlotte said, breathing deeply.

"That and the food. Eat once for yourself. Eat once for the germs. Eat once to gain weight," Lilly recited in the sing-song voice of a schoolchild. "It's a good thing waists aren't in style because I sure don't have one. Howard's coming before Christmas, and I don't have one decent dress to wear that fits."

"Listen to you complain!" Charlotte said. "The rest of us have to work at not losing weight. Fat is insurance, remember." Charlotte paused, her breathing becoming raspy." And you who gets dressed every day. . .and walks to town. . .and talk to others in the dining room. I haven't been off this porch in three years." Two angry red spots appeared on Charlotte's pale cheeks.

"How dare you flaunt how well you're doing while I must be content to wash in the bathroom for my day's entertainment. And Alice is looking forward to the day she's allowed to sit up for five minutes." Charlotte turned her head away, her heaving blankets indicating how much her tirade had agitated her lungs.

Lilly and Alice stared at the snow falling noiselessly onto the balsam branches. Alice studied the delicate flakes drifting onto her navy wool blanket. Had she heard right? Charlotte had been here for three years? She certainly didn't appear any worse off than herself.

Charlotte began to cough as Alice knew she surely would after such an outburst. "Oh, Charly, I'm so sorry!" Lilly flung herself on Charlotte's bed, embracing her in a hug. "Please don't cough so. Oh, God. She's shooting a ruby! Ring the bell, Alice." Lilly wiped Charlotte's face with a hankie, then swiped at the bright red blood splattered on the blankets. Charlotte was hemorrhaging, badly!

The sisters arrived and rolled Charlotte back into her bedroom, forcing Lilly to remain on the porch. She gripped the porch railing with her mittened hands and turned her tear-stained face up into the falling snow.

Soon they heard the familiar sound of Dr. Hayes's Franklin laboring up Helen Hill to Conifer Cottage and listened in silence to his heavy tread on the stairs. The footsteps stopped at Charlotte's room. Her terrible wracking coughs made it impossible for Alice to hear what Dr. Hayes was saying to Hilda and Ursula. Periodically, Ursula would scurry to the kitchen for more ice to slow the flow of Charlotte's hemorrhage.

Lilly hadn't budged from the railing. Some inner voice reminded Alice of two more TB commandments: "Don't get cold. Don't get wet."

"Lilly, please come out of the snow before something happens to you, too." Alice reached out when she saw Lilly's anguish. Lilly left her post on the railing and sat stiffly on the edge of Alice's bed.

"I'm such an insensitive clod. I knew Charlotte was feeling badly about spending another Christmas away from her little girls." Lilly sniffed and dabbed her eyes with a hankie. "Do you know her youngest girl has never spent a Christmas with her mother?" Alice's mittens patted Lilly's mittens comfortingly.

"Do you hear that?" Lilly sprang from the bed and went to the northwest corner of the porch where she could just see down Helen Hill.

"What?"

"Horses! It's the iceman." A chill ran down Alice's back. Charlotte had told her more than once about the terror all tuberculars felt when the iceman was summoned to some cure cottage. Every patient knew it meant ice was needed to stop a hemorrhage. Alice added her prayers to those she was sure other consumptives along Helen Hill were murmuring. One for the stricken consumptive. One in gratitude they had been spared for now.

"Oh, God!" Lilly said. "Suppose Dr. Hayes can't stop it?"

Almost a week went by before Charlotte rejoined them on the porch. When Hilda wheeled her out the first day, Charlotte looked terrible with dull eyes sunken into her white face. She looked far too frail to support the heavy blankets heaped upon her.

"We've had a little setback," Hilda said, making sure Charlotte's covers were firmly tucked in. "Dr. Hayes has ordered no sitting up for six weeks. No deep breaths. Now, ladies," Hilda stood up to her full six feet and stared down at Lilly. "If you want to see our patient recover, you know it means you must not conversation make."

"Yes, Ma'am," Lilly said. Hilda had barely left the porch before Lilly raced over to kneel by Charlotte's bed.

"Please forgive me," she entreated. "Just tell me what I can do. . .no, no, don't talk." Lilly put a mittened finger to Charlotte's blue lips. "But when you can, I'll do anything you ask. I can bring you things back from town. I'll write letters to your girls."

Ursula had slipped onto the porch and went quickly to Lilly, urging her away from Charlotte. "Come, Lilly," she said, placing an arm about her shoulder and helping her to her feet. "It's time to take your *spaziergang*. . .your walk."

Alice looked on from a sitting-up position in her very own cure chair. Five days of temperatures under one hundred had earned her the privilege. For a while she didn't think she'd ever get the darn thermometer to drop below a hundred and one.

Yesterday was the fifth straight day and her first with a completely normal ninety-eight six. Immediately after quiet hours, her cure chair, identical to Charlotte's sturdy, slatted chair, was delivered. She now had permission to sit up for the morning cure. Afternoons, she still must lie flat in her iron bed.

But it was definitely a step in the right direction. If she could keep the thermometer under a hundred for another week, she would earn permission to be in her cure chair all day. And if that went well, she'd start walking.

From her new vantage point in a cure chair, she could see over the porch railing. Conifer Cottage clung to a corner lot half way up Helen Hill on the high side of Shepard Street. Pelletier Cottage looked up at Conifer Cottage from the low side of Shepard, making it possible for Alice to observe the activities on the sitting-out porches of Pelletier. Lilly had told her they took in male consumptives and boasted she knew most of them.

Lilly certainly doesn't take curing rules seriously, Alice thought, and yet never gets any worse. You'd think she'd want to get well enough to go home. I don't want to spend my life on a porch. It's been seven weeks and I miss Joe so much. Alice watched snowflakes drift lazily out of a gray sky.

Where was Joe? She had visualized his arrival a hundred times. Even now she experienced a joyful catch in her throat when she replayed her favorite fantasy of their reunion. It'd be her old Joe and she'd recognize his step on the stairs as he ran to find her. Full of good spirits. Not the overburdened man with the lackluster eyes who put her on the train. She'd meet him at the door to the sitting-out porch and Joe would grab her in a big hug, lifting her off her feet. And she'd bury her face in his neck, enjoying the light rasping of his shaven face against her nose and inhaling his scent.

But her dream stopped there. There was a rule forbidding kissing. Of course she didn't want to pass this horrible disease to her husband but she badly needed to be kissed and loved.

Her favorite picture of Joe, the one in his doughboy uniform, sat on her dresser where she could blow him a kiss every night, and she could count on him being there looking at her with his open half-smile every morning. Even on her worse days, the cocky look in his dark eyes brought a smile to her own lips.

In the picture, Joe knelt on one knee in the front line of his troop. Small-boned and nimble, the straps of his heavy backpack squared his shoulders unnaturally. The sleeves of his uniform stopped a good three inches above his wrists. Alice had memorized every detail in the picture, even the way his veins stood out on the back of his fine-skinned hands.

Lilly, her cheeks colored by the nippy air, arrived for the mandatory two-hour afternoon nap humming a Christmas carol. "Why so sad?" she asked Alice.

"I think something has happened to Joe. When I left New York, he promised he'd be here in two weeks." Alice drew her lower lip between her teeth. "What do you suppose is keeping him?"

Lilly perched on Alice's bed. "Whatever it is, I bet he'll have a great story to tell when he gets here. You mustn't let yourself get worked up about it. Besides," she continued, "if you want to look good when he gets here, you know what it takes." Lilly rose and settled into her white-spindled cure chair, pulling blankets up to her chin.

"I know. Sleep, eat and think happy thoughts." But Alice found herself unable to close her eyes; she sat staring at the cold blue sky. Early afternoon, and already the pale sun was beginning its descent in the December sky. Her porchmates didn't talk in front of her, but she knew they secretly thought Joe never intended to come. She could see it in their eyes. They felt sorry for her.

Why does everyone tiptoe around problems? Alice clamped her teeth together so tightly her jaw ached. For the first time, nagging prickles of doubt about her husband's intentions demanded her attention. She needed to mull them over with someone. She sighed. How many times had she been told that worry hindered the cure?

Alice glanced at Lilly, who napped with a faint smile on her bright red lips. She should be happy, Alice thought. Her fiancé arrives tomorrow and he'll take her out of here. At least she's learned not to lord her good fortune over the rest of us.

Alice remembered the morning when Lilly was out and Charlotte had told her Lilly and Howard became engaged two years ago, just before Lilly was diagnosed as a tubercular.

"He's handsome, all right, I'll give him that," Charlotte had said. "That dark wavy hair slicked down just so to show off his face to its best advantage. He strolled in here last summer with his straw boater and silk tie and stood in the door waiting for Lilly to go to him." Charlotte had grown silent. Alice noticed her bear robe rising and falling with the exertion of talking.

"I can't quite put my finger on it," Charlotte started up again. "He just doesn't come across as very sincere. Lilly's family has a lot of money. Her father sends her a huge amount every month. And things like that fancy spindled cure chair. I think Howard feels he's snared a pretty woman capable of giving him the kind of life he deserves."

"Alice! This is Howard." Lilly dragged her fiancé to the sitting-out porch the next morning. "Isn't he the bee's knees?" Howard hung back, homburg in hand, smiling in Alice's general direction. His eyes seemed to be looking over Alice's shoulder at the snow-covered balsams.

"I've heard so much about you," Alice said. "You're to be congratulated on your engagement. Lilly is a wonderful girl."

Howard bestowed one of his perfect smiles upon Alice. "Well," he said, looking at his pocket watch, "our reservation is in ten minutes, Lilly."

"Then I guess we're off," Lilly said to her porchmates. "I'll tell you all about it in the morning." Her blue eyes glittered in the snow-bright sun.

"Excuse me, sir?" A thin young man weighed down by the bulk of a huge raccoon coat approached Howard as he helped Lilly from the car. "Could you tell me how to get to Church Street?"

Lilly, intrigued by the unusual placements of pelts on the coat, walked up to the stranger. "Church Street is the next cross street." Lilly looked closer at the man's drawn face. There was something about those intense eyes.

"Lilly, darling, we'll be late for our reservation." Howard came forward and steered Lilly away.

"Really, Howard, that was awfully rude. He didn't seem very well. I'm surprised he has exercise permission," she said, assuming the man was a fellow tubercular. "I was going to offer him a ride when you yanked me away."

Lilly sank into the padded chair the maitre d' held for her. "What a treat," she said, "sitting in a classy dining room with snow-white table linen set with sparkling crystal and polished silver. I bet that man in the fur coat would like to sit down for awhile." Lilly's red cupid's bow remained in a pout over Howard's bad manners.

Howard leaned across the table, his cold black eyes boring into Lilly. "I didn't come all the way to this, this frontier town to rub elbows with every lun. . ."

"With every what?" Lilly demanded, her cheeks growing hot under a layer of rouge. "You were going to say lunger, weren't you? And just what do you think I am, Howard? I'm one of the Saranac lungers, too. Does that make me repulsive to you?"

The next morning Alice and Charlotte fretted about Lilly's whereabouts. They finally decided Howard must have picked her up after breakfast.

But Alice knew something was wrong when Hilda wheeled Lilly from her bedroom onto the porch for the mandatory afternoon nap. Alice was anticipating a detailed accounting of the day. She was at a complete loss of what to say to the silent, staring Lilly. A blue plaid woolen scarf was wrapped about her neck, and her mittened hands lay motionless atop three heavy blankets. Alice had never seen Lilly without her red lipstick. She found her friend's down-turned mouth unsettling.

Alice looked over Lilly's head to Charlotte, still under orders to remain flat. Charlotte shook her head. All three porchmates, frustrated by the overwhelming shackles of their disease, stared at the inevitable falling snow this week before Christmas.

"He took his ring back," Lilly said an hour later, breaking the silence.

"Lilly, I'm so sorry," Alice said. "What a cad, just before Christmas and everything."

"He said he was sure I'd understand how difficult it had been for him, a red-blooded American, to be chained to an invalid."

Alice and Charlotte exchanged glances over Lilly's head but remained silent, waiting for their wounded friend to continue.

"Then do you know what he said?" Lilly's voice cracked with a heart-wrenching sob. "He wanted the ring to give to a girl this Christmas."

"Lilly. Lilly! Stop this instant." Charlotte broke her doctor's ban on talking. "Don't let Howard rob you of the progress you've made." Lilly tried to curb her crying, swiping at her red nose with her mittens.

"Lilly, honey. Why don't you get some tissues from my dresser?" Alice offered. Lilly rose like an obedient child, and did as asked. Alice reached out to squeeze her hand as she passed.

When Lilly returned, she had Joe's picture with her "This is your husband, right?"

"Yes, that's Joe." Alice felt uncomfortable talking about Joe when Lilly's feelings had been freshly bruised.

Lilly's plucked brows knitted together as she tried to solve some puzzle. "I think I saw him yesterday."

"Oh, Lilly, do you really think so?"

"I'm not sure, but there's something about those eyes. This man came up and asked directions to Church Street. He had a gorgeous raccoon coat."

"That couldn't have been my Joe. We don't have the money for a fur coat." Alice sank back on her pillow.

"I don't know, Alice. There is a resemblance. But this man was a lot thinner."

The porch trembled as Hilda stepped out. Standing with hands on hips, she reminded the girls it was the village's mandatory nap time and was sure their voices could be heard on Main Street.

"Conifer Cottage girls follow the rules," she admonished. "If you break the rule, you will be responsible for the fine."

"Well, how are my lovely lilies this afternoon?" Dr. Hayes inquired as he arrived at the end of the afternoon rest period.

The three porchmates brightened at the sight of their beloved pudgy doctor. His shaggy, graying hair met the collar of his tweed coat. It wasn't buttoned, Alice noticed, probably because it wouldn't meet over the maroon sweater of nubby wool he wore under it. He always came wearing a pair of worn slippers. Alice had wondered if Dr. Hayes wore slippers inside the galoshes he had on the first day she saw him. But Charlotte told her the sisters insisted he remove his boots and shoes at the door so as not to bring any germs in from other cure cottages. They kept a pair of slippers for him in a downstairs closet.

Ursula stood quietly, her faded yellow hair swept up in a sensible bun that somehow managed to stay in place throughout her long day. She had a pad and pencil ready to note Dr. Hayes's directives. She handed him Alice's temperature chart.

"Ah, this is a nice Christmas present you've given me, girl." Dr. Hayes beamed. "A very impressive string of ninety-eight sixes. And you've gained almost a pound. I should think that would warrant being able to wash in the bathroom, let's say. . .well, why not start tomorrow?"

"What a treat to clean up for the holidays. I wish there was something more I could actually do to get better quicker."

Dr. Hayes, stubby hands folded over his belly, slouched comfortably in the chair Ursula had drawn up to Alice's bed, giving the impression he had the entire day to visit with the young women.

"Do you think you'd be up to freezing it out?"

"I'm afraid to ask what that means," Alice laughed.

"Ursula would bundle you up at night before bed and then, instead of just opening the windows, she'd put you outside on the porch for the night"

Alice shivered at the thought. "If you think it would heal my lungs faster, I'll try."

"Doctors pretty much agree that one winter in Saranac is worth two summers. So it stands to reason that if you stay outdoors day and night the cure should go faster." Dr. Hayes stood, ready to move on to Lilly.

"Doctor, have you heard from my husband? Lilly was in town yesterday and saw a man that looked like my Joe."

"No, I have not." He patted her hand. "No doubt he'll be along any day now."

Ursula prepared Alice for her first night on the porch. After she donned her flannel pajamas, Ursula held out the pants to a sweatsuit. Next, she was instructed to sit on the edge of her bed while Ursula snugged the ankles with twine.

"Why does Dr. Hayes always call us his lilies?"

"I'm sure it's because he thinks you're all just as pretty as flowers," Ursula said. "You need to stand again, dear, while I stuff your legs with paper." Ursula began crumpling a Herald Tribune.

"But why lilies and not roses or petunias?" Alice persisted, as she layered on several sweaters and topped it all with a roomy overcoat, knitted cap, and two pairs of wool socks. Secretly, Alice didn't like being called a lily. Lilies were for funerals and she wished Dr. Hayes wouldn't greet the girls that way.

"I really don't know the answer to that," Ursula responded, helping Alice get into bed. Wrapped in rumpled paper as she was, Alice rustled noisily.

Ursula heaped on the wool blankets and crisscrossed two pillows over her face, leaving only her nose exposed. She then rolled the huge mound onto the porch.

"I've forgotten the petroleum jelly, dear. I will be but a minute." Ursula fluttered away, returning shortly and smoothing a large glob of grease on the underside of Alice's nose.

"I'm sure there's a good reason for this."

"Yes, indeed. The grease will keep your nose from freezing to the pillows," Ursula cheerfully responded. "I'll leave this bell so you can reach it easily. You lie there and breathe that good balsam air all night and you'll be surprised at the good it'll do."

"I will do whatever it takes for a year. Then, I'm going home," Alice chanted until her eyes became heavy.

Ursula returned to the kitchen after settling the girls for the night. She found Hilda wiping the counters with a carbolic solution.

"A little schnapps, Sister?"

"Ja. We have a problem to discuss."

Ursula pressed her lips together. She knew her sister's "problems" usually meant one of her girls was behind in her room and board. If a girl had to be confronted with it, the worry inevitably triggered a setback.

She'd like to thrash those uncaring families that forgot their girls were fighting for their lives! Lily's father was one of the worst. Yes, his check arrived the first week of every single month and right now the closet under the stairs hid a big box of Christmas presents from him, but he never came to visit his daughter. He didn't even call the girl for her last birthday. Just sent the expensive white wicker cure chair. She pushed open the door to the dining room a little more forcefully than usual, causing it to bang against the wall.

Ursula's worn fingers sought the key ring in her apron pocket. She selected the small brass key to the liquor cabinet in the black walnut breakfront. With a corner of her apron she wiped a section of ornate carving. She loved caring for the massive piece of furniture. The breakfront and a few pieces of lead crystal had come over from the old country where they had been proud possessions of many generations of Guenthers.

When the sisters' mother died, an aunt took in ten year old Ursula and brought her to America. Hilda stayed behind to care for her father, but the sisters were reunited after his death twelve years later, before the war.

Returning to the kitchen with schnapps and glasses, Ursula found Hilda at the scrubbed table reading the Adirondack Enterprise. Her wire-rimmed glasses clung halfway down her large nose as she read.

"It says here," Hilda pointed to a column, "Saranac Lake must provide more beds for incoming consumptives. Town fathers will have to shoulder the responsibility of building a new sanitorium unless more private cure cottages are opened. The results of the recent survey indicate Saranac Lake has a population of seven thousand, and curing consumptives number two thousand." Hilda raised her head from the paper and removed her glasses. "Our village becomes a city."

"You think we should take in more girls?"

"Nein. But it is good to know the need for our beds is great."

The sisters tasted their schnapps.

"Well," Ursula said, "what is our problem?"

"It's our new girl. Dr. Hayes said the funds Mr. Lattimer sent are nearly used up." Hilda went on to explain that Dr. Hayes had sent a bill to Mr. Lattimer, who wrote back saying that he only agreed to the initial payment."

"How can that be?" Ursula squeezed her laced fingers together. "Mr. Lattimer can't expect her to pay for her own cure!"

"You know she'll have to go to Ray Brook. We can't afford charity cases."

"Surely we can wait until after the holidays," Ursula said. "There has to be some kind of mix-up. Alice expects her husband any day now."

"Half the patients in the village expect their families any day, Sister. The letter Mr. Lattimer sent was from New York and I opened it today. He will not be here for Christmas."

"But the trauma of moving at Christmas. . ."

"Ja. You are right. We will put it out of our minds until the first of the year. Then we must be firm, Sister. You'd have us collecting those girls like stray kittens."

Ursula nodded unhappily, fearful Alice was too fragile to bear the regimen of the State Hospital at Ray Brook.

9

On the Saturday morning before Christmas, Alice cured on the sitting-out porch with Charlotte. The sun glinted off puffs of snow on the balsam. Lilly had walked into town, and a melancholy settled like a heavy blanket on the two young women secured on their stout wooden cure chairs. Alice watched water drip from the tips of icicles running the length of the porch roof.

"Listen to this," Charlotte said, holding up a little pink pamphlet. "'Never give up!'" She read. "'It is better always to hope, than once to despair. Fling off the load of Doubt's cankering fetter, breaking its dark spell.'"

"Couldn't be written by anyone sentenced to Saranac Lake."

"As a matter of fact, these pep talks are collected by two tubercu- lars." Charlotte passed the pamphlet over to Alice. "It's the latest Trotty Veck booklet. They give me a lot of comfort when I'm feeling blue."

"What does Trotty Veck mean?"

"Charles Dickens wrote about a messenger he called Trotty Veck who had perfect faith in his ability to deliver a message no matter how difficult or complicated."

"I'm sick and tired of everyone in this place pretending life is great." Alice tossed the pamphlet back to Charlotte. "I don't see how you can just sit here year after year and not want to scream your head off."

"There's no alternatives for tuberculars, Alice. The only hope I have of going home to my girls is to take this cure seriously and be optimistic that my lungs will clear."

"I want to do something. Every day it's the same old thing. . .wake up, eat, cure, eat, cure, go to bed." Alice's mittened hands kneaded the edge of her navy wool blanket.

"You are doing something," Charlotte said. "Following doctor's orders is what it's all about. You're even freezing it out."

"Alice! Are you up there? Al-ice!" Lilly called from somewhere outside. Alice sat up in her chair and peered out over the railing toward Pelletier Cottage. She saw Lilly jumping up and down on the first floor porch frantically waving her hands. Next to her stood a thin man engulfed in a huge fur coat.

"Look who's here!" Lilly yelled, the excitement in her voice carrying clearly up to the porch.

"What's Lilly up to now?" Charlotte asked from her prone position.

"Lilly has herself in a tizzy over some man in a fur coat," Alice explained.

"It's Joe!" Lilly called. Alice's throat went dry. She studied the man, but with just his head protruding from the shaggy coat, she saw only a vague likeness to her Joe.

"I'm bringing him up!" She saw Lilly grab the man's hand and drag him down Pelletier's steps.

Suddenly they disappeared from view. Alice covered her face with her hands.

"What's happening?" Charlotte asked.

"Lilly thinks she found Joe," Alice whispered, not daring to believe. "She's on her way up with him." She turned to Charlotte. "Could it really be?"

Both young women twisted around and stared at the door. They heard feet padding up the stairs and recognized Lilly's chatter. Above it all came Hilda's admonition to Lilly not to stress her lungs by running.

The French doors from Alice's bedroom flew open and Lilly burst onto the porch. Alice saw a huge fur coat fill the doorway, the man's face still hidden in the shadows of her bedroom. He stepped hesitantly onto the porch, his eyes darting about.

"Joe," Alice whispered, then with outstretched arms she called joyfully, "Joe!" Two steps brought him to her side and he dropped to a knee before her cure chair. Hungrily, they reached for each other. Joe pressed her head against the fur of his coat while Alice's arms found their way inside it. After a long moment they pulled back, eager to look at one another.

"You're so thin!" Alice cradled Joe's gaunt face in her hands.

"You look so much better!" Smiling and laughing, they alternated between hugging and touching.

Kiss me, Alice begged silently. Oh, Joe, forget the rules this once and kiss me.

God, I want to kiss you, Joe yearned. With her face cupped in his hands, he traced her lips with his thumbs. Alice gasped at the sensation and Joe stood quickly before he accepted the invitation her soft parted lips offered.

He removed his fur coat and pack. Alice experienced physical pain at the sight of her husband's bony body that even sweaters and long johns couldn't hide.

"I brought you something." Joe reached into his coat pocket and retrieved a scented burlap pillow and handed it to Alice. "Kinda corny, but they said the smell is good for you."

Alice filled her lungs with the familiar balsam scent before reading the message: "I pine for you and balsam too." Laughing, she hugged the pillow.

"Oh, Joe, I've missed you so. Come sit close to me on my chair." She moved her legs to the edge and patted the place where Joe should sit. He sat facing Alice and held her small hands in his.

"What took you so long? I've been terribly worried." Alice searched her husband's eyes, wanting to know everything instantly. His eyes had changed somehow, she thought. Behind the happiness of their reunion, she saw a deep tiredness, like the worn-out look of an old man.

It took a long while to recount their adventures since separating at Grand Central Station, every sentence punctuated by a touch. And then they would pause, fighting for control before a touch became the kiss Alice's disease denied them.

"But if you've been at the Club since Thursday, how come it's taken all this time to get here?"

"I was hoping you wouldn't ask," Joe said, reaching for her hand. "For some reason the Guenther sisters thought you were Alice Lattimer. Even your doctor didn't know you're Alice Devlin. I know you don't want to hear this, but I believe your father failed to mention that you were married to me when he sent the down payment. One more chance for him to show his disapproval of our marriage."

"I wish he wasn't so. . .mean."

"It took two days to track you down. You better believe I've set everyone straight."

When they were ready to rejoin the little world of Alice's cure porch, they looked about to discover the porchmates had slipped away when Joe came, giving the couple privacy for their reunion. Alice heard a little scratching at a window and turned to see Lilly smiling and waving from Charlotte's bedroom window. Alice smiled back.

Hilda strode onto the porch. "The husband has arrived, Ja?" Her strong white teeth flashed in the snow-bright light. She stuck the noontime thermometer in Alice's mouth and went about sliding the glass panels into place.

"It looks like he could some nourishment use," she observed, standing with hands on her large hips. "Will you join your wife for dinner, Mr. Devlin?"

Joe stayed until Hilda rounded up the dinner trays. Ursula wheeled Charlotte onto to the porch and Lilly followed. To give the couple some privacy, the sisters allowed Charlotte to have her dinner on a tray in the bedroom.

Now Lilly walked right up to Joe and said, "You're every bit as good-looking as your picture." Alice watched Joe struggle to find something to say to Lilly. She introduced him to everyone, but eventually Hilda announced it would be two o'clock in ten minutes.

Joe retrieved his pack and dug out a brown paper parcel. "Your sister mailed this to me at the Club," he said handing it to Alice.

"My first mail since I got here," Alice said, turning it first one way and then the other before setting it on her table

."Why don't you wait until after the nap to open it," Hilda took the package from Alice's hands. "Having your husband here is all the excitement you should have for the morning. You need to rest now."

"It will be something special to wake up to," Alice agreed. "I hope Nancy wrote a nice long letter." She turned her eyes back to her husband and reached for his hand.

"When will you be back?"

He kissed her fingers, saying, "One. . .two. . .three. . .four days till Christmas Eve. Do you think you can wait that long?"

"Not one minute longer!" Alice said. "Joe?"

"Hmm?" He smoothed the soft curls off her forehead and twirled a long lock around his finger."

"I don't have anything to give you for Christmas."

"How can you say that?" He cupped her face in his hands and looked deep into her troubled blue eyes. "There's color in these soft cheeks." He stopped to stroke her cheeks with the back of his hand. "Hilda says you're staying at ninety-eight six, and I haven't heard you cough since I got here. Those are pretty wonderful Christmas presents."

"I am going to get better, Joe. We'll be home for Christmas next year."

Ursula stood by the big oak door as Joe walked down the stairs, gripping the stout railing to ease his frostbitten feet.

"We're all so happy that you've arrived, Mr. Devlin. I'm sure Alice's cure will progress at a much quicker rate now that she doesn't have to worry over your safety. Will you be staying long?"

"Till I can take Alice back to New York with me," Joe said, slotting his coat buttons.

"That's wonderful." Ursula clapped her hands together. "It means so much to the girls to have their families nearby, especially during the holidays. Please plan on coming Christmas Eve and spending Christmas day with us. I'm sure we can find you a place to sleep."

"I'd like that. I need to get a better understanding of Alice's expenses, too." He reached into a coat pocket and took out his wool toque, pulling it down snugly over his ears.

"Ja, my sister wants that, too. But I'm sure it can wait until after Christmas." She opened the door and Joe passed through.

10

Joe found Tom Madden at his desk at 6:45 a.m. on Monday.
"Morning," said Joe.

Tom grunted without looking up from his papers. "Find some coveralls in the closet, then I'll show you around the garage."

Joe opened a likely door and found a closet packed with brown coveralls on hangers. Each had the LPC emblem. Locating a pair that fit pretty well, he was just doing up the last button when Madden shuffled the papers on his desk and stood up.

He studied Joe with cold eyes. Joe watched him stare at his feet and briefly wondered if the man could see the blackened, frostbitten toes through his shoes. Madden raised his head and appeared to be looking at a spot above Joe's right ear. Self-consciously, Joe ran a hand through his hair and cleared his throat.

"You need a haircut, Devlin," Madden said. "The Club won't tolerate unkempt employees. You're expected to wear clean Club coveralls any time you're working to be easily identified as a mechanic by the guests." He glared at Joe as though expecting an insubordinate reply. Seconds ticked away, then he turned for the garage. Joe followed.

Each of the five bays in the garage contained an eleven or fifteen passenger Cadillac.

"Go through them bumper to bumper," Madden ordered. His thick black brows gave his face a perpetual scowl. "I want these cars purring. I'll be in my office all morning, then I have to go away on. . .business. You're expected to work till five."

Joe started right in on a Cadillac touring car. Only glanced up once when, through the window, he caught the image of Madden coming down the stairs from the living quarters. Probably checking to see if I made my bed, Joe thought. But when he stopped at the noon whistle and ran upstairs to get his coat, he didn't know what to make of its ripped lining. Neatly cut. Why? What was Madden up to? Joe had examined the coat closely after getting it back from Earl. He was sure the lining wasn't ripped. The only damage appeared to be the brown bloodstains from Earl's mangled hand.

Geeze, how was he ever going to stitch it back right? And the bloodstains on the satin lining. . .how was he going to explain those to Mr. Bingham?

Joe spent the days before Christmas lubricating chassis and repacking wheel bearings. He checked belts and re-grooved tires. Occasionally he looked up to see Madden's bulk casting black shadows across the garage floor as the man stood at his office door watching.

Joe passed the time while carrying out the mindless maintenance by recalling happier days when he first brought his bride to their little flat overlooking Madison Square Park. Back then, the estrangement from their parents had given the newlyweds a welcomed privacy. Sometimes he walked away from the car he was working on to peer out the window overlooking Mirror Lake.

Madden found him at the window one day. "Problem, Devlin?" he called across the garage.

"No, sir." Joe jerked away from the window. "You don't get paid to look at the view."

Joe walked back to the car he was working on, grinding his teeth to prevent saying something he'd regret. He wished he didn't need this job so badly.

What can we do to get you some Christmas spirit?" Kate said when they ran in to each other at Finches for supper one night. "How about the movie tonight?"

"Can't waste money I don't have on a movie."

"Didn't Tom Madden give you a movie pass?" Kate began picking up their dishes.

"No." Joe drained his coffee and placed the cup on Kate's tray.

"Doesn't surprise me. Anyway, there's a movie every night in the Agora. Free for us employees." Kate nibbled at her thumbnail.

"I don't think. . ."

"Nonsense! I can't let you brood all alone here with Christmas just a few days away. It's the Thief of Baghdad, the Douglas Fairbanks film everyone raved about last summer. Did you know it made the Times' Ten Best List?"

Joe didn't know how to say no and let himself be dragged along. Seated in the darkened theater, surrounded by Kate's cheerful friends, Joe watched bare-chested Fairbanks, garbed in pantaloons, scale walls with a magic rope, fight off dragons and ride a winged horse.

As the film came to a close, Fairbanks, riding a magic carpet, escaped over the rooftops with his princess. The stars spelled out: "Happiness Must Be Earned." If that's really so, Joe thought, 1926 should be a very happy year for Alice and me.

Soft, feathery snowflakes lazed about the sky as the little group of moviegoers walked to their respective cottages. Behind Kate and Joe, a girl began singing a Christmas carol. Others joined in.

Joe found himself studying the dimples in Kate's face when he said good night to her and headed for the garage beyond the circle of employee housing. According to Kate, he was the only one staying over the garage. Kate shared a room with Louise on the third floor of Finches.

Kate was right. It was lonely. Joe lay on his narrow iron bed, fingers laced behind his head, staring at the ceiling. He moved his hips to avoid the spot where a broken spring pushed against the thin mattress. He hoped Alice wasn't this lonely. He knew she missed her mother and sister.

Joe had accepted being banished from the Lattimer household. He understood how devastated the Lattimers were when Joe, an Irish Catholic, whisked their elder daughter away to be married by a justice of the peace. It was the same story at his family's house where his own mother wouldn't let him cross the threshold after he married a Methodist outside the Church.

But a girl was different. What kind of father would refuse to let his daughter into the house? Weren't there all kinds of things a newly married girl needed to learn from her mother?

Still, it wasn't until he lay alone in his room over the garage that he faced the ugly truth. When his father-in-law's money ran out, he wouldn't be able to meet Alice's expenses.

Doctor's calls, medications. I'll be damned if I beg Mr. Lattimer for more money. I might be able to pick up some part-time work in the village, but how could I keep it from Madden? The Club rule book strictly forbade Club employees from seeking jobs in the village.

Puzzling over his finances, Joe heard the church bells from across the lake toll away the night.

11

Christmas Eve! Alice lay listening to muted Christmas carols. Joe had come! Her body reacted with a pleasant tingle of anticipation knowing she would see him again tonight.

Alice felt like a little girl again, waiting for the magic of Christmas. Briefly she worried if she was allowed to feel such joy. Would Hilda frown on such excitement? She quickly tossed the doubt aside.

Ursula found Alice quietly humming along with the carolers who sang on the Pelletier Cottage porch, a smile lighting her face.

"How about a red ribbon for your hair?" Ursula asked, handing Alice her comb and brush. Dr. Hayes had recently allowed Alice to raise her arms and brush her own hair. She found it tiring, and paused to rest several times.

"Isn't Christmas wonderful?" Alice asked, as she held her hand out for the ribbon.

"Wait till you see our tree when you come down tomorrow morning," Ursula said, clasping her hands together in delight. "You'll meet all the other Conifer girls and Sister and I have baked special treats."

"I've been smelling wonderful things for days. And Hilda smells like cinnamon and vanilla instead of disinfectant when she comes to take our temps."

"When we were children," Ursula said, pushing Alice through the doors, "our mother began preparing for Christmas a month ahead."

Alice looked out at a pearly gray sky with big soft flakes falling, making a pristine blanket for the wondrous day to come. Outside, the jingle of sleigh bells mixed with merrily tooting car horns. Laughter filled the air like the song of birds.

Alice was taken aback to see Lilly, wrapped in robes, her downturned mouth almost blue without its usual bright lipstick.

Lilly's eyes were closed, shutting the door on conversation. How come she's not over there singing with the men? Suddenly Alice felt guilty, like having only one piece of special candy that couldn't be shared. She had Joe, but Lilly would have a dismal Christmas with her engagement being broken so cruelly.

Charlotte appeared to be dozing also. Probably building up strength for her daughters' visit the day after Christmas. We'll have to make an effort to help Lilly through the holidays, Alice thought.

She reached for her sister's letter, wanting to read it once more before writing back. It felt nice to have something to do other than watch icicles grow.

Dear Alice,

I miss you so much! Even though Father forbade me to see you, knowing I could stop by your flat after school was a lot better than knowing you're hundreds of miles away. Mama and I made fruitcakes for all the aunts. I hope she won't miss the one I'm sending to you and Joe. Has Joe gotten there yet? It must be wonderful to know your husband loves you soooo much. I hope I can find a man who will love me half as much.

Mother and Father are fine. Father never mentions your name. But I saw Mama in your room. Just sitting there in your chair. She was looking out the window, so she didn't see me. I know she was crying, because she kept wiping her eyes. I want to hear all about Saranac Lake, and what you're doing. Get better soon!

Your loving sister,

She picked up her pen and notepad to write her letter. "Joe arrived in time for Christmas," she began.

The sky was barely light when church bells welcomed Christmas morning. Their joyous clamor rose clearly up Helen Hill on their ascent to heaven.

During the symphony of bells Joe appeared with breakfast trays for both of them.

"Merry Christmas, dear heart."

"Oh, Joe, it really is a merry Christmas. You're here and I can feel I'm getting better every hour. I know we'll be back in our flat for next Christmas." They toasted the arrival of the holiday with mugs of creamy eggnog sprinkled with nutmeg and topped with a candied cherry.

"I still can't believe you eat so much," Joe said, digging into his own stack of pancakes. "The last time we ate breakfast together you barely finished a slice of toast."

"Hilda won't tolerate anything but an empty plate," Alice said. "And something about the air gives me an appetite, too. But I never will get used to the raw eggs."

"They make you eat raw eggs?"

"Ursula says it's to 'fill the cracks.'"

The sun had risen while they ate and from the two churches at the foot of Helen Hill came a glorious rendition of "The First Noel."

The cherished carol spread over cure cottages throughout the village. Joe reached for Alice's hand and they listened in awed silence until the last strains echoed over the mountains.

Sounds of Hilda and Ursula bustling about the halls broke the spell.

"I want to get downstairs." Alice squeezed Joe's hand. "It'll be my first time since they carried me in the door."

She took the steps slowly, gripping the rail, and sank gratefully onto the landing's bench. Joe perched beside her and clasped her small hand in his.

"If you promise not to eat too much," he said, "I'll carry you back to your room." Alice smiled, too weak to return his banter.

Ursula came to the foot of the stairs. "Come on, dear, I want you to meet the other girls." Joe helped her to her feet and they continued the descent.

"I had no idea this would be so hard," Alice said.

She stopped again at the bottom of the stairs, not willing to loosen her grip on the ornately carved newel post to cross the hall to the living room. Gently Joe loosened her perspiring hand and placed it over his arm, urging her forward.

The large living room was full of people milling around. Ursula steered Alice to a comfortable chair tucked in the corner by the dining room and found a footrest for her. Two up patients she hadn't met came up and introduced themselves. Alice was conscious of the way they studied Joe and how important it was to them to know if he was her husband. They left soon after learning Joe and Alice were very much married.

Now Alice sat, with Joe standing at her side, looking at the fragrant balsam tree, its branches dressed in shiny balls and silver pheasants. Small white candles perched on the tips of the boughs. Little puffs of angel hair gave the tree a mystical air. It was placed in the window at the front of the house so its beauty could be enjoyed by those on the porch as well.

"How do you like our tree?" Ursula asked, her voice alive with Christmas joy. "Sister spent five evenings placing the lametta just so." She reached out and touched one of the tinsel icicles with a finger. "In Germany, Christmas Eve was the *Bescherung*, the gift opening," Ursula explained. "But with so many of our girls not being allowed up, Sister decided they shouldn't come down for Christmas Eve and Christmas Day. And we didn't want to leave anyone alone in her room on Christmas. So we have *Bescherung* on Christmas morning. Now, Mr. Devlin, if you come with me, I have some drinks for you and Alice."

There was a huge pile of presents under the tree. Mostly small boxes, all gaily wrapped and tied with bright yarn. Mixed among them were large dress-size boxes professionally wrapped in shiny silver paper and garnished with golden ribbons and bows.

Alice motioned Lilly over and whispered, "No one mentioned there'd be gifts. Joe and I haven't brought any."

Lilly alighted on the arm of Alice's chair and patted her hand. "It's mostly stuff the sisters get for all of us. No one expects you to bring presents."

"What about all those wrapped in silver paper?" Alice asked. "They must come from an expensive store."

"They're from my father." She stood abruptly. "He sent something for every girl."

"Your father? I've never even met him, Lilly."

"He does it every year," Lilly shrugged. "I think he feels it excuses him from being here." Her blue eyes glittered dangerously close to tears. She swiped at her nose and walked quickly away.

Alice felt Lilly's pain. She knew too well the hurt of being abandoned by your own father. Connie, whom she just met, had her husband with her today. But many were alone, like Lilly.

Alice looked for Joe in the group of people milling about. She was not going to be melancholy today. Joe was here. Their Christmas would be a happy one.

She saw Joe adding logs to the fire in the cobblestone fireplace. Boughs of fragrant balsam covered the mantel. On one side a colorful wooden Nativity scene had been arranged. Joe stood and turned toward Alice, smiling when their eyes met. Alice saw him stoop to pick up two glasses filled with a dark red liquid.

"Why the downturned mouth, dear heart?" he asked, returning to her side and handing her a glass.

"Oh, Joe, I'm so happy you came."

"Is that why you look so sad?" Joe smoothed a curl off her face.

"No," Alice smiled. "I feel badly that Lilly and so many of the girls are alone. And proud that my husband cared enough to come." And sad, she added to herself, that we haven't heard from our parents.

Hilda and Ursula served a wondrous Christmas dinner of pork roast and sauerkraut and so many side dishes it was impossible to sample them all. The sisters passed bowls and platters, encouraging second and third helpings. But it was Hilda's famous creamy kaesekuchen dessert that brought the oohs and ahhhs.

Most of the girls sat at the dining room table. Alice, Charlotte and Connie, who had been allowed downstairs only for this special day, had trays in the living room. Joe and Connie's husband ate from small tables next to their wives. Charlotte ate alone.

Alice glanced her way, noting the mechanical way Charlotte chewed her food, keeping her eyes straight ahead. She didn't want to share Joe with anyone after being separated for so long, but Charlotte was her porchmate.

"Joe," she began, and Joe put down his knife and fork to help Charlotte settle in a chair where she could be part of the little group.

Even Christmas didn't excuse the two hour quiet time. Joe helped the sisters settle the girls on the downstairs porch, passing around fur robes and mittens.

When he eventually sat down next to Alice's cure chair, he found her dozing in the bright sun in her new woolen bed jacket. It was Lilly's father's gift to Alice. From a man we've never met, he thought.

A stranger buys my wife a Christmas present instead of visiting his daughter. Must be nice to have enough money to erase guilt. Joe pressed his lips together. Wished he could buy his wife things like that. Was he always going to rely on others to supply nice things? When am I going to get around to being the man in this family? Maybe the second job he recently took on would change things. He thought back to last Saturday morning when he had set out from Placid to find Alice.

Joe had the road to himself that morning, it being so early. Several miles outside Placid, he heard a car, its tires squealing in the snow. He came upon a Pierce-Arrow touring car off the road with its nose in the soft, deep snow. The driver was alternately throwing the car in forward and reverse, then gunning it till the engine roared and tires spun. The heavy car sank deeper.

"Give you a hand?" Joe called, over the noise of the engine. The driver looked over his shoulder at Joe. He killed the engine and got out, his light brown eyes snapping with irritation. His wide mouth clamped in a grim line under a precisely trimmed brown mustache.

Like Joe, the man wore a coon coat, but his hung straight to his ankles without the fancy horizontal rows of pelts around the hem that Joe's coat had. The man's simple collar was buttoned and a scarf wrapped his neck.

"Never thought someone would be coming along at this hour," the man said, offering his hand. "Name's Armand Dasset."

"Joe Devlin," Joe said, shaking the man's leather-gloved hand. "Got a shovel? Let's see if we can't get you back on the road." Joe shoveled and pushed. Dasset snapped off pine boughs to place under the rear tires. Eventually the Arrow roared back onto the road. Dasset offered Joe a ride.

"Haven't seen you around before," he said, moving the powerful car through its gears. "No, sir. Just got to Placid last week from New York."

"What line of work you in?"

"Mechanic. Got a job with the Club's fleet."

"Mechanic, you say." Dasset glanced at Joe. "Would seem there'd be more call for that back in the city."

Joe hesitated. Kate's warning about being closemouthed echoed in his mind. In the end he decided to ignore it, and told Dasset his story as they drove along.

Most of Saranac Lake was still waking up when Dasset's Pierce-Arrow rolled into town. He suggested breakfast at the Riverside Inn while they waited for the town to come to life.

"My treat," Dasset said. "Least I can do for getting me back on the road."

Dasset looked around the big dining room from their table in the furthermost corner before confiding to Joe.

"I have three men working for me full time, another ten or so part time," he began. "I like to keep them on the road between the border and New York City." He captured Joe's attention.

"Rum running?" Joe whispered.

Dasset nodded. "It's imperative the cars are in top form." He raised his coffee cup and drank. His eyes never left Joe's face.

"Could use a good mechanic."

"I have a job, and the Club doesn't like its employees working anywhere else."

"I know that. Also know the expense of a cure, Joe. This would be nights. I'd send someone around to pick you up. They'd never suspect."

Hope I did the right thing, taking the job with Dasset, Joe thought, as he sat in the Christmas afternoon sun. It's not going to be easy to keep this from Madden. Can't be easy for Alice either, sitting here every day looking at the snow. He studied his wife.

He had to admit Alice did look beautiful in her new jacket. He wasn't sure if the vibrant blue wool made her eyes sparkle when she took the jacket from its box, or if her blue eyes sparkled at receiving such a grand gift. The lace-trimmed round collar buttoned high on her neck. Lace trimmed the lower edge of the full sleeves. The jacket was big enough for Alice to wear her flannel pajamas and a sweater underneath and still look festive for Christmas.

How can I complain? he thought. Alice has little enough to brighten her days. Joe wrapped his coat about his knees and picked up one of the books that the sisters had given him. Before long, in the sunny stillness, with a full belly and his wife close by, Joe napped.

Voices of approaching carolers woke Joe and Alice simultaneously. They looked at each other, still drowsy. Almost like waking up in bed together, Joe thought. Each sought the other's hand and joined them under Alice's bear robe.

Ursula brought a mug of hot spiced cider for everyone, and Hilda passed around trays of cookies. Hilda's big face beamed with pride.

"Only at Christmas we make," she said pointing to spicy, ginger-bread-like lebkuchen and the rich springerle. Alice wondered how Hilda's big hands and thick fingers managed to shape such delicate sweets.

"Please sing Saranac's 'Little Town of Bethlehem.'" Lilly called down from her perch on the porch railing when the carolers reached the foot of the porch.

"For you, Lilly, anything," a young man said, sweeping off his cap and bowing theatrically from the waist. He sounded a pitch pipe and the melody for "Little Town of Bethlehem" began, but the Saranac caroler had very different words:

"O little town of Saranac
　How still we consumptives lie.
　Above our coughs and temperatures,
　The world quickly passes by.
　We cure out on thy porches,
　Freezing off our ears.
　The hope of all consumptives
　Is going home next year.

O little town of Saranac,
Please give us back our health.
We breathe thy air, and brave thy cold
In hopes of going home.
The goal of ninety-eight sixes
Is as lofty as Mt. Marcy.
Thy air will clear our lungs for good
For this, we all give thanks."

12

Alice's eyes flew open at the sound of tire chains clacking up Helen Hill. Without moving her head, she followed the progress of the car's headlights creeping up the wall of her room and then spreading across the ceiling. Her eyes felt gritty and her temples pulsed in pain.

"No!" she protested. Pulling her arms from the warmth of flannel sheets, she groped for the bedside light. With a click, light pushed the darkness away. She found the temp stick in its usual spot and stuck the little bulb under her tongue.

Everything's been going so well, Alice fretted. Dr. Hayes said I could start walking this week. I'll lose it all with a darn old temperature. She glanced at the clock. Five. Another hour before she'd hear the sisters starting their day.

Just yesterday she was downstairs enjoying Christmas with Joe. And now this. She yanked the temp stick out of her mouth. Holding it under the yellow lamplight, she rolled it in her fingers. A hundred and two and something! As high as the day she came to this horrible place. She gripped the little stick in her hand, resisting the urge to throw it across the room. It wasn't fair that her life was dictated by what it said.

Two hours later, Alice woke again. This time to the touch of Hilda's big cool hand on her forehead.

"Ach. Not a good night, Liebchen?" Hilda extracted the thermometer from Alice's clenched fist. She held it to the morning light, shaking her head at what she read.

Alice didn't like the grim line of her wide mouth. Hilda took the notebook from the top drawer of the dresser and recorded the temperature.

"Just a little setback." She went about shutting windows. "A day or two in bed and we'll get it back down." She looked down at Alice, her mouth fashioned into its customary smile. She slipped her hands under Alice's arms and pulled her into a sitting position. Alice leaned forward while Hilda fluffed her pillows.

"Overnight I've lost everything I gained since I came here," Alice complained. She was exhausted with the effort of sitting up. "This whole thing isn't working for me."

"Did Dr. Hayes tell you the TB cure is easy?" Hilda drew herself up to her full six feet and fastened her hands on her hips. "You must never the battle give up."

Alice began a deep productive cough. Hilda handed her the ugly tin sputum cup. I don't have the strength to go through this again, Alice thought, perspiration beading her forehead at the effort. She felt a cool washcloth on her forehead. Hilda placed her other broad hand on the back of Alice's neck, urging her to lean forward.

When it was over, Alice averted her eyes from the thick gooey mess in the cup and sank back against her pillows. Hilda passed a clean cloth across her face and softly patted it dry. Placing Alice's hands under the blankets, Hilda drew the blankets up to cover her chest and left the room, closing the door softly behind her.

Alice shut her fevered eyes against the sting of the morning light glancing sharply off the snow on Pelletier Cottage's roof. Another impossibly long day, she thought.

The rattle of the breakfast tray and the scrape of a chair being drawn up to her bed broke the stillness. Alice squinted and frowned when she opened her eyes.

"Oh, Ursula, I can't eat."

"That's why I'm here to help. I brought a bowl of nice creamy hot oatmeal."

Alice groaned and turned her head away.

"I fixed it the way you like. With brown sugar and raisins. Just one spoonful before it gets cold."

Alice turned back toward Ursula and opened her mouth.

"Don't let this get you down, Alice." Ursula had a second spoonful ready. "You must pay as little attention to discouragement as possible." She spooned in oatmeal when Alice opened her mouth to speak.

"I've done. . .everything. . .Dr. Hayes. . .told me to," Alice said between mouthfuls. "Even those horrible nights wrapped up like a mummy on the porch."

Ursula put down her spoon and smoothed back Alice's hair. "All things are difficult before they are easy," she said. "The important thing is not to give up the fight." She stood and placed the empty cereal bowl on the tray. Returning with Alice's hairbrush, she sat on the edge of the bed and began to gently brush the snarls from Alice's long hair.

"You do have a number of things to be happy about. Now don't look at me like that. I'll bet there's at least a whole handful."

Alice closed her eyes. The brushing loosened her tight scalp. I suppose that counts as something to be happy about, she thought.

"Not only do you have a handsome husband," Ursula said. "But he cares enough to walk over a hundred miles after his car broke down to be with you."

"Joe is wonderful, isn't he?" Alice opened her eyes and the corners of her mouth lifted ever so slightly.

"You were enjoying his company so much yesterday that you probably didn't realize only three other girls had family visiting."

Alice had noticed several of the Conifer girls dabbing at their eyes in spite of the sisters' continuous effort to create a special day.

"I don't know how you do it," Alice said.

"Do what, dear?" Ursula stood to gather a glass of water and a small basin. She shook a little Pepsodent tooth powder on a brush and handed it to Alice.

"You're always so cheery, both of you. No matter how gloomy we are, you always find a bright spot."

"Not letting our girls become discouraged is one of the best medicines we can dispense."

"It is discouraging to live in fear of what that temp stick is going to say. . .three times a day." Alice rinsed her mouth and spit into the basin. "Or to be scolded at my weekly if I lose weight. I am discouraged."

"You're having a blue day." Ursula went about picking up. She returned with Alice's new bed jacket. "But one blue day will breed more." She helped Alice put her arms in the sleeves.

"You must kick those thoughts right out of your room. You're one of the lucky ones, Alice, with a husband who cares so much about you." Ursula went about opening the windows.

"I will do my best."

"Good." Ursula smiled and helped Alice to lie back down. "You know what my sister says."

"Oh, yes," Alice sighed. "TB feeds less willingly on cheerful tissue."

"She is right." Ursula's smile crinkled the corners of her soft gray eyes. "It's best for you to lie flat and quiet today." She raised all four windows. "I'm sure your noon temp will be lower."

I think my fever's dropped a bit, Alice thought, upon waking a few hours later. It didn't hurt to open her eyes. Her eyes traveled about looking for something to keep her mind off her setback. Turning her head to the left, she sought Joe's picture on the oak dresser. How carefree he looks, she thought. Even the miseries of war hadn't diminished his bright good looks. No, it took TB to do that.

She tore her gaze away from the picture. I'm just a burden, she thought, giving in to her gloomy mood. She studied the wallpaper next to the dresser and tracked the flowered vine that worked its way from floor to ceiling on a white latticed backdrop.

Twenty-six pink flowers on one vine.

The French doors leading to the porch faced her narrow iron bed. With two white-framed windows, the doors made up the entire west wall. Alice feared it would be days before she could be rolled out on the porch.

To her right, icicles hung halfway down the two windows on the north side of her room. Cold today, she thought, noting the icicles were not dripping.

Her restless eyes settled for a time on the small, padded slipper chair. Its low back barely touched the windowsills. She enjoyed sitting there with the late afternoon sun warming her shoulders.

It'll be a week before I'm allowed that treat, she complained to herself, feeling doubly bad thinking she somehow let Ursula down by not staying cheery.

"Whoops! I caught you thinking," Lilly said, as she stepped into Alice's room. "I'll have to tell Hilda. She said to bring you this eggnog." Lilly perched on the bed and offered the glass to Alice. "'We must some meat put on those bones.'" Lilly mimicked Hilda.

"Ja, I know." Alice joined in. "Fat is insurance."

The young women laughed.

"Laughing is not allowed today." Lilly cocked her head and shook a finger at Alice.

Alice laughed again and sipped her eggnog.

"Tell me your secret, Lilly," Alice said, serious again. "You follow hardly any of the rules and yet you don't get worse."

"I haven't gotten better in two years, either."

"But you're never confined to bed and you can walk and sing and. . ."

"I really am neglecting my cure," Lilly said. "I simply cannot compose myself enough to keep quiet. Yes, I'm supposed to walk and I'm allowed to sing 'occasionally', but I have to do better about really being still during quiet times." She stood abruptly and walked to the windows looking out to the north.

"I've decided to turn over a new leaf and cure faithfully." Lilly rested the heels of her palms on the windowsill. "I'm going to drink gallons of milk and walk slowly." She turned and looked at Alice with a fierce determination in her eyes. "I want to go home and start living."

The sound of children's voices came in the open windows. Both young women turned toward the porch. These voices were subdued, hesitant. Like children brought before the principal. Lilly opened the French doors and peeked around the corner.

"It's Charlotte's girls," she said.

"But they sound so. . .sad," Alice said. "Not like the day after Christmas."

"You forget Charlotte's been away from home for three years," Lilly said, still standing at the French doors. "And remember they aren't allowed to touch her. Charlotte can't even give them a hug." She stamped her foot and turned from the doors.

"Haven't you learned yet we are not allowed to think, feel. . .be real people?" Lilly's plucked brows furrowed in anger. She stormed from the room, grabbing a tissue from Alice's nightstand on her way out.

13

Joe stood looking out the window of his room over the garage.
Seemed like these mountains brought out the worst in him. First
he kills a man that's no more than a child and next thing he's agreeing to keep a fleet of rum running cars in top shape so their bootlegging drivers can escape the law.

What choice do I have, he thought, biting down on his cheek. Alice's basic cure cost more than what he made at the Club. Although
Ursula tried to make light of the financial picture, Hilda had no
qualms about asking how he intended to pay Alice's relentless expenses.

Ursula had been waiting for him at the oval-glassed door last
Sunday. She ushered him into the kitchen where Hilda sat at the
table, her glasses caught on the sharp arch of her nose, turning pages
in the account book.

"The money your father-in-law sent has been used up." Hilda
spoke frankly. "I've made a list of your wife's expenses."

Joe swallowed hard. The first item was room and board at Conifer Cottage—twenty dollars a week for a tray patient. He made nine
fifteen a week. The figures swam before him. Doctor's weekly visit,
five dollars; cure chair rental, two dollars, monthly X-ray, fifteen.

"I can see all this is quite a shock to you, Mr. Devlin," Hilda said.
"Are you aware the Ray Brook Sanatorium is free for all who live in
New York State?"

"I could never make Alice go there." Joe shook his head vehe-
mently.

"The facility is very modern and they accomplish great things."

"Great care is not the problem, Miss Guenther." Joe laced his fingers together, gripping them until his knuckles were white. "You see,

when Alice was a girl, she went to a sanatorium to visit a dying aunt. She still has nightmares about the horrible smells and screaming women. I promised my wife I'd never send her to a sanatorium." Joe passed a hand down his face. "She fears that more than the disease."

"See, Sister," Ursula exclaimed, "I knew our Alice was too fragile for the regimen of a san."

"We're not a charity cottage, Mr. Devlin," Hilda stated, unmoved by her sister's plea.

"And I don't accept charity, Miss Guenther." Joe pushed his chair away from the table and stood up. "I'll do what it takes to keep my wife's bills paid."

So here he stood waiting for a man called Charlie Rauch to take him to the place where Armand Dasset's fleet checked in. The slick plan Dasset had concocted rankled Joe. To anyone who inquired, Charlie Rauch was Joe's uncle who came to take Joe down to his place for a home-cooked dinner or a game of poker with the fellas.

Joe didn't like living under the pressure of watching what words escaped his mouth. Don't tell anyone around the Club that he had a tubercular wife curing in Saranac Lake. Don't let anyone know he was moonlighting for a notorious bootlegger. Don't cause Alice worry by letting her know he was struggling to pay her bills. Don't tell anyone he murdered a man.

He saw the headlights and quickly pulled on his coat and hurried down the stairs.

"Hey." The driver pushed aside the canvas side curtain and cigar smoke poured out. "Ready for a little poker?"

"Sure." Joe got in. Charlie turned the farm truck around and headed down Mill Hill. He took the road past the train station to the outskirts of town. The little man didn't talk, just puffed away on his cigar, filling the closed cab with its foul smelling smoke. When they turned in the drive of a simple white frame farmhouse, Joe was out of the car before Charlie cut the engine.

He filled his lungs deeply with fresh air and looked about. There seemed to be only one light coming from a back room of the house, probably the kitchen. Behind the house, light poured between the barn boards making yellow stripes on the snow. A large husky trotted up to Charlie, his curly tail wagging vigorously.

"Meet King." Charlie stooped to pat his dog. "Harmless if you're one of the family, but won't let you in the barn if you're not. Better pet him so he knows your scent." Joe did as instructed and the husky studied Joe with his blue eyes.

"Come on," Charlie said, walking toward the lower level of the barn that was built into the side of a hill. "Everyone will be down here." Charlie held open a small door set into one of the large barn doors and let Joe step into the barn first. Once inside, Charlie reached for a hay string that was attached to the wall and threaded through several fence staples before disappearing into a tiny hole in the ceiling. He gave it three sharp tugs. Joe heard a faint tinkling from somewhere above.

To the right, Joe saw the rumps of six horses standing in their tie stalls picking at the last of their hay. A roan draft mare turned her big head and nickered softly. Looking to his left, Joe noted a shiny Marmon Speedster and a beat-up Packard set up on blocks for the winter. Following Charlie, he walked around several sleighs and past a mound of fur robes and horse blankets hung neatly on a wooden railing.

Charlie opened a door and urged Joe ahead of him into a harness room smelling strongly of horses and oiled leather. Joe wondered where the automobile shop Armand talked about could be. Charlie pulled the string to an overhead light and Joe saw bridles, hames and collars hanging neatly on the walls.

Charlie went directly to the back corner and lowered himself to his knees, fumbling around underneath a saddle rack. Joe couldn't see what he was doing but thought he heard a barrel bolt slide across the floor.

The little man stood up and pulled on a saddle rack that was bolted onto the wall and at once the wall became a door. As it opened, engine exhaust and other familiar garage smells flowed out. Joe smiled, feeling much more at home.

Once again Charlie indicated Joe should go first. The door opened onto crude wooden stairs that were dimly lit from somewhere overhead.

"Charlie?" A voice questioned from above. "Is that you?"

"Yup. I brought my nephew."

There was a burst of guffaws and, as Joe climbed the stairs, he looked up into a circle of faces that were staring down at him.

"Joe!" Armand pushed his way through the group. "No problems getting here?" Armand clasped an arm around Joe's shoulders and introduced him around. Joe judged the men to be about his age, but there the similarity stopped. They were all dressed in the newest double breasted suits with polished shoes and dress hats set at cocky angles over slicked down hair.

Joe felt his hands go clammy when he was introduced to Phil Madden, a broad shouldered, shiny-faced youth. The kid couldn't be old enough to be out of school, Joe thought. But it was the pale blue eyes set under thick black brows that unnerved him. He was unmistakably Tom Madden's son.

"Relax," the kid said. "The old man doesn't know I'm here either. But I'd like to shake your hand." Phil held his hand out to Joe. "You must be a strong man to work for my father."

Fan belts and mufflers hung neatly on the walls. An expansive workbench held tools and wooden boxes full of automotive hardware. A pile of tires were stacked on the other side of the barn where four cars were parked.

A big round table, littered with playing cards, poker chips, glasses and whisky bottles, stood close to the woodstove, in the back corner of the shop side. Joe could feel the stove's warmth from ten feet away.

"We route the smoke through the forge in the blacksmith shed that's attached to the back of the barn," Armand said. "Charlie is a blacksmith and has a livery business going here. People expect to see smoke coming from his forge."

The barn doors, opening out to the back of the barn away from the street, seemed to be blocked by a U-shaped stack of hay bales, stretching almost to the roof.

"You have to move all that hay every time to take a car in and out?" Joe asked Armand. He wondered why it wasn't stored in the ample haylofts that flanked either side of the main aisle.

"Just a little added precaution," Armand smiled. "Charlie, show Joe how we open the doors."

The little man reached for a rope that ran through a big pulley that was hooked to the ceiling. It was rigged with thick ropes that attached to the bottom of the hay bales. Charlie pulled on the ropes. Slowly the center portion of the U-shaped stack, that Joe could now see was riding on a wheeled dolly, inched its way away from the door.

"We run a pole down through those stacks of bales," Armand said, "so they stay in place when we have to move quickly." As the space in front of the doors opened up, Joe saw a farm tractor parked at the door.

"To anyone snooping around," Armand explained, "it looks like a barn full of stacked hay with just enough room to back the tractor in out of the weather. Our cars pick up a road at the far end of the back pasture and we use the tractor to mask their tracks. This way the only car that comes and goes from the farmhouse is Charlie's Ford or his livery customers coming to rent a horse and carriage."

"Ellis here should head out for New York late tonight," Armand said, indicating the tall young man who followed Joe during his tour. "I'd like you to go over his car."

"Yeah, I was having trouble with backfiring just this side of Churubusco. It kept getting worse the rest of the way here." Joe looked at Ellis. The driver's hands were jammed in his pinstriped suit's pockets and Joe saw what looked like gravy spots on his tie.

"Thought I'd shit my pants the first time. Was sure it one of Broadfield's Boys shooting at me."

The three of them walked toward Ellis's car in the shop area as they talked.

"Ellis is carrying twenty gallons of 3-Star Hennessy," Armand said. "I can't have him drawing attention to himself all the way to New York, backfiring at state troopers."

"Where's the whisky?" Joe asked, looking around.

"Right where it sat for the trip across the border," Ellis said, striding to the back door of his car.

"Twenty gallons?" Joe couldn't see even one pint.

Reaching inside the back door, Ellis removed a thin seat cushion with a front flap that extended down to the floor. He motioned Joe over. Instead of the usual springs under the seat, Joe saw a metal container the width and breadth of the entire seat.

"3-Star Hennessy to the brim!" Ellis rapped his knuckles on the container.

"In two days," Armand said, "Ellis will be coming back with seven hundred and twenty dollars for our three hundred dollar investment. Plus a night out on the town in New York."

Joe stood back and shook his head. These guys are serious bootleggers, he thought, uncomfortable about the high degree of subterfuge going on in the big red barn. It was so far removed from the straightforward way he had lived his life. He passed a hand down his face and swallowed hard. Cars were the only thing he knew and he had to keep up with the expenses of Alice's cure. Straightforwardness wasn't paying the bills.

Joe shrugged out of his coat and opened the hood of Ellis's car. "Start her up," he said to Ellis. Joe listened to the engine for a few minutes before ducking under the hood and tinkering with this and that. Before long the engine began to sing a completely different tune. Joe stood up and wiped his hands on a rag.

"That's a lot more like it," Ellis said.

"Yeah," Joe agreed. "Someone messed with the carburetor to compensate for the bad timing." Joe lowered and latched the hood.

"Okay, boys," Armand said, "let's get Ellis on the road."

At once the group at the poker table came to life. Phil hooked the pulley to the barn wall and pulled back the hay. As soon as there was room to squeeze through the hay bales, Charlie pulled himself up on the seat and got the big tractor rumbling.

Ellis had already slid behind the driver's seat. The engine purred smoothly. He grinned at Joe. Armand opened the big door and Charlie drove out into the black night. Ellis had the hood of his car almost nudging the big tractor, impatient to start his run to the city.

Joe stood with the others, waiting for Charlie to bring the tractor back. Within minutes he was backing it in. One of the guys began winching the hay back in place.

"That was good work, Joe," Armand said. "Quick, too. I had a hunch I did the right thing having you join our group."

Joe didn't know what to say. He wasn't proud of what he was doing. Yet he accepted the bills Armand placed in his hand and stuffed them in a pocket.

"I'll have Charlie take you back," Armand continued. "From now on when we need you, your Uncle Charlie will call and see if you want to come to the farm for dinner or poker. It's a simple enough message that he can leave with Madden if you don't answer the phone."

"I appreciate the extra money," Joe said, "but I can't risk losing my job at the Club."

"We're used to being careful, Joe. I personally will make sure that won't happen."

14

"Hi," Kate said, setting her tray down across from Joe. Most of the Club's guests had returned to the city and only a handful of employees were eating supper on this snowy February night. "Haven't seen you in weeks. Tom Madden must be working you hard."

Joe looked up at her smiling face with its sprinkling of freckles. He thought it looked like God had lightly dusted her face with cinnamon. Kate looked so fresh, so. . .healthy.

"Soon as I finish one car he has five more lined up," Joe said. He looked quickly around to see if anyone was near enough to hear before confiding in Kate.

"I took another job, too," he said, just above a whisper. "Been at it about a month now."

Kate stopped stirring her coffee and leaned forward to hear.

"I'm fixing cars for Armand Dasset at night."

"The bootlegger?" Kate's eyebrows arched in surprise.

Joe put a finger to his lips.

"Darn right you better whisper. If Madden hears about this you'll find yourself on the street in no time. Why ever would you risk it, Joe?"

"You think I want to? I can't keep ahead of Alice's expenses on nine-fifteen a week. X-rays alone are fifteen dollars a picture."

"Poor Joe," Kate commiserated. "It really is tough sledding. How is Alice?"

"She had a setback after Christmas. Temperature and headaches. But now, oh, Kate you should see!" Joe brightened, like the sun breaking through the gloom of his problems. "She walks every day for a half hour and comes down for all her meals."

"Do you think they'll let her go to the Winter Carnival?"

"Carnival! That's all they talk about at the cure cottage. Alice told me last weekend that Dr. Hayes said she could go."

"Carnival is great fun," Kate said, dipping her spoon into a dish of chocolate pudding.

"Say, Armand is letting me use a car for the day. Why don't you come, too?"

"Oh, no. I can't tag along on a special day."

"Nonsense. Alice asked one of her porchmates to come. We'll have a swell day."

"Okay. If you don't think I'll be intruding."

"Great!" Joe reached across the table and squeezed Kate's hand. "I got to get back. Armand is sending a car for me about seven o'clock." Joe pushed back his chair and picked up his tray.

"I thought you might want to see the movie in the Agora."

"Another time."

Kate's hand still lay on the table where Joe had squeezed it, when Louise dropped into the chair Joe vacated.

"Is he ever going to ask you out?"

"Who?"

"Joe, who else?" Louise picked up her fork and cut into a wedge of blueberry pie.

"Oh. . .Joe and I are just friends," Kate said, remembering in the nick of time that the existence of Joe's tubercular wife was kept a secret from everyone connected to the Club. No one even suspected Joe was married.

"You mean to tell me a sheik like Joe just wants to be your friend?" She pointed her fork at Kate. "Come on, Kate, this is your roomie you're talking to."

Lilly skipped down the cure cottage steps ahead of Alice and Joe, her gray velours de laine coat swinging about her. Lavishly trimmed with gray squirrel, the bands of the fluffy fur circled the bottom and embellished the front edge, forming a deep collar Lilly could burrow her face in up to her nose.

"I'll get Frank," she called over her shoulder, heading for Pelletier Cottage. The sidewalks were full of a steady flow of Carnival-goers headed for the parade.

Joe held Alice's arm as they moved more sedately toward the showy Pierce-Arrow touring car Armand insisted Joe take for the day. Alice enjoyed her up patient status too much to risk a setback by overdoing. Her day-after-Christmas headache and temperature were still vivid. With her free hand she clutched the cloth coat to her body.

The coat was a Christmas present from her parents the year before she married Joe. The last gift she ever received from them. The blue wool had been the height of fashion, but ill-suited for warmth in this mountain climate. This morning Alice wore two sweaters underneath and wool stockings to combat the cold. Her face was buried in the wool scarf Lilly had loaned her.

Joe held open the passenger door of the Pierce-Arrow and helped Alice settle in the front seat.

"Alice, this is Kate Thurber," he said, tucking the lap robe about Alice's legs. Alice turned and looked into Kate's round cheery face.

"Hi," Kate said from the back seat, "Joe talks so much about you I feel I already know you. Hope you don't mind me tagging along today."

"This is my first venture into town," Alice said. "We'll make a regular party out of it."

Alice saw Lilly crossing the street, dragging a thin, dark-haired young man after her. He wasn't much taller than Lilly and carried a mandolin in his free hand. When they reached the car, Alice could see his large nose had as many bumps as a back road. She was immediately taken by the easy smile on his big mouth and laugh crinkles at the edges of his brown eyes. Alice wondered how long Lilly's newest boyfriend had been curing. The disease certainly didn't appear to be getting him down.

"Hi, everyone," Lilly said, a little breathlessly. "Meet Frank. Wait till you hear him play this thing. This is my porchmate Alice and her husband, Joe. Remember I told you Joe walked almost all the way from New York City?" Joe and Frank shook hands.

Lilly turned to Kate who was sitting quietly in the back seat. Her bright cupid bow mouth pouted as she studied the unknown young woman.

"I'm Kate Thurber," Kate spoke up, squirming a little under Lilly's scrutiny.

"Oh, yes," Joe said, coming to Kate's rescue. "Kate works in the Club dining room. She's been swell about showing me the ropes."

"Well, hello, Kate Thurber," Frank said as he handed Lilly up to sit beside Kate. "You'll have to tell us all about life at the Club since us Saranac lungers aren't allowed beyond the city limits." Frank pulled the door shut after him and immediately began picking on the mandolin.

"All set, dear heart?" Joe asked, taking his place behind the wheel. He reached over to squeeze Alice's mittened hand.

"It's wonderful you got such a grand car." Alice said, smiling into Joe's happy face. We can pretend we're normal people for today, she mused.

"It's an important day, taking my wife on her first outing."

"We'll be coming down the mountain for the fun." Frank sang his version of the old song.

"We'll be coming down the mountain. . ." Lilly and Kate joined in.

"Why aren't you singing?" Joe asked Alice. "Is something wrong?

"I'm not allowed to."

"Not allowed to sing?" Joe took his eyes off to road to look at Alice.

"Joe, please look where you're driving," Alice said. "Helen Hill is dangerous."

"I want to know why you can't sing?" Joe dragged his attention back to driving and lightly tapped the brakes. "Is this another rule from that. . .that old battleaxe? What about staying happy?"

"Oh, Joe, don't get so worked up. Hilda is not a battleaxe. Of course she wants us to be happy. And I am happy today." Alice paused to catch her breath. "It's just that singing is too much stress on my lungs."

"The others are singing," Joe said, still not mollified.

"They take more chances. I don't want to spend the rest of my life here, Joe."

"Joe'll drive a green Pierce-Arrow as we come," Frank still strummed away. The three in the back sang lustily, unaware of the tension in the front seat.

Those walking down Helen Hill toward the parade smiled and waved at the car full of singing carnival-goers. American flags fluttered from the upper windows of the private residences. The white porch columns of most cure cottages were wrapped in spiraling red crepe paper, looking like huge candy canes.

By the time Joe found a place to park near the parade route, Frank had led the group through five more verses. The young people climbed out of the car still singing and smiling like longtime friends.

Frank stuck his mandolin under a car robe and helped first Lilly then Kate down. Lilly immediately hooked an arm through Frank's and pulled him along after Joe and Alice, who had started toward the festivities. Kate was left to follow on her own.

Coming to a cross street, Alice looked behind and saw Kate, her hands jammed in her coat pockets, trailing behind.

"Kate," Alice called. "Come on up here and walk with us."

The three looped their arms together and crossed the street where every storefront was swathed in red, white and blue bunting. Joe bought cups of hot spicy cider from a sidewalk vendor.

"I hear the marching band!" The crowd surged to the sidewalk edge, seeking good viewing positions.

A pair of matched chestnut horses led the parade. Clouds of steam rose from their bodies as they jigged and chomped on their bits. Brightly colored ribbons fluttered from their harness as they pulled a two-seater sleigh, the back seat holding two fur-coated men who waved to the crowds lining the street.

"Must be what passes for dignitaries here," Lilly said to Frank.

"I believe you're talking about Dan Foster, the President of Saranac Lake and Dr. Francis Trudeau, Trudeau Sanitarium's attending physician," a woman standing in front of Lilly turned to inform her. "We happen to think quite of lot of them around here," she added a little frostily.

"Yes, Ma'am," Frank said. "No doubt they do great things for the village."

The woman stared at Frank for a moment as though deciding if he was poking fun at the officials. Apparently satisfied with his sincerity, she turned her attention back to the parade, waving as the sleigh moved pass.

Joe found a place for Alice in the front row of the parade watchers. Standing behind her, he wrapped his arms about her and together they watched the floats and marching bands parade by.

Across the street Joe caught sight of a slight, scruffy man in a grimy jacket. Something about the man seemed familiar, Joe thought, watching him pace back and forth behind the parade watchers. The hair raised on the back of Joe's neck. Something bad was connected to the man. The man chose that moment to look across the street and their eyes locked just as the next float filled the street. By the time it passed, the man had disappeared. But the twisted feeling in Joe's gut was slow to unwind.

A four-in-hand of huge white draft horses came into view. Sun glinted off the polished brass of the hames and straps of shiny jingling sleigh bells. The horses pulled a crepe paper decorated float bearing a banner proudly stating "We Have Come For The Cure." Huddled together against the cold, fifteen solemn faced young men perched on top. Their thin bodies were engulfed in fur coats.

"They don't appear to have caught the spirit of the day," Joe noted.

"They probably aren't well enough to wave to us," Alice explained. "I found it very tiring when I was first allowed to simply brush my hair."

Joe nestled his chin in Alice's soft hair and frowned. Her comment triggered a growing annoyance. Somehow Alice had drifted away from him since he put her on the train. Before that it was him and Alice against the world. Now – Joe pressed his lips together – he felt like the outsider. Like healthy people didn't quite fit in. Joe shook his head to dispel the black mood.

One of many fire engines rolled by, clanging its bell. Grinning firemen clung to its shiny sides, waving to the people. All the surrounding towns appeared to be represented. Even Lake Placid, normally so leery of bringing germs back to its pristine village, sent an engine.

A uniformed hockey team marched up the street, shouldering their long flat sticks with the distinctive hooks at one end.

"Don't miss the game," team members called out. "We're going to win!"

"Let's get something to eat before the game," Lilly said to the group. "I'm famished." Everyone nodded in agreement.

"I vote for Sadie's," Frank said. "She makes the best doggone chocolate cake." No one objected. Frank, with Lilly still holding his arm possessively, led the group to a small, dark coffee shop already bustling with hungry Carnival-goers.

After chocolate cake, the two couples and Kate made their way to the Ice Palace on the shore of Lake Flower.

"Do you think it's too late to find seats for the hockey game?" Lilly asked. "I don't think I could stand the whole time." The grandstand and bleachers on the shore side of the Pontiac Skating Rink were filling rapidly.

"Tell you what," Joe said. "Kate and I will find seats. Kate can stay and keep them for us and I'll run back and show you fellows the way."

"That's perfect, Joe." Alice said, smiling up at her husband. "I would like to be able to sit."

"I knew it," Lilly muttered.

"Knew what?" Frank asked.

Lilly turned away from Alice before responding. "Knew Joe would find a way to be alone with Dolly Dimples before the day was over."

"You're imagining things," Frank said. "That man adores his wife."

"Sure, but that's a farm fresh girl brimming with health if I ever saw one." Lilly looked over her shoulder, making sure Alice was still watching Joe walk away with Kate. "Healthy men get tired of being held back by us lungers. Believe me, I know firsthand!"

A starry winter night had fallen by the time the hockey game was over. From their seats high in the bleachers they could see colored lights glowing softly in the Ice Palace.

Alice tried to hide a yawn.

"Best get you girls back," Joe said. "I'd hate to have to face Hilda if she thought I kept you out too late. Why doesn't everyone wait here at the Ice Palace. I'll bring the car around."

"Great idea, Joe," Lilly said sleepily.

Joe had barely left Alice's side when a small man in a grimy jacket came up to her. She wrinkled her nose at his rank smell.

"Hey, lady," the stranger said. His weasel-like eyes darted around. "You know that man?" He pointed toward Joe's retreating back with an arm that ended with the cuff of his jacket.

"Of course I do," Alice responded. "He's my husband, Joseph Devlin." The man nodded and slipped away in the crowd.

Joe and Frank walked the girls up the porch steps while Kate waited in the car.

Joe hugged Alice close to him. Over his shoulder he could see Frank and Lilly kissing. An ache spread through his body and he held Alice tighter. Alice pulled Joe's great coon coat apart and snuggled against his chest.

Joe's hand moved down Alice's back and pressed her even closer. Immediately Alice pushed herself away and cupped Joe's face with her hands.

"We have to pretend we're just dating, Joe."

Joe groaned. "When can I at least kiss you?" he asked, noting the couple sharing the porch had no restrictions on kissing.

"I'm still contagious, Joe. I wouldn't wish this disease on anyone."

Joe grabbed her hands, kissing each fiercely.

"Please get better, dear heart," he said, and opened the door for Alice. Skirting the embracing couple he ran down the steps and helped Kate into the front seat of the Pierce-Arrow. Throwing it into gear, Joe roared down Helen Hill.

"Why are you frowning?" Frank asked. "Wasn't I very good at smooching?"

"No, it's not that. I don't like the way Kate has moved into Joe's life. And Alice is just too sweet to see what's happening."

15

"Come on, Joe, take a break," Armand said.

Joe peered out from under Stu's car to see Armand holding a glass of foamy beer in each hand.

"Thanks, but it's getting late. Stu's anxious to get these truck brakes on his car for his next run."

"Charlie brought sandwiches down from the house."

"Guess I can take a few minutes." Joe rolled himself clear of the chassis and stood up, arching the cramps out of his back. He wiped his hands on the rag stuck in his back pocket and took the beer. Together they walked over to the table, joining Charlie, Armand and three runners who were already devouring a platter of sandwiches.

"I hate this cold," Ellis said, wiping a glob of mustard off his tie. "I've had it with winter." He pushed himself away from the round table and, picking up his beer, went to warm himself by the woodstove.

"It'll hit fifty below this week before it lets up," Gaston said.

"Do you walk on water, too?" Stu asked. He twirled his rabbit foot key chain around his finger.

"Only when it's frozen." Gaston laughed softly. "I limit myself to weather forecasting." He reached across the table to refill his glass and the diamonds in his rings glittered in the overhead light.

"Been forty below the last two nights. No reason to think it'll be warmer tonight," Charlie said, talking around the soggy cigar in his mouth.

"Isn't it time to run that wedding booze down to Utica?" Ellis called out, his backside almost touching the stove.

"Most important delivery this week," Armand said. His crew waited for him to continue, their young faces eager with anticipation. "The deal is, Henry Poirier and his son are each driving a car out of Black Brook at daybreak on Saturday. I'm betting on fooling

Broadfield's Boys by traveling out in the open in broad daylight." He paused to bite into a thick ham and cheese sandwich, then ran a napkin over his mustache.

"I've seen Poirier's cars," Gaston said. "They're Essexes. Won't have a prayer in a chase. And if they're stopped, even a rookie will spot the hooch. There's no customized storage." He waved a hand in dismissal. "We shouldn't count on a bunch of amateurs."

"Normally I'd agree with you," Armand said. "This one time I based everything on Poirier being an upstanding citizen of Black Brook. Never ran booze. And since Stu here delivered the shipment to Poirier over two weeks ago, there's no reason to think Poirier has been singled out to keep watch on."

The men nodded their approval of Armand's reasoning.

"Poirier must get the load to Utica by Saturday in time for his niece's wedding. But there's a fly in the ointment," Armand said, taking several hefty swallows of beer. His men stopped chewing and waited expectantly. Ellis left the warmth of the stove and sat down with the others.

"Poirier called today all in a stew about the cold. Said his cars have been tough to start."

"Didn't I say you can't rely on an Essex?" Gaston interjected.

"Then you'll be happy to hear Poirier fears the cars won't start at all if it drops to forty-fifty below. And his niece is counting on him to deliver."

"If Charlie keeps the stove going here in the barn, you could count on any of your cars starting." Joe said.

"Not smart to use our cars," Armand replied. "We've made the mistake of working that area too heavily. Word's out Broadfield has troopers ready to pounce. It's not safe to drive our own mothers to church any where near Black Brook or Ausable Forks."

"I'd be willing to risk it, Armand," Stu spoke up. "Be a good test run with my new truck brakes. I'd go to Poirier's after midnight and. . ."

"No need to make a decision tonight," Armand said. "But don't stray too far from the phone. It may be a last minute decision." Armand topped off Joe's glass, letting the foam tumble over the brim.

Taking a swallow, Joe took the beer back to the shop. Would he ever get used to the fun these guys got out of playing hide and seek with the law? He heard Stu singing that crazy booze song in his twangy off-key voice:

"Take away my money,
Take away my shoes,
But lawdy, lawdy, mister
Don't take away my booze"

Joe picked up a Stilson wrench to tighten the backing plate to the top of the spindle. Now he was ready to connect the brake pedal rod. With that accomplished, he pressed the pedal. The brakes expanded, but not enough. He picked up a pair of pliers and gave the rod another turn.

Look at me. I spend my nights making sure their cars can keep ahead of troopers. Alice's cure eats up everything I can earn. But I won't be a booze runner.

"Much longer with those brakes?" Charlie broke into Joe's thoughts. "Kind of like to call it a night."

"I'd like that, too," Joe said, "but better plan on another hour."

"I'll take Joe home," Gaston volunteered. "No," Armand said. "Only Charlie drives Joe around. We can't risk Joe getting in trouble with the Club. Too many people suspect you're a runner, Gaston."

Early the next morning, Joe slipped down to the garage to make a call.

"I've been thinking," Joe said, when Charlie answered the phone. "I'd like to come by tonight and talk about the wedding."

"Sure," Charlie said, after a short pause. "Pick you up the usual time."

All through the day Joe kept refining his plan for a quick start on a fifty-below day.

"You realize Poirier is clear up to Black Brook," Charlie said, before Joe could even shut the truck's door.

"I remember hearing that. How far is it to Black Brook?"

"Forty miles or so."

"I remember seeing a kerosene heater at your barn," Joe said. "Any chance of there being a couple of pot flares, too."

"Yeah." Charlie turned his head to look at Joe out of his good eye. "I got one. What are you cooking up?"

"You'll see," Joe smiled. "I'll need another kerosene heater, too."

At the farm, Joe hurried to the barn, going through the small door set inside the two big barn doors. The roan nickered softly and Joe heard the splash of a horse letting loose a powerful stream of urine. He moved cautiously through the dark barn, making his way toward the harness room.

"Hey," Charlie called from the door. "You give the signal?"

"No, will you?"

Charlie gave the hay string three sharp pulls and Joe heard the responding tinkle overhead in the shop. Joe knew that unless the signal was given, the door to the repair shop would remain firmly bolted.

He fumbled for the tack room door in the dark, threw it open and raised his arms in search of the light string. With a quick tug the room was cast in a dim yellow glow. In two steps, Joe crossed the room and dropped to his knees to release the dead bolts on the floor. Standing, he pulled on the saddle rack and the wall opened. He took the steps two at a time.

"I don't know," Armand said, shaking his head. He and Charlie sat at the table in the barn listening to Joe's plan. "The principle appears sound enough but if it doesn't work. . ."

"It will," Joe said.

"The only way I'd consider it," Armand said, rubbing a knuckle across his mustache, "is if you're there Friday night to put it together. You'd have to stay over and see them off in the morning."

"I usually spend Saturday with Alice."

"Still can. Poirier needs to be on the road at sunup. You'll be in Saranac Lake in time for breakfast. Actually it'd be a smart move for you to mosey over to Saranac and spend the day visiting. If you're followed leaving Black Brook they'll soon see they're on a wild goose chase."

"Beats walking."

"You still walking to Saranac every weekend?" Charlie asked, puffing on a cigar until Joe turned his head to escape the foul smoke. "That's ten miles!"

"Don't forget the ten miles home."

"It's time you thought about getting a car," Armand said

"Actually I've had my eye on a new Stutz Sportster."

"I'm serious, Joe. Come to a booze sale. Police hold one in Placid every month. Confiscated bootleggers' cars go pretty cheap."

"I don't have cash for a flivver, much less a beefed-up rum running car."

"Don't be so sure. I've seen them go for as little as five dollars.

"That's still more than half a week's wages."

"Tell you what. You get the Poirier cars on the road by sunup on Saturday and you've earned yourself a twenty. I'll keep five of it aside and see what turns up at the next sale."

"Consider it done. But tell Poirier to start up the cars every day. Keep them running till they really warm up. I'll have those babies rolling at daybreak."

16

Joe could scarcely restrain himself from checking under the tarp when Charlie picked him up at the Club Friday night. The second he got to the barn, he jumped out of the truck and pulled back the tarp. Everything he asked for was there: kerosene heaters, pot flares, a sheet of tin and tin snips. Charlie handed him a map penciled on the back of an envelope and he was off.

Poirier's house was easy enough to find. Black Brook didn't have more than a couple of streets. Whole town can't have as many people as our one apartment building back home, Joe thought, pulling to a stop in front of a white frame house. Lights shone from all the windows. Peering over the snowbanks, Joe saw what Armand had described as the big barn where Poirier kept his cars, some chickens and a horse and carriage for the mud season.

Joe put the truck in first gear and maneuvered it between the snowbanks to the barn. Within seconds the barn doors were thrown open. Armand stood silhouetted in the yellow light, motioning to Joe to drive right in.

Joe squeezed the truck between Armand's Pierce-Arrow and Poirier's two Essexes.

"Okay, Joe," Armand said after introducing him to Poirier. "This is your show. What can we do to help?"

Joe took off his cumbersome coon coat. Then everyone pitched in to unload the truck. Although no one voiced their questions, Joe could see the uncertainty in the men's eyes.

It better work, he thought, experiencing his first doubt. The cars were positioned heading out the doors, one in front of the other.

"Put a kerosene heater in front of each car," Joe said, climbing in the first car. He set the hand brake and put it in gear, noting how hard it was to move the gearshift through the freezing oil. When he repeated the procedure on the second car, he wasn't able to put it in gear. He thrummed his fingers on the steering wheel.

"Problem, Joe?" Armand asked.

"Nothing I can't fix." He reached for the sheet of tin and tin snips. "How about jacking up a rear wheel on each car?" Poirier moved to do as Joe asked. Being in charge was nice, but Joe didn't like everyone hovering when he was trying to think.

Armand held the tin and Joe cut out a piece. "Bring along one of the pot flares," Joe said, taking his cut-out tin to the second car. He slid under the car and placed the tin above the gear case to protect the car.

"Light that flare, would you?" Joe took the lighted flare from Armand and set it under the gear case. He moved the tin shield slightly to the left. Couldn't have the flame reaching the car. Satisfied with the arrangement, Joe inched his way out from under the car.

"I couldn't move through the gears in this car," Joe explained. "Gear case oil's beginning to freeze. I'm counting on the pot flare to loosen it up."

Joe cut two large pieces of tin. Opening the hoods of both cars, he fashioned tin shields over the radiators and engines. Next he lighted the kerosene heaters and fussed with their placement.

"We'll leave these heaters going all night," he said to his skeptical assistants. "These tin shields should help direct the heat where we need it most."

Joe climbed back in the second car. "Lets see if the flare's had time to work." He put his foot on the clutch and the gear shift moved reluctantly from neutral to first in the sluggish oil.

"Good trial run," Joe said with a grin. "Now tomorrow morning, about half an hour before it's time for you to leave, I'll come out and light both flares.

"My plan is to start the engines in gear," he said, feeling confident his plan would work. "The engines will turn over with the starters until one cylinder catches, which helps rotate the rear wheels.

"Actually, the rear wheel will act like an extra flywheel and eventually all the cylinders will catch." Joe smiled. "You'll be on your way to Utica before sunup."

Armand clasped an arm about Joe's shoulders. "You sure know how to make these birds sing, Joe. Good thinking."

Joe didn't sleep well in spite of Armand's praise. He knew something could go wrong. Mrs. Poirier had given Joe a room to himself and the bed was comfortable with a goose-down comforter. He re-thought everything a dozen times, looking for loopholes in his reasoning.

He had never experienced such awful cold. They all took turns looking at the thermometer before turning in. Forty-nine degrees below zero!

Fretting won't help, he thought, punching his pillow. Everything drilled in him since childhood made him want to ask God for assistance. Couldn't do that this time. How could he ask God for help in aiding someone to break the law by running illegal booze? He pulled the comforter up to his ears and forced what he was doing out of his mind.

The mercury huddled at the bottom of the thermometer when the men assembled for Mrs. Poirier's eggs and ham in the pre-dawn dark. It couldn't register anything below fifty below. No matter how hard any of them stared at it, the mercury stubbornly remained in its little gray puddle.

All the Poiriers, dressed in their best clothes for the wedding, assembled to watch Joe work his magic. Piping hot stone pigs had been placed in each car.

Joe swallowed and climbed into the first car. Poirier's rooster chose that moment to crow. Everyone jumped as though Broadfield's Boys had burst through the barn door.

He put in the clutch and turned over the engine. "Come on, baby," Joe whispered. The engine responded like it was July.

"Hooray!" Poirier's son hollered. Joe beamed a smile at his audience. Mr. Poirier hugged his wife.

"Joe knows his cars," Armand told everyone.

The Poiriers got in. Armand helped Mrs. Poirier wrap the car robe about her legs and firmly shut the door.

"Have a great time." Armand rapped on the hood. Joe opened the barn door and the Poiriers drove to Utica.

Armand placed three five-dollar bills in Joe's hand and slapped him on the back. "Well done, Joe. Really glad you're part of this outfit. I'm keeping five back like we agreed. I'll find you a car at the next sale."

"Thanks." He took the bills and carefully placed them in his wallet, then went about setting the kerosene heaters and flares around their cars. No reason to think they'd start in this cold.

The plan was for Joe to hang around for a few hours before leaving. Armand would stay at the Poiriers' even longer.

"Actually," he'd Joe last night, "I'd welcome being stopped by one of Broadfield's Boys and found clean of hooch or money. It'd also give me the opportunity to identify which troopers have set their sights on me."

Now they sat around Poiriers' kitchen table drinking coffee and spooning honey on hot biscuits.

"Take the truck till Sunday night. Bring it back to Charlie and he'll drive you to the Club." Armand poured cream into his second cup of coffee. "Here's a little extra to take your wife to dinner." He peeled a few bills from his money roll.

"No, that's okay. We agreed on twenty."

"Hey, because of you there's a bride and groom downstate that'll have a great day. I want you to celebrate, too. Take Alice to the Hotel Saranac. Be sure to order the oyster stew."

17

A car of his own for the weekend! Granted the farm truck smelled of horses and pigs. But it beat walking, came with a tank of gas and Joe had more money in his pocket than he ever remembered having at one time.

Following Armand's directions, Joe drove west out of Black Brook to Clayburg where he turned south toward Saranac Lake. Just north of Bloomingdale he came across a car nearly blocking the road. Off to the side, a black horse stood with his tail to the wind. As Joe approached, two men dressed in identical mackinaws got out of the car and motioned him to stop.

Joe had heard Armand and the fellas talk about roadblocks the New York State Troopers set up to trap bootleggers. They were particularly effective in the winter when the deep snow prevented bootleggers from abandoning their cars to hightail it into the woods.

Well, he had nothing to hide. Except murder, he remembered with a start. His gripped the steering wheel.

"Morning, officer." Joe pushed the window curtain aside and forced a pleasantness into his voice.

"Where you headed, son?" The trooper stooped to look into the truck. His eyes darted everywhere.

"Saranac Lake." Joe was at a loss. Kate forever cautioned not to mention his wife had TB. Should he avoid it now? He heard the second trooper rummaging through things in the back of the truck.

"Where are you coming from?"

"Black Brook." Aw, geeze. Did that give Armand away?

"He's not from Black Brook," the younger trooper called down from the back of the truck. "I know everyone in that burg and I've never seen him."

"Didn't say I was from Black Brook." Joe felt a trickle of sweat run down his back. "I'm a mechanic at the Lake Placid Club." Joe swallowed hard, trying to make his story sound natural. "I try to pick up extra work. Mr. Poirier in Black Brook was having trouble with his Essex." That was the truth.

The senior trooper looked at his young partner for confirmation. "Checks out. Poirier has two Essexes." The trooper took the caps off the kerosene heaters and smelled the contents.

"Who is your boss at the Club?" The older trooper shot at him.

"Tom Madden."

"What's your business in Saranac Lake?"

Joe sighed. There was no escaping the truth. "My wife is taking the cure at Conifer Cottage.

"Tom Madden know about your wife?"

"No, sir. It's against Club rules."

"Well, guess that's between the Club and you. What's your name, son?"

"Joe Devlin."

"Sorry about your wife. You can go on your way now."

Joe waited till the trooper vaulted to the snow-packed road before letting in the clutch and driving off.

"Follow him, Cronk."

"You didn't think that flivver was a booze car?"

"No. I agree it's clean." Trooper Schermerhorn rubbed his gloved hands together, causing the leather to squeak. "Somehow I think he's connected with Dasset."

"Their cars are lightening quick."

"I know, I know. I don't think the truck is actually used to carry, but I'm pretty sure they've used it as a decoy." Cronk grimaced as Schermerhorn cracked his knuckles one at a time.

"I'm going to leave, too," he said, looking Cronk full in the face. "There hasn't been anything worth standing out in this cold for."

"Bet the mercury won't even hit zero today," Cronk agreed.

"I'll loop over through Vermontville and be back to the barn in Bloomingdale before dark."

"How far do I follow him?" Cronk headed for the car.

"Dasset keeps a shop somewhere. Lets see if this truck leads you to it. Don't let him see you," Schermerhorn called after Cronk. He stood watching the Ford drive out of sight before turning to his horse. The horse pricked a tiny ear at his approach and blew a soft nicker in welcome.

"Hope I'm wrong, Blizzard," Schermerhorn confided to his horse, "but I'll bet there'll be a steady stream of booze cars coming through here in less than an hour." The horse nuzzled Schermerhorn's pocket. He removed his gloves and fished out a sugar lump for the horse.

He stroked the horse's neck while he puzzled over Cronk. Too many leaks about where he planned to set up roadblocks for him to ignore. It didn't sit well to set up his partner, but he had to know for sure. He undid the tie rope from a tree and secured it around the gelding's neck.

Informants on the other side of the border had notified Schermerhorn that the McFadden gang had made a big purchase. He had the details of the six cars and the type of intoxicants they carried. Yet not one had passed him today. Schermerhorn had decided to send Cronk off with the news that he was leaving the area. He knew in his bones that Cronk would get word through to McFadden that it would be safe to get moving again.

He placed his foot in the covered stirrup and swung up in the saddle. The little horse immediately came alive. He snorted and tugged at the pelham bit, begging for permission to run. A smile broke the trooper's grim expression. With a subtle cue he gave the Morgan Horse the permission he sought and the two cantered down the snow-packed road.

If he was correct, Schermerhorn thought, enjoying his horse's good spirits, Cronk would make just one telephone call and the traffic from Canada would be picking up. Schermerhorn knew McFadden took more chances than most bootleggers to keep his customers in booze. It just didn't add up that his gang always slipped through.

All pointed to an informant inside Troop B. And now he had just set the trap for Cronk to fall in. He figured there'd be time for coffee up at the Stevens' farm before returning in time to greet the first runner. He could probably get Stevens to work with him.

Nearly an hour later, he brought his horse back to a walk and turned in the drive. Half way up, he heard the farmhouse door bang. The excited voices of two boys came to him on the cold air. Blizzard raised his head a little higher and quickened his step.

"Hi, Blizzard!" the boys called, each racing to be the first to reach the horse. The horse came to a standstill and lowered his head to the boys' height. They rubbed his ears.

"Can I ride Blizzard to the house? Please Trooper Schermerhorn."

"No fair! It's my turn. Right, Trooper Schermerhorn?"

"Must be fair," Schermerhorn said, "Tommy, you climb up here with me and Jack, you can walk him to the barn all by yourself."

The boys' father stood on the porch, his red union suit showing under a worn flannel shirt.

"Morning." Schermerhorn smiled up at the farmer. The man nodded his head. He clamped his arms to his sides and jammed his hands in his pockets. Something was bothering Stevens. "Blizzard and I could use some breakfast."

"Coffee's in the pot. The boys will see to your horse."

He dismounted and helped Tommy down before handing the reins to Jack. "Right hand on the bit," he instructed the boy, "and left hand at the end of the reins." He watched Jack solemnly lead the horse to the barn. His younger brother walked respectfully by his side. "Make sure you put a blanket on him."

"I didn't know anything about it," Stevens said, as Schermerhorn climbed the steps, taking off his gloves. Schermerhorn hadn't a clue of what Stevens was talking about but wasn't about to show his hand to the agitated farmer.

"Better start at the beginning," he said. Stevens nodded and held the door for Schermerhorn. The kitchen was steamy and smelled of wood smoke and wet wool drying too close to the stove. Over coffee and eggs fried crisp in bacon grease, Schermerhorn learned that when Stevens went to the barn to check on the livestock before turning in for the night, he found two men off-loading cases of alcohol in his hayloft.

"They had all but two cases stuffed in the mow when I got there," Stevens said, "or you know I would have told them to keep going. Said they worked with McFadden."

Schermerhorn nodded and kept the man's eyes locked in his gaze. Stevens kept stirring his coffee, scraping the spoon against the cup. He gave Schermerhorn the color and make of the car when asked.

"They said they'd have something for me if the goods was still there when they came back to fetch it." Stevens face reddened and he broke Schermerhorn's stare, taking a swallow of coffee. "It's hard to put any aside, farming with frost and snow cover month after month and a new kid most every year."

"You know you'll get forty percent of the fine when we catch them," Schermerhorn said. "And I will catch them."

The farmer raised his head. "Any idea what that might be?"

"They'll probably be looking at five hundred dollars plus six months in jail."

"That'd be considerable more than they offered. Not that I'd ever hold out on you," he hastened to add.

"Look, you help me out this afternoon and I'll put in a good word for you in my report," Schermerhorn said. "Might be able to increase the amount of the reward money."

"You can count on me."

18

The questioning at the roadblock upset Joe. He gripped the steering wheel till his hands ached. Never in his life had he felt queasy around the law. But so much had happened since he left New York. Yes, he had to shoot Bruce or get shot himself. But he didn't have to kill the man. . .more child than man. And not even bury him. And now he worked for a rum runner. What was it about these mountains?

He couldn't get over the casual way bootleggers handled their crimes. When he listened to Ellis, Gaston and Stu, running booze sounded like a kid's game of hide and seek. Only difference being they played it with high-powered cars. . .and guns. They're all heroes to Phil and he's just a boy, still in school.

If there was any other way to pay for Alice's cure, he thought, I swear I'd do it. It's not that I actually drive any of the booze cars myself, I just work on the cars. Like I do all day anyway. He brought the truck back to first gear and it labored up Helen Hill, its tire chains banging against the fenders.

Cronk's Ford moved quietly past Conifer Cottage as Joe climbed the porch steps. By the time the trooper had turned his car around and pulled to the curb a discreet distance from the farm truck, Joe had disappeared inside.

Cronk thrummed his fingers on the steering wheel and glanced at his watch repeatedly. He started the Ford and headed back into town, driving as quickly as traffic allowed. He maneuvered the car into a tight spot across from Luke's Pool Parlor, slammed the door and sprinted across the street.

Inside Conifer Cottage, Ursula told Joe that Alice was out walking with her porchmates. She settled him at the scrubbed kitchen table with coffee and a wedge of fragrant bienenstich with its crunchy almond-coconut topping baked on the yeast bread.

"Isn't it too cold to be walking?" Joe asked. "It must still be below zero."

"My goodness, no," Ursula said. She poked through cubbyholes in a desk set in a kitchen corner. "Read this while you wait for Alice." She handed Joe a pamphlet.

He read the title: "Regain Your Health in Air Conditioned by Nature." The pamphlet optimistically explained the options open to health seekers and the benefits of the pristine, cold mountain air.

The air may be free, Joe thought, but everything else is a king's ransom. There was a slight improvement in Alice's expenses, however. Now that she wasn't a tray patient and took her meals in the dining room, her board had dropped five dollars to fifteen a week.

Just then the front door opened and Joe heard female voices. And laughter. Joe jumped up from the table at the sound of Alice's laugh. Granted it was soft and fleeting. But it certainly held a happy, contented note. Joe smiled and strode to find his Alice.

He could listen to Ursula's glowing reports on Alice's improvement all day, but nothing filled his heart with gladness more than hearing her laugh again.

"Joe!" Alice said, and her smile reached her eyes.

He felt as though he was visiting a girls' school with the happy female chatter going on around him. They actually seem to like this place, he thought. He tried not to dwell on the irksome situation of getting Ursula's permission to take his wife away from here for the day.

If Alice was happy, that was good. Wasn't the other sister always saying TB feeds less willingly on the happy than on the gloomy tissue?

They had a marvelous day, imitating a normal couple. Arm in arm they strolled Main Street, stopping to peer in windows. Joe delighted at the surprise in Alice's eyes when he held the door at the restaurant for her.

The maitre d's voice became respectful when he took in Joe's luxurious coon coat. He thinks I'm a booze runner, too, Joe thought. It sure was hard to understand the way everyone welcomed the lawbreakers. Probably something as simple as a good coon coat symbolized money to spend. Well, today that's true. I do have money to spend.

They were given a window table covered with a white cloth that vied for brightness with the fresh snow clinging to the window. Ice clinked in the water goblets and the polished silver gleamed in the sun shining through the window.

"Can we afford this?" Alice leaned across the table and whispered.

"Sure can." Joe picked up his menu. "We're going to start with the oyster stew, then I want you to order anything on the menu. Don't look at the price."

It felt so good to have the money to bring Alice to a place like this. The next time a windfall like this came along, he planned to use it for a new coat—something as fancy as Lilly's.

Inside Luke's Pool Parlor, Cronk went immediately to the back room and knocked.

"Yeah?"

"It's me, Carl." He opened the door and headed for the phone on Luke's cluttered desk. "I need to use your telephone." Luke nodded and gestured toward it. Carl grabbed it off the desk and barked a number to the operator. "Yeah," he spoke into the mouthpiece, "the road's clear." Carl's face turned ugly at the reply. "Dammit, of course I'm sure." He banged the earpiece back on the receiver and slammed the telephone onto Luke's desk. He stalked to the door.

"Big hurry?"

"Supposed to be tailing a guy." He all but ran from the pool hall to his car and roared up Helen Hill to Conifer Cottage.

"Shit!" Joe Devlin and his truck were gone.

"Anything special you'd like to do this afternoon?" Joe asked as they left the restaurant. They walked arm in arm to where Joe had parked the truck in the narrow alley behind the restaurant.

"Could we drive to Placid? I'd love to see where you work. So I can have a picture in my mind of where you are during the week."

"To Lake Placid it is." Joe opened the truck door and settled Alice in the seat. Earlier he had fabricated a story that the truck belonged to the Club and he had permission to drive it.

"They must think a great deal of you, Joe," Alice had said, "to let you use the truck for the weekend."

Joe let it go at that. What was one more lie? But hadn't he been told time and again that TB patients needed to be free from worry if the cure was to be successful?

Joe drove slowly around the Club's sprawled-out buildings. "There's over two hundred buildings," he said. "Course a lot of them are closed up for the winter and the roads aren't rolled."

He stopped in front of the garage. Leaning across Alice he pointed to the upstairs windows. "My window is the third from the right."

"Is it a nice room? I've become to accustomed to lots of open windows. It's hard to think of a room with just one."

"It's okay. Clean, warm. Bath just down the hall. But it's missing the most important thing for a bedroom."

Alice turned blue eyes to her husband's face.

"You. I'll never really be whole again till you're beside me every night." He cupped her small face in his gloved hands. "I miss you so much, dear heart." He pressed his lips against her forehead, aching to do more.

"I am getting better, Joe. I bet we're back home in New York in less than a year. . .making babies." She pushed gently against his arms, breaking the embrace.

Joe put the truck in gear and drove up to Finches. "The laundry is in the cellar," he explained. "Even the help get all the clean sheets and towels they want. We eat on the first floor and the dorms for the single men and women are on the second."

"Is that where Kate lives?"

"Yup. She goes home to her father's farm for her days off. He manages one of the Club's dairy farms. There's something like ten farms in all." Joe let in the clutch and headed for the main building.

"I heard the other day that the Club owns ten thousand acres. Has its own electric power plant, too." Joe pulled the truck out on Mirror Lake Drive.

"A complete little village," Alice observed.

A twenty-foot tall cobblestone retaining wall rose from the edge of the road. A wall of steps, so many it took Alice's breath away, clung to the side of the cobblestones from Mirror Lake Drive up to the porte cochere entrance of the Lake Placid Club. At the top of the steps a large sign stated: "Jews and Consumptives not welcomed."

Joe heard Alice's quick gasp. He reached for her hand, but she kept it on her lap. Why did he have to drive by that sign? A black cloud settled over them. Out of the corner of his eye, he could see Alice wrap her arms about her thin body, hugging her elbows. He wished he had prepared her for the Club's banning of tuberculars.

"That's about all I can show you till some of this snow melts. Want to stop for a hot chocolate?"

"I think I'd rather wait till we get back to Saranac," she said. Where consumptives aren't on a blacklist, she said to herself.

19

Stepping back out on the Stevens's farm porch in Vermontville, Schermerhorn pulled down the earflaps on his sealskin hat. The two men headed for the barn.

Schermerhorn's eyes roamed the inside of the barn, rank with ammonia built up from cows confined too long. His eyes teared up. Blizzard would smell like one of them by the time they left. . .hell, he would, too. It'd take forever to get a smell like this out of his mackinaw.

"This is how we'll play it out." Schermerhorn turned to the farmer. "Open the barn doors so they can drive right in. Then close and latch the doors. But make sure they don't feel you're locking them in or they'll bolt for sure."

"What can I say? They don't much care for the cow stink." He hunched his shoulders, lowering his neck into the meager warmth of the frayed corduroy collar of his brown duck jacket.

"Tell them you have to keep the barn warm. Shouldn't have a problem believing that. It's sure to be twenty below tonight." Schermerhorn walked to a corner closet and opened the door. He removed the pitchforks and shovels, stepped in and pulled the door shut after him.

"This will work fine," he said. "When I hear them come, I'll shut myself in here. After you've locked them in the barn, I'll come out. You and I can stand with our backs to the door and McFadden's men will be trapped. Quick and easy."

Stevens nodded and rounded up his boys, taking them into the house. Schermerhorn shut the door behind Stevens and headed for Blizzard. The horse raised his head at the trooper's approach.

"Looks like we'll be here awhile longer, fella." He patted the horse's blanketed rump and walked on to where his saddle was swung over a stall partition. He took the Winchester 30–30 from its holder and carried it back to the closet. Next he checked the Colt .45 and placed it back in the holster on his waist. Ready.

Car doors slammed like rifle shots. Schermerhorn jumped from his perch on a milk can and peered out a crack in the barn door. Couldn't see a thing but heard voices and then the bang of the house door.

He strained to understand the mumble of voices, but only Stevens' nervous whine carried on the cold air. Hope McFadden's men didn't pick up on it. Schermerhorn retreated to the closet, pulling the door shut after him. He heard the snow squeak under the car's tires as it drove up to the barn.

Hinges creaked and the big door scraped across the snow. The purr of a powerful engine grew louder then stopped, followed by the ratcheting of a hand brake being set. Exhaust fumes mixing with the ammonia reek seeped around the ill-fitting closet door.

Good work, Schermerhorn thought, when he heard the repeat performance of scraping and creaking that signaled the closing of the barn doors.

"Whew! What a stink. Don't shut those doors. We'll suffocate on that godawful smell."

"Too cold not to," Stevens answered.

Schermerhorn heard the wooden thud of the bar falling into place. In one swift movement he moved from the closet and trained his Colt on the man facing him.

"Holy shit." The man fumbled for the gun concealed somewhere within his coat, realized the futility and raised his hands.

His obese partner oozed out of the Packard. "You snivelling turncoat," he wheezed at Stevens. "McFadden isn't going to be happy about this."

"I'm none too happy myself that you're not putting your hands up," Schermerhorn said.

The man glared at Schermerhorn and inched his arms upward, exposing wrists creased with fat.

"One at a time, drop your guns. You first." He waved his Colt at the driver. The man reached inside his coat, pulled out a gun and let

146

it drop to the ground. "Get your hands back up. Now step back." He repeated the procedure for the fat man and instructed the farmer to pick up the guns.

"I understand you've come to retrieve some merchandise," Schermerhorn said, keeping his Colt leveled at the bootleggers.

"I'm sure we could arrange to leave some good bonded stuff."

"Don't add bribery to the charges." Schermerhorn's face hardened as he took a step forward. "Get it loaded. . .now."

The driver shrugged out of his coat, folded it with the satin lining on the outside and laid it on the hood of the Packard. Next he removed his fedora and set it on the coat and passed his hands over his dark, patent-leather hair. Glowering at Schermerhorn, he shot his cuffs and climbed the ladder to the hayloft.

The driver carried the cases down the ladder. The fat man, grunting under their weight, waddled to the Packard. Scotch, rye, champagne. All expensive goods.

"You don't have to act so virtuous just because you're wearing purple and gray," the fat man said as he carried the boxes past Schermerhorn. "Most folks in these parts don't think having a drink is committing a crime."

"And I suppose doubling the price you pay for booze in Canada is all right, too?"

"Hey. . .demand is high." He stopped and faced Schermerhorn, his fat face red and sweating. "Some troopers," he said softly, "have learned ways of doubling what they make in a year."

"Name one."

"I've heard rumors," he wheezed, breathing hard through his mouth. Schermerhorn chewed on that tidbit while the man set the box in the Packard.

"Give me a name," he said, when the fat man passed by again. "If it pans out my report will say you cooperated." The booze runner stopped to face Schermerhorn and started to reach inside his coat.

"Don't try that," Schermerhorn said, raising his Colt. Everyone froze as the click of the safety cut through the tension in the barn.

"Calm yourself," The fat man quickly withdrew his hand and held up both palms." "Just need my handkerchief."

Schermerhorn kept the Colt aimed at the fat man's sweating forehead. By the time he shook out the handkerchief and thoroughly wiped his jowly face, the fat man was breathing more normally.

"Cronk," the fat man said. "Carl Cronk's been alerting McFadden about roadblocks." He paused. "Bastard called this one wrong."

Schermerhorn's shoulders drooped under his heavy mackinaw. Cronk. . .his partner. He kept his Colt poised, ready to act, but let his mind mull over the Cronk situation.

Night had fallen by the time Schermerhorn had the four of them in the car with a delighted Stevens at the wheel. The farmer's entire family lined up on the porch, waving as Stevens cautiously drove the fancy Packard to Saranac Lake.

Schermerhorn brooded over turning Cronk in to Captain Broadfield. The Commander was a strict disciplinarian and took great pride in the high calibre of his troop. Cronk simply didn't cut the mustard.

At the Saranac Lake Police Station, Schermerhorn put in a call to his Commander in Malone. Unfortunately, Captain Broadfield had gone for the night. He'd have to decide the best way to handle Cronk on his own.

It's possible Cronk didn't suspect he was on to him. But when Cronk learned he'd caught McFadden's men, it might get him to thinking. Well, nothing to do but keep Cronk right at his side. They weren't due back at the Malone barracks for another five days, but he'd drum up some reason to come in early.

20

"I feel like a child being told to go out and play," Alice commented to Charlotte. The two young women made their way down Conifer's porch steps for their morning walk. "If the rest of the world knew what we were made to do, they'd put our keepers in jail."

"Goodness, you're as bitter as the cold this morning." Charlotte's face was buried nose deep in the scarf stuffed in the shawl collar of her brown coat. "It's such a treat to get off the porch after three years of just sitting that I don't care what the weather is."

"Don't you ever want to scream about being sentenced to this life? I can't imagine being here for three years."

"Everything is somehow easier to bear since I've been allowed to get up." Charlotte looped her arm through Alice's and they joined the group of consumptives out taking the air. "I should think you'd be in a good mood after your outing with Joe yesterday. Luncheon and all."

"That was the best part of the day," Alice said. She told Charlotte all about the elegant meal. "They must think pretty well of Joe at work. Giving him a truck to use." She pulled her arm away from Charlotte to adjust the scarf around her neck. Alice wore three sweaters under her old blue coat but it still wasn't much of a defense against an Adirondack cold snap. "And to think he had money to pay for a fancy lunch," she continued, linking her arm back through Charlotte's again. "We were never able to do that in New York."

They walked along in silence for awhile, their feet scrunching on the packed snow. Snippets of conversation and laughter from the growing crowd of walkers carried on the cold air.

"The Saranac crowd is always so cheerful and optimistic," Charlotte observed. "So, what did you do after lunch?"

Alice sighed. "I asked Joe to drive over to Lake Placid. I've been curious about where he lived and worked."

"I've heard so much about Placid. What did you think of it?"

"They're all healthy over there, Charlotte. And they don't want people like us around."

"What do you mean?"

Alice told her about the sign at the Lake Placid Club's main entrance.

"That's just one hotel, Alice."

"I don't know about that because as soon as I saw it I asked Joe to take me home. Home!" Alice stopped in the middle of the sidewalk and turned to face Charlotte. "Did you hear me say that? I felt threatened and wanted to come back to Conifer where I feel safe and accepted. Conifer has become my home."

"I know that feeling," Charlotte said. "Come on, we're making everyone walk around us." They walked silently for a few steps before Charlotte continued.

"I haven't told a soul yet. Not my husband or anyone. I don't want to be disappointed if it doesn't happen, but Dr. Hayes has been hinting I could go home this summer."

"Oh, Charlotte, what good news." Alice squeezed her friend's arm.

"My lungs have been bad for so long, I can't believe I could be ready so soon after being allowed up for barely a month now. And after that hemorrhage in December. Dr. Hayes is surprised at the speed of healing after stagnating for so long. Can you believe no spots on my last X-ray?"

"You must be so happy."

"Yes. . .and more than a little apprehensive, too. Like you said, Conifer Cottage has become home. I'll be going to a home run by another woman. My girls have been trained not to come near me. Are they going to forget that overnight? And John. It's been almost twelve hundred days since we've slept in the same bed."

They came to a stop at the bottom of Helen Hill. "Let's go this way today," Alice said. They crossed Church Street and walked past the great grey stone structure of St. Bernard's Church.

"Clearing our lungs is only the first step, isn't it? We concentrate so hard on it that it's easy to forget what it takes to join the world again."

"Well, I know I have to build up my stamina if I plan to keep up with my three daughters. I'm trying to walk a few minutes longer each day. It will be hard enough adjusting to life in Schenectady without dealing with exhaustion."

"It's not going back, it's starting from the beginning, isn't it?"

"Look!" Charlotte touched Alice's arm. "Isn't that Connie across the street? See? With that tall man in the fur hat."

Alice looked and recognized Connie, the tiny girl she and Joe had Christmas dinner with. She had turned up her shiny, scrubbed face to say something to the man she walked with.

"I'm sure it is. But that's not her husband she's so cozy with."

"No doubt it's her cousin. I heard she was seeing someone."

"Seeing her cousin? The man she's holding hands with is her cousin? They aren't acting like any cousins I know."

"Cousining." Charlotte took a good look at Alice. "You really don't know, do you? Hard to imagine. You spend so much time with Lilly and you don't know about cousining? No one tries to hide it."

"Hide what?"

"I'm talking about Saranac Lake cousins. Like Lilly and Frank."

"Lilly and Frank are cousins? Charlotte, you're talking in riddles.

""I wonder if this is what it'll be like to explain the birds and bees to my daughters," Charlotte smiled. "Now, dear, there's something you're old enough to know." Charlotte pulled Alice off the sidewalk into a driveway. She grasped Alice's hand between hers. "Saranac Lake cousins are two people who are romantically related."

"But Connie's married."

"And so is Frank. The local saying for married cure patients like Connie is: 'She left her spouse behind when her train pulled out of Utica.'"

"That can't be so. I met Connie's husband last Christmas. His name is Mike."

"Alice you are naive. It's a. . .discreet way of acknowledging romantic involvement. Let's us tuberculars feel good about ourselves."

"I can't believe Hilda and Ursula put up with that right in their house! So many rules and then turn the other way when such a major rule is broken. And Lilly and Frank, acting like lovebirds right out there on the porch. I didn't know he was married."

"You know Dr. Hayes—everyone who takes care of us for that matter—makes a big to-do about keeping us happy and light-hearted."

"Oh, yes. TB feeds less willingly on the happy. But it's good to break marriage vows?"

"You're different from the majority of us, Alice. You have Joe right here."

"But we don't. . .do that. I wouldn't want Joe to get TB. The doctor in New York said we should use gauze between our lips if we kissed."

"Then you need a cousin, too. Someone to take away the feeling of being damaged goods. Someone who already has TB." Charlotte steered Alice back on the sidewalk and they continued their walk down Main Street.

"Do you have a cousin?"

"No," Charlotte answered, "but now that I'm up I wouldn't mind finding one. Let's stop for a hot chocolate before tackling the return trip up Helen Hill."

Alice nodded absently, her head still whirling with the things Charlotte told her. They stopped in at Sadie's and stood inside the door for a moment while their eyes adjusted to the dim light.

Alice stuffed her mittens in her pockets and slowly unbuttoned her coat. She had only been to Sadie's once before, during Carnival, her first time in town. Joe drove everyone in that fancy Pierce-Arrow. That was the day she met Kate, too.

If it was all right for tuberculars to have cousins, was there a rule for the healthy spouses of tuberculars, too? All of a sudden she saw Kate in a different light. Dimpled, rounded. . .healthy Kate. Who saw Joe every day, for all Alice knew about what went on at the Club.

21

"Funny the troopers didn't bother to search Charlie's truck," Stu said, stroking his chin with the fur of his lucky rabbit's foot key chain. Dasset's group sat around the table in Charlie Rauch's barn listening to Joe's account of the roadblock outside of Bloomingdale.

"Those Series A Chevy trucks are so underpowered," Armand said, "the law wouldn't dream there's anyone out there foolish enough to shoot a load in one."

"They caught some guy in Ausable Forks driving a Road King Motor Truck," Ellis said. He picked at the dirt under his fingernails with a pocketknife. "It was camouflaged with strips of two-by-fours at the rear end and both sides. Even smart enough to nail more two by fours across the top. He was carrying a hundred cases."

"So smart he got caught, eh?" Gaston said

"He made a couple of major mistakes," Ellis said. "Like traveling at midnight instead of daytime when you'd expect to see a truck delivering lumber."

"That would do it," Gaston said. He tilted his chair on its back legs.

"That, and he made so many runs—three a week—the troopers began to wonder where all the new construction was happening."

"Doesn't pay to be so smug," Armand said. "Start acting cocky and it'll be your downfall."

"You hear about the raid at Green Onion?" Stu asked. He waited for everyone to look at him before continuing. "The feds found some pretty entertaining ways of searching for the goods," Stu chuckled. "Just a nice group out to have a good time. No big time cases and gallons. Feds barge in and began feeling up everyone's legs."

153

"No shit?" Ellis said.

"Truth. Someone must have tipped them off. They lost no time in frisking up the ladies' legs and found pints in their garters."

"Now that's a job I could get into," Ellis said.

Stu stood and grasped the lapels on his suit, waiting for the snickering to quiet down. "Course they had to check the men out, too. Heard the men really played it up, saying things like 'Oooh. . .that feels so good!'"

"Serves them right for breaking up an innocent party," Gaston said, righting his chair.

"Guess they had to pay big time for their clowning around, though," Stu said. "Feds carted the whole party down to the jail. Locked them up overnight and gave each a fifty dollar fine."

Joe and Gaston left the group and returned to the shop area where Joe had been adjusting the fan belts on Gaston's car.

"What do you do besides work?" Gaston asked, propping his elbows on the front fenders of the car so he could talk to Joe.

"Not much time or money for anything else. Between working here three, four nights and spending Saturdays and Sundays with Alice, I'm out straight most of the time."

"Ever been to Canada?"

"No."

"Come with me. We'll go Friday."

"I work Fridays."

"After work. It's an easy two-hour drive. I know a good roadhouse with great steaks and music. We'll stay at my parents' farm in St. Antoine-Albe."

Joe took his head out from under the hood. "It does sound good. I'd want to be back early enough to see Alice before noon on Saturday."

"I'll have you there quicker than if you hitchhike."

Friday afternoon crept by for Joe. He couldn't remember how long it had been since there was something to look forward to on a Friday night. Finally he pushed himself out from under a car, put his tools away and turned off the shop lights. The light was still on in Madden's office so he rapped on the door.

"Going now, Mr. Madden," he called through the door.

"You finish the five-passenger?"

"Ready to roll. See you Monday."

"Seven sharp."

Joe all but bolted out the door and sprinted up the steps to his room. He shrugged out of the brown coveralls and stripped off his clothes, leaving them where they fell, and headed for the shower. He spent more time than usual getting the grease out from under his nails.

Whistling, he swiped the steam off the mirror and worked up a lather to shave. That accomplished, he gave his hair a good dose of hair tonic, parted it in the middle and slicked it back in place. "Fine looking fellow, Devlin," he said, observing his efforts.

Back in his room, Joe saw the lights of Charlie's truck coming up the road. Charlie was to take Joe to the barn where Gaston waited. He hung his towel on the doorknob and quickly pulled on clean clothes.

Wish I had one of those fancy suits, he thought, as he buttoned his flannel shirt. Seems like I have a wish list as long as my arm. Car, coat for Alice.

No worries for tonight, he admonished himself. They'll keep for tomorrow. Tonight I'm having some fun.

The young men sped for the Canadian border in Gaston's souped-up Buick. The Canadian customs agents smiled when Gaston pulled up.

"Evening, gentlemen," Gaston said, rolling down his window. Joe could see he enjoyed showing off his easy camaraderie with the agents.

"Staying long?" the agent asked.

"Overnight."

"Have a good time. Give my best to Anne." The agent thumped on the roof and waved him through.

"That was easy," Joe said. "Who's Anne?"

"Oh, a long-legged Sheba I know." Gaston ran the Buick up through its gears. "You'll meet her tonight. But first we'll do our buying, eh?"

They drove on through the night, talking easily about girls and cars.

"I think we should talk about the story we'll tell if we get caught with the goods," Gaston said.

"Caught." A sour taste rose in Joe's throat. "You said this would be an easy trip."

"It will be. But it's best to be prepared for anything. Dasset would have my head if he knew you came with me tonight." Gaston wove his car through the Montreal traffic, eventually turning onto Sherbrooke Street. "I sure as hell wouldn't want to face him if you get arrested."

"Isn't it a little too late to be thinking of that?"

"No. Now listen to how we'll handle it." Gaston pulled the Buick under a big sign that read "Ian Flanders & Sons, Ltd., Wholesalers of Fine Liquors." He turned off the key and looked Joe in the eye.

Gaston had developed a story in which Joe went to Montreal to visit a girl he'd met when she came to Placid. Gaston was at the same roadhouse where Joe and the girl were and Gaston offered to give Joe a ride back to Placid. Joe was to insist he never met Gaston before tonight and certainly wasn't aware what the Buick was carrying.

Making up such a tale was bad enough. The possibility of needing such a story to escape being arrested sent a chill racing down Joe's spine.

"They keep long hours," Joe observed, when Gaston finally let him out of the car, content that Joe understood what to say if they were caught.

"Most of their business is with their friends across the border. They know we prefer to travel at night and are most accommodating."

Mr. Flanders came from a back room to greet Gaston with a handshake and a smile. Joe stood in the background and watched Gaston order cases of liquor and cordials and pay for it with a wad of greenbacks he pulled from his pocket.

A smiling Mr. Flanders poured Canadian Club for them while they waited for Gaston's order to come up from the warehouse. Joe had never tasted such smooth stuff. He rolled it around his tongue before allowing it to slide down his throat. He didn't remember draining his glass, but he must have, and the next thing he knew they were back in the Buick, driving over the Honoré Mercier Bridge.

"Ready for a good steak?" Gaston asked.

"You bet."

Gaston drove south on Route 138 for a time and pulled into a roadhouse. He wedged the Buick into a narrow spot in the crowded lot. Joe squeezed out of his door and hurried to catch up with Gaston. The roadhouse door opened and Joe was engulfed by music and smoke. People having a good time. Eagerly he stepped inside and unbuttoned his coat.

"Gaston!" A tall, slim girl wrapped her long bare arms around Gaston's neck and kissed him fully on the mouth. "You have been neglecting me." Her crimson mouth pursed in an attractive pout. She looked down at Gaston, whose head was about eye level with her bosom.

"I'm here now," Gaston said, "and I brought my friend, Joe. Joe, this is Anne."

"Ah, Joe." Anne turned to look at him. Her angular face was capped with smooth black hair and heavy bangs cut just above her eyes. "You are alone? We can't have that on a Friday night."

Joe found himself herded to a table. Soon Anne reappeared with a tray of drinks and a girl she introduced as Collette, who smiled shyly and slipped into the seat next to Joe. Her fair hair was parted in the middle and held smoothly in place by barrettes. Below them her curls fluffed out, leaving just the pink tips of her ears showing. Joe turned away and took a swallow of his Canadian Club. Across the table Gaston and Anne were talking. Gaston ran a finger up and down Anne's arm.

Suddenly Joe felt uncomfortably warm. He opened his shirt collar and picked up his whiskey.

"I've never seen you around before," Collette said. Joe turned his head and inhaled her sweet flowery perfume. He briefly wondered if her full red mouth was as soft as it looked.

"This is my first trip," he managed to say. Fortunately their steaks arrived and Joe cut into his hungrily. The girls had already eaten, but sipped away at their drinks while Joe and Gaston enjoyed their meals. Joe saw Anne lean toward Gaston and run a long-nailed fingertip back and forth across the back of his neck while he ate.

Geez, Joe thought, and lowered his eyes, attempting to concentrate on the steak. He took a deep breath to still the pulsing in his loins but only succeeded in filling his head with Collette's heady perfume. He reached for the only thing to drink on the table and found he had emptied his glass of whiskey.

"I'll take care of that for you." Collette clasped her soft hand gently over Joe's, which was still clutching his glass. He looked at her and fought his desire to taste those soft lips. Collette leaned ever so slightly and touched her lips to Joe's mouth. The touch of a feather, yet Joe felt on fire.

"I'll be right back." Collette smiled and left the table.

"Collette seems like a nice girl," Gaston observed from across the table. He smiled and tilted his head. "Good food, good drink, good women. . .what more is there?"

"Good music," Anne said. "Come on, I want to dance." She tugged at Gaston's arm. He groaned good naturedly and followed her to the crowded dance floor.

Joe brought his attention back to his steak. I'll be all right when I get some food inside me, he thought. He hadn't eaten anything since noon and here it was ten o'clock. That and three. . .no, probably four. . .Canadian Clubs.

Before long, Joe found himself on the dance floor, his arms around Collette's pliant, healthy body. He let her drag him through a Charleston and now they were pressed together in a fox-trot. It took every ounce of self-control to keep from exploring her body, covered so lightly in a thin chemise.

Gaston touched Joe's shoulder, breaking into the seductive swaying of the dance and the closeness of Collette. "They say it's snowing pretty hard. We better leave."

"So," Gaston asked, as they brushed several inches of snow off the windshield, "what do you think of our Canadian girls?"

"Very friendly."

Gaston laughed. "They do know how to warm up a winter night, eh?" Guiding the big car out of the parking lot, he turned his attention to driving in the deepening snow. He crept along looking for a left turn.

"I've known this road all my life," he said, "but snow distorts everything. Ah, there it is." The headlights picked up a small sign for Route 201. Gaston gingerly stepped on the over-loaded car's brakes and made a left turn. Soon he turned in a long drive. The Buick sashayed and veered into deeper snow.

"I guess this is where we stop," Gaston said. "We'll dig it out in the morning. Think you can walk to the house?"

"Sure. Can't be worse than the pass into Placid." Joe got out of the car and pulled his coat around him. He let Gaston lead the way up the drive to his family's farmhouse.

22

Before she opened her eyes on Saturday morning, Alice knew it was snowing. There was a muffled quiet in a snowstorm. Birds waited the storm out, huddled in the inner branches of the evergreens. Traffic came to a standstill. Any sounds that existed were absorbed in the all-encompassing white insulator.

But hadn't there been enough snow? It was March, after all. Back in New York she'd be looking for signs of the first daffodils in the park across from their flat.

She dropped her legs over the side of the bed and searched for her slippers with her toes. Standing up, she pulled on her bathrobe and went about shutting the windows. She could barely see Pelletier Cottage through the big, wet snowflakes.

She wished she could call Joe and tell him not to walk over today. Much too stormy. But Joe had told her that it was difficult for employees to receive telephone calls. All of a sudden the turbulent thoughts she had yesterday about cousining and the real nature of Joe's friendship with Kate came rushing back.

If Joe stayed at the Club today, would he and Kate be together? And if Kate had already gone home to her father's farm weren't there dozens of waitresses and maids who would be snowbound. . .with Joe? What would they do when they weren't actually working? And then there was that ever-present seed of doubt that had been trying so hard to germinate: was she being unrealistic to think Joe could resist all that temptation when he was forbidden to kiss his wife?

Resolutely she pushed the disturbing thoughts from her head and tried to think of something positive instead of fretting over events she couldn't control. She picked up her toothbrush and other toilet things and went to the bathroom for her morning wash. Remembering Saturday breakfast was fluffy pancakes topped with melting creamy butter and swimming in maple syrup, Alice hurried with dressing and joined her porchmates in the dining room. All three young women were enjoying up patient status now.

Funny, Alice mused on her way downstairs, in New York a wife's status was measured by the house she kept and the way her husband's clothes were ironed. Here status was measured by the privileges earned, which indicated a degree of health recovered.

A foot of snow didn't change Conifer's routine one iota. By ten o'clock the sisters were gently pushing the up patients out the door for their morning walk. Alice had heard the scrape of shoveling earlier, but the porch and stairs already had a new covering.

Charlotte and Alice decided to make a circuit of the streets at the top of Helen Hill, agreeing that if they went into the village the return climb to Conifer would be too difficult in the deep snow. Cure cottages clung like trees to the sides of Helen Hill. The houses filled their small lots, each wrapped with big porches and garnished with every imaginable configuration of second floor and often third floor sitting-out porches.

Gaining permission to sit on the first floor porch was the goal of every patient. Wrapped in fur robes, settled on a cure chair, a patient could visit with others curing at the cottage and, even more important, the surrounding cottages. It was the place to see and be seen. Alice recalled Lilly pointing out several girls who actually met their future spouses on cure cottage porches.

Finding the deep snow tiring, Charlotte and Alice started back to Conifer. They heard Frank's mandolin even before Pelletier came into view.

"Let's stop at Pelletier's," Charlotte said.

"Can we do that? Just invite ourselves over?"

"Lilly does. Come on," Charlotte urged. "I want to see some new faces."

On Pelletier's porch they found Lilly curled at the foot of Frank's cure chair. She jumped up, delighted to see her porchmates, and introduced them to the fellows, all snug under their fur robes. Lilly made a big to-do about settling the two girls on an empty cure chair right in the middle. Even found them a bear robe to share.

Frank strummed along while the pale young man next to Alice smiled at her. She learned his name was Tom. He was from New York and this was his first week as an up patient. She liked his lazy smile. Following his lead, Alice offered her vital statistics, but found herself omitting the fact that she was married. Charlotte had turned around on the cure chair and Alice heard her talking to the fellow on the other side.

Is this how it all starts? Alice wondered.

As the excitement of getting to know one another subsided, one by one they started humming, then singing softly along with Frank. They looked out at the falling snow, their noses getting chilly, and did exactly what they had come to the Adirondacks to do: sit and sit and sit.

Frank picked absently for a time then eased into "Old Black Joe." The entire porch sang the melancholy song. When it was over, Frank kept going. This time he sang alone:

"Gone are the days, when my lungs were good and strong.
Gone are my friends, with whom I've cured so long.
Gone from this earth, to a better place I know
I hear the devil softly calling, 'Come down below.'
I'm coming, I'm coming, but my cough is getting worse
I hear the undertaker calling 'bring on the hearse.'"

The porch was silent. Followed by coughs and a few nervous laughs.

"Frank, that is so depressing," Lilly said.

"Oh, come on, Lilly, can't we poke fun at ourselves?"

"TB isn't fun," Alice said. "Dying isn't fun." She flung off the bear robe and stormed off the porch.

"Alice!" Lilly called after her.

Safely inside the vestibule at Conifer, Alice yanked off her boots and hung up her coat. On her way to her room, she passed Ursula using the carpet sweeper in the upstairs hall.

"Has Joe called?" Alice asked.

"No, dear."

"I hope he doesn't try to come today." I can't imagine there'd be anyone he could catch a ride with, she thought. He'd have to walk the whole way. "Please let me know if he calls so I can talk to him."

Alice shut the door to her room and immediately felt caged. She flopped into the slipper chair and tucked a blanket around her legs. Picking up a copy of True Story she forced herself to read.

The sound of laughter out in the street caught her attention and she turned her head to look out the window. The gang at Pelletier was building a snowman. Both Lilly and Charlotte were joining in the fun. She saw the man Charlotte had been talking to earlier touch her arm. Charlotte smiled up at him.

As Alice watched, Ursula called them in for dinner. Lilly scooped up a snowball, throwing it toward Frank, then looped her arm through Charlotte's. Alice lost sight of them as they crossed the street.

She washed her hands, tugged a comb through her curls and hurried downstairs. She wanted to find a place at the table where Lilly and Charlotte couldn't be near her. She knew they'd want to talk about her scene at Pelletier's. She'd scream if Charlotte started to quote from her endless supply of cheerful little mottos. Someday I'll burn all her "Trotty Vics," she vowed.

If Alice's porchmates were surprised she chose not to sit near them, it didn't show. She bent her head, concentrating on her food, only talking when courtesy demanded. She was the first to leave the table and went directly to her room. She was needlessly refolding clothes in a dresser drawer when Charlotte knocked on the door.

"It's not good to stay upset," Charlotte said.

Alice gritted her teeth. "It's all a big game to them."

"We'll never get well if we dwell on our disease all the time. A dose of quiet fun is good for us."

"You and your happy little mottos." Alice shoved the open drawer back in place. "I'm sick of it. Sick of Saranac Lake and the little gods that run it. 'You will be happy,' she mimicked, 'you may forget your husband and take a cousin.' This place isn't real."

"Calm down, Alice." Charlotte reached out to touch her shoulder. "You'll work yourself into coughing or worse."

"Maybe worse is better," she shrugged Charlotte's hand away. "At least it'd be over."

"I know you don't mean that. You've got a wonderful husband who changed his whole life to be with you."

"Oh, Charly, what has happened to Joe?" Alice's anger fled and she crumpled in Charlotte's caring arms. "It's not like him not to call if he can't come," she sobbed. " I'm so worried he's stuck out there in this storm."

"That might be true of some other man," Charlotte said, "but we know your Joe is capable of walking hundreds of miles in the snow."

23

"Joe. Wake up." Gaston's voice seemed to echo from a deep tunnel. Joe's mouth felt woolly and tasted even worse. His eyes didn't want to focus.

"Just a little longer," he mumbled.

"No, now." Gaston yanked back the blankets.

"Come on, Gaston. It's too cold for games. I feel awful."

"Some fresh air and your head will feel better."

"You're crazy."

Gaston pulled Joe to a sitting position and shoved a cup of black coffee in his hands. Joe sipped at the coffee and made several attempts to open his eyes.

"Get dressed. I'll meet you downstairs."

Joe fumbled with his clothes and found his way down a flight of stairs he had no recollection of climbing. He followed Gaston's voice to the kitchen. A plump woman stood at an immense black cookstove frying up a skillet of greasy potatoes. Joe's stomach lurched. He leaned against the wall and covered his mouth. Gaston laughed.

"Let's get you outside. You can meet my mother later." He helped Joe into a jacket that smelled of cows and sweat then handed him a pair of rubber muck boots.

Joe stood on the porch and filled his lungs with the cold air. Soon his stomach settled and the two set off for the barn. When he took his first step off the covered porch he floundered up to his knees in fresh light snow. It came down at a furious rate. Was there no limit to the amount that could fall in this godforsaken country?

The steamy barn smelled of silage. Gaston set Joe to watering the cows and then went to help his father with the milking. Joe performed the task methodically, his head too muddled from last night's whiskey to sort things out.

Last night came back slowly, starting with unaccustomed drinks at the liquor store. And that good-smelling Canadian girl. Joe felt his face burn at the liberties Collette took Let's be honest, he told himself, I enjoyed every minute of it. It's been a year since Alice and I have been able to. . .act normal. Then it hit him, today must be Saturday. Alice would be expecting him!

But the snow. . .would the roads be passable? He picked up his pace, anxious to be on his way. Later he'd worry about whatever happened last night. He found Gaston putting a harness on a huge gray draft horse.

"Gaston, I have to get to Saranac Lake this morning."

"First we have to get the car back on the road. . .don't suppose you remember much about last night." Gaston chuckled. "What a shame. You were having such a great time."

"You're right, I forgot about the car." Joe chose to ignore the other remark. "What's your plan?"

"We'll get you in the driver's seat," Gaston said, as he threw thick leather tugs over the horse's rump. "Then Nanette here and I will pull the Buick out and get it turned around." He hung a tow chain over the mare's hames and led her out of the barn.

The two men trudged along behind Nanette as she broke a path down the drive. Gaston held the long lines to the mare's bit lightly in one hand, guiding her to the car. Both men carried shovels over their shoulders.

The Buick was buried up to its windshield in the snow. Joe groaned at the work ahead of them to free the car. Gaston turned the mare so her big rump faced the driving snow. He halted her and looped the lines around the hames.

More than an hour of shoveling and tire spinning passed before Nanette pulled the Buick back onto the drive. The men cheered loudly and joyfully slapped the mare on her neck.

"Look, Joe, this snow isn't letting up and nothing has moved on the road since we've been here." Gaston put into words what Joe didn't want to think about. "I think Nanette will tow the car back to barn and we'll wait till the snow lets up before moving on."

"I guess there's no choice," Joe agreed. "If I can use your telephone I'll let Alice know I probably won't get there today."

"No telephone lines out here."

"I never should have let you talk me into coming with you." One thing I know for sure, he thought, I'm never going to drink like that again.

"Hey, I'm sorry the way things turned out, Joe. Most likely this snow is covering Saranac Lake, too."

"I've walked ten miles in snow more than once this winter."

"Come on, Joe. Would she really expect you to walk ten miles in a storm like this just to visit?"

Joe got back in the car, slamming the door so hard the whole car shuddered. He took it out of gear and let Nanette tow him to the barn.

The snow had stopped! Joe expelled a great lungful of air in relief. Looking out a window of the farmhouse, he could already see patches of blue in the afternoon sky.

"It'll be some time yet before the roads are passable," Gaston said, placing a tight rein on Joe's hopes for getting to Saranac Lake.

"We can't risk crossing where the border guards are," Gaston added. "The goods are barely hidden in the back seat. My plan was to take a cow path through the woods to an unguarded crossing." Gaston pushed himself away from the table where he and Joe had been playing cards. He went to the window and looked out at the snow. "The crossing is only a couple of miles from here but I doubt it'll be passable before tomorrow morning."

"So it'll be afternoon before we get to Saranac Lake," Joe said, realizing the couple of hours the trip normally took would be doubled or more with the poor road conditions. But there wasn't a damn thing he could do about it.

"Yes," Gaston said, "but there's a lot of shoveling to do while it's still daylight." The men pulled on jackets and boots, tugged knitted toques over their ears and went out in the snow. Picking up shovels at the door, they dug a path to the barn.

Joe leaned on his shovel and judged the distance between the barn, where the Buick had waited out the storm, and the road passing the farm. Five, six hundred feet up one side and five, six hundred feet back the other. Well, it wasn't going to get any shorter looking at it. He bent his back and began scooping great shovelfuls off the drive.

Gaston's mother had another greasy meal ready for them when they finished. The food she served was either fried or swimming in a greasy gravy. They appeared to be pleasant people, Gaston's mother and father, but not understanding a word of the French-Canadian dialect they spoke had made being snowbound difficult. Joe smiled when their eyes met, but what else could he do? With much smiling, he cleared his dishes off the table and went upstairs to pass the time before they could leave.

This time when Gaston called him, Joe came instantly awake. Finally time to go. Still buttoning his shirt, he ran lightly down the stairs.

Joe drank the hot coffee, but turned down the eggs floating in bacon grease. "My father is taking the team and going with us till we pick up a good road on the other side," Gaston told him, dipping his toast in egg yolk. "If we get stuck," he explained, "we'll have the horses to pull us out."

In less than an hour, the strange convoy started down the drive; the big, gray draft team, hooked to a bob sleigh, led the way. A bright half-moon was low in the starry sky, casting long, black shadows on the white snow. Good thing; it made hooking the tow chain onto the car that much easier. Only a half hour since starting out and twice the Buick had to be pulled free from drifts.

The road left the farmland and wove through a forest. The snow wasn't as deep under the big trees and they moved along without incident.

The horses stopped. Joe watched Gaston's father climb down from the sleigh.

"This is where we cross the border," Gaston said. "My father is opening the gate so we can pass through."

"Hook the gate back up, eh?" Gaston asked after they crossed. Joe got out and went back to hook the chain in place. He smiled at the simple fence that marked the division between the two countries: three strands of barbed wire and a chain gate. Those who used this crossing, Gaston said, were conscientious about hooking the chain back up to keep Canadian cows from going south.

Gaston's father stayed with them until daylight, when they came to the edge of a small settlement. The roads were passable and Gaston felt they were finished with the worst.

Without the horses slowing their progress, they traveled a bit faster, although the snow had narrowed the road to one lane. Now that the sun had come up on a cloudless day, they didn't even have the headlights of approaching cars to warn them as they drove the curvy road. They only came across an occasional car and a couple of horses and sleighs, but it was tricky.

The road straightened out for a bit and they saw a car coming, blowing up great plumes of snow in its wake. Joe got nervous when the car showed no signs of slowing down. Gaston eased the Buick down through its gears. Suddenly the oncoming car swerved, its rear end whipping side to side.

"Crazy fool hit his brakes," Gaston said. He gunned the Buick and drove it off the road. It came to a stop nose deep in the snow. Gaston jumped out swearing and shaking his fists at the car, now speeding out of sight.

Joe pulled shovels from the Buick and silently offered one to Gaston. He glared at Joe, snatched the shovel from his hands and shoveled furiously, mumbling in French all the while.

"Looks like you could use some help." The voice startled Joe. He looked up and saw two tall men in huge mackinaws and fur hats standing not three feet away. They both led black horses. Joe recognized the purple saddlepads of the Black Horse Brigade.

The sight of the troopers went through him like a shot of the whiskey he and Gaston carried. He looked over at Gaston. His friend stood frozen to the spot, like a startled deer. But only for an instant.

Gaston hurled his shovel, full of snow, at one of the troopers and bolted for the woods. The horse snorted and turned tail, nearly knocking Joe down.

"Stop!" The command was followed by the sharp crack of a gun. Joe watched Gaston lunge through the snow. One trooper climbed on his horse and spurred it across the field after Gaston. The other kept his pistol pointed at Joe.

"Step away from the car," he said. He placed Joe in handcuffs and then peered into Gaston's car.

The Buick was loaded with top bonded goods. Would he be arrested with Gaston as a bootlegger? Could he make the story Gaston had contrived sound real? He'd better be ready to say it just like they had rehearsed. He really did not want to speak the words that indicated he was involved with a Canadian girl. Of course he wasn't. And Alice would never hear it. But still it made him feel unfaithful. Panic replaced his fear. The fine would be in the hundreds of dollars. Jail time, too.

Joe watched Gaston struggling back through the deep snow, the trooper riding his horse close behind. When he reached the Buick, Gaston was cuffed, too. He leaned sullenly against the car. Joe couldn't get him to look his way.

The troopers talked softly between themselves. They were an imposing pair. Tall, ramrod straight, with pistols and gun belts around their mackinaws. Their clean-shaven faces were grim. When they looked at Joe with hard, confident eyes, he knew he'd have trouble stumbling through the lies Gaston had dreamed up.

The troopers split up. One mounted his horse and herded the two men in front of him, back to the border village. The other trooper stayed with the car to guard the booze till help could be sent from the village.

The snow crammed down Joe's galoshes melted as they walked. His feet sloshed in a puddle of cold water. The last of the black carapaces on his toes had sloughed off only recently, leaving the frostbitten spots a vivid pink and tender. The affected toes were very susceptible to new frostbite; Joe knew he had to keep them warm and dry.

The trooper ushered them up the steps of a small general store. A group of men leaning back on chairs sat around a big potbellied stove. They dropped their chairs back to all four legs and stared at Joe and Gaston.

"Hey," one called out, "get yourself another booze car? How many does that make, Jim?"

"Hundred and sixty-two," the trooper said. "Any of you men want to make a buck? My partner's down the road with these bootleggers' car. He needs some help to get it back on the road."

"How about a bottle instead of a buck?" Good-natured guffaws followed the remark.

"Now you know I can't do that, Luc."

A young man with a heavy black beard stood up. He grasped his suspenders from where they looped below his waist and pulled them up over his shoulders. "I'll do it," he said.

While the trooper arranged to have his horse taken care of, Joe learned his name was Sergeant Jim Welch. He and his partner were responsible for seizing more booze cars than any other members of Troop B.

"Well, we got caught by the best, eh?" Gaston smiled thinly. Finally Sergeant Welch took Joe and Gaston to a back storeroom.

"Remember," Gaston whispered when the trooper turned his back to accept three mugs of coffee from a stout woman whose wool sweater didn't quite meet across her sagging breasts, "you've never met me before."

The trooper released them from their handcuffs. Gratefully Joe sat down, pulled off his galoshes and shoes and peeled off his sodden socks.

"Frostbite?" Sergeant Welch asked. Joe nodded. Without a word he picked up Joe's socks and took them out front. Joe watched as he conferred with the stout woman. She turned and looked at Joe, then took the socks and shuffled over to place them near the potbellied stove.

"This looks good, Joe," Gaston whispered, as he watched the goings-on. "You've got Welch feeling sorry for you. I'll do my damnedest to make sure they know you weren't involved."

They saw the woman go behind the counter and return with a piece of toweling. She handed it to the trooper, who nodded his head in thanks and returned to the storeroom.

Welch questioned Gaston while Joe dried his toes. He listened as Gaston insisted he was working alone, not associated with any gang. Every chance Gaston got he stressed that the first time he met Joe was at the Canadian roadhouse where Joe and a girl were dancing. He insisted Joe had asked for a ride back to Saranac Lake.

The interrogation went on for several hours. Welch shot questions at Joe then walked away to get more coffee. The next round of questions seemed to be headed in a different direction. Somewhere along the line, Joe admitted he had a wife curing in Saranac Lake.

Welch jumped on that bit of information, making Joe feel like a class A heel for chasing a Canadian girl when he had a wife spending her days in a cure cottage. Like he was cheating on his wife.

"What kind of men are you troopers?" Gaston asked. "You know you can't touch a lunger. Can't you understand what it must be like month after month with no woman?"

Joe understood Gaston was trying to help, but hinting that he couldn't control his urges while Alice was sick didn't sit well with him.

Eventually the troopers herded them back into Gaston's Buick and drove to Saranac Lake, where they went straight from the car to a cell. The metal cell door scraped shut over the cement floor. Joe heard the key turn in the lock and they were left alone. Gaston immediately lay down on one cot, covering his eyes with an arm. Joe sat on the other, holding his head in his hands.

24

"The snow has stopped," Ursula said, as she joined her sister in the kitchen. The Saturday afternoon rest period was almost over and the sisters would soon be checking their patients. For now Hilda sat at the kitchen table, the Adirondack Enterprise newspaper spread out before her.

"Alice is getting herself all worked up about Joe," Ursula said, pulling out a chair and sitting down. "You saw the way she kept to herself at dinner. Didn't speak to a soul."

"He'll be along soon."

"I don't think so. It's almost four o'clock." Ursula sat stiffly at the edge of her chair. Her hands, locked together, rested on the scrubbed table. "He's always here long before noon. I think we should telephone him before Alice comes down and wants to place the call herself. Joe would lose his job if the Lake Placid Club knew he had a wife taking the cure."

Hilda took off her glasses and rubbed the bridge of her large nose. "Ja, you are right." She went to the kitchen desk and located Joe's number at the Club's garage. She gave the number to the operator. No answer. Hilda hung up after ten rings.

The sisters conferred and eventually decided it would be wise to call the Saranac Lake Constable to check on the condition of the road to Lake Placid. Constable Duprey informed Hilda the road crews from both villages were starting work now that the snow had stopped. If a man was trying to walk to Saranac Lake, Hilda was told, he could hitch a ride on the snow roller.

"We will tell Alice everything," Hilda decided, after repeating her telephone conversation to Ursula. "It should ease her mind knowing the road crews are out rolling the snow."

"She'll wonder why he hasn't telephoned."

"I wonder, too," Hilda said. "It's out of our hands, sister." She stood, folded the newspaper neatly and placed it on the kitchen desk. "We've done what we can. We must act like there isn't a whisper of a problem."

Upstairs, Alice came awake with a start. Joe! Where was Joe? The snow had stopped and he still wasn't here. If only he'd telephone she'd be content knowing he wasn't lying unconscious in the snow.

She heard Charlotte and Lilly stirring. She shut her eyes, hoping her porchmates would think she was still asleep and not bother her by trying to find something cheerful to say.

Her mind explored every possible reason Joe wasn't here and no matter how she looked at it, there were only two explanations: he had set out in the snow and was stuck in the empty stretch of road between the two villages; or he was having so much fun playing in the snow with Kate and others, that he forgot all about her.

Either way was upsetting. One explanation worried her sick over his safety. Joe's story about being pulled unconscious from a snowbank was all too vivid. The other explanation made her furious.

Alice looked around and discovered Lilly and Charlotte must have gone downstairs. Good. She had the porch to herself. Getting up, she went to the porch railing and looked out on her little world. As far as she could see in either direction, people were out shoveling snow. At Pelletier, a woman was sweeping the first floor porch and a man was shoveling snow off the porch roof. On Helen Hill, a small boy cleared the sidewalk in front of the Noyes Cottage, tossing huge shovelfuls in the street.

Alice paced the length of the sitting-out porch, her mittened hand clearing the railing of its covering of snow.

"Alice?" She turned and saw Lilly standing in the porch door. "We want to play bridge. Come be a fourth."

"You don't want me around. I'm not cheerful enough." Alice stopped pacing and glared at Lilly. "And if I hear one more time 'it's not good to worry' so help me I'll. . ."

Lilly left, slamming the French door so hard the glass rattled.

Alice flung herself down on her cure chair and cried noisily into her mittens. Soon her hands dropped to her lap and she let her head fall back. Tears continued to stream down her face. She lay, chilled, but too exhausted to pull up the fur robes.

"Alice! Oh my dear, what have you done to yourself?"

Alice forced her puffy eyes open. She shivered and started to cough. Ursula had the sputum cup ready and placed a hand on her forehead while Alice brought up globs of the yellow phlegm. When it was over, she handed Alice a tissue then helped her back inside.

Alice's lips were blue. Ursula quickly helped her undress and get into her flannel gown. Sticking a temp stick in Alice's mouth, Ursula hurried from the room, returning just moments later with a hot stone pig taken from the back of the cookstove.

Alice was coughing again. Ursula placed the sputum cup in her hand and retrieved the temp stick where Alice had dropped it on the quilt. She wrote one hundred and two in the notebook.

When she had made Alice comfortable, Ursula hurried downstairs. She found Hilda preparing supper.

"We must call Dr. Hayes," Ursula said, heading for the telephone. "Alice's temperature is a hundred and two. And she's streaking." After talking to the doctor, Ursula went to sit with Alice.

Dr. Hayes came immediately. He put the stethoscope to Alice's chest and listened to the gurgling in her lungs. He drew a brown bottle from his bag and administered a spoonful of the liquid.

"What is this?" Alice asked.

"Something to help you get a good night's sleep."

"I can't sleep. Joe's missing."

"We'll let you know the moment we hear from him," Ursula said, smoothing Alice's tangled curls from her damp brow.

"I'm hoping the opiate will quiet her cough," Dr. Hayes told the Guenther sisters when he came back downstairs. "She has herself worked into a tizzy over that husband of hers. I must say not checking in is not what I'd expect of Joe."

"Ja," Hilda nodded, "that's what we also thought."

"I do hope he hasn't had trouble trying to walk from Lake Placid." Ursula's hand fluttered at her throat.

"Well, check on her every hour," Dr. Hayes said. "I don't like the signs of that streaking one bit." He pulled on his galoshes. "I'll be by to see her in the morning after I have a chance to look at the X-rays we took a few days ago. I suspect they may not tell a pleasant story."

The up patients were very quiet at the supper table. Dr. Hayes's unscheduled visit didn't go unnoticed, but Ursula and Hilda were united in their standard 'just a little setback' answer.

"How bad is Alice?" the girl across the table from Charlotte asked after the sisters went back to the kitchen.

"She's streaking," Charlotte answered.

The girl stopped spooning mashed potatoes on her plate and stared at Charlotte. "But she's been up and walking for. . .months."

"Alice follows every one of the rules," another girl said. "Why I saw her in Sadie's with Charlotte just the other day."

"Oh, shut up, would you, Doris." Lilly threw her napkin on the table and stood up. "Who ever promised if you followed the rules you'd get to leave here? Grow up! The only way you'll ever be free of TB is if you die of something else." Lilly hurried out of the dining room. In the silence she left behind, the girls heard the front door slam.

After supper, Hilda finished scrubbing her kitchen counters with a carbolic acid solution, then sat down with her sister to discuss Alice's situation.

"We do the best we can," Hilda said, "but you must not let the girls get to you this way. It's not good for the other girls to see you less than cheerful."

"It's Joe I'm upset about," Ursula said. "I thought he was different. He must realize Alice is worried about him with nothing to think about except when he'll walk in the door."

25

Church bells called their congregations to Sunday services. Alice fought her way up through a drugged sleep and found it hard to breathe.

She focused her eyes on the picture of Joe on her dresser. Usually just looking at his smiling face gave her a feeling of well-being. But this morning her worry worked into rage at Joe for not calling. She turned away from the picture and looked out the north window. Already the sky was blue.

Worry about Joe's well-being was a frequent and unwanted visitor. I don't think I have the strength to live through it again, Alice thought.

The years Joe had fought in the war, Alice waited it out with several of her friends whose boyfriends were soldiers. Together, they fretted over daily reports about the suffering in the muddy trenches and rumors of thousands of young men gassed. Joe had been one of the lucky ones, escaping without injury.

Then waiting in Saranac Lake for Joe to join her before Christmas had been unbearable. Confined to bed. Watching icicles grow. Learning the strange ways of a cure cottage. Counting snowflakes to fall asleep. She never wanted to experience such loneliness again. But Joe came. All the way from New York. . .walking after his car broke down, frostbitten and hijacked.

Today was different. Joe wasn't across the ocean or hundreds of miles away. He couldn't be more than ten miles from her. Why hadn't he called? Anger ricocheted back to worry. Dear Lord, please keep him safe.

Alice heard slippered feet scuffling to and from the bathroom as the up patients prepared to go down to breakfast. She was glad she had to stay flat. She didn't need the temp stick to know she still had a fever and she'd scream if she had to look at the concern in everyone's faces.

God bless Ursula for understanding! She was there to hold her head while Alice raised a great amount of the yellow, gooey mess. But Ursula didn't chatter and tell her what a good productive cough that was. She wiped Alice's face with a cool cloth and didn't insist she had to eat the entire bowl of oatmeal.

Later, Hilda gave Alice a bed bath. Alice gritted her teeth, waiting for the lecture about TB feeding on gloomy tissues. But the big woman was mercifully quiet, sloshing her with warm soapy water, gently drying her with towels warmed on the radiator. Then those big hands gave her a wonderful alcohol rub, releasing the tension gripping her body. The sharp vapors cleared her head of the last traces of the opiate Dr. Hayes had given her.

Hilda helped Alice put on a clean fresh gown and brushed the snarls from her black curls. Next she shook tooth powder on her toothbrush and stood patiently while Alice brushed her teeth.

"Thank you," Alice said, handing her brush and glass back to Hilda. "You've made me feel much better. I'm sorry I've been so. . .disagreeable."

"Things always look better when the sun comes out," Hilda said. She straightened Alice's blankets and made sure the sputum cup had a fresh cardboard liner and the call bell was within easy reach.

Alice willed all worrisome thought out of her head and drifted into a semi-sleep. Some time later she vaguely became aware of people talking. It finally registered that it must be Lilly and Charlotte on the sitting-out porch. And they were talking about her.

"I don't care what you say," she heard Lilly say. "If I find out he's been sitting out this snowstorm with that Dimpled Dolly he's going to get a piece of my mind."

He'll get a piece of my mind, too, Alice thought, as she heard Charlotte murmur something. Probably one of her "Trotty Vic" platitudes. She smiled when she heard Lilly echo her thoughts: "God, Charlotte. Please not another of those sickening sayings."

Ursula hurried into Alice's room just then, a smile crinkling her gray eyes. "Joe's on the telephone," she said. "Hilda is coming to carry you downstairs."

"Oh, Ursula!" Alice was already sitting up. "Help me on with my robe. . .please. Is Joe okay?"

"He's fine. Now don't hurry so."

The phone in the kitchen seemed miles away. "Joe will surely hang up if you don't let me get there."

"I'm sure he'll wait. He sounded very anxious to talk to you."

Alice heard Hilda's firm step on the stairs and, like a child, reached out her arms to be picked up. Hilda scooped her up in her strong arms and started back down the stairs. Ursula went ahead and placed a chair by the telephone in the kitchen.

"Joe!" Alice snatched the telephone the moment Hilda placed her in the chair.

"Are you all right, dear heart?"

"Much better now that I hear your voice. I've been so worried about you. I thought you tried to walk over in all this snow." Alice listened while Joe told a story about going to a speakeasy with a man he works with. They drove way up to Plattsburgh.

"Almost to Canada," Joe said. It was snowing so hard when they were ready to come home, they decided to stay the night at his friend's parents' farm. They didn't have a telephone. And of course with the deep snow, there was no motor traffic on Saturday.

"I never should have gone, Alice. I'm so sorry you worried about me."

Alice hung up feeling much better after hearing Joe's version of what happened. Beaming, she repeated what Joe had said to the sisters. As Hilda carried Alice back through the living room, she found all the up patients gathered around the foot of the stairs waiting to hear her news. There was a collective sigh of relief when they saw Alice's smiling face.

Alice didn't mind having to go back to her room. Joe was all right. And just listen to the girls' chatter, she thought. Her friends were happy for her.

Downstairs in the living room, Lilly didn't join in the girls' discussion about Alice's wonderful husband. She sat in a far corner of the living room, flipping the pages of a magazine.

"Aren't you happy for Alice?" Charlotte asked her.

"I'm happy Alice is finally getting some peace. Worry over that sainted husband of hers caused this setback. But I can't believe she's so naive. . .swallowing Joe's story." She dropped the magazine on the table and began shuffling a deck of cards.

"Why are you always so cynical?"

"Believe me, I know firsthand what healthy men think about us lungers." Lilly sat at the table and began dealing cards. "I'm sure Joe went to that speakeasy all right. Bet he only told half the story, though. Come on, Charlotte, you can't be as blind as Alice. If he didn't take that Dimpled Dolly along, you can bet he found some flapper to keep him company."

"Don't you so much as whisper this to Alice." Charlotte sat across from Lilly and picked up her cards for a game of gin.

Joe felt dirty. He hung up the telephone and the trooper herded him back to his cell. It was one thing to keep unpleasantness from Alice. It was an entirely different matter to actually lie in order to keep her from hearing upsetting facts. Joe waited for the trooper to open the cell door. He passed through and sat on the bunk, head in his hands.

Hilda had been mad. Told him how agitated Alice had become over the weekend. Geeze, he couldn't tell Alice the troopers had taken him to jail because he and Gaston were carrying booze! Or got drunk at the speakeasy and got carried away with a brazen dance hall girl.

He heard voices and looked up to see Sergeant Welch walking toward the cell. Gaston sat up on his bunk.

"Devlin," Welch said, "we're letting you go."

Joe jumped up from his bunk. Seemed the troopers were due in Lake Placid and now that the road was passable, they would take Troop B's Ford. Joe could have a ride back to the Club.

He wasn't being let off as easily as it first appeared, though. During the drive, made twice as long with the bad roads, Joe had been subtly grilled. He became aware the troopers weren't completely convinced he wasn't involved with the bootlegging.

They let him out at the garage with a final warning that if he was found in a car carrying booze, he would be fined and jailed. They didn't drive away till Joe climbed the stairs and went inside.

"Alice still is not doing well, Doctor," Ursula said several mornings later as she opened the door for Dr. Hayes. "Her temp still hasn't dropped below one hundred."

"I suspected as much. The X-rays we took last week show that the persistent spot on the top of her left lung has worsened with the obvious beginnings of a hole. I've come today to suggest we do a pneumothorax procedure."

"What a shame," Ursula said. "She was doing so well."

"I'll go up and explain the matter to Alice. Please prepare the pneumo instruments."

"Alice, my dear," Dr. Hayes said, pulling a straight-backed chair close to her bed. "I think it's time we took more serious measures to clear your lungs."

"I'm so tired of all these setbacks. I'm ready for most anything."

"Good. Thinking positively is a big help." He cleared his throat and locked his hands around his expansive middle. "I don't like the spots I'm seeing on your left lung. It needs a complete rest. There is a procedure that allows that to happen. It's called a pneumothoraxy."

"An operation?" Alice drew her lower lip between her teeth.

"Not really. A simple. . .procedure. You'll stay right here at Conifer."

"Exactly what do you do?"

Dr. Hayes cleared his throat again and patted Alice's hand. "I'll slip a hollow needle between your ribs into the chest cavity."

Alice attempted to jerk her hand away.

"There, there, it's not so bad. Over in a minute. Then I simply inject a little air through the needle to fill the chest cavity. That pressure will cause your left lung to collapse and get the rest it needs to heal."

"Won't breathing be even harder with just one lung?"

"If you take things easy, you'll hardly notice the difference. Your right lung will handle it nicely. But you must be careful not to overdo. I'll keep track of the air pressure and when it goes down, I'll repeat the procedure."

"For how long?"

Dr. Hayes cleared his throat. "A year or two." He stood up, scraping the chair across the floor.

"A year?"

"Possibly longer."

Ursula came into the room with a tray of bottles and something that jangled. Alice's eyes widened at the ominous change in routine. What was Ursula carrying? Alice watched as she set it on the dresser. Why was she shutting the windows in the middle of the morning?

"What are you doing?" she whispered, her throat going dry.

"Ursula will prepare you for the procedure," Dr. Hayes said.

"So soon? Can't I have some time to think about? Talk to Joe?"

"You mustn't fret so," Dr. Hayes said. "I've performed this procedure countless times. I'll be back as soon as I've scrubbed my hands."

"Ursula?" Alice pleaded.

"Now, Alice," Ursula said, as she helped Alice to sit up. "Dr. Hayes is right. This is just what your bad lung needs. Raise your arms." She pulled the nightgown over Alice's head, then helped her to settle back on the bed. "I can tell you firsthand that it has helped a number of our girls." She laid a clean towel across Alice's chest and pulled the sheet up to her waist.

"We're ready, doctor," Ursula said when Dr. Hayes entered the room, dressed in a white operating jacket. A white cap covered his hair. Ursula swabbed something cold on Alice's chest.

Alice began to perspire when Dr. Hayes pressed his fingers over her ribs. It was hard to believe the doctor she had come to trust was rushing her into this. Why couldn't he wait till Joe could be here?

Alice felt Ursula at her side, passing a cool washcloth across her forehead, then taking one of Alice's hands and holding it between her two firm dry hands. Alice turned from Dr. Hayes and looked up at Ursula. Immediately she was reassured by Ursula's smile and the complete lack of concern in her soft gray eyes.

"You'll feel just a little discomfort," Alice heard Dr. Hayes saying. She drew in a breath and braced against it.

"You mustn't move now, Alice," Ursula said. "If you feel the pneumo needle too much, just squeeze my hand hard."

Alice bit down on her lip and dug her nails into Ursula's hand as the needle pierced her skin.

"There we are," Dr. Hayes said. "The needle is in the chest cavity and safely away from the lung. Now we'll introduce a little air."

At first the pressure was just a little discomforting. As the air pressure in the chest cavity increased and her diseased lung was forced to shut down, Alice felt like an immense weight had been placed on her chest. She struggled for a breath.

"There now," Ursula crooned, "relax. Take little sips of air." She stroked Alice's forehead. "Try not to fight it."

"Most successful, my dear." Dr. Hayes beamed down at her. "I want you to lie completely flat and quiet for a day or two." He pulled off the white cap and shrugged out of the operating jacket. "We'll see where we go after that. I'm optimistic, Alice. Very optimistic." He patted her hand. "I'm sure Ursula will see you're comfortable."

As soon as Dr. Hayes left the room, Ursula helped Alice back into her nightgown and administered a little of the opium he had prescribed to help her rest.

"I'll be back to check on you soon," Ursula said. She picked up the tray and left Alice alone.

"We've got to talk," Hilda told her sister later that week when Ursula brought down the last of the supper trays. Hilda leaned her shoulder into scrubbing a pot.

"Oh, dear," Ursula said, "is one of our girls getting behind?"

"No. It's Joe." Hilda sprinkled scouring powder in the pot and added a little hot water. She removed her arms from the sink and dried them on her apron.

"Should I get the schnapps?"

"Ja." Hilda cleared the kitchen table of platters and bowls waiting to be washed and sat heavily in her chair. She sipped at the schnapps.

"Joe's name was in the newspaper's Bootleggers column today. They seized twelve cases of liquor in the car he was riding in."

Ursula gasped and pressed her hand to her mouth. "It must be a mistake.

""Nein, Sister. You know this column is not gossip. Just a list of captured bootleggers with the amount of their fines and sentences." She tipped back her head and drank the last of the schnapps from her mother's leaded crystal glass.

"For some reason they released Joe but booked a Gaston Proulx, the driver of the car. He was caught and brought to Saranac last Sunday. All this when he told Alice a fairy tale."

"We mustn't let Alice find out."

Hilda nodded. "I picked up the newspaper from the living room right away. But I worry about Lilly's friends at Pelletier. One of them is bound to read it. We can only hope they won't associate his name with Alice."

"I really don't understand all this American fuss over alcohol," Ursula said. "Everyone in the world benefits from alcohol in moderation." She paused to sip her schnapps. "But we can't let Alice worry about her husband being arrested. Will you speak to Joe?"

"Ja. The very next time I see him."

26

The faint pinks of dawn streaked the gray sky when Joe started out for Saranac Lake the next Saturday. It was difficult walking in the deep ruts that automobile traffic had carved in yesterday's slushy snow. Last night the weather had turned cold again, turning the slush into rock-hard grooves. But, Joe noted, there was only one set of tire tracks. Like traveling both ways on a single set of train rails. What would happen when cars going opposite directions met? While puzzling over that, he turned in surprise at the sound of a car coming up behind him. He stepped up out of the ruts, slipping on the thick ice.

It was Dasset's Pierce-Arrow, coming at a fast rate. The big car ground to a halt on the icy road, its tires held prisoner in the deep ruts.

"Get in," Dasset said.

"Didn't expect to see you out so early," Joe said.

"I don't want you coming around Charlie's," Dasset said, moving the car up through its gears. "I'm pretty sure you're being watched."

"Watching. . .me?"

"You don't really think they bought your story?"

"They let me go."

"Sure, so you'd lead them to me."

Joe chewed on that for a while. Once, just once in the months since he got to this godforsaken place, he took a night off away from his worries about Alice and how to find the money for her cure. How could a simple night out turn into such a hornet's nest?

"I don't want you coming to the barn for a couple of weeks." Joe brought his attention back to what Dasset was saying. "You need to act like we don't exist. Those troopers know what they're doing."

"Yeah." Joe told Dasset that the trooper who picked them up had brought in over a hundred and fifty booze cars.

"That'd be Jim Welch. He's good. Schermerhorn's not far behind. I think it was Schermerhorn who stopped you at the roadblock. I heard he caught McFadden's men red-handed that same day. Seems they had gone to a barn just a few miles from the roadblock to retrieve some goods they ditched in a hayloft. Schermerhorn was waiting for them."

"I'll wait for Charlie to call me, then. It'll be hard doing without what I make working for you, but I don't need trouble."

"I want you back as soon as things have quieted down," Dasset said. "I'm not at all sure we can keep the cars going without you. But things slow down a lot this time of year. Roads are too unpredictable. . .mud, ice. Probably a couple more big snows, too. We usually have to shut down operations for a couple of weeks during spring thaw."

Joe bit his cheek. He needed every penny he made working for Dasset for Alice's cure.

"Damn," Dasset said, "I was hoping I'd be the only car on the road this early." A car coming from the direction of Saranac Lake, its tires held fast in the same set of ruts Dasset was using, was headed straight for them.

"Didn't expect to see anyone out so early this morning," the other driver said, when he reached Dasset. He and Dasset wasted no time getting pickaxes and shovels from their cars. All three men set to work chipping away at the ice to create a turnoff.

The other driver started up his smaller car and inched it into the turnoff. Joe picked up the tools and climbed in the Pierce-Arrow. Dasset drove it forward and waited to be sure the other car made it back into the main tracks. The other man tooted his horn, and drove off. Joe and Dasset resumed their trip.

Dasset let Joe out at the edge of town. "Don't want it to look like I'm driving you over," he apologized.

Joe walked along Lake Flower, still frozen solid, and turned up Shepard Street, which climbed much more gently than Helen Hill up to Conifer Cottage. If he was lucky, he might be early enough to have breakfast with Alice.

Upstairs in Conifer Cottage, Lilly flung open Charlotte's bedroom door, then stormed out to the sitting-out porch. She stood, hands on hips, looking down at Charlotte in her cure chair.

"What's got you so upset?" Charlotte asked.

Lilly let out a gutsy sigh, plunked down on her wicker cure chair and proceeded to examine her red nails.

"Lilly?" Charlotte asked again. Lilly jumped to her feet and stood at the porch railing, looking down Helen Hill.

"When I was with Frank last night he showed me the Bootleggers Column in the Enterprise." She turned to look Charlotte full in the face. "Charlotte, Joe was picked up for sneaking booze over the border."

"That's hardly scandalous. Just about everyone does it at one time or another."

"No, no." Lilly flipped her hand in dismissal. "You don't understand. Bootlegging isn't important. In fact they even released him because he was just a passenger."

"Well, gracious, Lilly, what has you so upset?

""The day he was arrested is important." Lilly turned from the railing and perched on Charlotte's cure chair. "The Saturday snowstorm. The Saturday Alice worried herself into a temperature and Joe gave her some cockamamy story about waiting out the storm in Plattsburgh."

Charlotte stared with round, wide-open eyes and mouth.

"Joe had no intention of being here. He was in Canada."

"Alice must never know."

"Never know?" Lilly jumped to her feet. Hands on hips she stared down at Charlotte. "Alice has every right to know why her husband is traipsing across the border." She turned toward the railing in time to see Joe headed for Conifer.

"Here comes that. . .that self-righteous cheat."

"Lilly, promise me you won't make a scene. It'll cause everyone harm."

"Okay," she conceded, her plucked eyebrows nearly meeting in a fierce scowl. "But it's not right."

Joe rang the Conifer doorbell. He heard Hilda striding down the hall. When she opened the door the good smells of bacon and home made bread came with her. While Joe sat on the bench to remove his galoshes, Hilda told him about the pneumothoraxy and interrogated him about the Bootleggers Column in the paper.

Joe looked up at the big woman, her arms folded, tapping her fingers on her muscular arms. He told her the truth. . .everything except about Collette. What else could he do with Hilda's formidable presence looming over him?

"Ja," she said. "You did the right thing not to cause Alice undue worry. TB feeds less willingly on the cheerful."

When Hilda released him, Joe mounted the stairs feeling guilty that Alice's brooding over his whereabouts made her have this pneumo thing. Sticking a needle right through her ribs and pumping her with air. When he asked Hilda why they had to rush into it, she told him it was important not to let Alice dwell on something unpleasant.

Nothing prepared him for what he saw when he walked into Alice's room. All the windows were closed and the room stank of vomit. Alice sat on the edge of her bed, her thin legs dangling over the side. Ursula sat close to her, one arm around his wife's shoulders, the other holding a cloth to her forehead. Alice didn't see him. Lengths of her knotted curls hung over her face as she coughed and gagged into the sputum cup.

Joe's stomach lurched. A sour taste rose in his throat. He turned and left the room, colliding with Lilly, hurrying down the stairs, late for breakfast.

"Joe. Racing off?"

"No, Alice is. . .Ursula is helping her. . .she must have thrown up her breakfast." Joe stumbled with the words, wrestling with the churning in his belly.

"Sounds like a normal morning in a cure cottage," Lilly sang, sugary sweet. "If you don't cough up that slimy mess before breakfast, then it comes up right after. . .bringing breakfast with it."

"Is Alice like this every morning?"

"All week. Since she worried when you didn't come or call. You know, when you were in Plattsburgh. . .or was it Canada?" Lilly walked off, leaving Joe sick with remorse.

Canada. It hit Joe what Lilly had implied. She must have read about him in the Bootleggers Column, too. If she told Alice. . . .

He waited in the hall until Alice stopped coughing. When he heard Ursula's comforting murmurs, he tapped on the door frame.

"Oh, Joe's here. How nice." Ursula smiled. "Alice has been looking forward to this morning all week long."

Alice held out a hand. Joe reached for it and Alice began to cough. She snatched it away to cover her mouth with a tissue.

"Perhaps it'd be best," Ursula said, handing Alice the sputum cup, "for you to wait down stairs until Alice is more comfortable."

Joe nodded and fled Alice's room. I'm to blame for her setback. Snippets of last Friday night's adventure came to mind, the steak, drinking, Collette's vibrant body pressing against his on the dance floor. He couldn't face Hilda or the girls. Especially Lilly.

He grabbed his coat and went out on the porch. He filled his lungs with the cold air and pulled on his coat. Jamming his hands in his pockets, he stared out at the street.

How did I get into this mess? he thought. I never should have let Gaston talk me into going to Canada. It just sounded good to have a night out. Look at the trouble it caused. If Sergeant Welch had kept me one more day, I'd have lost my job for sure.

Dasset doesn't want me around. Where am I going to come up with the extra money now that Alice is back being a tray patient? That's an extra five dollars a week. And the pneumo thing. Sure was a pretty expensive trip to Canada.

27

From the window of his room over the garage, Joe looked out at the gray clouds discharging their load of cold rain. The once sparkling cover of white snow had turned into dirty granular piles. Large yellow spots littered the snowpack on Mirror Lake. No one was about on the cheerless day. Not one car had gone by all the while he stood at the window. Even the usual strollers who trudged around Mirror Lake had been kept inside by the cold, dismal rain.

Joe had just returned from risking a call to Alice on the garage telephone. He sure as hell wasn't going to take the chance of having Alice work herself into coughing up blood again because he couldn't get to Saranac Lake when she expected him. Alice wasn't allowed to come to the downstairs telephone so Joe had to relay through Ursula that it was raining too hard for him to walk over. He wished he could have spoken directly to Alice. At least he could have told her he loved her.

He couldn't walk over and back in this drenching rain with nothing but Mr. Bingham's coat to wear. And there wasn't an extra cent to buy a rubber raincoat. Every penny of his nine-fifteen a week had to go to Alice's cure. Now that she was back being a twenty dollar a week tray patient, that left him eleven dollars short every week. On top of that, he hadn't even seen Dr. Hayes' bill for the pneumothoraxy. And Hilda told him the procedure would be repeated every couple of weeks.

Yesterday, while he was in Saranac Lake, he had stopped in a store to price jackets. He found a brown duck jacket with a blanket lining and an interlining of oiled slicker cloth. The ticket said it was wind and water proof. Just what he needed. But at almost five dollars, Joe would have to wait until Dasset called him back to work.

He pressed his head against the cold pane of glass. Three weeks since his joyride to Canada and Alice was still hadn't regained her up patient status. When he saw her yesterday, she didn't cough once, but that darn temperature didn't want to drop below a hundred. Hilda said it'd be at least a week after her temperature returned to normal before Alice could be an up patient. And then her weekly board would return to fifteen dollars.

He turned from the window and flopped down on his narrow bed, setting the springs to twanging. When was Charlie going to call? He needed the extra work badly. Hilda didn't look any too pleased yesterday when Joe was short. She pressed him to say when he would make up the difference. What could he say? As soon as the troopers quit following me I'll go back to work for the bootlegger? Sure.

He laced his hands behind his head and shut his eyes, but he couldn't escape to sleep. Completely unbidden, an image of Collette appeared behind his closed eyes. He sat up and rubbed his eyes to chase the image away. It seemed he wasn't able to escape the guilt of his trip to Canada by napping. The dreary day would not pass. He decided to go down to the garage and putter around.

A new drum of oil had been delivered, so Joe set about changing the oil on a touring car. I should have gotten into something else, Joe thought, as he went about the mindless chore. But there wasn't anything very challenging to do in maintaining the Club fleet. Maybe when the summer guests came and started driving the touring cars, he'd have some more interesting work.

Ever since Joe had come up with a way to start the Poirier cars, Dasset was willing for Joe to experiment. Sure there was the basic lubricating and regrooving tires, but Dasset gave generous bonuses when Joe found ways of beefing up brakes and getting more speed from his cars. Could use one of those bonuses right now!

Joe started when the ring of the telephone broke into his thoughts. He wiped his hands on a rag and went to answer it.

"Garage."

"Joe? This is Charlie. Doing anything today?'

"No. Just hanging around."

"Your aunt thought you might like a home-cooked dinner."

"You bet!"

Quickly, Joe jotted down the oil change on the touring car's work order. *Hope Dasset has enough work to keep me going all day. . .all night, too.* He turned off lights, shut and locked the door and raced upstairs. He shrugged out of the Club's coveralls, combed his hair, taking time to part it neatly down the middle, and stood at the window, impatient for Charlie's truck to appear.

After picking up Joe, Charlie took a circuitous route to the barn, stopping in the village to buy some cigars. He told Joe to get out and buy a newspaper. Charlie shot the breeze with his friend behind the counter while Joe opened the paper and leaned against the wall, pretending to read. *Geeze, he didn't want to waste the afternoon in the news shop.* He shook the newspaper and cleared his throat. Eventually Charlie ambled back to the truck and the two drove slowly off.

At the farm, Charlie made Joe go into the house first. After what seemed like hours, he allowed Joe to go to the barn with him. Once inside the barn, Joe pulled open the tack room door and raised his arm to locate the light string in the windowless room. He quickly dropped to his knees and slid open the barrel bolt, then stood up and opened the door, breathing in the familiar garage smells of new tires and oil.

"Joe." Armand met him at the top of the stairs. "Good to have you back." He clapped Joe on the shoulder and led him through the shop area back to the woodstove. The fellows were warming their backsides at the stove and drinking beer.

"Hey, Joe." Ellis came over to him. "You lucky son of a polecat. Let me shake your hand." The group crowded around Joe, wanting to hear all about his capture and release. Stu put a beer in Joe's hand. He looked at it warily, hesitating a moment. The last time he drank was that night in Canada. . .with Collette. He closed his eyes and tilted the bottle to his mouth. The cold liquid fizzed down his throat.

"Ah," Joe smiled. "It's great to be back."

"You hear about Gaston?" Armand asked, sitting down at the table. Joe shook his head. The men dragged chairs away from the woodstove to sit around the table.

"Two hundred big ones and two months," Ellis rushed to answer.

"You got off easy," Stu said, running his rabbit foot key chain under his nose.

Easy? Joe drank from the bottle to keep from telling them all the trouble his joyride had caused Alice. They all knew Joe had a wife taking the cure in Saranac Lake, but Joe knew talking about one's tubercular spouse wasn't popular.

"I got you a little welcome back surprise," Armand said. The men smiled and bobbed their heads. "Come on, let me show you." There was a great scraping of chairs as the whole group rose to take Joe to his surprise.

Armand placed his arm around Joe's shoulders and they walked around the misleading bales of hay to where cars were stored. He stopped in front a pea green Cadillac with black fenders.

"New car?" Joe asked.

"Your car," Armand said.

"My car?" Joe pulled away from Armand and looked at him. "What do you mean? I can't even pay Alice's board. I sure as hell can't buy a Cadillac."

"Don't get all worked up," Armand said, smiling. "This car went through the booze sale the Saturday you and Gaston were snowbound in Canada. It was snowing so bad here, next to no one showed up for the sale. It went for the five bucks you already set aside to buy a car."

"I thought you'd use my five bucks for some beat-up tin lizzie," Joe said. "Not a Cadillac!"

Armand told Joe the car had belonged to a man who didn't normally carry goods. Last fall the owner bought champagne for his baby's christening. Someone tipped off the troopers and when they tried to stop him, he took his new Cadillac off across a stony field.

"Barreled into rocks," Armand said. "Broke the driveshaft."

"That will take time to fix," Joe said.

"I'm sure," Armand agreed. "I arranged to have someone else bid on it and buy it in your name. Charlie towed it over here in the middle of the night after word came that the troopers left town. I don't want anyone connecting you and me."

"Yeah." Ellis pushed himself between Joe and the pea green Cadillac. "My girl took the call the troopers made to Broadfield from the National Hotel. Broadfield sent them to Ausable Forks a few days ago."

"I was waiting to learn something concrete about the troopers leaving town before bringing you back here," Armand told Joe. "Ellis' Gladys is pretty darn reliable."

There were times Joe had been in the barn when Gladys, a telephone operator, had reported to Ellis when she handled a call involving the State Police. Dasset promoted Ellis's friendship with her. "Valuable asset," Dasset told Joe. "That girl is a prime reason we're able to have so many uncontested runs."

"I own a 1925 Cadillac," Joe said to no one in particular. And I don't know where the money for next week's cure cottage board is coming from.

"Perfect car for you, Joe. No one will think twice about a mechanic buying a non-functioning car like this. And it doesn't have a booze car reputation with the troopers."

Joe walked around the car. His car. He ran his fingers over the satiny finish. He opened the door and slid behind the wheel. His car. He looked up and saw the fellows looking back at him.

"Fits just right," Joe grinned. He got out and pulled himself underneath the chassis. He groaned at the damage he saw. Part of the driveshaft stuck through a hole in the oil pan.

"Pan's been ventilated," he said.

28

Big improvements in one week's time, Joe thought, as he started out for Saranac Lake the next Saturday morning. He smiled and took long strides, freed from the cumbersome weight of the coon coat. It felt good not to have to mince along on his frostbitten toes. His toes were shiny pink and tender but didn't pain him unless they got wet or cold.

The Adirondacks were definitely shrugging off winter. He could see the snowpack high in the mountains and sure, it still froze every night and there were patches of snow under the evergreens, but when the sun came up he could smell the earth. He hadn't seen brown earth since he left New York. . .five months ago.

Joe was disappointed that Armand wouldn't let him work every night. He needed the money.

"No sense looking for trouble, Joe," Armand cautioned, even though Gladys passed on the word that the troopers had left Lake Placid. But Joe did have enough money in his pocket to pay all but ten dollars of Alice's bill. He fretted over his decision to keep five dollars aside to buy the brown waterproof jacket he had seen in Saranac Lake last week. He should be using it to pay the Guenther sisters.

But he needed something for the rain. He'd be in a fine fix if he got caught in one of those downpours on his way to see Alice. It'd be some time before he got his Cadillac running, so he had to continue to walk. No, the jacket was something he really needed. Not like those swell pinstriped suits that all the fellows at Dasset's had. That'd have to wait. By next weekend I should be caught up, he thought.

Joe whistled while waiting for someone to open Conifer's door

"Good morning!" he said, when Hilda's large frame filled the open door. "Isn't it a great day?" Hilda nodded and stepped back, making room for Joe to enter. She held a rolling pin in one hand. Did

Hilda greet everyone with a rolling pin? Or was it saved for those who were behind in their bills?

"You'll be happy to know I have money for you today," Joe said. He sat on the bench to remove his galoshes.

"Ja, that is good. Come with me and we will write in the books."

"I don't have the entire amount," Joe said, as he followed Hilda into the kitchen.

"Mr. Devlin." Joe nearly bumped into the woman as she turned abruptly to face him. "My sister and I are not millionaires." She waved the rolling pin under his nose. "We need money to keep Conifer Cottage running."

"I'll have everything paid up by next weekend." I hope. Armand better have work for me.

Hilda studied Joe in silence for a moment, and fastened her hands on her hips. "We will one more week wait. If you cannot keep your wife's bill up to date, we will have to consider alternative cures."

Joe nodded and cleared his throat. He couldn't let them send Alice to the Ray Brook Sanitorium.

The kitchen was steamy and smelled of carbolic acid as two day girls cleaned up after breakfast. Joe saw circles of rolled-out biscuit dough on the flour-covered table. It made him feel more at ease to realize the rolling pin was being used for the biscuits and not him.

Hilda placed a large black ledger on a clean corner of the table and fetched two ink bottles and a pen from a cupboard. She motioned for Joe to sit at the table next to her. She settled her substantial body on a chair. Taking her time, she carefully dipped her pen in the black ink and scratched notations in her account book in a surprisingly feathery hand. When she finished, she blotted the page and placed the stopper back in the black ink. Then she looked up at Joe and opened the red ink with a pop. Dipping her pen in the ink, she drew a bold red slash under the outstanding amount, blotted it and turned the book so Joe could read it.

"You have my word," Joe found himself saying. "I'll have all the money next week."

"Plus the twenty dollars for this next week's care?"

Joe cleared his throat. "Plus the twenty dollars for this week's care," he echoed.

Joe took the steps two at a time. He knocked lightly on Alice's door and opened it at the same time. In a glance he could see Alice and Charlotte bundled on their cure chairs on the sitting-out porch. Joe felt a stab of disappointment. He had hoped to have Alice to himself and not have to share her with the others. The porch was so tiny it was impossible to have a private conversation.

Alice turned her head at the sound of Joe's step, her face lighting with joy. She wore the blue bed jacket Lilly's father had given her for Christmas. Joe sat on the edge of the cure chair and brought her two mittened hands to his lips.

"I hear you've got your temp under a hundred," he said, noting that the fevered red spots of last Saturday had vanished.

"All the way back to normal," Alice said, squeezing Joe's hands. "I'll start walking again tomorrow and". . .she paused to catch her breath. . ."the next time you come I should be an up patient." She took off her mittens and smoothed the hair from Joe's forehead.

"That's swell." Joe looked up at Charlotte. "Doesn't Alice look better? Isn't it something the way everything looks better now that winter's almost over?"

"It's been a long winter," Charlotte agreed, laying her open book face down on her bear robe. "It must have been pleasant walking over today, not fighting the snow or slipping on ice."

"It was. Heard birds singing, too." He felt Alice tug at his sleeve. He brought his attention back to her.

"I was pretty discouraged with this setback, Joe." Her fingers picked at the edge of her blanket. "This darn old place gets on my nerves more and more." Her chest heaved with the effort of getting air into the one lung trying to do the job of two. "I wish I could go home."

"We are going home, dear heart. But when you're well and strong.

"I'll stick it out for a year. . .like we planned. . .but then it's bye-bye Saranac. I'll be twenty-four in ten days."

Alice's birthday? Joe thought with a start. Geeze, it is. I've got to find something really nice for her.

Joe brought his attention back to what Alice was saying. "I can't imagine taking years out of my life," she lowered her voice to a whisper, "like Charlotte. She's been here over three years, Joe."

Joe didn't know how to respond. Everyone was hinting he should plan on Alice being here for at least five years; but he could never share that with Alice.

"I've lost four pounds. If I keep it up, I'll be below my entry. But I'm getting so I don't care at all."

"Alice, don't talk that way. I care. What about the children we want." Joe grabbed at anything that might perk Alice up.

"How could I handle children if every time they have a problem I get a temp and streak blood?"

"That's why you're here, to heal those holes in your lungs. Then you can handle problems like a nor. . .like mothers handle."

"Like a normal person?" She said quietly and turned her head away. "That is the point, isn't it? I'm not normal."

"You sure aren't."

Alice turned back at the unexpected reply. He took her face in his hands and looked into the sad blue eyes. "You're special." He raised his head and kissed her forehead.

"I don't know about being special, but I do have a special husband."

Joe stayed until Ursula came around to settle the young women for the two-hour quiet time. He planned to buy the waterproof jacket and hurried down Helen Hill to Main Street. Walking along he thought about what to get Alice for her birthday. Twenty-four, he mused. That means our fourth wedding anniversary is coming up, too.

He thought back to the black-haired girl who had met him at the boat when he returned from the war. He remembered the warm sunshine of her smile. And the plans they had. All dashed apart. First her parents cutting all ties with Alice when they eloped. Then his own mother shutting the door in his face for not marrying in the Church.

Perhaps it was wrong to encourage Alice to run away with him and ignore their parents. As far as his parents went, he knew he did the right thing. But a girl is different. If he was honest with himself,

Joe had to admit it was just months after they eloped that Alice began having persistent tubercular coughs.

He shouldn't have been so insistent just because he didn't want to live without her. Didn't? Still don't in spite of her frequent bouts of depression. He tried to overlook the whine that frequently crept into her voice. There were times it took all his self-control to stay by her side after trudging ten miles through a snowstorm just to listen to her complaints. It was hard to be eternally cheerful with the relentless bills.

And that's the heart of the problem, Joe mused. Alice doesn't have any idea of what it takes to keep her in Conifer. It'd surely give her another setback if she knew the illegal things he had to do to pay the bills. But I'll do whatever it takes five time over to get my Alice healthy again.

He constantly reminded himself that sitting out in the cold all day took a lot of determination on Alice's part. And he still couldn't believe the tales of how they wrapped his wife in newspapers so she could "freeze it out." The cure was Alice's job and came with as many rules as his Catholic faith.

Joe walked in the store and asked to try on the brown duck jacket with the slicker cloth interlining. The first one he tried was a good fit. He buttoned it carefully and was pleased that the sleeves came down to his knuckles. He liked the way the soft corduroy collar closed snugly around his neck.

"I'll take it," he said, digging in his pocket for the money he had set aside.

"That'll be four seventy-five," the clerk said, rubbing his hands together. "There's a matching short-billed cap for just a dollar ninety-five. Keep your head dry."

"Just the jacket. And I'll keep it on." He walked out of the store into the sunshine. He was pleased. The sun was warm on his face. Alice was improving. He was back repairing cars for Dasset.

But what to get Alice for her birthday? He strolled along Main Street looking in windows, then turned down Broadway. Alice probably wouldn't be well enough to be allowed to go out to dinner, so that was out.

He stopped at a display of hats. Joe thought the hats girls wore now looked like helmets. He wasn't sure Alice could pull one down over her long hair. Still, he looked at a red leather hat with a matching red wool scarf. She could wear it when he took her driving in his Cadillac. But no, women had to try on hats. Joe walked on past stores offering chocolates, perfumes and powders.

Then he came upon a black coat displayed in the gleaming window of a women's apparel store. Just as fancy as that gray fur thing Lilly wore. He went inside.

"The black coat in the window," he said to the lady, "how much is it?"

"You have excellent taste, sir. That's one of our very best coats." She stepped up in the window display and took the coat off the mannequin.

"It was featured in the January issue of Vogue," she said. "In a season of bright colors, this black broadcloth stands out as very smart." The coat had simple straight lines and was trimmed at the neck, cuffs and hem with foot-wide bands of fur. Joe reached out to touch the longhaired fur. It was as soft as Alice's hair.

"It's imported Turkish fox," the saleslady said.

Imported, Joe thought. That's nice. The fur on Lilly's coat was squirrel. Joe liked the way this coat buttoned all the way down the front and Alice could snuggle her neck into the furry collar.

"How much?"

The saleslady retrieved a card from a pocket, "One hundred and ninety-five dollars."

Joe raised his eyebrows and swallowed.

"Winter is practically over," the saleslady continued. "Perhaps your wife would prefer a lovely camel hair spring coat with a silk crepe lining. It's very reasonably priced at sixty-eight dollars. Bois de rose is such a cheery color and very popular this year."

"No, I really want something warm. . .with fur. My wife. . ." Joe hesitated before remembering he was in Saranac Lake where it was okay to talk about tuberculars. "My wife is taking the cure and needs to stay warm."

"Well, of course." She scurried to the other side of the store. "How about this fox scarf. Very smart. It's lined with silk for twelve ninety-eight." The saleslady draped it around her neck and stroked the fox's head. "There is a matching muff for nineteen ninety-eight." The fox's shiny eyes winked at Joe from the saleslady's neck.

"I'll think about it," Joe said and left the shop. He had seen ladies at the Club with those foxes around their necks, the foxes' little paws dangling on the ladies' bosoms and their fluffy tails wagging as the ladies walked along.

The fox scarf may be very smart, Joe thought, but he didn't want to wrap those animal heads around his wife's neck. He wanted the black coat. He walked back up Broadway and headed out of town toward Lake Placid.

He shouldn't have promised Hilda that he'd pay off Alice's bill completely next week. The way things were going, he'd hardly have the money for a box of candy for her birthday.

29

Joe stooped to scratch King behind the ears before going into the barn. The husky looked at him with his blue eyes. "That's right, King," Joe said. "Don't you forget this face."

Armand met him at the head of the stairs and led the way to the table.

"Where is everyone?" Joe asked, looking around.

"I'm shutting things down for a while," Armand said. "I do it every year during mud season. It's not worth trying to make runs."

"Why did you call me in?" Joe looked around the empty barn. His pea green Cadillac stood alone in the shop. No cars to work on, he thought, shoving his hands in his pockets. I'll never be able to pay Hilda this week.

"Never can be too cautious." Armand place an arm around Joe's stiff shoulders and led him toward the table. "I want to establish a routine where you still come by to see your aunt and uncle once or twice a week." Armand sat down and immediately shuffled a pack of cards. "If anyone is keeping an eye on you, they'll see a pattern of you coming by every week."

Joe leaned his elbows on the table and passed a hand down his face.

"Relax. A little poker will be good for you."

"Don't feel much like cards. I came here to work. I was really counting on the money." Joe told Armand about getting behind on Alice's board and wanting to get her something special for her birthday. "You sure you don't have something for me to do?"

Armand shook his head. "No, I told the guys to stay away for at least two weeks. Get seen using their cars for normal things. Take their girls to a movie show. Take their mothers to church."

"Joe could take my truck," Charlie spoke up, "and begin to stock-pile the goods at Champlain transfer station. Him needing money so bad and all." He scratched away at the ruff of strawberry roan hair that circled his head, then pulled a card from his hand and tossed it on the table.

"No. I promised Joe I wouldn't let him risk getting caught. That fiasco with Gaston was close enough."

"Wouldn't be like really running," Charlie said "Just a couple of miles from the border."

"Drop it, Charlie," Armand said. "It's not a good idea. We don't even have any cars."

"Joe could use my truck. I've had a notion to build a false bottom for the truck, anyway." Charlie puffed away on his cigar. His left eye was nearly closed in a permanent squint against the foul smoke climbing up the side of his face.

"Forget it, Charlie. Those guys have seen more false bottoms that you could possibly dream up."

"Not this one." The wooden false bottom for the bed of his truck would act as a decoy. If the law decided to rip it up with crowbars, they wouldn't find a thing. The real false bottom would be a metal container welded under the body and the only access would be by re-moving the seat in the cab.

"You might have something there," Armand conceded. "The trip pays fifty dollars. If you and Charlie could have the truck ready by Friday it'd be a likely night for you to be seeing that girl in Canada, should anyone ask. It'll be consistent with what you and Gaston told Welch."

"I'm not seeing any girl in Canada," Joe said, jumping up from the table. "I need fifty dollars to pay the cure cottage bill. And I still don't know the cost of those pneumothoraxes. Next Tuesday is her birthday. I'd like to get her something special. It costs nearly two hundred dollars." He swallowed hard. "At fifty dollars a trip, I'd need to make four more trips."

"Before Tuesday?" Charlie took the cigar out of his mouth and raised his woolly eyebrows.

"If you could spare the truck, I could go Saturday night, twice on Sunday and a final trip on Monday."

"Too risky," Armand said

"Wouldn't be unusual for a young buck like Joe to be real fired up for some French poontang."

"Look," Joe said, placing his hands on the table and staring hard at Armand and Charlie. "What do I have to say to convince you guys that there is only one woman in my life and that's Alice?

"Whatever you say." Armand raised his hands in a gesture of surrender. "But surely no one around these parts is going to think the worse of you, knowing your wife's cure will take years."

Joe slumped in a chair and held his head in his hands. "I love my wife. But just visiting her, not really having her is hell. Sure I look at pretty women. . .and I'll admit there's times I'd like to do more. But Alice comes first."

"Don't apologize for being a man," Armand said. "Let me loan you the money on account. Make a trip a week."

"No. I won't borrow money."

"I made you a promise when you first came to work that I'd make sure you'd never do anything that might cause you to lose your job. Now I'm telling you that making more than one trip a week is the surest way of spending time in jail and losing your job that I can think of."

The telephone rang. They all stopped talking and stared at the phone on the wall as though expecting it to speak.

"Probably just one of the guys," Charlie said. He laid his cards face down on the table and rose to answer.

"Better be damn important if it is," Armand said. "I made it clear they were to avoid all contact with this place."

"Rauch Livery." Charlie stretched his neck up to speak into the mouthpiece. Joe watched the old man's eyes twitch as he listened to the caller, then change direction and hook up with Armand's.

"For you." Charlie held the earpiece toward Armand.

Joe shoved his hands in his pockets and went over to his car. He kicked a tire.

"Bet you can't wait to get this beauty on the road," Charlie said.

Joe grunted and slid underneath his car. He didn't want to talk.

Charlie dropped down on his haunches so Joe could hear him. "Armand's talking to Wild Oats, one of our regulars down in Underwood." He waited till Joe stopped banging before continuing. "They need some goods this weekend."

Joe kept working.

"If Armand doesn't deliver, they'll find a different source. . .like McFadden. Then there's always the chance of Armand losing Wild Oats as a regular."

"So he'll have to call in Stu or Ellis."

"You don't get it, do you, kid? Our crew needs to lay low for a while. So who better to make the trip but you with my truck rigged out like I said."

Joe swung himself out from under his car. "Me? Make a run?"

"Why not? A new face with a beat-up farm truck? Who's to care?"

"How much?"

Charlie shrugged. "Depends on the size of the order. But I'd bet my Aunt Martha's bloomers your share would be at least the two, three hundred you're looking for."

"I'd make the run. Just this once to get caught up. But who am I kidding? Armand will never let me."

"Leave that to me. You stay busy tinkering with your car."

Joe thought about how he'd reply to all the reasons he knew Armand would have for not letting him shoot a load. Armand simply has to decide to hire or not hire me. That's his responsibility. I'm a grown man, I'm responsible for me. I can make my own decisions.

Joe was sick of doing what everyone else thought he should do. He wanted to get Alice the coat with the imported fur. He closed his mind to Armand's and Kate's warnings. He closed his conscience to the nature of his undertaking.

"Joe! Come on over here," Armand called from the table.

Joe stood up. He breathed deeply. He needed control over his emotions. He needed to wait till Armand asked him to make the run.

"If there was any other way to get the goods to Elizabethtown, I'd never ask you to make a run. If you and Charlie can have the Chevy ready to roll by Friday. . ."

"You got a deal." Joe grabbed Armand's hand and pumped it vigorously.

Thursday night Armand slowly walked around the truck. He rapped on the new wooden truck bed, firmly secured with shiny new bolts.

"You know all this new wood and bolts is going to be too tempting. Some trooper's going to use a crowbar on it," Armand said.

"That's okay," Charlie said, his cigar bobbing in his mouth as he talked. "The way I figure, the new bed gives the law a place to look. When they find it empty they'll quit."

Armand got down on his knees for a better view of the underside. The booze compartment was completely concealed. Next he opened the passenger's door and felt along the back of the seat. He couldn't find anything indicating access to the booze compartment.

"By God, it'll pass," Armand said, standing back. Joe grinned at Charlie and clapped him on the back. Charlie grunted and clamped down on his soggy, unlit cigar.

"I doubt they'll give it the going-over they give the typical booze car," Armand said. "These Series A Chevy trucks have a reputation for being seriously underpowered."

"I need to call Alice so she won't go to pieces when I don't show this Sunday." Joe went to the telephone and jangled the operator. "Saranac Lake 496." When Alice came to the telephone, he told her since he wanted to be with her on her birthday next Tuesday, his boss said he'd have to work Sunday.

Joe was excited. His mind raced like quicksilver over the details of this new venture.

30

Schermerhorn felt good about his new partner, Bill Dutton. A little wet behind the ears, but took direction well. Of course Schermerhorn always gave bonus points to a man who had respect for his four-legged partner.

He glanced over at Dutton as they cantered down the road just south of Au Sable Forks.

Wished he had Dutton's easy way with women, he thought, raising his hand to pull a big rubbery ear, then laying a finger on the length of his fleshy nose. Convinced women didn't find him attractive, he found it difficult to talk to them. There was that telephone operator in Lake Placid, he mused, a smile coming to his stern mouth. Gladys. . .she talked so much there wasn't much need for him to do anything but admire her looks. But it probably wasn't smart for a trooper to take up with a telephone operator. Too many of them kept the bootleggers informed of a trooper's whereabouts.

Schermerhorn shook Gladys out of his mind and turned to glance at Dutton, hoping the rookie hadn't caught him in a daydream. He filled his lungs with the crisp morning air that held traces of spring in it. Felt good to be moving away from winter. Also felt good to be rid of the burden of Cronk. Like finally freeing one of the Troop's Fords from a snowdrift.

Schermerhorn judged it'd be another week or two before booze car traffic picked up. Only the most desperate bootleggers would risk shooting their loads before the mud dried up. Sure, the Whiskey Trail from the border to Albany and New York was paved, but not many other roads.

For now he and Dutton just rode out in a different direction every day. Broadfield believed the simple presence of his troopers curbed crime.

He had to hand it to his Commander. Did a great job getting the newspapers to build up the Black Horse Brigade's reputation. He still chuckled over Broadfield's latest quote in Au Sable Forks' Adirondack Record. So good, he committed it to memory: "The runner who barks his pistol at a state trooper will be inviting a hail of lead from men who know how to shoot."

Schermerhorn's attention was drawn up the road to a horse and wagon tilted precariously in the mud. The driver was flaying a long-lashed whip about his horse.

A bolt of pure anger jolted Schermerhorn into action. "Get him," he said to Blizzard and touched his neck. The gelding leaped forward, stretching his neck out in a dead run. Bessie, her ears pinned back, ran shoulder to shoulder with Blizzard.

The driver turned to see the galloping horses and gave his own struggling horse a vicious crack of the whip. The terrified animal made a frantic lunge, freed the mired wheel and galloped down the road, the driver cracking the whip at every stride.

The troopers urged their horses on, easily overtaking the exhausted horse.

"Stop the horse," Schermerhorn ordered, and the younger trooper pushed his mare up to the horse's head. Schermerhorn pressed Blizzard close to the spinning wheels. Leaning far to the right he grabbed the driver by his collar, yanked him off the wagon seat and dumped him on the ground.

Dutton brought the steaming horse to a stop, vaulted from the saddle and stroked the exhausted animal's neck. Welts stood out on the farm horse's rump and pink-tinged sweat ran down his matted coat. He struggled for air and the whites of his eyes flashed in terror.

"You son-of-a-jackal," Schermerhorn said. "I'll see you never touch that horse again."

"I only done what any man would do to get my wagon out of the mud." The man struggled to his feet, filthy as a pig after a good wallow in the mud. He slapped his hat on his thigh, trying to dislodge some of the goo, then reached in the back pocket of his overalls for a dirty handkerchief and passed it down his unshaven face.

"Get that horse off the road and unhook him," Schermerhorn said to Dutton.

"How'll I get my wagon home? You've got no right to interfere . . ."

"We've got every right to keep you from abusing that horse. Right now you're going to get a little lesson in how to take care of that horse. . .starting with leading him home."

"Walk home? It's five miles or more."

"Hey," Dutton called out from where he was poking around in the bed of the wagon. "We've got a dozen bottles of Canadian ale here. Our friend must have been in a hurry to get it home."

Schermerhorn, with his Colt poking the man between his shoulders, walked over to the wagon. He glanced over his shoulder at the sound of a car coming down the road. Not many cars willing to risk getting mired in the spring mud.

He recognized it immediately as the Chevy farm truck that he knew in his bones was related to Armand Dasset. Looked like the same man behind the wheel as when he had stopped it at the roadblock outside of Bloomingdale. Wasn't his name Devlin?

The driver looked their way, then quickly jerked his eyes back to the road. He's hiding something, Schermerhorn thought, and watched the truck lurch slowly down the rutted road, noting the raw blond lumber bolted to its bed. A false bottom? Too obvious for a slick bootlegger like Dasset.

He debated leaving Dutton here with the horse beater and going after the truck, but quickly dismissed the idea. A gut feeling told him to be patient and not alert Dasset he was keeping track of him.

Joe drew in his breath when he came upon the troopers standing with a mud-covered, overalled man. Geeze, he thought, these guys are around every corner!

He gripped the steering wheel and stared straight ahead as he drove past. Without thinking of the consequences, he pressed the throttle to the floor. The engine strained but didn't pick up speed. The load of booze taxed the underpowered truck to its limits. Only after he had safely driven past did he realize he hadn't been breathing, and he exhaled in a noisy whoosh.

This truck is worthless carrying a load, he thought. I couldn't even outrun those horses. He had to admit Charlie and Armand were right. No trooper would think someone would be so dumb as to shoot a load with a Series A Chevy. These seriously underpowered trucks had trouble getting out of their own way.

If I ever do this again, he thought, turning onto the paved road, I'll use my car. Really is a beauty. All these years working on cars and I've never even driven a good one. Now I own a very good one. Well, it will be good once I fix the connecting rod.

In an effort to increase speed, Joe cranked open the split windshield, cutting down the wind resistance. He adjusted driving goggles over his eyes and pushed the truck to its limit.

Like to see the trooper, even in one of their Ford roadsters, that could catch me in my Cadillac. He drove along dreaming of speeding down the Cascade Pass. His Caddy was one of the best handling vehicles around.

Since I have to rework the driveshaft anyway, Joe thought, I could add a chamber. . .a tunnel. . .two of them. One on each side of the driveshaft. Bet they could hold several hundred quarts of booze. Fixed up like that I could make the big money runs to New York City. I've seen Dasset hand Gaston four hundred after a New York run. What I wouldn't do with that kind of cash!

Like to see the look on Hilda's face if I handed her a couple hundred greenbacks at a time. That's what I'd do, too, make it all ones. Big fistful! Get one of the pinstriped suits for myself and new stuff for Alice. Drive her out to the Swiss Chalet for dinner every Sunday. Wouldn't it be swell?

Suddenly a tire blew with a bang, cutting Joe's daydreaming short. He knew flat tires were a major risk when he put in extra air. Filled hard as rocks, they helped the truck go a mite faster.

Squatting in the mud at the side of the road and spinning the lug wrench, he looked up at the sound of an approaching car. It stopped behind Joe's truck. Troopers got out of both front doors simultaneously and adjusted their Stetsons.

Joe swallowed hard. This time he did have something to hide. One trooper walked slowly around the truck; the other came up to Joe.

"Think they'll ever come up with a tube that won't blow so easy?"

"I'll be the first to buy them," Joe said, not raising his eyes from the chore of prying the tire off the wheel. He picked up the tube and went to the back of the truck for the vulcanizing kit.

Both troopers joined him there. One casually rapped on the new wood. "New truck bed?"

"Yeah." Joe struggled to swallow his nervousness. "My uncle hauls manure. Rots the boards pretty quick."

"Where you headed?"

"Elizabethtown." Joe fumbled with a patch and glue. He couldn't go about the simple job of patching a tire with two troopers looking over his shoulder.

"What takes you to Elizabethtown?"

Geeze, did they see his hands shake as he lit a match to heat the glue? He dropped a glob on the patch and slapped it over the hole in the tube before he replied.

"Shoes. Horseshoes." Joe looped the tube over his arm, picked up the tire pump and went about inflating the tube. "My uncle is a blacksmith. The spring mud is sucking shoes off right and left and. . ." Joe paused to fit the tube just right, "my uncle is too busy nailing them back on to drive all the way to Elizabethtown for kegs of shoes and horseshoe nails."

The troopers backed off while Joe got the inflated tire back on the rim and finished the job. He strained to hear what they were saying. When Joe stood, they came up to him.

"We'd like to look under that new truck bed," one said.

"Why would you want to do that?" Joe took off his cap and ran his arm across his sweaty brow. "Besides, I'm not carrying any tools that could pry those boards off."

"We think you could be carrying illegal intoxicants."

"Booze?" Joe squeaked, his throat closed up.

"That's right. We'll follow you into Elizabethtown. There's a filling station on the right. Pull in. We'll find something to take a couple of those oak boards off with."

Joe was glad he could busy himself with cranking up the truck. He was sure the troopers would read guilt all over his face. Once he got the Chevy moving, with the Ford Roadster tight on his tail, he took deep steadying breaths.

"What do you have to worry about?" he lectured himself out loud. "They're looking under the boards. They'll never find the real false bottom."

At the filling station, Joe stood back trying to casually lean against a wall while the troopers cut a few bolts with a cold chisel. Using a drop light they poked around the insides. This was the test and it looked like he was going to pass.

But when a trooper dropped to his knees to look underneath, Joe's knees buckled. Good thing he had the wall for support. He and Charlie had spent a lot of time packing the liquor bottles in burlap. If the troopers rapped on the container, it should sound solid. Seconds seemed like hours before the trooper pulled himself upright and conferred with his partner. Finally one strode over to Joe.

"You're clean."

Joe nodded, attempting to present an I-told-you-so look.

"My partner's getting someone to bolt those boards back in place. Then you're free to go." The trooper turned to his Ford and got it cranked up by the time his partner joined him. Joe was relieved to see them drive off in the direction they had come. He wouldn't have to be looking over his shoulder as he went about his business in Elizabethtown. He'd still have time to stop at Jean-Paul's on the way home.

Joe wasn't sure he'd recognize the turnoff to Jean-Paul's cabin, since he hadn't been any too clear in the head the last time he passed through here. His fingers probed the base of his head where Bruce. . .he'd never forget that name. . .had knocked him out, leaving him for dead on the side of the road.

Bruce was dead. Buried under some pine boughs. But his brother Earl was still out there. Joe knew Earl would make good his ugly threats if they ever met up again. He didn't dwell on it, but Joe never believed Earl had made it out of the woods that day without snowshoes. But he might have. Now here he was driving through Earl's neck of the woods. Hoped he could get through this stretch of road without another flat.

A vision of the vile man came to mind, and for the first time he matched it up with the sneaking, grimy man who seemed to be stalking him when he took Alice and the group to the Carnival. It finally came to him that the man in Saranac Lake had to be Earl, looking for the chance to revenge his brother's murder.

The back of Joe's neck prickled. Maybe he shouldn't try to find Jean-Paul's cabin and chance getting the truck mired in the mud. But the need to thank the trapper and his wife overrode his fear, and when he saw a rutted road curving to the right, he braked the truck and turned. The road, hardly more than a path, followed the stream that would take him to the cabin.

Suddenly he was in a hurry to find the French Canadian couple who had saved his life. He wanted to tell Marie about Alice. And Jean-Paul. . .well he had something he wanted to give his friend. . .his *mon ami*, as Jean-Paul would say.

He shifted down and jostled along the road, setting the barrels of horseshoes to clanging. When the cabin came into view, Jean-Paul was on the porch with Louie at his side.

"Jean-Paul! It's me. . .Joe Devlin."

"Holy *Mere!*" A smile lit the little man's face. Louie bounded off the porch, tail wagging. "*Comment ça va?*" Jean-Paul walked to Joe and clasped him by the shoulders. Louie whined and pushed between the men.

"Marie," Jean-Paul called out, and the longhaired woman appeared at the door, wiping her hands on her skirt. "Look who has come to visit. Come, *mon ami*, tell us all about your winter. Marie has prayed before the Virgin for you and your woman every day."

"First I have a present for you," Joe said. He raised the truck seat and lifted out two quart bottles of 3-Star Hennessy. He pulled off the protective burlap and offered them to Jean-Paul.

The trapper's black eyes glowed. "I think you have much to tell, Joseph Devlin." He reached for the bottles and the men walked to the cabin.

It felt like a homecoming. Sitting at the rough-planked table, Joe told his story. How he had come to work for Dasset and why he was driving the Chevy. How hard it was working for a man like Tom Madden.

"Why do you bother?" Jean-Paul asked. "You can make large amounts of money moving the booze. A little more fun, too?"

"I'm tempted," Joe smiled. "I've got some ideas I want to try out on my Cadillac, then I plan on asking Dasset to make regular runs. So maybe I'll be stopping by more often."

"And your heart, Joe," Marie asked, "will it be happy with the new path you are taking?"

"No. I haven't slept easy for some time now." Joe sat back and splayed his hands on the table. "Back when we learned Alice had TB and should come to these mountains to cure, the cost was overwhelming. But what an adventure to go to the Adirondacks! In the city you hear so much about the cold, the wilderness. I felt Alice and I would face it together and lick this TB.

"But that was before I realized the cure cottage rules kept a distance between us." Joe leaned forward and held his head in his hands. "Nothing in our experience prepared us for this new life."

"I think it is time to leave you to your talks." Jean-Paul took a parting sip of the Hennessy and sighed with appreciation. "What do you say, Louie, the air she be a little clearer outside?" Joe and Marie turned to watch the trapper and his wolf leave the cabin.

"We used to take a worry or a fear," Joe said, after Jean-Paul and the wolf left. "and spend hours talking up one side and down the other till before long it didn't appear half as fearsome." He raised his head and smiled as he recalled happier times. "Of course most of our talks were in bed where we could hold one another." He passed a hand down his face as though to remove the smile before continuing. "Now I'm not allowed to talk about anything unpleasant, much less curl up in bed with Alice."

"Dear Joe," Marie said. "The boy that came to this cabin on frostbitten feet last winter is showing signs of becoming a man. A good, caring man. One I'm proud to say I know."

"It's not easy." Joe pushed away from the table and went to stand at the river-stone fireplace. "I'm always at odds with myself. Surely God wants me to do everything in my power to take care of Alice. See that she has what she needs to cure. But the only path he leaves me is working outside the law with the rum runners." Joe paused and raised a hand to touch the feet of the Blessed Virgin who looked down from a niche in the stones. "The toughest part is doing it all on my own."

"I believe God knows you have become a man and is giving you problems a man must face. They are only for you to make as only you must live with the consequences. Lead with your heart, Joe, and let your faith carry you through."

"Be aware, *mon ami*, that Earl is looking for you," Jean-Paul said, as Joe got ready to go. "Be sure he will try something should your paths ever meet again. I should confess, mon ami, that when the snows left I buried what was left of Earl's brother. No sense in inviting questions."

Joe told him about thinking he had spotted Earl during Carnival. Jean-Paul agreed it was probably Earl.

"Have you not heard of the break-ins in Saranac?" Jean-Paul asked. "I know it is Earl. He steals supplies woodsmen need and peddles them at their camps. I've seen him at a logging camp. They will catch up with him one of these days. He lost his hand. My guess is he lost the hand that Louie grabbed day we met at my lean-to."

Joe couldn't drive Earl from his thoughts during the remainder of his trip to Placid. Even after generous servings of 3-Star Hennessy, he kept alert, his eyes darting from side to side. He was getting so he could hold his liquor better than when he and Gaston had made the trip to Canada.

He pushed the truck to its limits up the steep mountains, all the while keeping an eye on the hood's temperature gauge. Even so, he knew it would be a simple matter for someone to jump into the bed of the truck. He didn't want to be ambushed again.

Only when he came into the village did the tension ease out of his shoulders.

31

"Miss Twinkle Toes said it's time we got out of the house and go for our morning *spaziergang*," Lilly announced, as she came into Alice's room one morning and flounced on the bed. She propped her head up on her elbows and watched Alice straighten clothes on hangers. "Will you look at all the new clothes!" Lilly jumped off the bed and pulled a sleeveless, swishy dress from the closet.

"When did you get this?" She held the dress to her flat chest and preened before the mirror over Alice's dresser.

"Joe bought it himself at one of those ritzy shops in Lake Placid. It's the new bois de rose color and look at all those hand-sewn little tucks around the neckline."

"He must be doing well, buying you new things every week."

"Joe has another job. . .mostly nights," Alice said. She turned and looked Lilly in the eye. "If I tell you something, you must promise not to repeat it to a soul. . .not even Frank." She took the dress from Lilly's hands and placed it back in the closet. Alice sat on the bed and patted a spot for Lilly to sit next to her.

"Joe repairs cars for a rum runner."

Lilly moved her head slowly up and down, her eyes never leaving Alice's face as if she was waiting for more.

"It's not as though he's actually transporting the stuff," Alice continued, perplexed by her friend's uncharacteristic silence.

"I think it's time you heard the whole story."

"What do you mean?" Alice pulled back from Lilly, tensing for an unknown blow.

"Charlotte didn't think I should tell you, but remember that Saturday back in March when Joe didn't come? The day it snowed so hard?"

It was Alice's turn to nod slowly.

"There was lots more to what really happened to Joe than simply going to a speakeasy and getting snowbound. Joe and another fella were caught taking booze over the border."

"No!" Alice jumped from the bed and faced Lilly squarely. Two deep red spots glowed on her cheeks. "You're making things up. It's not nice."

"It was in the paper, Alice," Lilly said softly and reached out a hand to her friend.

Alice scowled and folded her arms tightly across her chest.

"Rum running is not the end of the world," Lilly said. "I don't know a single person who thinks having a cocktail is committing a crime. What do you think Ursula and Hilda have locked up in the sideboard?"

Alice dropped her hands to her sides and crossed to the window. "I guess you're right. It's Joe keeping secrets from me that I don't like. Am I the only one that doesn't know what my husband is up to?"

"That's what I told Charlotte. You had a right to know. But you were having your first pneumo and you know how the sisters drill into us to talk only about cheerful things."

Alice pressed her fingers against her chest, wondering if you could feel the tiny pneumo scars through her overblouse.

Hilda appeared, hands on hips. "Outside you go. Now." Hilda stood waiting for Lilly and Alice to leave the room. "Charlotte is waiting downstairs.

""I'm going to miss Charlotte," Alice said. "By this time tomorrow she'll be on her way home to Schenectady. She's become closer than a sister."

"More like a mother with those do-good things she's always spouting."

They found Charlotte perched on the porch railing talking across to the men at Pelletier.

"Bags all packed?" Alice asked.

"I guess so."

"You don't sound very excited," Lilly said. "When I'm released. . .if I ever am. . .I'll be out of town before sunset."

"Like a Buster Keaton picture show?" Alice asked.

The porchmates laughed.

"Come on, let's get out of here before Miss Twinkle Toes chases us off the porch."

"It's wonderful to be going home," Charlotte said, "but I'm really scared I won't fit in."

"It's your husband and daughters, for gosh sakes," Lilly said, "not a house of strangers."

"Yes, but they've gotten along without me for years. My girls have been turning to someone else with their problems. For almost four years. Every member of my family has been warned not to come too close, to leave the room if I cough. At most I'll be a guest. Maybe even a guest they distrust."

Charlotte's misgivings revealed a scary prospect. Alice realized all her efforts were directed toward getting well enough to go home. It never crossed her mind there'd be an entirely new set of hurdles to face after her lungs healed.

By some mutual, unspoken consent, the young women didn't walk down into the village this morning, but rather chose the sanctuary of the streets lined with cure cottages that wove around the crown of Helen Hill. They walked shoulder to shoulder in the street, only moving to the sidewalk when an automobile came by.

Occasionally a tubercular curing on a porch called out to wish Charlotte good luck. More often, Alice noted, a male patient called an invitation to Lilly to come join them on the porch. Lilly waved and smiled at them all, but stayed with her porchmates. They were all threatened by the impending change.

Charlotte told them about her appointment at the beauty salon for that afternoon. "I'm going for a modern look," she said. "Marcel my hair and learn to handle all that new makeup. I want you both to come to my room and see the wine-red crepe dress I bought. It's trimmed in gray and I got gray stockings to match. Even a picture hat and dangling earrings."

"Your going-away outfit?" Lilly teased.

"Don't think I haven't worried about that, too," Charlotte said. The porchmates walked in silence for a time before Charlotte spoke again.

"I know it sounds scandalous to you, Alice, but I'm really glad I found a cousin. Tom has boosted my confidence that I can still function. . .as a woman."

"Will you tell your husband about Tom?"

"Goodness, no!" Charlotte came to an abrupt halt in the middle of Pine Street. "I certainly don't want to hear what John's been doing all these years."

"Why do you assume he's. . . ?" Alice asked.

"Slept with a woman, or women?" Lilly jumped into the conversation. "Come on, Alice. I'm not even married but I can't imagine a healthy married man saving it for his wife's return to his bed."

"But Joe. . ."

An automobile honked its horn, chasing the young women up on the sidewalk.

"Alice, are you blind?" Lilly asked. "Don't you ever wonder about Kate?" Charlotte jabbed Lilly in the ribs with an elbow and Lilly fell silent.

"Joe is different than an absentee husband, Lilly," Charlotte said. "Goodness, Joe's over here several times a week."

"Yes," Alice said, "but we never. . ."

Neither of her friends had a comment. They filed out on the street again and turned back toward Conifer.

"Say," Alice said, suddenly brightening. "Joe is coming by tonight. Let's all go out to the Chalet and celebrate Charlotte going home. The whole gang. . .Frank and Tom."

Charlotte had already gone to the beauty salon by the time Lilly and Alice woke from their afternoon nap.

"It won't be the same without Charlotte," Alice said.

"Bet there's a new girl in her room within a day. Now that Charlotte is really going home, it makes me want to try harder," Lilly said.

"You so seldom have a bad day," Alice said. "I don't understand what's keeping you here. I'm ashamed to admit it, Lilly, but I hope you don't go home before me."

"Humph. I'm not going anywhere unless I take curing more seriously. Right here and now I vow not to run up and down stairs. Let's make a pact to help each other get out of this place before winter."

"Good idea," Alice agreed. "Now that I'm up I don't follow all the rules if I'm feeling good."

"Hmmm. We've got to spend more time sitting."

"'Concern yourself with Today,'" Alice said, quoting Trotty Veck. "'Grasp it and teach it to obey Your will.'"

"Yes, Mother Charlotte," Lilly laughed.

32

Alice pulled herself up to a sitting position and went over last night's going-away celebration in detail. She was pleased she had thought of it and proud it was her husband who drove the party out to the Swiss Chalet in his Cadillac.

A social success, she said to herself, enjoying the memory. Never mind that she found it disconcerting to see Charlotte enamored with her cousin. Holding hands, dancing the fox trot so closely. All just hours before Charlotte would be going home with her husband.

Of course Lilly didn't seem to mind, Alice thought, swinging her legs over the side of her bed. She was carrying on the same way with Frank. As usual, Frank and his mandolin were popular. Simply having Frank around turned any gathering into a party. Alice stepped into her slippers and reached for her robe. The band had even asked him to join them for a few numbers. And Joe had produced some booze that he poured into everyone's lemonade.

Alice started off the evening determined to confront Joe with the real truth about the snowy Saturday in March. But after awhile it didn't matter anymore; she was ready to accept that Joe was simply sparing her any worry. And they were having such a swell time.

It must be hard on Joe, she mused, with my cure costing so much and me being pretty useless. She'd never admit it to anyone. . .barely acknowledged it herself. . .but if rum running was responsible for all the nice things Joe kept bringing, she was willing to look the other way.

But Joe took his religion so seriously. She wondered how he handled the guilt of breaking the law. Even a law that few people took seriously. Certainly everyone she knew felt it was a big game to take a drink and not get caught.

She vowed she'd never add to her husband's burden by questioning him about his other job. Just be appreciative and loving about the fruits of it.

Loving! Unfortunately that's where the big problem lay. She couldn't kiss Joe without endangering his health. And Lilly was right. Joe, a healthy young man, needed. . .it. Was she truly supposed to look the other way until she was no longer contagious?

Maybe that was another reason to find a cousin. She couldn't feel so righteous about Joe if she, too, were. . .seeing someone. Kind of evens things out, she mused. Yet her situation was different. Most healthy spouses appeared at most a few times a year. Now that Joe had his own car, she saw him two or three times a week. If she started cousining, she'd have to sneak around between the times Joe came to see her.

A soft knock at her door broke into Alice's thoughts. Charlotte walked in.

"Look at you!" Alice said, clasping her hands together. "John will be taking home the prettiest woman in Saranac Lake."

Charlotte blushed, but looked terribly pleased. "Is this makeup all right?" She studied her face in the mirror over Alice's bureau. "I never was one to paint all this stuff on my face. I hope I didn't make a mistake plucking away nearly all my eyebrows." She ran a red-tipped finger over the narrow arch of one brow.

Laughing, Alice took Charlotte gently by the shoulders and turned her friend around. "You look lovely. That red is a good color for you. I know John will be pleased and proud."

"I know you don't like to think about it, but my. . .friendship with Tom has given me the courage to start my life with John. Please don't turn away, Alice."

Alice looked out the window, keeping her back to Charlotte. She really didn't like to discuss cousining.

"I truly believe you should find a cousin to help you feel like a desirable woman. Joe doesn't have to know about it. He'd appreciate the change in your attitude."

"You may be worried about picking up with John," Alice said, wrapping her arms tightly about her thin chest, "but I know our

'Mother Charlotte' won't have any trouble keeping her girls on the right path with your supply of Trotty Vecks."

"Don't change the subject, Alice. I just wanted to share with you the confidence I have now because of having a cousin."

Alice had nothing to say.

"I also came so I could say goodbye before John gets here. Please don't come out on the porch to see us off. I know I'll cry and make a mess of all this stuff on my face. I've already asked Lilly the same thing."

Finally Alice turned back to her friend, screwing up her face to keep from crying.

"Oh, Alice, don't make this more difficult than it is."

Alice swallowed hard and pulled herself together. "We've said it all over the last few days. You're a dear friend I'll remember always." They hugged fiercely. Charlotte pulled away first, straightened her picture hat and quickly shut the door behind her.

Within minutes the door opened again. This time it was Lilly, her eyes bright with tears. Wordlessly the young women clung to each other.

They stayed in Alice's room through breakfast. God bless Ursula, Alice thought, for not insisting they come down to eat. Even through the closed door, they heard the excitement of Charlotte going home. . .healthy, cured! The good news charged through the halls. Alice was sure every patient at Conifer was vowing to adhere to the rules so they, too, could go home.

They held their breath when strange footsteps. . .a man's. . .made several trips to Charlotte's room and carted suitcases that bumped their way through the narrow halls.

Together they went to the porch railing and looked down at the car that would take Charlotte out of their lives. They saw John help Charlotte settle in the front seat. How attentive he seemed! Charlotte glanced up at the porch and blew them a soft kiss. The remaining porchmates waved a reluctant goodbye.

Without a word, both young women collapsed on their cure chairs. Even the balsam seemed to be sighing along with their own sniffles and sighs.

A commotion at Pelletier broke their thoughts. Chairs scraped across the porch and agitated male voices carried clearly across the narrow street.

"Lilly!" The urgency in the voice caused Lilly to leap to her feet. She leaned out over the porch railing. "It's Frank. He's shooting a ruby!" Lilly flung open the door and bolted from the room.

Alice heard Ursula's calm voice, then Lilly's in near hysteria. "You can't stop me. Frank's my friend."

Alice recognized Lilly's quick steps down the front porch's wooden steps and the fear in the sound of her friend racing across the street. And still Alice could not move from where she sat before Lilly was summoned to Frank's side.

Dear, sweet Frank. With his big bumpy nose and thick glasses. He appeared so well last night. Cheerful, funny. Poking fun at being a tubercular with his silly verses and songs. Smooching with Lilly on the dance floor. Surely this could be no more than a little setback.

Are we never past the danger of hemorrhaging? Fear spread through her. Would she ever be free of this disease? Alice shivered and perspired. She hugged her arms tightly to her chest as though willing her lungs not to tear.

The flurry of activity at Pelletier had been replaced by a quiet murmuring of male voices. And the crying of one woman.

Alice knew. Frank had died.

She should go to her friend. But she couldn't move. She heard footsteps. . .were they Ursula's on the porch steps? A little later, a soft sobbing and Ursula's unmistakable comforting voice carried to where Alice sat.

Soon Lilly climbed the stairs, the quick, lighthearted step Hilda was forever admonishing her to curtail had swiftly changed into the defeated tread of an old woman. Alice heard Lilly approach her room and still she could not go to her friend.

Minutes, recorded by the loud ticking of Alice's bedroom clock, passed slowly. Alice didn't have to look to know the car coming to a stop was the undertaker pulling up in front of Pelletier Cottage. Car doors closed softly.

Some time passed before Alice heard a scuffling of several pairs of feet in the street and more doors opening and closing with the same care.

Next came the silence. Complete silence. No murmuring voices drifting up from porches. No feet shambling softly on the sidewalks. No footsteps on the creaky, bare steps and halls of Conifer. Helen Hill had lost one of its own. And Frank had taken his mandolin music with him.

With considerable effort, Alice rose from her cure chair. She must comfort her friend. She went to Lilly's room and knocked gently on the closed door.

"Lilly?"

"Go away."

"You shouldn't be alone." Alice tried turning the doorknob to discover it locked. "Please unlock the door."

"Go away."

33

Excitement quivered in the dust motes of Charlie Rauch's barn. Joe was about to make his first run in his Cadillac and the entire Dasset gang had assembled to see him off.

Over the months Joe had not only repaired the driveshaft but also designed and positioned secret chambers on either side of it. He beefed up the springs and installed truck brakes to handle the heavy loads of booze he would be carrying. Caught up in customizing, he took the loud ah-u-gah horn from a junked truck and installed it. He couldn't resist trying it out in the shop over the barn, and when he did the horses below whinnied shrilly in fear.

He incorporated every device for increasing speed he could think of, like exchanging the Cadillac's solid windshield for a split one that he intended to keep cranked open to cut down wind resistance.

Joe chose heavy-duty inner tubes and fitted them on the rims with the skill of a surgeon. He pumped them up to their limits so they could sing over the mountain roads and stowed sufficient spares to handle a minimum of four blowouts. Anticipating that his Cadillac would require large amounts of gasoline, he strapped on three five-gallon cans.

Armand had given Joe a list of cooperative farmers along the route where he could obtain gasoline in exchange for a little booze. He folded it carefully and placed it in the glove box. Joe hadn't neglected the Cadillac's exterior either. The pea green body gleamed from cans of rubbing compound patiently applied. The rich upholstery had been oiled and buffed, and every day Joe placed a single fresh flower, taken from the Club's dining room, in the little silver dashboard vase.

It was quite possibly the fastest car about to enter the traffic of sleek, powerful automobiles darting through the mountains in the night. Joe's palms sweated; he was anxious to start and alternated between wanting to test his car in a confrontation with the troopers and hoping he could get through unnoticed.

Joe and Armand had loaded the hooch hours ago, and Armand made Joe sit down and go over the route, pointing out a couple of alternates in case he found trouble along the way. His destination was a hotel a few miles north of Albany.

Joe was taken by the way Ellis sought him out, offering his famous diamond horseshoe tie tack, his good luck charm, and then, not five minutes later, Stu wanting to hand over his lucky rabbit foot key chain. He firmly refused both. He had engineered his own luck: a pea green 1925 Cadillac with glossy black fenders and an eighty-five horsepower engine modified to fit a rum runner's needs. But it was a nice feeling to know they cared.

Gaston, recently out of jail and laying low for a while, approached Joe, too. "I don't think I have any luck to offer you," he said in his quiet way.

Finally Armand gave the signal. The Cadillac sprang to life as though eager as Joe to begin the night's adventure. Joe thrilled at the sound of the powerful engine, rhythmical and confident, he thought. He cranked open the split windshield and adjusted goggles comfortably over his eyes. Next he pulled on a worn pair of leather gloves, Charlie's contribution, and waited for Ellis and Stu to finish winching the decoy hay bales out of the way. Geeze, they were taking their good sweet time!

Gaston and Armand pushed open the barn doors and Charlie drove the tractor out into the night. It was like the lead pony bringing his nervous thoroughbred to the post for the Kentucky Derby.

Under the cover of the tractor's noisy engine, the elegant Cadillac purred out of Charlie Rauch's livery stable to begin its maiden race.

Joe fought the urge to speed out of town and guided the big car sedately in the early June night. But after crossing the Chubb River he couldn't resist testing its climbing power. Topping the hill, he guided his car through the gears and gave it a free rein. The Cadillac flew across the Plains of Abraham. It was a different sight than when he had plodded across the Plains on snowshoes six months ago.

Forty, fifty. Doesn't that beat all—nudging fifty-five miles an hour with a full load of booze!

Joe was so exhilarated with the Cadillac's performance he nearly missed seeing the car parked on the corner of Heart Lake Road, where the Plains met the dense forest wall. He took his foot off the throttle and glanced sharply to the right. Definitely a car, but much too dark to identify.

In moments headlights jabbed at his back. Had the car he glimpsed lurking in the dark been waiting for him? He pressed the throttle and the Cadillac responded easily, increasing Joe's lead. Soon the headlights disappeared for long moments as Joe maneuvered his heavy car down the road snaking its way through the mountains. What a thrill to be in control of the road. To drive the car that couldn't be caught. His car.

He had hoped to gain experience handling the Cadillac around the many bends in the road, without the pressure of being followed. For all his expertise with cars, Joe seldom drove one. Certainly not one the caliber of the Cadillac. And here he was, careening down a midnight-dark road.

It crossed his mind that the automobile tailing him was not just another automobile. Kind of late at night for aimlessly driving in the mountains. Too late for those suppositions now. He'd shown his hand. Now he had to win.

The curves were coming at Joe faster than left-right punches. Tires screeched. Joe heeded their warning and reined in the powerful car, knowing the over-inflated tires were badly stressed. His pursuer, obviously someone more familiar with the sharp turns, made significant gains and when the road straightened briefly, Joe heard the distinct crack of a rifle. And another. The second bit into the Cadillac's back window. Joe instinctively hunched over the steering wheel.

He thanked God for the cover of the next bend in the road. But the rifle shots unnerved him and he jerked the Cadillac sharply to the left, only to feel it begin to sway. He couldn't be so crude or he'd overturn for sure.

Joe picked up speed again when the road straightened, but before he slammed into the next sharp right curve, the stalking headlights found him once more and another shot rang out, thudding into the car's body. Definitely closing the distance.

Joe longed to get out of the mountain pass. Where the hell was Keene, anyway? If he ever reached the straight valley road south of Keene, he felt confident the Cadillac would outdistance whoever was following him.

A large white building appeared on the left. The church, Joe thought, his car roaring down the hillside. The inn and crossroads would be next.

Crossroads! He made an instant decision to take the road to the right if he could reach it before the persistent headlights captured him again. Dasset said the road—he called it Hulls Falls Road—would meet up again with the valley road. Could he slow the car in time?

He stood on the brakes and hauled the wheel to the right. Everything depended on making the turn before his pursuer saw his move. He held his breath as the Cadillac lurched to its outside wheels. He took his foot off the brakes and turned the wheel to the left. Seconds passed before the big car steadied and Joe dared to breathe again. He switched off the lights and slowed to a crawl in the dark, ready to speed off should the headlights turn in after him.

Within seconds he saw a streak of light in his rearview mirror. Then blackness. The headlights had not turned. He waited a little longer before switching on his headlights and picking up speed.

He unfastened a hand from the steering wheel, flexing his fingers, noting his hands were soaked inside their leather gloves. As the adrenalin left his body, he felt spent. But good. The Cadillac had performed well. Clung to the road beautifully even in his inexperienced hands. And power! Joe knew the car was capable of going even faster than he could handle it on the twisting road.

A light flashed through the trees. A car coming toward him?

Joe gripped the steering wheel. Suddenly a bang. He crouched over the wheel and his car pulled sharply to the right. A flat tire! Far better than being shot at, he thought, straightening up in his seat. He slowed to a crawl, not willing to stop. He knew he must be shredding the tire and mangling the rim, but he couldn't risk staying in the road.

There was the light again. Now it shone on the right. Coming out of the woods, Joe realized it was a light in a house, not a car. He pulled in the driveway and picked his way slowly behind the large barn, hiding his car from the road. He switched off the headlights and killed the engine.

More lights came on in the house. Then a porch light followed by the door opening. A very tall man, silhouetted in the open door, swept the lawn with a light.

Joe waved and got out to meet him.

"Need a place to hide?" the man said, something familiar about his voice.

"Dr. Decker?"

"I know you?"

"I'm Joe Devlin. You treated my frostbite last December."

"Sure! The mechanic walking to Saranac Lake. Could have used this beauty back then," he said, running a hand over the Cadillac's hood. "You. . .uh, changed professions?"

"Couldn't meet all my wife's bills on nine-fifteen a week," Joe smiled. "You doctors don't come cheap. They're expecting this load in Albany tonight." Joe dropped to his knees to look at the ruined tire and mutilated rim. "This rim's going to take some fixing."

"Might as well wait till the light of day. Come on in. I want to hear everything. Your car's safe here."

Joe located a bottle of White Horse Scotch and the two men went up to the house.

A crowing rooster woke Joe the next morning. It seemed hardly minutes since Dr. Decker had shown Joe to a bedroom. The two men had sat around the kitchen table, the scotch bottle between them, discussing the Lake Placid Club, tuberculosis cures and rum running.

He pulled on his trousers and quietly left the house, taking care to keep the screen door from banging. When Dr. Decker found him, Joe had the tire off and was examining the mangled rim.

"Whew!" Dr. Decker whistled when he saw the rim. He offered to take it to the local blacksmith up on Bartlett Road, north of Keene. The man had a lathe that could be used in smoothing it out.

"Replacing this back window is a different cup of tea," Dr. Decker said. "Not at all sure I can trust the man at the hardware to keep his mouth shut when I ask him to cut a new glass." He ran a hand over his unshaven face.

"I don't dare drive with it broken," Joe said, picking at the broken shards and laying them on a newspaper. "I'm sure whoever did it is already looking for a car with a shot out back window."

"I'll do my best. Maybe I can convince the fella it's a new window for my barn."

Joe paced the large wraparound veranda, anxious to be on his way. Mrs. Decker came out offering lemonade. Joe smiled and politely refused.

"You're going to wear the paint right off my veranda," the exasperated woman finally said, before Joe realized his pacing was annoying.

"Have you seen the falls?" she asked. "They're a local point of interest. Quite impressive this time of year with the river still full."

"My car isn't operable."

"Goodness, you don't need a car. Follow the cow path." She pointed to the north. "Scarcely a ten minute walk."

"Yes, Ma'am." Joe didn't want to go sightseeing, of all things. But he could take a hint. The doctor's wife would like some peace.

The ruined rim sure had put the kibosh on his carefully laid plans. It'd be mid afternoon or later before he made his delivery. Then he'd really have to push to get back to the Club. Madden expected him at work by seven sharp. The Club was beginning to fill up with summer guests and the fleet of touring cars were a popular way to picnic and take in the scenery.

Joe was wondering if he should try to telephone Dasset when he pushed his way through dense evergreens and saw Hulls Falls thundering below him. The black water plummeted over the falls and churned into white foam as it crashed around huge piles of boulders and rocks. The noise was overpowering. Joe stood mesmerized by the force. He wanted to get closer and looked about him for a way to reach a flat rock at the falls' edge. He picked his way down the sharp incline, grasping evergreen branches to keep from stumbling.

Once on the flat rock, he sat and removed his shoes and socks and plunged his legs in the rushing water. The shock of the icy water made Joe jerk them out. He lowered his feet more cautiously the next time *When Alice is stronger, we'll drive here in the Cadillac for a picnic*

Kate will get me a basket lunch from the Club dining room. I'll get a bottle of champagne.

He took his feet out, letting them dry in the sun and the warm rock before putting his shoes and socks back on. The power of the falls drained the tension from him. He ambled back to the house and was content to rock on the veranda till he heard Dr. Decker's old Chevy rumbling down the road.

"The remainder of the run went like clockwork," Joe reported to Dasset. "You know, I think my Cadillac is the fastest car around."

"Don't get too cocky," Armand said, peeling off bills from a big roll and handing them to Joe. "It takes more than speed not to get caught. Take your share and buy Alice that special present."

"You bet. And I'm going to pay her cure cottage bill in advance, too. Can't wait to see the look on that old battle-ax's face."

34

"Let's get a canoe and paddle across the lake," the tall, angular girl said, wiping the corners of her wide mouth with a napkin. She and another girl were among the last Club guests lingering over lunch in the dining room. "We'll get an ice cream soda at the drug store."

"I'd rather take bikes around the lake," her friend answered from across the luncheon table. She spooned the last of a cold custard. "By way of the garage," she added.

"Garage? Whatever for?"

"You haven't seen him?"

"Who?"

"Him. . .the dark silent mechanic with cocker spaniel eyes."

"Mechanic! Really, Lucinda. With all the gorgeous men at the Club practically begging for your attention you want to chase after a mechanic?"

"I'm sure he's destined to be something else," Lucinda said, a wistful smile on her red lips. "Like a movie star."

"How did you find this movie star mechanic?"

"George and I were at the porte cochere waiting for his car to be brought around and Joe. . .that's his name. . .drove up." She ran the tip of one manicured finger around the rim of her water goblet.

"How could you even look at a mechanic when you have George? There's a man who has everything."

"He's just too. . .boring." Lucinda dismissed George with a graceful flick of her hand.

"This mountain air has affected your brain, Lucinda. Every girl in Manhattan has her eye on George."

"I don't care. Joe is. . ."

"All right. We'll get bikes and take a look at your mechanic."

"How about a race?" Emily called over her shoulder. Her shiny brown hair swung in the breeze. "Loser pays for the ice cream sodas."

"I don't want to perspire," Lucinda said from her bicycle. "Or have the wind muss my hair."

"I can see this will be a lot of fun." Emily pumped her bicycle effortlessly.

"Don't be such a pickle. I want him to notice me." Lucinda paused, finding it hard to talk and pedal. "I can't arrive gasping for breath and red in the face."

"I thought breathless and blushing would be good." Emily stood up on the pedals and her bicycle surged ahead. "I'll wait at the top of the hill."

A short while later, Lucinda pulled her bike to a stop under a towering white pine.

"Now what?" Emily asked.

"The garage is just around the corner," Lucinda said, as she poked inside her purse, retrieving a nail file. "If one of my tires were to be flat, I certainly would have to stop for help."

"This Joe doesn't have a chance." Emily propped her bicycle against the pine and sat cross-legged on the ground while Lucinda let most of the air out of her back tire. "But answer me this." She sifted brown pine needles through her fingers. "What will you do after you spark his interest?"

"Why, I intend to get to know him." She looked at Emily, compassion filling her big eyes, "and learn about his great tragedy." She dropped the nail file back in her purse and took out a mirror. Holding it this way and that, she patted an errant marcelled wave back in place.

"What great tragedy?"

"Oh, I don't know. Your questions can be exasperating, Emily. I haven't even met the man yet." She raised her head and gazed at the distant mountains. "Something has happened to etch such a sadness on that handsome face." She placed her purse in the bicycle's wicker basket and started to push it down the road. "It may be fate that sent me to bring some happiness into his life."

"Get a look at what's coming down the road," Allen said, rolling his eyes. He and Joe were washing road grime off a touring car. "A couple of ladies in need."

Joe looked up and saw two young women walking their bicycles toward the garage. The shorter one was a looker, all right. Her caramel-colored hair curled prettily around her oval face.

They walked straight up to where Joe and Allen stood, soapy sponges in their hands.

"I seem to have a flat tire," the shorter one said, tilting her head so she looked at Joe through fluttering eyelashes. Joe noted that her eyes were the same deep golden caramel of her hair. Dressed in cool lime trimmed in crisp white, the girl was a sweet-smelling summer breeze.

"I'm sure you're terribly busy, but would you take a look at it?"

"Yes, Miss," Joe said, dropping his sponge in a pail and running his wet hands down the pants legs of his coveralls. Lucinda followed Joe into the garage while Emily waited in the shade with Allen

."Have you worked here long?" Lucinda wiped the chrome bumper of a car with her hankie before sitting on it.

"Since just before Christmas, Miss." Joe pumped air into the flat tire.

"My name's Lucinda." She arranged her pleated skirt so it ruffled about her crossed knees. "Are you a native?"

"No, Miss. I'm from New York." Joe hefted the bike so he could spin the tire in a trough of soapy water.

"What a coincidence." She clapped her hands together and rested her chin on her red-tipped nails. "So am I."

"There don't seem to be any punctures. You and your friend can be on your way." He steered the bike out of the garage and wiped off the seat with his rag.

Lucinda pursed her mouth together. "Just as we were getting to know one another," she pouted, but rose good-naturedly and followed Joe out of the garage.

"Do you ever drive the touring cars?" she asked.

"Sometimes."

Lucinda got on her bicycle and joined Emily. "Good-bye," she called over her shoulder. "Thank you!"

"I think she's taken a shine to you," Allen said, watching the girls pedal away.

"Humph. . .what would a Club guest want with the help? Naw, she's just practicing her flirting. There wasn't anything wrong with that tire. She must have let the air out on purpose."

"Well, what do you think of him?" Lucinda asked, eyes shining.

"He does have a certain earthy masculinity. Did he confide his great tragedy to you?"

"No," she pouted. "He was much too quick fixing the tire. Maybe I should have poked a hole in it." The girls came out of the Club grounds and pedaled toward the village.

Finding an empty table in the drugstore, both girls ordered strawberry ice cream sodas.

"Joe told me he drives the touring cars." Lucinda dabbed at her forehead and upper lip with a hankie.

"Hmm."

"Wouldn't you like to take a drive somewhere. . .in the woods? We could have the kitchen pack a picnic." She dug into her purse, brought out a slim black cigarette holder and fastened a Lucky Strike to it.

"What about my picnic? Will you go?" Their sodas arrived; frothy pink foam bubbled over the edge of the tall glasses. Big scoops of ice cream perched on the brims. Emily eagerly reached for hers, drinking deeply through the straw.

"Umm. . .good! I don't know, Lucinda." She spooned ice cream into her mouth. "I think you're taking this too far. Beside, what am I supposed to be doing while Joe confesses his great tragedy?"

"Daddy won't give our picnic a second thought if I say you and I are going for a drive to. . .sketch the mountains."

"I'm supposed to play chaperone?"

"You could ask Winston to come along. You're always taking walks in the woods with him."

"And you don't think Winston will find it a little odd. . .leaving George at home?" Emily pointed the long-handled ice cream spoon at Lucinda. "Every one of the Club's thousand guests would banter that choice gossip around. Your father would whisk you back to the city on the night train. You know he intends to play a major role in selecting your husband."

"Well, I have to do something." She sipped up the last of the ice cream soda and ran the tip of her tongue along the length of the straw.

"Devlin. . .come in here," Madden bellowed into the garage from his office door.

Joe pushed himself out from under a car. He wiped his hands on the rag stuffed in the back pocket of the regulation coveralls and walked over to his boss. The other mechanics stopped their tinkering and watched Joe thread his way through the cars.

"Good luck," Allen whispered when Joe passed him.

"My boss called to say a guest complained about one of my mechanics." His eyes were blue chips of ice and his grim mouth was tightly clamped on a toothpick. "I run a tight ship here, Devlin. I don't like complaints from the guests." He glared at Joe as though daring him to speak. Joe didn't rise to the bait. He looked Madden in the eye and waited for him to continue.

"What's this about refusing to take two of the Club's guests on a drive along the Ausable?"

Joe swallowed. He knew that girl was going to be trouble. "Got a pile of work here. The brakes are shot on the yellow nine-passenger, there's at least four cars long overdue an oil change. . ."

"I didn't realize you had been promoted to job foreman, deciding to send Allen in your place." He kept Joe locked in his glacial glare.

"I don't know these roads well. Not like Allen who's lived here all his life."

Madden nodded, and spat pieces of the toothpick close to Joe's left elbow. "Don't care much for girls, Devlin?"

"No, sir. I mean I like them fine." He stumbled over the unexpected question. "But the Rule Book says employees aren't suppose to fraternize with guests."

"Don't be a smartass, Devlin." He poked Joe's chest with his stubby sausage finger. "I know what the Rule Book says. I know it says we do everything we can to give the guests a memorable vacation. If those ladies request you, they get you."

"Yes, sir. Can I get back to work now?"

"You know, Devlin, come to think of it, I never see you with any of the girls. You know your Rule Book so well, you must know what the Club thinks of queers." A snarly smile contorted his mouth. "What do you suppose they'd think if they knew a healthy young man never spends any time with the fair sex?"

Joe jammed his fists in his pockets to keep from socking the man. "I like girls just fine, sir. But I was hired on my ability to fix cars, not my popularity with girls." He turned and walked back to the car he was working on.

35

"**N**eed to talk about it?" Kate stood before Joe, her dinner tray in hand. Joe sat with his chin resting on white-knuckled fists. Kate could almost hear the thunder of his unspoken anger crashing about his shoulders.

Joe's expression didn't change, but with a shrug of his shoulders he motioned for Kate to sit across from him. She ate in silence, waiting for him to speak.

"If I thought I could swing it just working for Dassett, I'd quit this place tomorrow," he finally said.

"Madden giving you a hard time?"

"If suggesting I'm a queer, then yes, I'd say he's giving me a hard time."

"What?" Kate's fork dropped on the plate with a clatter.

Joe told the story of the girl purposely letting the air out of her bicycle's tire and Madden's ugly suggestion as to why Joe refused to drive her into the woods for a picnic. Kate felt Joe's embarrassment at the word Madden had used.

"It must be so hard for you to deny to the world that Alice even exists."

"Honestly, Kate, I don't know how much more of this I can take."

"Alice is improving, Joe. Think of that last time you took both of us for a drive. Alice looked so good. Didn't cough the entire time. I bet you're back in New York before Christmas."

"It's well and good to talk such sugar around Alice. Every one drills in the importance of being eternally cheery. But when I hear how many years most of those cure patients have been here, I don't know why Alice should be different. She still has to get those pneumo treatments every couple of weeks." He leaned forward before saying quietly, "I've made a few runs."

Kate's eyes sparked with anger. "How can you risk the fines. . .and jail, if you get caught? Who will look after Alice then?"

"I figure the risk is worth the money and, oh, I don't know, Kate. Racing down the roads at night is about the only time I really escape everything that's happening to me and Alice."

"Look," Kate said, leaning across the table, stopping short of touching his clenched fists. "Why don't we kill two birds with one stone." Joe raised his eyes to meet hers.

"There's a Club picnic just for employees tomorrow night. Come with me." Kate saw Joe about to object and raced ahead. "Don't you see it's perfect timing?" She began to tick off all the positive reasons on her fingers.

"It doesn't interfere with seeing Alice on weekends," she began, choosing Joe's most important objection to any suggestion. "It's more. . .sensible entertainment than making runs." She looked Joe squarely in the eye, making sure he understood what she thought of rum running.

"Madden often comes, "she continued. "If not, word will be sure to get back to him about you being there with a girl. And since I know Alice, I won't be expecting you to act. . .like a date." Kate lowered her eyes on this last point, hoping Joe wouldn't notice her cheeks coloring. When she looked up, Joe was staring over her shoulder.

"Can you think of one good reason for not going?" She tried to nudge him into talking. "It'll be fun, Joe. We'll go by boat to Moose Island. Lots of singing. . .great food. A really swell time."

His gaze shifted back to her. He pressed his lips together and fashioned a halfhearted smile. I wish I could do something to make that smile reach his mournful eyes, Kate thought.

"Sure. Let's give it a try."

Kate could see his fists relax. Her heart did a quick little flip-flop and she grinned so widely her eyes crinkled. It was kind of like she had a real date.

"I'm glad to see you gussied up for your first date with Joe," Louise said.

"I'm not gussied up."

"Sure. And you wear chiffon scarves in your hair all the time, too."

Kate's eyes widened at Louise's remark. Was she being entirely honest with herself? She ran a hand through her thick auburn hair, pulling off the long blue chiffon scarf. This wasn't a real date. Joe was married, for gosh sakes. What was she thinking?

"Would you like to borrow my bust binder?"

Kate turned sideways at Louise's remark. Her very noticeable and unfashionable breasts spoiled the popular lean, flat look.

"I'm afraid I'm beyond help."

"If you'd paid more attention to what you ate," Louise said, sinking on her bed and smoothing rayon stockings up her lean legs. "That diet I found in Vogue did the trick for me." She attached the stockings to garters embroidered with the same red of her dress.

"Don't forget I had to room with you while you starved yourself. It wasn't all that easy."

"Vogue says," Louise went on, ignoring Kate's remark, "men won't dance with women in whalebone and I intend to dance."

"Honestly, Louise, you read that magazine like it's the Bible."

"I like to know what's fashionable. Will you let me do your makeup?"

"It's just a picnic, not a fancy dress ball."

"If you don't get at least a dozen compliments tonight then I'll never ask again."

"Oh, all right." Kate sat on the edge of her bed and let Louise paint her face. "I've never worn so much lipstick," she said when Louise allowed her to look in the mirror.

"Oh, come on, Kate. You work in the dining room. It's how all the women are doing their faces."

Resigned, and slightly worried Joe might think she was trying to attract him, Kate picked up a comb and tried to force her heavy hair into lying in a smooth cap on her head.

Louise reached up to the top shelf of the closet and retrieved a simple blue cloche hat with a white bow. "Here," she said, "try this on." Kate sat the hat on her head.

"Like this," Louise said, tugging the hat tightly down on Kate's forehead.

"It's too tight."

"I keep telling you to get your hair thinned. You'll get used to it."

Kate, Louise and a young man were waiting for Joe when he drove up. Everyone was in a party mood. That Louise was a hot sketch, he thought. What was her date's name? Dan. Yeah, Joe had seen him in Finches.

"Swell car," Dan said, passing his hand over the leather upholstery.

A sizeable crowd had already gathered at the marina when Joe drove into the parking lot.

"What are you staring at?" Kate asked, as they walked toward the boat.

"You look very. . .attractive in blue," Joe stumbled. A vivid picture of a laughing Alice, her soft black hair caught in a big blue bow the summer he met her, flashed through his mind. I shouldn't be doing this, he thought, and shoved his hands into his pockets.

"Thank you," Kate said, suddenly shy. This is ridiculous, she thought. I've known this man for six months. And you've known for six months that he's very much married, she scolded herself. You can't let Louise's idea become real.

By the time the launch reached Moose Island, the yearning to be part of a carefree group of people their own age pushed the secret Kate and Joe shared to a distant corner of their minds. Joe jumped lightly onto the dock and turned to offer Kate his hand. It was easy to form a foursome with Louise and Dan, and they started with a game of horseshoes.

After a while, the good smells of sausages and hot dogs sputtering on the grill drew them to the line waiting to fill their plates. Dan took the cloche from Kate's head to mark a spot at the picnic table.

"Feels good to be rid of that," Kate said, running a hand through her hair.

"You have pretty hair," Joe said, finding himself wanting to touch it. He gripped his plate a little tighter. "I don't know why you'd want to cover it up." Kate's hair picked up the rays of the setting sun, giving it a warm glow.

Louise gave Kate a knowing little jab in the ribs and she felt her cheeks color. Dan never stopped shoveling in spoonsful of food while he questioned Joe about cars. Louise nudged Kate under the table. When she looked up, Louise rolled her eyes and mouthed, "He likes you."

Phil Madden slid on the seat next to Joe. "Hi, fellas," Phil said. "You look great, Kate," he remarked, leaning around Joe for a better look.

"Thanks," Kate mumbled. Louise caught her eye and smiled triumphantly.

Phil lowered his voice and spoke quietly to Dan and Joe. "Got a little hooch on the other side of the island."

"Yeah?" Dan's eyes lit up.

"Canadian Club."

"Wow, what'll it cost?"

"My contribution to the picnic." Phil waved his hand in dismissal.

"Swell," Dan said, turning to Louise. "Want to go for a walk? Phil, ahh. . .has something to quench our thirst on the other side."

"Sure!" Louise, Dan and Phil rose from the table and turned to wait for Joe and Kate.

"We'll go if you want," Joe said to Kate

"No. No thank you. I'd rather not," Kate said. "That's expensive stuff for a kid to have," she added after the group had walked off.

"He works with Dasset."

"Joe, Phil is still a schoolboy!"

"I know. He doesn't drive any of the booze cars. Just helps out."

"And that justifies it?"

"Don't get all huffy with me. I didn't hire him." Joe didn't like the fury he saw in her eyes. She stared at him silently for a few moments, then got up and flounced away, leaving him looking at the sway of her hips.

He watched her join another girl at the water's edge. Before long a man came and spoke to the girl and the two walked off hand in hand to join the dancing. Kate stood where they left her, looking out over the lake. From where he sat, Joe could see her run her hands up and down her arms.

She must be cold, he thought. He picked up her sweater and walked toward her.

"Thought you'd want your sweater," he said, as he approached her from behind. Kate started at the sound of his voice and swung around to face him. He had never before seen such anguish on her face.

"Look." He had rehearsed what he wanted to say. "I don't want to spoil this picnic and I do appreciate your concern. Honestly, Kate, I don't know what I'd do if I didn't have you to talk to."

"It's all right." She placed a hand on his arm. "I know things are difficult for you." She raised her eyes to meet his. She couldn't tear her eyes away from the pain, the confusion and something else. . .was it longing? Would he take her in his arms? Her heart leaped at the prospect. But in a moment a picture of Alice, dear, frail. . .and Joe's wife, came to mind to still her heart. Unconsciously she took a step back, her emotions as tangled as an unraveled scarf.

"My whole life has become nothing but one big lie." He handed her the sweater. "I'm constantly on guard about what I'm saying. You're the only person I can be myself with."

Kate busied herself putting on the sweater. "Some of that. . .deceit would go away if you'd stop working for Dasset."

"Kate, if I could come up with any other. . ." He hesitated.

"Is 'legal' the word you're looking for?"

"All right, yes. Any other legal way to pay all Alice's bills, I'd do it in a minute." They had begun to slowly walk the edge of the lake. The moon had risen, casting its white light on the still waters of the lake.

"You've never explained why Alice doesn't cure at the Ray Brook San. Since it's free, your job at the Club would see you through."

Joe sighed and shoved his hands in his pockets. He explained, as he had to Ursula months ago, Alice's irrational fear of any sanitorium.

"We all feel sorry for the life Alice is forced to live in Saranac Lake." They walked, shoulders touching. "But Alice has one very precious blessing in her husband. You've sacrificed a great deal. You're a very special man, Joe Devlin." And I hope Alice appreciates what her husband has gone through, she thought to herself, all the while wondering if there was one more Joe Devlin out there that she could claim.

"This is just the 'worse' part of 'for better or worse,'" Joe said, trying to lighten the mood. "The rest of our life will be not 'better' but 'best.'" Kate smiled up at him.

"Thanks for being my friend, Kate." He reached for her hand and they turned back to where the sound of singing rose with the campfire smoke. Kate's eyes widened at Joe's words. Yes, it was only right that Joe defined their relationship, but a small part of her, deep in her heart, hoped the door to something more wasn't locked.

Louise, back from the walk to the other side of the island, saw them coming and waved, indicating room for Kate and Joe to sit next to her and Dan. Joe speared marshmallows on a stick and hunkered down to toast them in the fire.

"I like them burnt on the outside," Kate said.

"Where've you two been?" Louise whispered. "Smooching?"

"No. Just talking."

"Sure. Tell it to Sweeney."

Joe stood before Kate with the stick of burnt marshmallows. Kate slipped one off and bit into it.

"Yum," she smiled, licking the sticky sweet off her fingers. "Just right." Joe ate the others in quick succession and went back to toast more.

"You'll bust my bust binder if you keep that up," Louise whispered. Kate chose not to listen.

Joe sat next to Kate with the next stick of marshmallows. She could feel his hard body pressing against hers. He took a marshmallow off the tip of the stick and offered it to her. Without thinking, she merely turned her head and bit into it. Joe jerked his hand away when her lips touched his fingers. She blushed and turned her head away.

"I thought you were going to bite my finger off," he said, attempting to make a joke. He couldn't believe the jolt that ran up his arm at the tantalizing touch of her soft lips.

Kate turned back and smiled, not quite daring to look him in the eye. Joe reached out and touched the corner of her mouth where a dab of the candy stuck. Kate was sure he could hear the pounding of her heart. She watched, mesmerized, as Joe licked the errant marshmallow off his finger.

Their eyes locked. But there was nothing they were allowed to say.

36

"This is the last time," Emily said. "No matter who is sitting in the driver's seat, we will carry on with our picnic. I felt ridiculous telling Winston we couldn't go last time because you didn't like the driver." The girls were waiting under the Club's porte cochere for the car Lucinda had ordered to take them to their picnic on the Ausable River.

"Joe will be driving," Lucinda assured her. "The concierge knows I simply wasn't interested in any other chauffeur."

"I think you went overboard with that outfit. Hardly something to choose for a picnic in the woods."

"Yes, well, you know full well that the setting has nothing to do with today's purpose." She played with a long rope of polished amethyst beads.

"Oh, yes," Emily said, "you're still waiting for our chauffeur to divulge his great tragedy." She laughed and rolled her eyes. "And dressed in lavender pongee will definitely help?"

"Most men like women to be feminine," Lucinda said. "I'm not comfortable, like you are, to be a hiking partner or sports buddy to the man in my life."

"Yes, but heeled pumps for the woods?" Emily raised her eyebrows and stared at Lucinda's purple pumps and lavender silk stockings.

"They complete the outfit," she said. "Honestly, Emily, you can be so exasperating."

Winston joined the girls just then. A tall young man, dressed in tweeds and an argyle vest. A short-billed cap covered his narrow forehead.

"I was able to locate a celebratory libation," he said, lifting the top of the picnic hamper he held in front of the girls. Winston had nestled a green wine bottle in with the fried chicken and potato salad. "I'll immerse it in the cold waters of the Ausable the moment we arrive at our destination."

"I think we're going to have a grand time," Emily said, linking her arm through his. "I've heard it's a lovely spot with nice walking trails into the woods." She wore knickers with matching cotton stockings covering her knees and stout walking shoes on her feet. Winston looked at her, his appreciation for her hiking outfit shining in his eyes. He smiled and squeezed her arm. Politely he turned his attention to Lucinda.

"Lucinda," he said, "you're looking lovely. Are you joining us for a picnic on the Ausable?"

"I wouldn't miss it. But I think I'll leave the hiking to you and Emily. I've heard the scenery is breathtaking and I'm hoping to capture it on my canvas." She indicated an easel, paint box and several small canvases stacked at the curb.

"Here's our car." Lucinda said, waving to the driver of a five-passenger Cadillac. Before Joe could turn off the engine and hop out, Lucinda opened the back door and began to stow her supplies. "Here, Winston," she said, "why not put the picnic hamper on the seat?" Winston did as asked.

"Oh, my," Lucinda said, standing back after all the picnic supplies were loaded, "there won't be room for three of us in the back seat. I'll sit in front," she volunteered, and quickly opened the passenger-side door and sat down.

"We could put all this in the trunk," Winston said.

"No, no. I couldn't risk spilling our lunch on my canvases."

"If I placed all that in the front seat," Joe intervened, understanding completely what Lucinda was up to, "I would make sure it traveled safely."

"My goodness, such a to-do. Everything is packed and I'm already settled right here. If the rest of you would get in, we could be on our way."

"Yes, Miss." Joe marveled at the way this girl maneuvered people. Her friends didn't appear to notice anything unusual. Or perhaps they were in on her scheming. And look at how she dressed for a picnic in the woods! He gripped the steering wheel and yanked the car away from the curb. This girl was trouble.

"What a perfect day for a picnic." Lucinda threw her head back and looked up at the sky. One golden arm hung gracefully over the door. "Do you enjoy getting out of the garage for a day?"

"Yes, Miss."

"Please call me Lucinda," She turned her head toward Joe, but he continued to stare at the road without a trace of emotion on his face. "After all, we will be picnicking all day."

Joe didn't respond.

"Do you like working at the Club?"

"It's a good job."

"What do you do when you're not working?"

Joe's eyes widened at the question. He couldn't say he went to see his tubercular wife. He couldn't say he worked on rum runners' cars. What did Club employees do when not working?

"We have passes for the movies in the Agora."

"Do you?" Lucinda sat up in her seat. "I'll have to look for you the next time I go."

"They don't let us sit with the guests." Joe saw where this was leading.

"I'm sure there's no restrictions about where a guest chooses to sit," Lucinda said. Joe hazarded a glance in her direction. She was looking straight ahead, smiling like a cat preparing to lap a bowl of cream. He clamped his mouth shut and turned back to the road.

"Is this the Ausable we're following?" Winston leaned forward to ask.

"Yes," Joe answered, relieved to be freed from Lucinda. "The east branch, to be exact. It's the same river that goes through Ausable Chasm. They say that's an awesome sight. I think you can even get a boat through part of the rapids."

"Let's plan to make that trip another day," Lucinda said.

Joe shook his head. Every time he opened his mouth this girl found another way to be with him. And he already knew what happened when he tried to avoid her. It still made his stomach churn when he thought about his confrontation with Madden. Since when did mechanics have to be escorts for bored young ladies?

He slowed the Cadillac and took a turn to the right. Allen had told him the road to the picnic site would be less than a mile from the turn. He found the narrow dirt road, barely more than a path, that threaded through the pines. He brought the big engine back to first gear and moved slowly over the bumpy roots of the white pines. Soon the trees gave way to a grassy clearing on the banks of the river.

Joe parked the car on the edge of the clearing and turned off the key. No one moved as the beauty and stillness of their surroundings encompassed them. Along the grassy clearing, majestic pines crowded the riverbank, overlooking the black water gliding silently by. Above the treetops, the splendid, symmetrical peak of Whiteface Mountain completed the landscape.

"This looks great!" Winston broke the spell. "Look, Emily, I can see a trail leading off into the woods on the other side of the river." Doors opened and banged shut.

"We could walk an hour out and an hour back. By then we'll be ready to do justice to this lunch." Winston enthusiastically took charge. "I can see some great possibilities for your canvases, Lucinda. Whiteface Mountain is a popular subject."

"Canvases? . . .Oh, yes, of course. Joe could you set my easel up over there?" She waved vaguely toward the river. Joe quickly picked up Lucinda's painting supplies, glad to have something to take him even a short distance away from her. How was he going to handle the two hours Winston planned to leave him alone with Lucinda? Emily and Winston carried the wine and bottles of Coca-Cola to the river's edge and immersed them in the water.

"Well, Emily and I are off. We'll be expecting the beginnings of a great landscape when we return," Winston said, taking Emily by the hand and striding toward the river. "Should I cut a walking stick for you?"

Joe couldn't hear the girl's response, but in moments he saw the couple sitting on the riverbank removing their shoes and stockings. He heard their laughter as they stepped into the water. Joe stood, captivated by their obvious enjoyment. He wished he could spend a day like this with Alice. Maybe at the falls he had discovered on his first run in the Cadillac. Splashing in the water, sitting in the sun.

And particularly away from the battle-ax for an entire day. Maybe Alice would let him kiss her.

Joe stopped and shut his eyes. Please, God, don't let my body betray my love for Alice. He found himself reciting this prayer regularly as pretty young women like Collette and this spoiled Club guest made advances. And Kate. Sure she didn't make any advances, but she was so. . .healthy, so easy to be with. Now he understood why all-girl or all-boy schools were so popular. They certainly encouraged the young people to keep their minds on the job at hand and not on what their bodies yearned for.

"Jo. . .oe." Lucinda's cloying voice brought him back to his situation. He'd have to keep his wits about him not to be caught in the sticky web this girl was so intent upon weaving. It could be as challenging as keeping alive in the trenches.

Walking as slowly as he thought he could get away with, he made his way to her outdoor studio. He was surprised to see Lucinda had actually placed a canvas on her easel and was attempting to set up her folding chair in front of it.

"I can't seem to make this work." She smiled up at Joe. He took the chair from her and in one quick movement latched it open and set it before her easel, wondering all the while if she knew the first thing about painting.

"How about getting us a couple of bottles of the soda Winston put in the river?" Joe nodded and walked away quickly. When he returned, Lucinda was on her chair and choosing brushes and paints.

"I think I'd like to paint that pointy mountain. Do you remember what Winston called it?"

"Yes, Miss." Joe handed her a soda, making sure their hands didn't touch. "That's Whiteface Mountain. Should make you a pretty picture to take back to the city. I'll leave you to your work and get busy with mine." Joe turned to go.

"Work? I thought you'd stay and we'd get to know one another."

Joe was ready for her this time. "My boss is pretty strict about us keeping busy when we're not actually driving." He smiled ruefully, pretending he'd much prefer to sit and keep her company. "I'm to give the car a good polishing while you and your friends enjoy your picnic." He walked quickly away before she could dream up some reason for him to stay. He smiled for the first time that day. It felt good to beat the little minx at her game.

He felt her eyes on his back but didn't look in her direction while he made a big to-do about taking rags and rubbing compound from the trunk. He took off his chauffeur's jacket and rolled up his sleeves and starting spreading the compound on the Cadillac. He'd polish the car twice if it meant staying away from Lucinda.

He kept his head down till he heard Winston and Emily splashing back across the river. They called out to Lucinda, who immediately began putting her brushes away.

Joe kept polishing away as the girls spread blankets on the grass and unpacked the food. Winston brought the cooled bottle of wine from the river. How he wished he and Alice could be part of a simple summer pleasure like a picnic by the river. They would, the moment Dr. Hayes gave permission.

He allowed himself the fantasy of putting Alice in Kate's place at the Club's picnic. But it was hard to place his wife in the outdoor setting. She couldn't have played horseshoes. She wasn't allowed to sing. And she never would have been allowed to stay out so late. Would it always be this way? Would they always have to view life from the sidelines instead of jumping right in, like Winston and Emily hiking across the river?

"Joe," Lucinda called. "Time to eat." Joe replaced the top on the tin of rubbing compound and joined the group. He had known it would be impossible to attempt to sit anywhere but close to Lucinda, so he didn't even try. He was rewarded by a big smile.

"Isn't it great Winston thought to bring wine?" Lucinda handed Joe a glass, making sure their fingers touched.

"Hmmm. It's quite good, too." Winston said. "I was reluctant to buy more than one bottle. Some of the stuff you get is pure vinegar."

Lucinda piled Joe's plate with chicken and potato salad. He kept his eyes down and ate steadily, hoping to stay out of the conversation.

"Where did you have to go for this?" Emily asked, taking another sip of her wine.

"Saranac Lake. Tom and I went to this place called Luke's to shoot some pool. They have a soda bar, and a big supply of booze. If you know how to ask."

"Could we go?" Lucinda asked.

"It's hardly a place to take ladies." Winston looked genuinely horrified at the thought. "It's a real dive."

"Goodness, I wouldn't want to go in. Emily and I could stay in the car and maybe they'd have a nice liqueur to finish our day with."

"You know, it might be fun," Emily said. "I've never been to Saranac Lake."

"You do know it's loaded with tuberculars?" Winston said. "I've seen people hold handkerchiefs over their noses while they drive through town."

"Don't be such a flat tire," Lucinda said. "I don't believe we could get sick just sitting in the car. Besides, you went."

"I think Lucinda's right." Emily said. "It's not like all those people are walking around coughing in your face. Don't the really sick ones just sit on porches all day?"

"All right. But you must promise to stay in the car."

"Of course!" Lucinda clapped her hands and Emily squeezed Winston's arm. Joe closed his eyes and sighed. He buttoned up his chauffeur's jacket and pulled the hat firmly on his head. He ached to speak his mind. To dump this spoiled rich girl and her friends back at the Club. To throw this uniform in Madden's face and. . .and then what? He longed to confide to Alice the growing list of contradictions that made up his life, but knew that was impossible.

Joe saw before him a picture of Hilda shaking a finger under his nose: "TB feeds less willingly on the cheerful." For a moment he envied Alice, who was free to admit what she was, to be accepted, have friends, someone to talk to.

Armand knew Joe's whole story. Well, almost. Not about killing a man. But Armand didn't invite confidences, he got a faraway look every time Joe brought up the strictures of TB.

Then there was Kate. She was so easy to talk to despite the fact that she grew angry when Joe talked about rum running. Her open, smiling face came to mind. Yes, he thought, maybe she'll be around to talk to tonight.

Joe let Winston tell him where to drive, pretending he didn't know the exact location of Luke's. The truth was, Joe handled most of the booze runs to Luke's, since he was in Saranac Lake so often to see Alice.

As he drove, Lucinda inched her way as close to him as possible. He wished he had thought to stack something between them. He turned his head away from her. Saranac Lake's sidewalks were full of people strolling after the afternoon rest period. They were pale and thin, yet he saw smiles and a camaraderie his life was lacking.

An expensively dressed brassy blonde walking between two men turned and watched Joe drive down the brick street. Her cupid bow's mouth was pursed in distress.

"Someone you know?" one of the blonde's companions asked.

"Yes, and not with his wife."

"Come now, Lilly. Since when are you against a little cousining?" The girl opened her mouth to argue, but apparently thought better of it.

"You're right. We're not supposed to worry. Doctor's orders."

37

Captain Broadfield stood in front of the map fastened to his office wall. Troop B's responsibilities covered a vast area abutting the Canadian border. Densely wooded mountains predominated, with a minimal tracery of twisting roads. He had seventy men out there; most were mounted on the black horses his Black Horse Brigade was famous for.

The map was stuck with dozens of flagged pins identifying the last known location of each two-man team. Today was the Captain's day to plan Troop B's itinerary for July.

So many factors to consider in computing the most advantageous equation. He couldn't expect the field patrols to average more than 20–25 miles a day. Add to that each trooper's two week annual leave and it became an impossible situation to have Troop B's territory adequately covered.

The ringing phone interrupted his contemplation.

He grabbed the phone and put the receiver to his ear. "Captain Broadfield."

"Yes, Captain. This is Constable Duprey from Saranac Lake."

"What can I do for you, Constable?"

"We have a man incarcerated here confessing to a string of breaking and enterings that have been plaguing me since the first of the year."

"Good work, Constable. Sounds like you have the matter well in hand. Troop B's mission is largely the running down of smugglers of intoxicants. Is your prisoner a runner?"

"Well, it's a long story."

Broadfield clamped his mouth shut to avoid saying something unprofessional. At this point he expected the local constable to state that they'd found a half pint on the prisoner's person when they picked him up. Dammit, his men were spread thin enough without getting involved with a village's petty thief.

"Tierney. . .that's the man's name, Earl Tierney. He's missing his right hand. I asked how it happened in an effort to get the man talking. I find you get these guys off guard by talking about themselves," the constable added, "and before you know it, they spill the whole story."

"And were you successful with Tierney?" Broadfield prompted him along.

"Like opening a valve," he responded, the pride in his voice coming across the wires. "Tierney starting talking, all right. A lot didn't make sense. But when I got to thinking about it later, it appeared too strange not to have some truth to it."

"Just what did Tierney say?" Broadfield urged. Would this man never get to the point?

"Tierney claims a trained wolf attacked him during a scuffle in the woods outside of Keene last winter when he tried to stop a man he's calling Joe Devlin from shooting his brother."

"And you believe his story?"

"I admit Tierney sounds demented, but no matter how many times I questioned him, he stuck to the same story. Seems the wrist the wolf chewed on got infected. That's how he lost his hand. He's also telling me this Joe Devlin has a wife curing at Conifer Cottage off Helen Hill. I checked the TB roster and sure enough there's an Alice Devlin registered at Conifer."

"And how is this connected with bootlegging?"

"Tierney claims that Devlin is mixed up with Dasset. I can't make sense of how he's come to that conclusion and maybe it's all just a vendetta against the man he believes killed his brother."

"Does your prisoner know how to find Devlin?" Broadfield sat down at his desk and began to make notes.

"Says he works at the Lake Placid Club garage. I'm sure Tierney is just biding his time to take his revenge on Devlin. Told me his brother. . .the man Devlin is alleged to have killed. . .wasn't right in the head ever since their father threw the kid down the stairs in a drunken rage. I guess the brother. . .think he called him Bruce. . .was little more than a baby at the time. Tierney had been looking out for his little brother ever since."

"Thanks for the tip, Constable. I have troopers scheduled to arrive in Placid tomorrow. I'll get them right on it."

"Glad to help you guys out. You're doing a great job, Captain. I can remember a few years back before Troop B came. People took their lives in their hands if they drove after dark. Those bootleggers don't give a shit who they run off the roads."

"Troop B has a fine group of men. Many are veterans of the war, you know."

"So I've read in the paper. Called them Broadfield's Boys."

Broadfield squared his shoulders. "Glad to know we're appreciated. I want to get right on this Joe Devlin lead. Thanks for passing it on."

"We've all got to work together."

Broadfield propped his elbows on the desktop and ran a finger down the arch of his nose. Schermerhorn and the rookie Dutton were due at the Lake Placid Zone Station tomorrow. He hesitated to use the telephone. He knew all the Malone operators and felt he could trust every one. However he wasn't at all confident about the Lake Placid operators. Couldn't tell which ones got paid by bootleggers. On the other hand, the mail would take at least two days and Schermerhorn could be on his next loop by then. He decided to risk placing a telephone call.

"Lake Placid 239," he said into the mouthpiece.

"National Hotel," a voice eventually crackled across the connection.

Schermerhorn had trouble making his knees bend to climb the porch to the National Hotel. Long day in the saddle. The fifteen mile climb from Keene was steep and he and Dutton stopped frequently to let their horses drink. The horses were settled in the livery and now a hot bath and meal were looking real good. He always looked forward to doing his route on Blizzard. But after an especially long day, he'd get to thinking that driving one of the troop's Fords might be better.

"Aren't you ever tempted to keep just one bottle aside?" Dutton asked. "Seems a shame to turn over all that top shelf stuff we took from those New Yorkers."

"It's thinking like that cost Cronk his job."

"Yeah, but just one quart of good Scotch?"

"Let's get this straight, Dutton." Schermerhorn turned and caught the rookie in the glare of his uncompromising gray eyes. "It's our job to stop bootleggers and confiscate the intoxicants."

"Message for you," the man behind the desk said, when Schermerhorn came to the desk for the keys to the rooms kept aside for the troopers.

Schermerhorn took the folded paper and turned aside from Dutton to read it.

"A girl in every port, eh?"

"Yeah," Schermerhorn went along with the misconception. He read the short message from his commander and slowly tore it into small pieces. Joe Devlin, he thought. Name sounds familiar. We'll go see Tom Madden tomorrow.

38

"Ahh, the schnapps," Hilda said, noticing the glasses Ursula had set on the kitchen table. "We need to talk?"

Ursula nodded. She filled two of her mother's lead crystal glasses.

"What is so terrible to take the smile from my sister's face?" Hilda eased her big body onto the kitchen chair.

"It's Alice." Ursula looked down at her fingers splayed on the scrubbed table.

"Ja. Tomorrow is the picnic." Hilda removed her glasses and pinched her large nose. "We will a nice basket pack."

"I've heard Alice talking to Lilly about. . .about *geschlecht-sverkehr*." Ursula's face turned pink. "Tomorrow. With Joe, of course."

"Has Dr. Hayes given the permission?" Hilda sipped from her glass, then swirled the delicate stem in her fingers.

"I don't know." Ursula wrung her hands. "Alice isn't like Lilly. She doesn't talk freely about such things."

"Ja. But you must instruct Alice to talk to the doctor."

"Have you decided what to wear?" Lilly asked when she came into Alice's room and plopped in the chair.

Alice pulled a striped two-piece sports frock from the closet and held it up in front of her.

"I like it," Lilly said. "That bois de rose color looks great on you. How are you doing with the other decision?"

"Not so good," Alice said, sinking on the bed and curling a leg under her. "Ursula must have heard us talking. She said I must get permission from Dr. Hayes if I want to. . ."

"Let me guess. . .you got Ursula's *geschlechtsverkehr* talk? Is it so hard to say 'make love with your husband for the first time in going on a year'?"

Alice blushed. "I'm not going to ask for that permission from Dr. Hayes."

"Atta girl."

"But I do wish I knew the right thing to do."

"It's perfectly legal, you know."

"Yes, but is it the perfectly healthy thing to do. . .for Joe and me. Maybe it would be too exciting for me."

"I should hope so!"

Alice blushed again. "That's well and good for you to say. Remember I only have one working lung."

"My advice is let the day play out on its own. You and Joe will know when the timing is right."

"So," Allen said, sidling up to Joe as the mechanics put their tools away for the night. "You got something big planned for your day off?"

"Not really."

"That's a lot of bunk. I've known you for months now and it's the first time I've heard you whistling on the job."

"Yeah, well, you're wrong." Joe never stopped to think anyone in the garage cared enough to notice his moods. But how could he tell Allen about Alice? Can't talk about tuberculars around the Club, much less discuss picnicking plans with a tubercular wife.

"Don't get testy."

The next morning, Joe placed the red rose he snitched from the dining room in the Cadillac's silver dashboard vase.

Champagne, towels, a blanket, Joe went over his list. Next to pick up his wife and the picnic lunch Ursula insisted on and off to Hulls Falls. Maybe they'd stop at the Inn in Keene on the way home for a little dancing. Maybe even stop in to see Jean-Paul and Marie.

He'd have to be careful not to let Alice overdo. But, geeze, an entire day alone with his wife without Hilda putting the kibosh on everything they did.

There had been times Joe was allowed to take Alice off for the morning. Kate had invited them to join her at the farm her father managed for the Club and the three of them had a swell time walking in the sweet-smelling pastures at the foot of the purple mountains. The girls picked buttercups and Indian paintbrushes.

It made Joe happy to see what good friends Alice and Kate had become. He knew Alice was close to her porchmates, but he suspected they mostly talked about their sickness. With Kate, Alice seldom brought up her disease and instead talked of going home. And because Alice had grown up in the city, she delighted in learning about farm life. But he always had to return Alice to Conifer in time for the afternoon quiet time.

No time restraints today. Joe eased the Cadillac down Helen Hill and paraded along Main Street with Alice by his side. Today they would be like any other carefree couple out to enjoy the summer day.

"It's like going on a date," Alice said.

"A very special date," Joe agreed. "But you must promise to tell me if you begin to get tired."

"No, Joe. Today I want to feel like we're a normal couple. No TB talk."

Joe supposed it was good for Alice to be so positive, but he would do his best to make sure his wife didn't overdo. He drove the big car sedately, its polished pea green finish gleaming in the cloudless day.

"This is where Kate and her father picked me up when I walked up last winter," Joe said, when they reached the Plains of Abraham plateau. "I had just snowshoed from the village at the bottom of this mountain pass."

"Whenever I feel sorry for myself, everyone at Conifer reminds me of what you went through to get to me."

"We'll lick this thing, Alice."

Joe slowed at the foot of the hill in Keene and turned right onto Hull Falls Road. Yesterday he had let some air out of the Cadillac's tires so the ride on this back road would be more comfortable for Alice. And he'd like to get through today without a blowout.

"When I first came I couldn't stand all this quiet after a lifetime in New York." Alice looked at the sun poking through the rich green of the trees as they drove along. "I've been thinking, Joe. Would you consider staying here after I'm free to leave Conifer? It'd be a wonderful place to raise a family and you already have a great job. Certainly you're making more than you ever did in New York."

"I've never thought about it. We always talked of going back to the city," Joe said. Alice doesn't realize, he thought, that most of what I make comes from booze runs. I'd have to quit that and all the extras it brings if we were to start a family.

"We're here." Joe eased the car back to first gear and pulled off the side of the road. He cut the engine.

"I can hear the falls," Alice said, and was out of the car before Joe could help. "It can't be far."

It pleased Joe to no end to hear the lilt in Alice's voice. He stooped to pick up the picnic hamper and car robe from the back seat.

"Hurry, Joe. I want to see everything."

They took off their shoes and socks, wriggling their toes in the warm brown pine needles that carpeted the forest floor. Joe took her hand and together they wove their way around the trunks of the ancient pines as they made their way toward the sound of the river.

He wanted to see her face when she first glimpsed this special, private place. Coming to a ledge overlooking the river, they stood for long moments, staring down at the sun-bright water sliding across smooth river rocks and foaming as it crashed over the falls.

"It's beautiful, Joe. So full of life."

Joe had forgotten how steep the bank was. But even as he wondered if he should be carrying Alice down, she took the first tentative step over the edge. Joe set down the picnic hamper and helped her down the steep bank and out on the table-top boulder he had discovered on his first trip to the falls.

He noticed the river was calmer than on his first visit, but the rush of the falls was still too noisy for Alice to try to be heard. They sat hand in hand on the flat rock, content to let the power and beauty of the summer day wash over them.

After a bit Joe stood and stripped down to his undershorts and slid into the quiet black pool at the rock's edge.

"Uhh! Cold!" Hugging his arms to his bare chest, he danced in the waist-high water.

Alice smiled at her husband and folded his clothes in a neat pile, watching him sink below the surface then explode upward, sending spray over her.

"Oh, Alice," Joe said, when he saw her tug her blouse over her head, "It's awfully cold." Alice stood and slipped out of her skirt. Dressed in just a short chemise, she sat on the edge and dipped her toes in the water, only to jerk them back.

"I told you it was cold."

Alice put her feet back in more slowly. Soon she held her arms out to Joe.

"Are you sure?"

She nodded vigorously. He helped ease her into the water, holding on after her feet touched the sandy bottom, afraid the current might be too strong.

Her mouth opened wide at the cold. Joe thought he heard her magical laugh mixing with roar of the falls. They danced and played like children. When he saw goosebumps rising on her arms and her lips losing their rosy color, he lifted her out of the river.

He carried her up the steep incline to where they had left the picnic hamper under the white pines. Alice shivered and sat on the blanket he spread over the pine needles.

"We shouldn't have stayed in the water so long," Joe said. He sat beside Alice and began rubbing her with a towel.

"It was what I wanted to do. And don't you say a word about what I'm not allowed to do."

"Well I want to take off this wet chemise before you catch cold." Alice lifted her arms and Joe tugged the wet clothes over her damp curls.

Soon they were both undressed. How did this happen? Joe thought, amazed. His hands dropped to his sides. The sight before him was both endearingly familiar and yet strangely new in its forest green setting.

Alice looked frankly at him with those wonderful round blue eyes. Slowly she reached out a hand and touched his mouth. Joe watched her lips part and a smile grow, reaching all the way to her eyes.

"Alice," he said, laying her gently back on the blanket. Slowly he touched and stroked, remembering what pleased her and eager to give that pleasure so long denied.

His fingers touched the small pneumo scars along her chest. "My poor, brave Alice," he said.

"Not today, Joe." Alice took his hands and moved them to cover her small breasts.

So many nights alone in the bed with the broken spring over the garage he had wondered if this would ever happen again.

Dear, sweet Alice. She joined in with enthusiasm that matched his. At first the restrictions of the past year made them hesitate to kiss but soon their young bodies demanded more. Joe kissed her lips a dozen times and then the little hollow in her throat that always made her gasp in pleasure. He pulled back to look in her shining blue eyes and his heart filled with joy at the love and happiness he saw reflected there. Today they would not deny themselves. They yielded to the aura of the river's freedom and joined to the music of the falls.

They slept in one another's arms till the afternoon sun sifting through the pine branches woke Joe. Dressing quickly, Alice set out the food Ursula had packed and Joe retrieved the bottle of champagne he had left in the river.

"What a marvelous place," Alice said. "It's so nice to be. . .alive again."

"I hope you didn't get too cold. Say, how would you feel about stopping to visit Jean-Paul? I'd like them to meet you."

"And leave this place? Joe, I'm serious about considering not returning to New York and staying up here. I've learned to appreciate what the air can do for me." Alice moved closer to Joe and snuggled against his chest.

"When I first got off the train and was carried into Conifer Cottage I thought of Saranac Lake as a bitter medicine I had to take every hour of the day if I were to be free of this disease." Alice sifted pine needles through her fingers. "But now I've come to understand how good the air is for me. And it's comforting here, close to people who understand."

"That's a pretty big speech," Joe said. "You've been giving this a lot of thought."

"It's been important to picture what life could be when I leave Conifer." She pulled away from Joe and began to pick up the leftover food. "Something to aim for. Those times we've spent with Kate on the farm. . .it's a wonderful, simple life. Especially if we can have friends like Kate."

"A lot of the peacefulness is due to the rules about never bringing up anything unpleasant," Joe said.

"I know that. 'TB feeds less willingly on the cheerful.'" She held the champagne bottle up against the setting sun. "Enough for a few more sips."

Joe held out the glasses "But," he said, as Alice emptied the bottle into the glasses, "in a life away from Conifer problems have to be talked about."

"Everyone I've seen appears to carry out their lives at a more reasonable pace. I'm sure there will be problems," she sipped the champagne, "but the tranquility of these mountains would make them easier to solve."

After a bit she added, "Maybe we could save up and you could open a garage of your own someday."

"I'd like that." Joe thought the most heartening part of this whole talk was Alice talking so enthusiastically about the future instead of complaining about her disease. Staying in the Adirondacks would have its merits.

"We'll talk about it again," Joe said. He drained his glass and placed it in the picnic hamper. "But for now. . .how about the visit to Jean-Paul? He lives in the woods next to a brook."

Joe drove the Cadillac cautiously down the narrow path to Jean-Paul's cabin. Pine branches swiped at the car. He tried not to think of the scratches on its finish.

"That's a mighty grand car, *mon ami*," Jean-Paul greeted him. "Business is good?"

The two couples settled on the porch sharing the last bottle of champagne. After awhile Marie asked them to stay for supper and Joe quickly agreed, remembering the simple, savory meals she prepared.

"Please let me help," Alice said, rising when Marie did. "It's been so long since I've worked in a kitchen."

Marie smiled and reached for Alice's hand. "I would enjoy the company of a woman."

"I hear that our friend who stole your coat has been picked up by the Saranac Lake police," the trapper said after Alice and Marie went inside.

"Earl? What did that weasel do now?"

"They got him for stealing from the supply stores and selling it to the woodsmen. I told you about it last time you were here."

"Well, at least I don't have to be looking over my shoulder for him any more."

"So, with a car like that you must be making profitable runs."

"You bet. Sure is nice to pay Alice's bills and buy her nice things. Alice doesn't know I make booze runs."

"She'll not hear it from me."

39

"Yeah," Tom Madden growled, at the knock on his office door. The door opened and two broad-shouldered troopers filled the little office.

"Mr. Madden?" the Sergeant asked.

"Yes." Madden stood and looked up at the troopers. Then his eyes were drawn down to their gun belts with the regulation Colts strapped in their cases.

"You have a Joe Devlin in your employ?"

"He's a mechanic."

"We'd like to talk to him."

"He's in the shop." Madden moved toward the door. "I'll bring him in."

"Perhaps you'd just tell him we'd like to talk to him." With a slight movement, Schermerhorn blocked Madden's passage. "We'll take him outside and ask him a few questions."

"Anyway you want it."

The troopers backed out of the office, settled their Stetsons on their heads, and allowed Madden to lead the way.

"Devlin!" Madden stepped into the garage and shouted. "The law wants a word with you."

Joe's breakfast rose in his throat and took away his ability to speak. Slowly he stood up from where he was working under the hood of a car. He looked at Madden and the two troopers towering behind him. He had never seen Madden's smile look so genuine. Everyone stopped working and turned their full attention to Joe. He slammed the hood and it echoed in the silent garage.

When he thought he could trust his legs to carry him, he walked toward the troopers. They know, he thought. Somehow they found out I make booze runs. He couldn't bring himself to look them in the eye, so he busied himself with continually wiping his hands on a rag.

Or Earl had told them about Bruce.

"Joe Devlin?" the Sergeant queried as Joe approached. Joe nodded.

"We'd like to ask you a few questions." Joe nodded. He thought the trooper looked familiar. Then again, they all looked the same under the Stetsons.

Madden stood in the garage door and watched the troopers lead Joe to where the black horses were tied to a tree. Madden took a clipboard and walked quickly in the opposite direction, circling the garage until he came to a group of cars waiting for service, just out of sight of Joe and the troopers. Head down, walking among the cars, pretending to make notes on his clipboard, Madden heard the Sergeant question Joe:

"How long have you been working here?"

"Since just before Christmas."

"Where are you from?"

"New York." Joe kept his hands behind his back, kneading the oily rag.

"What would make a mechanic leave the city?"

"My wife's taking the cure in Saranac Lake."

"Now I know where we've met. You came through my roadblock at Bloomingdale last winter. How's you're wife doing?"

"Better, thanks." Joe shifted his eyes up to face the trooper. "We're hoping to be back in New York by Christmas."

"Seems to me you were driving a Chevy truck, last we met."

"Yes, sir. Belongs to my uncle."

"You have relatives up here?" the Sergeant shot the question. "Yours or your wife's?"

"Uh. . .mine. Charlie Rauch."

"That'd be the blacksmith? Runs a little livery?"

"Yes, sir."

"Ever hear of a man named Earl Tierney?"

Madden didn't know what the troopers were looking for, but even this far away from them, he could see Joe's discomfort with that last question. But the troopers had just supplied him with what he'd been seeking: Devlin had a wife taking the cure in Saranac Lake. He quit the pretense of making notations on his clipboard and started back to his office. He now had the necessary ammunition to fire Devlin. The Club's fathers would back him a hundred percent.

"Mr. Dewey," he barked eagerly into the mouthpiece. His sausage fingers thrummed the desktop while he waited for the Lake Placid Club's telephone operator to complete the connection.

"Tom Madden here, sir. I just learned several disturbing facts about one of my mechanics." He explained Joe's transgressions, then took the earpiece away from his ear at Dewey's explosive remark. "Yes, sir, that's what I thought. Just wanted to be sure I did the right thing. He'll be out of here within an hour."

"May I help you?" asked Ursula.

"Yes, Ma'am." Schermerhorn removed his Stetson and rubbed the brim with his thumb. "I understand a Mrs. Joe Devlin is curing here?"

"Alice has been with us since November." Ursula's hand fluttered to her neck. "There couldn't be a problem with Alice."

"No, Ma'am. No problem. Just looking to ask her a couple of questions about her husband."

"Joe? That nice young man? Do you know he walked from New York City to be with his wife?"

"His devotion to his wife is commendable. But there are a few questions my commander needs the answers to and I'm sure his wife could supply them."

"Ursula? Do you a problem have?" Hilda moved past her sister and stepped onto the porch, locking eyes with Schermerhorn. It unnerved him to be standing at eye level with a woman.

"This trooper wishes to speak to our Alice. Something about Joe."

"What kind of questions?" Hilda folded her muscular arms. "We can't allow our girls to become upset."

Schermerhorn shifted his weight to one foot, and found himself slightly shorter than the large German woman who smelled like carbolic solution. He pulled himself up to his full six feet.

"I won't need more than five minutes of her time."

"Five minutes with you, Herr Trooper, could mean five weeks of setbacks. We go to great lengths to keep our girls protected from all unpleasantness. TB feeds less willingly on the cheerful than the gloomy."

"Perhaps you would be willing to tell me what I need to know. So we don't risk upsetting Mrs. Devlin."

"Perhaps." Hilda folded her arms, but didn't release the trooper from her uncompromising stare.

"What's the average weekly cost of Mrs. Devlin's cure?"

Hilda and Ursula exchanged glances.

"Now that she is no longer a tray patient, basic cost is fifteen dollars a month. Plus the doctor's visit at five dollars. Cure chair rental is two dollars."

"Would twenty-five dollars be a reasonable amount?"

Both women nodded.

"And who is responsible for Mrs. Devlin's expenses?"

"Why, Mr. Devlin, of course."

"Don't you find that interesting with Mr. Devlin bringing in nine-fifteen a week from his job at the Club?"

"We never gave it much thought," Ursula said. "We certainly never came out and asked him how much he earned."

"In the beginning behind he got with costs," Hilda said.

"But lately he's always on time, isn't he, sister?" Ursula said. "Takes Alice to dinner and buys her nice things."

"Do you know the sources of this extra income?"

The sisters shook their heads.

"What are you suggesting?" Hilda asked.

"Not really sure. There's been some talk to indicate Mr. Devlin is involved with a bootlegging gang."

"I doubt your sources are reliable, Mr. Trooper."

"Well, thank you, Ma'am. You've been most helpful." He set the Stetson back on his head and took a minute to adjust it. He had hoped to talk privately with Devlin's wife. The unspoken innuendos from such a interview usually told him volumes more than words.

But, come to think of it, this town went to such extremes to keep their patients from worrying, maybe Devlin keeps his rum running to himself. *If I read those German hausfraus right, they sure don't know anything about it. They almost have Devlin sainted.*

And as far as the alleged murder went, he and Dutton had looked all around the lean-to for the remains of a body. Although Joe could have been in the area at the time of the murder, nothing could be done about that without a body.

He'd stop by Rauch's Livery next.

40

"When will I learn?" Dr. Hayes chastised himself after examining Alice.

Ursula had summoned him to Conifer Cottage. The morning after her outing with Joe, Alice woke with a fever and breathlessly complained her throat was blocked.

"I should not have granted permission for Alice to go off for the day with her husband." He stood in vestibule, commiserating with Ursula. "She obviously overdid and got a chill. I suspect she even took a dip in that cold river. I fish that part of the Ausable with Charlie Decker. Cold as. . .well, quite cold.

"I vowed after I lost a young girl last winter that I would be very sure a patient was well enough to take on more physical activity before I permitted it." Dr. Hayes told Ursula about the girl who had died. Only sixteen. She couldn't wait to show him the new dress and shoes her parents sent. Begged him to let her walk down Main Street in them. She'd probably be alive today if he'd refused.

"It's damn hard to see these young people. . .barely more than children. . .denied the simple pleasures healthy youngsters take for granted!"

"It's hardly your fault that Alice is having another setback," Ursula said. "I wouldn't be surprised if she even had. . .*geschlechtsverkehr* with her husband."

"She what?"

Ursula's pale face turned a splotchy red from her neck to the roots of her colorless hair. "Had. . .relations. . .with her husband."

"Much too much excitement." Dr. Hayes pressed his lips to a thin line and shook his head. "The most difficult part of my job is seeing the hundreds of young people placed in my care spending their youth on a porch." He paused, his shoulders slumping, before continuing. "They beg with their eyes until they're strong enough to plead with words to be allowed to spend a few hours pretending they're normal."

"You mustn't be so hard on yourself," Ursula said. "We all know it's important to keep them happy."

"We walk a fine line, Miss Guenther. A very fine line." He stood a little straighter and squared his shoulders. "Alice has a reasonable chance if I do a thoracoplasty. I have told her to prepare to leave for the hospital."

"She must be terribly upset." Ursula turned to leave. "I'll go to her right away."

"I suspect she'll be all right for a time. Lilly was with her when I left."

"Then come with me to the kitchen," Ursula said. "You could use a cup of coffee."

"No time to linger, I'm afraid. There's a young woman at Ledger Cottage on Academy Street waiting to see me. She's hoping I'll grant exercise permission today. . .the first time she'll be allowed off the porch since she came here. She was shipped from New York on a cot in the baggage car when she was sixteen. That was ten years ago."

"Someday there will be a medicine, a cure for tuberculosis."

"Not in time for the thousands already here. So, enough of what we can't do. I'll schedule Alice at Saranac General. Can I leave it to you to contact her husband?"

"Certainly."

"This is turning into a terrible mess," Ursula said to her sister as they settled on their favorite corner of the porch. "We need to inform Joe about the thoracoplasty. When I placed the call, the man who answered the telephone told me Joe has been fired."

"Nein. . .someone is a joke playing." Hilda, eyes closed, glasses clutched in her hand, was stretched out on a cure chair. "Sister, the police will fine you for the noise that rocker is making. This is rest period, not exercise time."

"I asked the man's name." Ursula stopped her agitated rocking. "He said he was Tom Madden, the garage foreman. He doesn't sound like the kind of man inclined to joke. I'm worried the trooper was right." Ursula leaned forward in the straight-backed rocker and lowered her voice. "Perhaps they found Joe out to be a bootlegger. The Lake Placid Club is so strict about drinking, they would have fired him. What should we do? Alice is frightened. She wants Joe to be here when she goes to the hospital."

"We will have to be her family, sister. Like we are for the other girls."

"We can't have Alice worrying about Joe on top of the operation. Remember what a bad setback she had last winter when she couldn't find him?"

The screen door slapped and Lilly marched across the porch, stopping before Ursula and Hilda, hands on hips.

"Lilly," Hilda's deep voice attempted a whisper. "You must obey the rest period."

"Where is Alice's saintly husband?" Lilly hissed. "Alice is up there all alone scared stiff. He should be with her."

"We don't know where Joe is," Ursula said. "We can't seem to reach him."

"Have you tried his girlfriend?"

"Lilly, you go too far. Please lower your voice."

"Your saintly Joe has a healthy—complete with dimples and freckles—female friend who probably knows where he is." Lilly told Ursula what she knew about Kate and where she might be found.

In the stillness of the mandatory rest period, Alice sat up in bed, filling page after page in her writing tablet. She was well aware that writing was strictly forbidden in her condition, but she wanted to send a letter to her sister before the operation.

Lilly had told Alice about a bunch of people she knew who had the operation. She had to admit they were all up patients. Cheerful. At least the ones Lilly chose to tell her about. Was there an equal number who didn't make it?

This wasn't going to be like the bedside pneumo treatments. She would have the operation in the hospital. Lilly also said it was done without being put to sleep, just a local. Did that mean she would hear everything going on? Dr. Hayes said they would remove three ribs on the left side. She would have to lie flat with sandbags on her chest for some time.

She hated the way no one will ever say how long you'll be ill. Everyone was talented in ways to talk around problems. Just be patient, they'd say.

Dr. Hayes did say that her left lung would stay collapsed forever. She would never be able to exert herself. Could she play with her children? Could she even have children? Would she be permanently deformed like the girl she and Lilly came across on one of their walks. No. Lilly said she had six ribs removed. Dr. Hayes is taking just three.

To her sister Nancy she wrote about the wonderful day at the falls and meeting the French Canadian trapper and his trained wolf. Then, hoping Nancy might show the letter to her mother who might, in turn, tell her father, Alice bragged about how well Joe was doing. Making money to buy nice things and putting some aside for the future.

"The climate is good for me," she wrote, "and Joe is doing so well that we've been talking about staying here to raise our family after I'm cured. But I've had another setback and the Doctor wants to perform an operation called a thoracoplasty." Maybe her mother might worry enough to come see her. Well, no. Father would never allow that. But maybe her mother would write or call. Ursula was nice and Lilly was like a sister. But she wanted her mother.

41

A rapid knocking at the door caught Tom Madden by surprise.

"Come in," he barked. The door whooshed open and Mr. Bingham, clearly agitated, stood before him.

"I understand you fired Joe Devlin."

"Yes."

"Would you care to justify firing the most capable mechanic the Club has ever seen?"

"Can't deny Devlin's ability," Madden groveled. "But Club rules. . ." He leaned forward to speak confidentially. "We learned his wife is a lun. . .has TB. Curing in Saranac Lake."

"I know all about Joe's wife."

"Well." Madden leaned back in his chair, throwing his arms out, palms up. "You see, Mr. Bingham, the Club has a strict policy about tuberculars."

"Don't quote Dewey's bunk to me. Joe works in the garage. . .hardly a place to endanger guests."

"But that wasn't all," Madden continued. "Troopers came by to question Joe about being involved with a rum running gang."

Bingham laughed unkindly. "You self-righteous. . .you and I. . .half the country deals with illegal intoxicants."

"Yes, but the Club rules about drinking. . ."

"I've had enough." He banged his fist on the desk. "I've a good mind to let Dewey know about your connections with rum running."

"Don't be hasty, Mr. Bingham." Madden leaned forward again and lowered his voice "By the way, were the goods we sent by train just before Christmas satisfactory? I found the money, just like you said I would," Madden emphasized, "in the lining of your coon coat."

Bingham stared, his jaws working, eyes smoldering. "You're out of your league here, Madden. I will drop the matter. But you and I will never do business again." He glared at Madden till the foreman broke the stare.

"Unfortunately I'm still forced to deal with you regarding my car. I drove my Pierce-Arrow up from New York yesterday expecting to find Joe to service it. Is there a mechanic in the Club's employ I can trust?"

"I'll put Allen right on it. He's the best." Madden stood and walked out of the office. With Bingham on his heels, he instructed Allen to take a look at the Pierce-Arrow.

Bingham hovered near Allen while he raised the hood. The young mechanic whistled softly.

"You'd better look at this, sir."

"I know where Joe is," Allen said, when he and Mr. Bingham had their heads under the hood. "He's staying with Rauch, the black-smith."

"Where?"

"Down by the train station. Big sign for his livery stable. You won't miss it. I know he wants to return your coat, sir."

"Thank you, young man," Mr. Bingham said loudly enough for all to hear. He stood up and pulled out a money clip. "I think my car is in good hands." He peeled off a few bills and handed them to Allen. Lowering his voice again he said, "As soon as you take care of the car I'll drive down to see him."

The yellow Pierce-Arrow slowed after passing the train station, its powerful engine rumbling softly. Bingham turned in the drive for Rauch's Livery and cut the engine.

"Hello," he said to the woman who came to the porch door. "I'm looking for Joe Devlin."

"I'll fetch him for you," she said. "Please sit. I'm partial to the lat-tice-back rocker, myself."

"Joe! Come out from under that car."

Joe pushed himself free of his Cadillac and stood up. He pulled a rag from his back pocket and wiped his hands. "I guess you heard, huh?" Joe asked, seeing the scowl on Armand's face.

"I heard that someone in a pea green Cadillac ran the troopers off the road near Chazy after they signaled the car to stop."

"I wasn't about to stop. I was carrying the four hundred and eight quarts you wanted at Luke's."

"I didn't give you that run," Armand barked at Joe. "I knew it would be risky."

"I have the fastest car."

"Why would you take a risk like that run? Want to guess how many pea green Cadillacs are roaming these mountains after midnight? And how many are riddled with bullet holes?"

"None I know of," Joe said, wiping the hood and left fender of his car. "Bet you can't tell where it took the bullets."

"What's come over you, Joe? You're inviting trouble with the law."

Geeze, Joe thought during Armand's tirade, the record's stuck on the same lecture Kate gave me this morning. You'd think I was some kid.

"I promised you I'd keep your activities low key. . .behind the scene." Joe brought his attention back to what Armand was saying. "Because you didn't want to risk your job at the Club."

"Well, I don't have a job to worry about anymore."

"I never should have let Charlie pressure me into allowing you to shoot that first load. It's changed you somehow. Got in your blood."

"Alice's cure costs. . ."

"They'll be hard to meet when you're in jail. . .after you pay the fine."

"Look," Joe said, losing his temper. "Leave me alone. I can make my own decisions. If you had taken some interest in what seventeen-year-old Phil was up to, maybe he wouldn't be sitting in the Plattsburgh jail on a $2,000 bond for transporting. And you won't even bail him out because it'll point a finger at you."

Armand's arm shot out and grabbed the neck of Joe's shirt.

"Go ahead," Joe said, his hands clenching into fists at his side. "New York City was a swell place to learn all about fistfights."

"Excuse me." Maisie Rauch's timid voice broke the tense silence. "There's a man to see Joe. He's waiting on the porch."

Armand's hand fell to his side and he turned to face Charlie's wife. "Troopers?"

"Goodness, no. No one from these parts. A gentleman driving a yellow Pierce-Arrow."

"Sounds like Mr. Bingham got here," Joe said. He started for the stairs.

"We'll finish this later, Joe," Armand said to Joe's back.

"Mr. Bingham!" Joe ran up the porch steps and shook the man's hand. "Good to see you and the Pierce-Arrow."

"Heard Madden fired you," Bingham said. The two men settled onto wooden rockers. "I want to know two things: how's the wife and do you have work?"

"Good news on both counts. Alice is doing well. I was able to get her away from the cure cottage for a whole day. Had a swell picnic by a falls in Keene that I discovered while on my new job. I'm working for a booze runner. Keeping the cars on the road and shooting some loads."

"Madden hinted you were tied up with a rum runner," Bingham said. "I must say I never expected it of you, Joe."

"Alice's expenses. . ."

"Don't apologize," Mr. Bingham smiled. "It's just a different Joe Devlin than the one I loaned my coat to in New York last November."

"Oh, yes. I'll get your coat." Joe stood up and the wooden rocker bobbed noisily. "Your coat and I have had some adventures. I want to tell you up front that the lining has some stains and the bottom of the lining somehow got ripped and I haven't been able to mend it very well."

Mr. Bingham chuckled. "If I had known you were going to. . .change professions, you wouldn't have a ripped lining to deal with." Bingham went on to explain that his poker group had placed a booze order with Madden and hidden the money in the lining of the coon coat. "You delivered right to Madden's door for us. But that's the last business I do with him."

"This coat saved me from freezing to death several times." He handed the coat to Mr. Bingham and recounted the story of his trip from when the open Ford roadster went off the road to when he killed Bruce.

"I've worried about explaining the bloodstains to you ever since," he concluded.

"It was clearly self-defense. You have changed, Joe. Oh, don't go looking so culpable. I think it is a change for the good. You've matured. Toughened up."

"You're the first one I've met today that can see good in the way I've had to become." Both men turned their heads at the sound of a car turning into the yard.

"Before we get interrupted here, for the record, you've proven you have what it takes to be a survivor. That's not bad."

Joe was surprised to see Allen sprinting across the yard and up the porch steps. Seeing Mr. Bingham, Allen snatched off his cap.

"Hello, sir. How's the Pierce-Arrow?"

"Top shape, young man."

"Excuse me. I have a message for Joe." Allen and Joe moved a short distance away. "It's about your wife. Geeze, Joe, I never knew you were married."

"Allen, what is it."

"Kate came to the garage to tell me your wife needs an operation. I guess she's pretty upset about it. Kate wanted me to come find you right away."

Joe raced down the steps, then remembered he'd left Bingham on the porch. "I've got to go," he called. "I'll explain to both of you later." Damn, he thought, berating himself for forgetting to tell Hilda where he could be found after Madden got him fired. He had planned to give her Rauch's telephone number when he went to see Alice in a day or two.

Joe hit the open stretch on the road to Saranac Lake and pushed the Caddy to its limits. Empty, it hit sixty easy. Alice was doing so well at the falls. Laughing her silvery laugh, making plans for the future. He shouldn't have let her go in the cold water, he thought, punching the steering wheel with his fist.

Maybe they shouldn't have made love. She seemed to like it as much as he did. As he approached the Ray Brook Sanatorium, he noted a car about to pull out in front of him.

Joe slammed on the horn. Too late he realized he had almost forced another Troop B Ford off the road. Sure enough, the Ford pulled out behind him and furiously flashed its lights. Easy to out-run them, Joe thought. But Kate's angry, disapproving face appeared before him, followed by Armand's rage. He took his foot off the throttle and stepped on the brakes, easing the car back. He pulled off the road just before the railroad tracks.

Troopers got out both doors, adjusted their Stetsons and strolled toward the Caddy. Joe took a deep steadying breath and went to meet them. Knowing his car wasn't carrying booze, he hoped they'd search it. On the other hand, he didn't want to waste time getting to Alice.

Geeze! It was the same two who had questioned him at the Club just before he was fired.

"Joe Devlin, isn't it?" Sgt. Schermerhorn asked.

Joe nodded and watched the other trooper move to the front of his car, running his hand slowly over the hood and left fender.

Right where I took the bullets. Joe had to cover his mouth to keep from smiling. He was good at bodywork. They'd never see any signs in his Caddy's finish.

"Going a little fast, don't you think?"

"I just got word my wife isn't doing well. . ."

"Curing at Conifer, right?"

"Yes, sir." Armand was right. These troopers were keeping track of him. He watched the other trooper go through his car, then thump on the spare tires. Joe knew some runners carried booze in the spare tires.

"There's a report on a pea green Cadillac that ran troopers off the road outside of Chazy."

"You don't say? I never heard of another car like mine around." Pride in the Cadillac's touch up job and the absence of booze gave Joe courage. He'd play their game.

'Neither have we."

"Those troopers must have made a mistake. The shadows on these mountain roads play tricks on what you see."

"Well," Schermerhorn said. "Better see to your wife. I don't want any reports from Constable Duprey about a pea green Cadillac speeding through the village."

42

Joe slammed the car door and raced up the steps of Conifer Cottage.

"Joe!" A voice from the porch called as he was about to knock on the door. "Alice is gone. . .to General Hospital." Joe changed directions and hurried to where Connie reclined on a cure chair. "They took her last night. No one has been able to find you."

"I've changed jobs. How do I find the hospital?"

Connie told him the way and Joe was off, tearing down Helen Hill, hoping he didn't have to stop for cars when he crossed Church Street at the bottom of the hill.

A nurse was giving Joe Alice's room number when Dr. Hayes walked up.

"Joe. A few words before you see your wife?"

"Is Alice all right? She seemed so good when we had our outing."

"Unfortunately these acutely fluctuating ups and downs are the nature of tuberculosis. Why don't we sit down over here?" Dr. Hayes placed a hand on Joe's elbow, urging him toward a seating area. "Would you like a cup of coffee?

"No, no thanks." Joe looked down the corridor in the direction of Alice's room. He wanted to see Alice, not talk to the doctor.

"It'll just take a few minutes."

Joe's shoulders sagged. He walked over and sat down heavily. "I was told Alice needs an operation?"

"That's right. A thoracoplasty." Dr. Hayes cleared his throat. "We already removed three ribs this morning. Alice is resting quite comfortably now."

"Already operated?" Joe jumped to his feet. "Removed ribs? What's going on here? Jumping in so fast to mutilate my wife. She was fine the last time I saw her."

"Joe, calm yourself. You'll not be doing your wife any good in this state of agitation. Please sit down and I'll explain everything to you."

Joe glared at Dr. Hayes, breathing hard. Eventually he sat down, his eyes demanding the truth.

"The day after your outing, Alice had a temperature and began streaking. The X-rays were not good."

"But that pneumo thing. That was suppose to rest her bad lung."

"It usually does. And Alice did improve nicely. But I'm afraid the outing was too stressful. The only course of action left was the thoracoplasty."

"But why the rush? It was the same with the pneumo."

"A tubercular's state of mind is a very important factor in successful treatment. Anxiety over impending medical procedures can accelerate the problem, often to the point where the patient has worried herself into dying."

"Why wasn't I told?"

"It's my understanding the Guenther sisters have been trying to reach you for several days."

"You've cut out her ribs?"

"Three. This allows her chest wall to lie upon the diseased lung, keeping it deflated."

"Forever? She'll be. . .disfigured?"

"Yes to the first question. There will be a scar, of course, below her left shoulder, but with just three ribs removed, her appearance will only be slightly altered."

"Just three ribs?"

"There have been instances where it was necessary to remove nine ribs over a period of time to achieve success."

"I'd like to see Alice."

"Of course." Dr. Hayes rose to his feet. "Please keep your visit short. The operation has tired her a great deal."

Joe pushed open the door to Alice's room. He was surprised to see Lilly sitting in a chair, thumbing through a magazine.

"Joe," Lilly said, rising to her feet. "How good of you to find time to come." Her eyes flashed in anger as she flounced out of the room.

"Alice, dear heart." In two steps Joe was at her bedside. "I'm so sorry I wasn't here earlier." He bent down to kiss her forehead and took in the smell of her unwashed hair. Her blue eyes were huge in her thin, pasty-white face. Geeze, he thought, she must have lost ten pounds since the picnic. The circles under her eyes looked like blue bruises. She lay so spiritless on the hospital bed, dressed in huge white pajamas, arms listlessly at her side. He didn't know why two canvas bags lay on her chest.

He pulled a straight-backed chair up to the bed. Sitting down, he picked up a limp hand and clasped it between both of his.

"They took three ribs."

Joe leaned forward to hear the words Alice whispered.

"I won't ever look the same." Her mouth quavered. Tears slid slowly from the corners of her eyes and disappeared in the tangle of black curls.

"Oh, Alice, you'll be the same." He wiped the tears away with a thumb. "No, that's not true," he teased. "You'll be better."

"I shouldn't have let Dr. Hayes do it." Alice turned her head away. "So tired. No patience for years of this."

"It's not like you to be so selfish."

Alice turned back to look at Joe. He was pleased to see some emotion in her eyes, even though it was anger. "You are my first. . .my only love, Alice." Joe raised her hand and pressed it to his lips. "I can't picture a life without you in it." He watched as the anger subsided and, like a kaleidoscope, her eyes reflected the tangle of emotions she didn't have the strength to utter.

"I forget you've gone through so much, too," she said at last. "Everyone is always reminding me how wonderful you are. You deserve better."

"No, dear heart. You've got it wrong. I found the very best. Something beautiful and musical came into my life when I first heard your laughter that summer at the inn. Your laughter makes my heart sing. It's what kept me going during the war. It's what made me run up the stairs to our flat at the end of the day. And it gave me the determination to walk to Saranac Lake to see that your laughter is restored."

As he spoke, Joe watched her eyes close and the tense lines leave her face. He thought he saw the corners of her mouth turn up ever so slightly as he took her mind off the misery of the operation. Her breathing deepened and Joe knew she slept. He hoped she dreamt of happier times.

He got up, careful not to scrape the chair across the floor, and left the room. As he walked down the corridor, he saw Lilly sitting with her legs crossed at the knee, her top leg jerking up and down. She's angry, Joe thought.

"Thank you for staying with Alice," Joe said as he approached. "She's sleeping quietly now."

"She needed someone with her," Lilly said.

I'm not going to argue with this one, Joe said to himself. To Lilly he asked, "Would you like a ride back to Conifer?"

Lilly shrugged her shoulders, but got up and gathered her purse and magazine. They walked to the Cadillac, keeping a distance between them. He opened the passenger door and waited for her to settle on the seat. Lilly didn't so much as glance his way. He resisted the urge to slam the door shut.

He slid behind the wheel and turned to Lilly. "I'm glad you've been such a good friend to Alice all these months. . .almost a year now." Joe kept his eyes off her, making no effort to start the car. "But why are you always so sarcastic with me?" He toyed with the car keys as he waited for Lilly to talk.

Lilly was a long time in answering, and her words were hesitant. Bruised, Joe thought. At once both more mature and more childlike than Joe had ever heard her.

"You're making me be honest with myself," Lilly said. "I don't like what I see. I distrust you because you're healthy." She laced her fingers together and held them primly on her lap. "I keep waiting for you to abandon Alice."

"Abandon? How could you. . ."

"Please. . ." Her hands flew apart and she held them palms up. "This is hard enough for me. You see, I'm accustomed to being abandoned by the healthy people in my life, my father, my fiancé." Lilly was quiet for awhile, running a red-tipped finger around the neck of her sleeveless dress. "Why should you be any different? I know you'll eventually get tired of this Saranac Lake life and take up with some healthy girl. You have lots to choose from." She turned to look at Joe for the first time. "At the Club."

"Christ, Lilly. You must stay up all night to come up with this crap."

"Stop lying, Joe Devlin. You'll have to go to confession. I saw you driving right down Main Street with some vamp practically sitting on your lap."

"That was a Club guest my boss ordered me to drive."

"Horsefeathers! I may not be allowed in the Lake Placid Club, but I do know employees can't socialize with the guests."

"Believe me, I was under orders to chauffeur her and her friend around. That's the whole of it."

"Well, what about the dimpled Miss Thurber? How come you dragged her along to Carnival? And Alice told me you take her to Kate's farm every week"

"Kate's a friend. . .a friend of Alice's too. The Thurbers accept tuberculars. Even take one in as a boarder sometimes. It's a pleasant place to spend a few hours away from Conifer."

"Tell it to Sweeney."

"Lilly, Alice is the only woman I ever loved." Joe reached across the seat, took Lilly's shoulders and made her turn to look at him. "I'd do anything to help her to lick this thing. If someone told me years ago that I'd end up working for a rum runner, I sure would have laughed at him. But here I am doing just that to see that Alice gets what she needs. I know you. . .girls. . ."

"Is 'lungers' the word you're looking for?"

"Quit it, Lilly." Joe shook her shoulders. "It's hard enough to find the words for what it's like. I was trying to say I know it's not easy to spend every day sitting on a porch watching life go by. And it's not easy for me to have silly women like the Club guest you saw with me in the car making advances."

"That's why I rely on Kate so much. She's the only one in my life who knows I have a wife taking the cure. She's my friend. . .only a friend." Joe stopped to make sure Lilly was taking in the words "I would never betray Alice." Joe released Lilly and sat back behind the wheel. He stepped on the clutch and reached to turn the ignition key.

"Wait," Lilly said, touching his arm. "I get so jealous of healthy people like you, it turns me into a witch. Healthy people are accepted. People don't cross the street to avoid a healthy person. I spend years hanging around Conifer. . ."

"Mostly Pelletier's, from what I can see." Joe said. He put the car back in gear and waited.

"Yes. Those times at Pelletier's I can pretend I'm a normal woman. Not damaged goods." Lilly stopped talking and twisted a ring around her finger. She continued much more softly. "You may not be as saintly as the other girls at Conifer seem to think you are, but I do admire you for moving up here to be near Alice. Then I do get angry when I think I see signs of you acting like the other men I know."

Joe was confounded by Lilly's shifting judgments of him: jealousy, hate, admiration. He tried to understand what it must be like for Alice and her porchmates, living out their lives on a porch. What they were allowed to do was governed by a little temp stick. That and ten times more rules than the Ten Commandments.

"Well," Joe said. He stepped on the clutch again and turned the key. "I'd better get you back to Conifer before Hilda comes looking for you."

43

Joe didn't remember dropping Lilly off at Conifer or even the drive back to Charlie's. Alice filled his mind. A year ago he thought all he needed to do was get Alice out of the city and up in the mountains.

Then it became a struggle to keep up with the cure costs. I never could have made it without working for Armand, Joe thought. Keeping the booze cars on the road brought in good money. He was pleased to finally get Hilda off his back. All those angry red slashes in her account book were behind him.

But it wasn't until he began making booze runs in his Cadillac that the real money started coming in. He spent most of it on nice things for Alice. Or taking her to swell places to eat. . .dine. Sometimes they'd pick up Kate and the three of them would drive around the countryside in his fine car. Those two girls never ran out of things to talk about.

Truth is, Joe thought, I haven't set any aside. The thoracoplasty and hospital stay were going to be expensive. I've got to make some big runs. That's not going to be easy. I'll have to patch things up with Armand. Even so, I know Armand's right. Every one of Broadfield's Boys is keeping track of my car. Yet, that's exactly why I built those channels alongside the driveshaft. Let them stop me. They'll never find anything.

Joe shifted down and turned into Charlie's drive. Now that he no longer worked at the Club, Armand decided they'd be open about Joe staying with his "uncle" and he no longer had to go through the complicated steps of hiding his car in the barn.

"Joe!" Armand met him at the head of the barn stairs. "How's Alice? I heard she needed an operation."

Joe, relieved that Armand appeared willing to forget their unsettled confrontation, told him about the thoracoplasty.

"The operation and hospital stay are costing a lot," Joe said. He cleared his throat before continuing. "I need to make some booze runs."

"Ahhh, Joe!" Armand raised his arms, splaying his fingers. "Let's not go around on that again. You know every trooper in the Adirondacks is keeping track of a pea green Cadillac. I never should have gotten that car for you. It'll be the downfall of all of us."

"I've given it a lot of thought," Joe said, working hard to keep his voice even. "I'll give you that the troopers are keeping an eye on me, but you've got to admit they've never found a drop of booze in my car."

"Concealing booze alongside the driveshaft is unique," Armand said. "but now that you're openly staying with Charlie, you can bet Broadfield's Boys are keeping a sharp eye at the traffic coming and going from here. They already suspect something's going on in the barn."

"Armand has a point," Charlie interrupted. "If it weren't for King we'd be out of business."

"Troopers came here?" Joe asked.

"Yup." Charlie rested his hairy arms on the table, settling down to tell the story.

"Must of been right after the troopers visited you at the Club," he began. "We were all here, hustling to get Stu and Ellis on the road. Big order. . .clear down to Albany." He shifted the unlit cigar to the other side of his mouth. "King started an awful ruckus. When I looked out, sure enough there were two troopers staring at the barn."

Charlie told how after a bit his wife had come out and passed time with the troopers, giving Charlie a chance to get out of the loft.

"I swung open the barn doors like there was nothing to hide, and went to see them. They hung around the longest time. Poked into every corner. I put on my shoeing apron and took a horse to the shop out back. Generally went about my business like their being here was no bother."

"I never heard about all this," Joe said, when Charlie finished.

"You're much too busy outrunning the troopers, Joe," Armand said. "They will catch up with you. Let me lend you the money. Let the troopers get interested in someone else before you start making runs again."

"No. I won't borrow money."

"You're already making good money keeping the cars on the road. Our cars are moving hooch several times a week. There's full-time work for you."

"You might as well give me a run. If you don't, I'm sure I can find someone who'd like me to move some goods."

Armand jumped up from the table, sending his chair crashing to the floor. "Let's be real clear. One, I'm the boss. Two, I will not be swayed by threats."

"Fine." Joe stood and stalked out across the hayloft. He stomped down the stairs and slammed the tack room door shut. Moments later the Cadillac roared out the drive, gravel spewing from its tires.

"Never should have gotten him that car." Armand punched his fist into his hand.

"Joe's in a real bind," Charlie said.

"Don't you start. You started it all by talking me into letting him make his first hooch run."

"Why don't you let Joe do some middle of the day runs?" Charlie presented a plan in which Joe could move some goods in broad daylight, just taking booze from the stockpile in the barn and delivering it to speakeasies in Saranac Lake. "Any troopers keeping track would know he wasn't crossing the border or going far from his wife's side."

"All right," Armand conceded. "Set it up. Tell Joe when he comes in tonight. But," Armand shook a finger under Charlie's nose, "you'd better make sure he thinks it was all my idea. And no speeding."

"Right, boss."

Ever since the thoracoplasty Joe had started going to daily Mass. He felt at peace when he prayed in the serenity of St. Agnes, with its gracefully arched ceilings and filigreed white altar. He joined the scattering of early morning parishioners in the comforting rituals of the service.

After Mass, when Father McCabe went into the sacristy to take off his green vestments, Joe walked up to the altar and lit a votive candle. Kneeling at the marble altar railing, he blessed himself and buried his head in his hands.

Please God, he prayed, give Alice the strength she needs to recover. You know I'm willing to share the burden of this cross You've chosen to give her. I know our marriage doesn't please You and I know I should expect suffering as a result. But please, Lord, let it be my suffering.

Joe blessed himself again and pushed himself up from the railing and walked slowly out of the silent church. He was surprised to see Kate kneeling in the back pew. She smiled and stood to walk out with Joe.

"I don't have to be in the dining room until noon today," Kate said. "I came to Mass to pray for Alice. How is she, Joe?"

"Depressed. Still has a temperature. Dr. Hayes is going to move her back to Conifer today. He thinks she may be more comfortable there."

"I'd like to go see her when you think she's up to it." Kate buttoned her wool jacket against the frosty fall chill, then tugged her hair free of the big collar.

"I know seeing a cheery face would help, he said, looking down at Kate's round face with its sprinkling of cinnamon freckles." Alice always seems a little better after spending time with you, too, he thought.

"She was improving so much this summer." Kate turned and started down the church steps. "Those times you stopped at the farm for our midday meal, she ate as much as the men. And full of plans for the future."

"Can I give you a ride back to Finches?"

"Swell."

Joe drove down Saranac Avenue, turning left at the bottom rather than driving through the village. He drove slowly. Relaxed. Turned to look at Mirror Lake edged with its colorful skirt of reds and golds and the rich, velvety evergreens.

"The colors are so vibrant this fall," Kate said. "I think it's the prettiest time of year. I could sit for long hours absorbing the colors. Something to remember during the long winters."

Joe thought she belonged to the autumn with her bright russet hair resting on her green coat collar.

"I never got to tell you how rotten I think Mr. Madden was getting you fired. I swear that man drinks vinegar for breakfast."

"I never understood why he was always so sour to me. It's good not to have him looking over my shoulder."

"They say he was very different years ago. Played piano in the Club band. Sang. Before his wife ran off with some man staying at the Club."

"I guess that could change a man. And now his son's in jail for transporting. Allen says Madden is furious that Phil won't name the bootlegger he's working for. Refuses to come up with the two thousand dollar bond unless he does."

"I don't know how you can work for a man that'd allow a seventeen-year-old boy to be a rum runner."

"Kate, cars are all I know. The only chance I have to pay for the operation and hospital stay is to shoot some loads. Believe me, I plan on stopping as soon as I can afford to."

"I'm sorry." Kate put a hand on Joe's arm. "This is not the time to chastise you."

They were quiet for awhile as Joe slowed and turned into the Club's service entrance.

"Suppose I take you to see Alice tomorrow right after their quiet time? I could have you back at the Club in time for supper."

"Swell. I'll wait for you at Finches."

Alice saw the alarm in Kate's face when she came to visit. She had seen it on everyone's face since returning to Conifer. She watched her friend's eyes take in the heavy shot bags that covered her sunken chest then reluctantly return to look at Alice's face. She can't find anything pleasant to say, Alice thought, looking at Kate's open mouth and the utter dismay flowing from her eyes.

Alice worked at a smile, trying to put her friend at ease. She was glad Kate had come. She hoped she would be strong enough to discuss what needed to be said.

"It must be good to be back at Conifer," Kate said. She pulled a chair close to Alice's bed and sat on its edge. Earlier Ursula had rolled Alice's bed through the French doors onto the sitting-out porch to enjoy the cloudless autumn day with its delicious warmth of summer.

"So peaceful here," Alice agreed. "The nurses were efficient. But nobody knows how to care for me better than the Guenther sisters." Alice told her friend how Hilda had given her a soothing bed bath and one of her famous alcohol rubs. Then Ursula had washed and towel-dried her hair. "She just about put me to sleep while she brushed the snarls out."

"You'll be getting stronger every day now."

"I'm not really sure about that anymore. That's why I'm glad you came today."

"Is there something you need? Joe said he had some things to do in the village before stopping by."

"In a way. And I'm glad we have this time to talk privately. Kate, it would give me a lot of peace of mind if I knew Joe won't mope around if. . .if I don't recover."

"Alice, you mustn't talk like that! You know how important it is to stay optimistic."

"Optimism put me on the train almost a year ago. Optimism kept me obeying all the cure rules and made me try all the outlandish rituals like freezing it out. Now it's time to be honest with myself about the possibility of not making it."

"Don't you dare give up, Alice Devlin. You're not the only one making sacrifices here. If you knew the half of what Joe does to pay. . ." Kate's hand flew to her mouth.

"Like working for a rum runner? Carrying illegal booze?"

"You know?"

"Some he's told me. Some I heard from Lilly. Some I suspected. How do you think it makes me feel to know he's compromising his religious beliefs to pay the bills? On top of marrying me outside his church."

Alice lay quietly, catching her breath after the long speech.

"The day we spent at Hulls Falls, we decided to stay here in the Adirondacks to raise our family."

"Oh, that'd be swell."

"If I don't make it, I want Joe to get on with his life. I can't think of a nicer person to plan his future with."

"What are you suggesting?"

"Kate, I don't know how to say this, but I'm too weak to take hours to get it out. For months I've seen how easy you and Joe are around one another. Don't get me wrong. I know you both have principles that wouldn't allow you to do anything. Although there were times last winter when I wondered how Joe was spending his free time in Lake Placid with you right there. And Lilly was always hinting that Joe might be taking an interest in you."

"Oh, Alice. There was never. . ."

"I believe you. But I want you to know I think you and Joe would be great together. Please promise you won't spend years mourning me. I know what's it's like to spend one's days on the sidelines of life. You need to be strong for Joe. Help him put this year behind him." Alice fell silent.

"All this talking is too tiring for you," Kate said. "You're saying things that won't make any sense when you get better."

"These things must be said now. I doubt I'll be getting better." Alice paused. Kate had to lean closer to hear when she began again.

"My TB has forced Joe to make many changes in his life. I know they are at odds with his religion. The only thing I can offer Joe is his freedom to pursue your friendship."

"Alice, you shouldn't be worrying about things like this now."

"Can't put it off. Please. Some water."

Kate helped her sit up and sip from a glass. She lay back exhausted with her eyes closed.

"I know you care enough about Joe to keep him from rum running. I want him to make a life here. But so afraid he'll take up with Mr. Dasset again. You're the only person who really understands what he's going through."

"Have you spoken to Joe about. . .this?"

"Not yet. Soon."

44

A week after her talk with Kate, Alice opened her eyes to steady rain dripping off the porch roof. Her cheeks were hot and her nose was cold. Such a dismal day.

Two hours till supper, then two hours till bed. Bed. . .she hadn't left bed since the day after Joe took her to the falls.

She was so depressed this afternoon after weeks of temps and the lingering pain of the thoracoplasty that nothing in her dwindling supply of happy thoughts succeeded in lifting her spirits. Even the perfect day at the falls. If only Joe had brought her home sooner. Joe? Why was it his fault? I didn't want to leave either. For a brief afternoon they had pretended to be a normal couple. The first time they'd made love in over a year.

The familiar sound of Dr. Hayes's Franklin climbing Helen Hill broke into her consciousness. Alice frowned when she heard it come to a stop in front of Conifer Cottage. Only an emergency brought Dr. Hayes out on a house call on a Saturday.

The car door slammed loudly in a world just waking from its mandatory nap. In moments she heard his steps on the stairs. They sounded weary, deliberate and slow. Had the dismal day affected his unswerving good spirits? Ten months of his weekly visits and she had never seen him less than cheerful.

The soft rap on her door startled her. She turned her head. Dr. Hayes smiled but his eyes told a sadder story. Alice's heart jumped about in her bruised chest.

Why was he here? Why wasn't Ursula here to take notes? She wouldn't let him take more ribs. It was bad enough that Joe would never have a healthy wife. He didn't deserve a deformed one as well. If that's why Dr. Hayes had come, she'd just have to tell him she wasn't strong enough.

"Alice," he said, drawing the chair up to her bed and sinking heavily upon it. He propped his pudgy hands on his knees, elbows askew. He looked so sad. Alice feared he was about to cry. The corners of his mouth turned upward in a parody of a smile.

"Resting comfortably?" He bent forward and pressed a cool hand to her forehead.

"I feel stronger than in the hospital, but my temp is never completely normal."

Dr. Hayes nodded and settled back in his chair. He pulled a handkerchief from his breast pocket and took off his glasses. Methodically he polished each lens.

Alice bit her lip to keep from screaming. "What is it, Dr. Hayes? Another thoracoplasty?"

He shook his head without looking up. Finally he placed his glasses back on his nose.

"I dearly wish the removal of additional ribs would help. Often it does, but I don't believe it would in your case." The doctor's chest expanded in a huge sigh. "I've read your X-rays. There's so many spots. New ones." Another huge sigh threatened to burst the buttons on his jacket.

He reached for Alice's fluttering hand and caged it gently between his two. "There's nothing more to be done. The damage is too extensive."

Alice's blood raced through her veins. Why couldn't Dr. Hayes be specific?

"What am I to do. . .lie here for years?"

"No sense fooling ourselves that one more winter in Saranac Lake would help."

"There's no possibility of getting better?"

He shook his head.

Her ears buzzed. She thought she had prepared for this possibility, but having the ugly decree spoken was devastating.

"What am I to do?"

"Why don't you have your husband take you back to New York? You haven't seen your parents in some time. I believe I've heard you talk about a sister you'd like to see. . ."

"Before I die," Alice whispered. Die. The word bit into her like the slash of a whip.

"Would you like me to call your husband?"

"Call Joe?" She found it hard to concentrate on what Dr. Hayes was saying. "No. . .no. He'll be here tomorrow. I'd like to time to think about it first."

Dr. Hayes opened up his bag and fumbled around. He selected two white pills and poured fresh water into a glass. With a hand behind her shoulder he helped Alice rise up to swallow the pills.

"How long?" she whispered.

"A month or two at the most," he whispered back. "Would you like me to send Ursula up?"

"No."

"Well. Good-bye, then. You don't know how it pains me to have brought this news. I'll be back to see you on Monday." He made an abrupt about-face and disappeared out the door.

Alice was bewildered, then the drug took over. She fought against closing her eyes as though she must keep track of where she was headed.

The need to cough forced Alice awake the next morning. Beads of sweat turned the fine black hair framing her face into tight curls. The effort of dragging herself into a sitting position and coughing into the ugly sputum cup took her breath away. A good productive cough, the snippet of the TB patient's creed, came to mind when it was over.

I don't have to worry about that any more, she thought, dabbing her forehead with a tissue. The memory of Dr. Hayes's visit flooded her consciousness. She sat still with a tissue pressed to her mouth as the full ramification of what the doctor had come to say spread to every corner of her being.

Her heart pumped wildly. It pounded in her ears, rebelling at Dr. Hayes' declared death sentence. The endless days of following every rule for a cure meant nothing. . .nothing! The excruciating pain of the two operations was not a step forward but just unadorned torture. And the wasted money. Money they never had. Money Joe was drawn into rum running to obtain.

311

She dropped her hands to her lap and kneaded the tissue into a sodden mess. She wasn't supposed to think unhappy thoughts. No, she thought, that was yesterday. *I'm freed from all those rules.* A bitter smile barely lifted the corners of her mouth. *I can think and act as I please.*

A few golden leaves drifting past her windows caught her eye. The short mountain summer had quickly colored into autumn as she wrestled with the thoracoplasty. The misty dawn sky deepened into the splendid blue of a clear day as Alice watched the leaves' aimless descent and thought about the future.

Joe would be free, too. Would he give up rum running? The biggest burden of this whole thing was Joe resorting to illegal ways of paying the bills. She was responsible for turning Joe into such a reckless lawbreaker.

As of today he was released from this millstone. What would he do? She must not put off talking to Joe about not wasting another day of his life. There had been more than a few times during the winter and spring when the thought of Joe and Kate pursuing an obvious attraction while she lay helplessly in a cure chair made her angry.

I owe it to him, Alice thought. *I must not waste any time in convincing Joe to follow his heart with Kate. They are so right for each other.* She was pleased she had taken the opportunity to speak frankly to Kate about the future.

"It won't be about Joe and Alice anymore," she remembered telling Kate. "I hope it will be about Joe and Kate."

"*Guten morgen*, dear," Ursula said. She smiled down at Alice and offered her the temp stick.

"It doesn't matter a whit what my temperature is," Alice said. "I've been released from following rules." Her mouth quivered in attempting a carefree smile.

"Well. . ." Ursula's eyes widened and she dropped her hands to her side. Her perpetual smile momentarily fluttered from her mouth.

"I've been freed from all this," Alice waved her hand about, "all this discipline and rules." She was forced to stop and catch her breath. "Since I cannot be cured, I plan to spend the time I have left with as few restrictions as possible."

Alice realized Ursula's repertoire had no words for this situation. She watched the older woman place the temp stick back in the glass and turn to shut the windows.

"I'm going to ask Joe to take me home. I want to see my mother and father and Nancy before. . ." She pressed the hankie to her mouth.

When Ursula turned to face Alice, her pale eyes were rimmed in red. "The regimen of a cure will keep you feeling your best till. . .up to the end." She wrung her hands. "Oh my sweet little Alice." She dropped to the bed and hugged Alice close. "I've prayed every day that your lungs would heal and we'd send you home to raise your family."

Alice clasped the caring woman and her tears flowed freely.

"You've been so good to me. It's not your fault my lungs won't heal." Placing her hands on Ursula's shoulders, she gently pushed her back.

"Just before you came,' Alice said, "I began to feel a kind of. . .peace. No more wondering, struggling." She offered one of her hankies to Ursula.

Ursula blew her nose and dabbed at the corners of her eyes. "Well, I must start the breakfast trays." She patted Alice's hand and stood up.

"Please, Ursula, don't bring me any more of those raw eggs."

"Goodness, it's stuffy in here." Lilly sashayed into Alice's room as Ursula left and dropped into the chair. "How come all the windows are closed? What do you think of my new hat?" She tugged at the brim of her green felt cloche. It was an exact match for her green and gold wool sweater.

"You're writing. You're not allowed to write." Lilly sat up to have a better look at her friend. "You're not even supposed to be sitting up." Lilly got up and stood at the foot of the bed. "Something is kerflooey in here. Alice, what's up?"

"I don't have to follow the rules anymore."

"You just had a rib operation, what do you mean you don't have to follow the rules? Now lie back down and I'll put the shot bags back on your chest." Lilly turned and pushed up the windows and flung open the porch door.

"Lilly, I have something to tell you." Alice shifted her legs to one side and patted the comforter. "Come sit." Alice saw her friend's back stiffen. Her hands dropped to her sides and she slowly turned to face Alice. Her bright cupid bow's mouth was a red slash in her pale face. Her eyes were huge with alarm.

"No," she whispered. "You can't leave me, too." Her hands reached out to grasp the iron bed railing. "I don't want to know."

Alice closed her eyes. The sound of someone coughing came in the open window. Slippered feet softly scuffled down the hall to the bathroom. A doorknob was released, its latch snapping into place.

"Does Dr. Hayes want to take another rib?"

Alice, her eyes still closed, shook her head. "Please," she opened her eyes and held her hand out to Lilly. "Let me hold your hand so I can tell you."

Lilly released her grip on the railing and walked hesitantly to Alice's side. Alice reached for Lilly's listless hand and tugged her down on the bed.

"Dr. Hayes came by last night. I'm not going to get better."

"Well, I know you won't be well enough to go home this Christmas, but by next year. . ."

"Lilly," Alice squeezed her hand, "please let me finish. This is the first time I'm saying it out loud." Alice stopped, ran the tip of her tongue around her lips. "I'm going to die."

Lilly's red mouth opened and an agonized sound of despair rose from her throat. She pulled her hand away and rushed from the room, slamming the door after her. Alice heard the squeak of Lilly's bedsprings next door and the unmistakable muffled sounds of crying into a pillow came clearly through the bedroom's open windows.

Hilda must have heard, too. Alice listened to her solid steps on the stairs and down the hall to Lilly's room.

What have I done to Lilly? I never thought she'd act so violently. After all, it's me who's dying. Oh my gosh, how will Joe take it?

Lilly's sobs and Hilda's murmurs were the sobering background to Alice's thoughts.

Hilda strode into Alice's room. "You should not have Lilly told," she said, hands on hips. "It may cause her a serious setback."

"Not tell her? What am I to do? Walk out of here one day and never return? Never say goodbye?"

"There is no hope of a cure if one dwells on death."

"No one, Miss Guenther," Alice paused for a breath, feeling the familiar gurgle in her lungs, "will stop me from saying goodbye to my friends." The urge to cough overtook her. She snatched a tissue from the nightstand and prepared for the onslaught.

Just then Ursula entered the room with a dinner tray. "Why aren't you helping Alice?" She thrust the tray at Hilda, forcing the larger women to unfasten her hands from her hips. "Get a face cloth," she ordered her sister. Ursula picked up the sputum cup and gently folded Alice's hand around it. She smoothed Alice's tangled curls off her face and snatched the wet face cloth from her sister's hand. Hilda opened her mouth to speak, then turned and stomped from the room.

Placing the cool cloth on Alice's brow, Ursula helped her raise the gooey mess. When it was over, Alice looked at the red-specked contents of the cup.

"I'm bringing up blood." She looked at Ursula and handed over the sputum cup. "Ursula, you must tell me."

"Tell you what, dear?"

"What it'll be like. At the end."

"Oh, no. I couldn't do that. We mustn't dwell on things like that."

"Don't you understand it's over for me? All that Trotty Veck malarkey isn't going to help. I want to know."

"Well." Ursula pursed her lips and struggled with the forbidden request. Coming to a conclusion, she softly closed the bedroom door and came to sit on Alice's bed.

"You might not even know what's happened," Ursula began. "One night you'll go to sleep, but instead of waking up to hearing the steam rise in the radiators or to windows being shut, you'll wake up in heaven. Your temperature will be gone and you'll never cough again." She offered a small smile of encouragement to Alice.

"Ursula. . .the truth."

"It is the truth that many tuberculars slip silently into the next life while they sleep."

"How?"

Ursula took a deep breath and released it slowly. "Medically, an artery will rupture. . ." Ursula bit her lower lip.

"And?" Alice relentlessly pursued the truth.

Ursula turned her head away and mumbled, "The patient will drown in her own blood."

45

"Push me out onto the porch," Alice whispered.

"You don't have to do the eight-hours-of-air-a-day any more," Lilly said. Nevertheless, she left the comfortable slipper chair where she had been reading aloud to Alice from a True Story and pushed Alice's bed through the door.

"I like our porch. Peaceful." Alice found talking a struggle.

"Look at the leaves fall," Lilly said. "Like bits of sun."

"I've never heard you talk so poetically." Alice looked at Lilly fondly.

"Well, it is pretty, the way the yellow leaves are caught in the dark evergreen boughs."

"I'll miss our balsam. It smells so good." Alice couldn't repress the cough tickling her throat. Lilly helped her sit up and handed her the sputum cup.

"Thank you," Alice whispered when it was over. Lilly took the cup from Alice's hands. Neither spoke of the heavy lacing of blood in the thick slime.

"Your hands are freezing," Lilly said. "I'll get you another robe."

How will I manage without the Saranac crowd, Alice thought. Everyone here knows without thinking exactly what to do. Mother's never been near a tubercular. Even Joe doesn't really understand.

And how will my father treat Joe? Will I spend my last days watching my father and my husband glare at one another? Suppose they won't let him stay at the house? I don't want Joe to just visit. I want. . .I want to spend my last days with Joe. Share a room with him, like when we first married.

I can't expect it to be perfect, she thought. At least they finally are allowing me back in the house. Imagine it taking my death to accomplish that.

Alice had been surprised at her mother's quick response to the letter she wrote to Nancy.

Of course Alice must hurry home, her mother had written. It had taken all this time, but eventually Mr. Lattimer came to face the truth that Joe cared very deeply for his daughter, and was well able to care for her and meet the expense of a cure. "Your father would never say it out loud," Mrs. Lattimer wrote, "but I know he's come to think highly of Joe."

At least it was a change for the better since her wedding day, Alice thought.

"Caught you thinking," Lilly said, carrying a heavy bear robe.

"Hmm. Of when Joe and I married."

"Oh, tell me about the wedding." Lilly fussed with arranging the lap robe just so.

"Our fathers had a fistfight."

"What?"

Very slowly, resting between each sentence, Alice told the story of her wedding day. How her father had stopped them on the street in front of the house of the Justice of the Peace.

"Joe and Father argued. . .People had to walk around us." She haltingly told of feeling so embarrassed with people staring. Then Joe's father had appeared just as Mr. Lattimer tried to take Alice away.

"I think Mr. Devlin had been drinking," Alice said, "and got mixed up as to why he was there." Instead of behaving like it was Joe he was mad at, she recalled, Mr. Devlin walked right up and punched Mr. Lattimer in the nose."

Lilly laughed.

"It wasn't funny." Alice stopped to slow down her breathing. "When my father fell back from the blow, he still had a grip on my sleeve. Pulled the entire sleeve off the dress."

"Your wedding dress?"

Alice nodded. "Made it myself. I'm not a good seamstress."

"There's got to be more."

"Please," she said, "may I have some water first?" Lilly jumped up and poured a glass. She helped Alice sit up and stayed with her while she drank. Then Alice laid back and shut her eyes while Lilly placed the ten-pound shot bags back on her chest.

"Both fathers started swinging at each other," Alice continued after a bit. "Joe tried to break it up. His own father socked him in the eye."

"No!"

"Yes. Police came. Took our fathers away. Joe had a black eye before he said 'I do.'"

"What a story to tell your chil. . ."

"Children? Not for Joe and me."

Lilly rushed from where she had been leaning on the porch railing and perched on Alice's bed. "That was an awful thing for me to say."

"I know what's ahead for me. But you can make it out of here, Lilly. Do it for both of us."

"Maybe I don't want to. What do I have to go home to? Watching Howard strut down the street with his healthy fiancé on his arm?"

"You could be one of the healthy ones, too. You're so close."

"Tell that to Sweeney. You're only free of TB if you die of something else. . .Oh Alice, I didn't mean to talk of dying."

"It's all right," Alice said. Poor Lilly, she thought. She's always putting her foot in her mouth when she gets upset. The thought of dying didn't panic Alice nearly as much as it appeared to bother those around her. I'm tired of the continual ups and downs. Of being such a big expense to Joe. To Lilly she said, "There comes a time you know you must let go. My time is. . .nearby."

The friends sat quietly for a time. The golden leaves fluttering in the blue sky were something to savor. The last ones I'll ever see, she thought.

"It's Joe I worry about," Alice said after a while. "He deserves a chance at a real life with a real wife. And those children you talked about."

"I have a feeling Joe can look out for himself," Lilly said.

"We've talked about it."

"About what?"

"What Joe will do after."

"And?"

"The day we went to the falls we talked about staying here in the mountains to raise our family. I think he should stick to our plan. Open his own garage."

"Wouldn't he prefer to go back to the city where there's lots of work for a mechanic?"

"There are nice people here."

"Alice Devlin, are you placing your husband in Kate's arms?"

"Oh, Lilly, I'll be long gone. Joe can't spend his life mourning me. Life has been hard enough for him this past year. He deserves a chance at a real marriage. Kate's a good, kind woman. And a Catholic."

Lilly sat quietly for a bit before speaking. "Joe's a good, kind man, too. We had quite a talk when you were at the hospital." She got up and started pacing the small sitting-out porch. "I've thought some rotten things about him. I know now I was wrong. He does love you very much. But you shouldn't be fussing about what Joe will do with his life. . .later."

"I owe it to Joe to encourage him to get on with his life."

"Have you spoken to Joe about this?"

"Yes. He found it difficult to discuss. I came right out and told him I knew they were well suited. When we all went for drives or stopped at Kate's father's farm I could see how they acted with one another."

"You accused Joe of. . ."

"Of course not. They're far too principled for that. I told both of them that."

"You've spoken to Kate, too?"

"Yes. I worry about you, too, Lilly. You haven't been close to anyone since Frank died. You're so close to licking this curse and finding a good man to live with."

"No life commitments for me." Lilly held up her hands, palms out. "I've tried it and the misery when something happens. . ." The cupid's bow mouth turned down. "I never want to go through it again."

That's exactly what I'm trying to ease for Joe, Alice thought. I know Joe and Kate are attracted to one another. I don't want them denied happiness out of some misplaced guilt.

"I want to confess something." Lilly broke into Alice's thoughts. "I used to tell Charlotte that I thought Joe wasn't the saint you and Ursula made him out to be. Now I know I was just jealous. He really adores you. You were. . .are lucky to have that."

"I don't know how to better thank him than setting him free to start again."

"Joe loves you too much to think about taking up with Kate. You have to let him pick his own pace."

"He was angry. Real storm in his eyes. Refused to talk about it."

"Good man," Lilly said.

"You haven't begun to pack," Ursula said. "I thought Lilly was doing this with you." Ursula opened drawers.

"I only need a few things. I'm going back to die. All these clothes are much too big since my rib. I'm lower than my entry weight. New girls will come into Conifer who'll want something nice once they're up patients."

"You'll certainly take your new coat?"

Alice smiled and nodded. "I'd like my sister to have it when it's over." Alice loved the smart black broadcloth coat Joe had bought for her twenty-fourth birthday. She remembered how proudly he told her that the fur trimming the cuffs and hem was imported Turkish fox. And even though winter was pretty much over when he gave it to her, she wore it well into summer when Joe took her out.

"See the long-sleeved blue heather dress?"

Ursula moved the hangers about and pulled out a fine wool dress with a wide collar and cuffs of silk jersey. "This one?"

"It's one of my favorites," Alice said. "So soft."

And all the details. All the tiny buttons down the front, the dark blue of the collar." Ursula held the dress against her body and peered in the small mirror above the dresser.

"Perfect color for you. I want you to have the dress."

"Me! Why where would I wear such a lovely dress."

"You deserve something pretty, Ursula. I bet there's someone who'd enjoy seeing you wear it." Alice saw a shy smile on Ursula's face; she was obviously pleased with the dress. It was a glimpse of the pretty woman a younger Ursula must have been. Before the years of caring for tuberculars in this harsh climate.

"There was a young man, once."

"Tell me," Alice said, patting the bed, inviting Ursula to sit. Still clutching the dress to her, Ursula sat on Alice's bed.

"Years ago, before Hilda came to America, I worked at the Noyes Cottage." Ursula raised her head and looked at Alice with a glow in her soft gray eyes. "That's where I met Wilbur. He was a patient."

Alice lay entranced, hearing this new side of Ursula. The woman told of Wilbur taking her to church socials and when he was almost cured they went canoeing on Lake Flower and Wilbur proposed.

"We made plans to stay on in Saranac Lake and open our own cure cottage."

"And?"

"Two months after he proposed Wilbur died."

Alice reached out to squeeze Ursula's hand. This dear, sweet woman never got to experience what she and Joe had, Alice thought. No wonder Ursula was always saying I was one of the lucky ones.

"Afterwards I found out he had already bought Conifer Cottage. . .in my name." Ursula stood up and walked to the windows, looking out on the street. "I believe he always knew he wasn't going to make it and did this wonderful thing for me." Ursula pressed a tissue to her eyes. "There isn't a day goes by that I don't think of him."

"Well, who knows. In that dress someone's going to come knocking on the door." Goodness, Alice thought, wasn't I just saying that same thing to Lilly?

"Do you think so?" Ursula's eyes were bright with wonder and she hugged the dress to her chest. Leaning closer to Alice, she whispered, "I'm nearly thirty-four."

Suddenly Joe appeared at the door. "Joe. . .I didn't think you'd be by today," Alice said.

"Wanted to see if there was anything I could do for you today, dear heart." Joe sat on the bed facing Alice. Ursula left with the blue dress draped over her arm.

"The most important thing for me now is to know you'll move on with your life after I'm gone.

"Alice, how can you expect me to think about taking up with Kate at a time like this?"

"Because there is no more time." Alice closed her eyes and gathered her strength.

"It means a lot to me after all you've given up for me. She's a good woman, Joe."

Neither spoke.

"Dear heart, please don't ask me to do something I cannot do. It's not that I don't like Kate. And even though I will not be forced into a promise, the day may come that it will fall in place. But for today, I'm sorry, but I cannot promise you what you ask."

Alice opened her eyes and reached for Joe's hand. "I understand," she whispered. To Joe, her touch was like the wings of a butterfly. Like when he had helped her out of the boat so many summers ago. He would never again hear the laughter he had fallen in love with that day.

Alice drifted in and out of sleep. She was exhausted with all the preparations for leaving. As when Charlotte went home, Alice didn't want any good-byes in the morning. Please, she had begged Ursula, don't let the girls be on the porch. Joe would carry her downstairs and out the door. That'd be it. Now, with Joe at her side, she watched her last sunset at Conifer.

46

It didn't feel right to make plans for his life. . .after Alice. It was hard to deny his wife this last promise, but Joe was content that he made the right decision in telling Alice exactly how he felt about taking up with Kate.

One last time, the pea green Cadillac climbed Helen Hill and eased to a stop in front of Conifer Cottage.

It took some time to pack Alice's belongings in the car in such a way that she could make a bed out of the back seat. All the girls stayed behind their closed doors as Joe carried Alice down the narrow hall. She clasped her hands about his neck and buried her head in his shoulder.

Geeze, she was light, Joe thought. Couldn't weigh a hundred pounds. Was she strong enough to make this three hundred mile trip? Ursula, biting her lower lip, met them at the door. She followed them down the porch steps and opened the car door.

Alice turned her eyes up to her sitting-out porch while Ursula fussed with her makeshift bed. There was Lilly, with her hand over her mouth, looking down at her. When their eyes met, each young woman raised a hand.

Joe settled her on the back seat and Ursula directed him in the proper placement of the heavy shot bags.

It was time to go.

Joe shut the car door. When he turned, he found Ursula looking at him with such sorrow in her faded gray eyes. Before he knew it, he reached out to hug the woman. He thought he might cry when he felt Ursula softly patting him on the back.

"Thank you for all you've done," he said, stepping back and squeezing her hands.

"I'm so sorry it wasn't enough. Take good care of her, Joe."

Joe wished Alice could be in the front seat with him. He wanted to look in her face, hold her hand. When he did turn to glance at her, her eyes were shut, the long black lashes lying against white cheeks. He drove slowly. Surely the slightest rut would bounce her right off the seat. Then, when he descended the mountain after leaving the Plains of Abraham, he worried Alice would slide forward off the seat. No racing down the road today. Joe kept the Cadillac in a low gear, gently stepping on the brakes before entering each bend in the road.

Even though he had seen it a dozen times, coming upon the beauty of the black lake reflecting the autumn colors caught him by surprise. He pulled the car off the road. He had to share this with Alice.

He carried her from the car and sat her on a flat-topped boulder overlooking the silent lake a hundred feet below them. A mountain rose from the far side. The lake clearly reflected its steep flank, lushly covered with evergreens and a sprinkling of graceful white birch. The air was fall-crisp and smelled of wet leaves. Of life coming to an end.

Alice leaned back against Joe. Sunshine yellow leaves drifted lazily from the white birch trees and settled on the lake.

"Do you suppose it's this beautiful every autumn?" Alice asked.

"For more years than we could count." Joe said. "God has loaned you to me for a very short time." He stopped to pick a birch leaf from where it had settled on Alice's hair. "But this lake, these mountains will always be here." Joe fell silent, absorbing the timelessness of the scene before him. Last winter he had trudged this same road on snowshoes. He remembered the loneliness of his night spent among the countless evergreens. But at least he had a goal last winter. He had to get to Alice.

Soon Alice would be gone.

He was angry when she first suggested he pursue his friendship with Kate. She had pressed Joe's hand against her cheek and said, "Life isn't about Joe and Alice anymore." For days he had churned with the agony of life without Alice. She had been uppermost in his mind since he first heard her laughter that summer at the lakeside inn.

"Here," he said, "let me help you turn around." Joe took Alice's hands, supporting her as she turned away from the lake. When she was settled, he took out his pocketknife and opened the blade. He went to the white birch that grew alongside the boulder and slowly carved: "Joe loves Alice, now & always." When he was finished, he fashioned a big heart around it.

Joe was pleased to see a spark of light in her blue eyes. Maybe, he dared to hope, with him caring for her every day, she might not have to die. He folded up his knife and dropped it in a pocket. Maybe they could just visit her parents and come back to the mountains. He settled beside Alice on the boulder.

"Will you think of me when you pass by here in years to come?" she asked, nestling into his shoulder.

"Dear heart, you'll always be a part of my life." Joe closed his eyes and inhaled, memorizing the smell and feel of her soft babyfine curls.

"Remember the good times, Joe."

"They're safe," He took her hand and traced an "X" over his heart. "Tied with a ribbon the color of your eyes and stored in a special pocket of my heart."

He scooped his wife up in his arms and settled her back in the car. They were almost in Keene when she called his name. When he looked back, he saw the fear in her eyes before he noticed the blood-stained tissue she held against her mouth.

She was hemorrhaging! Ursula had said this is how Alice would probably go. He stood on the brakes and pulled the Cadillac off the road. Think, he demanded. What did Ursula say to do? Ice. . .that was it.

No ice. There was a stream back up the mountain a short distance. Had to be cold water. Joe pushed his car in reverse and it screamed up the hill. He stopped, jumped out, shrugged out of his jacket and ripped the shirt off his back, all the while running to a small stream that raced down the mountain. He dropped the shirt in the water and pulled his undershirt over his head and plunged it into the water as well. Scooping them up he ran back to Alice.

"Alice, dear heart, I'm here." She was so white. Her mouth almost blue. He fumbled with her suit buttons and placed his cold wet shirt on her chest. Please God, don't take her yet. Alice's eyes fluttered open at the touch of cold water.

"Ursula said you need ice in your throat, too." Joe wadded up his undershirt. "Try to suck the cold out of this." He needed more cold water. He didn't dare leave.

"Joe Devlin?"

Joe jumped, smacking his head on the door frame of the car. He backed out to see two troopers standing before him.

"My wife. She's hemorrhaging. I need water from that stream."

The troopers sprang into action. They spilled Canadian Club from several bottles recently confiscated at a roadblock, filled them with water and hurried them back to Joe.

Joe poured the cold water over his shirt, wrung it out and gently placed it back on Alice's chest. When he did the same with the undershirt he kept in her mouth, he didn't see any signs of fresh bleeding. He was terrified. He pulled a robe over Alice's chest and backed out of the car.

"Thanks," he said to the troopers, noting for the first time one was that Sergeant Schermerhorn, who seemed to be keeping an eye on him.

"Can your wife travel now?" Schermerhorn asked. "We ought to move her down to the village."

"I don't know. I need ice. She shouldn't travel any more today."

"There's an ice house off Lacy Road north of Keene," Schermerhorn said. "But I'm not sure who'll let a lun. . .your wife in for a night."

"Keene? I've lost track of where we are," Joe said. "We're near Keene?"

"Yes."

"I have a friend in Keene who would put us up."

"Then why don't we split up like this," Schermerhorn said. Joe was relieved to have the trooper take charge. Quickly Schermerhorn explained that he would take the Ford, get ice and meet Joe at the friend's house. Dutton would drive the Cadillac so Joe could ride in the back with his wife.

"Let's do it," Joe said, and quickly drew directions to Jean-Paul's cabin in the sand.

Schermerhorn drove slowly down the narrow path to the trapper's cabin. The Ford rocked over the exposed roots of the towering white pines. The back seat carried a block of ice in a sawdust-filled wooden box.

He saw sun glancing off the tin roof before the actual cabin came into view. That must be Jean-Paul, Schermerhorn thought, taking in a small man with a trim black beard standing on the porch. His hands were in his pockets and a rifle hung casually off one arm. A big gray dog sat at the man's side.

He got out of the Ford and strode toward the porch. My God, he thought, eyeing the softly growling beast and noting its yellow eyes, that's a wolf.

"Hello," Schermerhorn said.

"*Comment ça va?*"

The trooper explained that Joe was coming with his dying wife.

"Marie," the trapper called, and went inside, leaving Schermerhorn alone with the wolf. Suddenly Earl Tierney's far-fetched story of how he lost his hand to a wolf came to mind. Could this be the wolf? Schermerhorn had no doubt those powerful jaws could cause considerable damage to the small bones in a hand.

And Joe Devlin called this trapper a friend. Was it Joe Devlin who had murdered Earl's brother like that bum insisted? There was much about Joe Devlin that Schermerhorn didn't have answers for. Like the whole other issue of possibly working for Dasset and trafficking in illegal intoxicants.

The wolf starting growling again, bringing Schermerhorn sharply back to the problem at hand. He heard the rumble of a car and soon the pea green Cadillac came into view.

Schermerhorn started down the steps only to be stopped by the wolf, who snarled menacingly. The trooper held his hands palms out toward the wolf and backed up the porch just as the trapper and a small black-haired woman came out of the house.

"Louie," Jean-Paul said, "come." The wolf stopped his growling and pushed his big head under the trapper's hand.

Schermerhorn was alone on the porch, chipping pieces from a block of ice as Joe and the trapper's woman settled Alice on the cabin's only bed. The trapper was building up a fire and Dutton had asked permission to stay in their Ford. "I'll do whatever's needed," Dutton had said, then lowered his voice before continuing, "I feel kind of queasy around tuberculars."

Inside, Marie sent Joe to clean up at the kitchen pump while she found a clean nightgown for Alice.

"You've been so kind to both of us," Alice whispered, while Marie helped her put her arms in the nightgown's sleeves.

"I knew Joe was a special man from the first time my Jean-Paul dragged him home half dead." Marie held a mug of cold herbal tea for Alice to sip. "I was very taken by his determination to be by your side. Hobbling into the mountains on frostbitten feet." Marie set the mug down and helped Alice to settle back on the pillows. "If you mean that much to a man like Joe, than you, too, must be special."

Marie picked up the two ten-pound shot bags. "Joe said to place these on your chest?"

"They can't help anymore," Alice murmured. "Not much time left." She ran her tongue across her bottom lip. "Joe must learn to let me go. Please. . ."

"I'll send Joe right in."

Joe knelt before the statue of the Virgin that Marie kept in the niche at the right of the river-stone fireplace. His eyes were closed and his head bent on his folded hands. Still bare-chested, he shivered now and then in the cold.

"Alice wants to see you," Marie said, dropping one of Jean-Paul's flannel shirts across his back.

Joe stood, jabbing his arms into the sleeves as he hurried through the curtain dividing the living quarters from the bedroom. She's leaving me, he thought, as he sat gently on the side of the bed. Alice's eyes fluttered open.

He tried to smile and reached for her hand.

"You're all cleaned up and prettier than ever."

"Don't remember me like this."

"Dear heart. . ."

"No, Joe." She stopped to cough. "I know it's time to go."

"But the ice. . .we've stopped the bleeding."

"Joe, please accept it. I have." Alice coughed and fell silent, catching her breath. "I will leave more easily knowing you'll get on with your life."

"Alice. . ."

"You've done all you can for me." Joe heard the gurgling in her chest. "Nothing more to do. Thank you for sharing your life with me."

"Oh, Alice, dear heart. You are my life."

Alice coughed and gasped for air, then coughed once more, bringing the bright red flow of her life with it. Her eyes closed and her shoulders relaxed.

Joe bent his head to the bed and sobbed. Forcing himself to do Alice's bidding, he brought to mind the young, healthy woman he married. He heard her laughter, and captured it to be relived again. It wasn't so much that she spent her days laughing, Joe realized, but rather that Alice had a lyrical way of speaking. She had a way of finding something good in whatever she talked about.

Joe remembered being captivated by the way Alice could find joy in such simple things, like preparing a meal or handing him a crisply ironed shirt to wear to work. Such everyday chores brought that golden light, like sunlight dancing off the water, to her blue eyes and a heartwarming lilt to her words.

When Marie woke him with a touch to the shoulder, the room was dark. He stood, stiff and forlorn.

"I loved her so much."

Marie took him in her arms. Soon he took a deep breath and walked to the porch.

"She's gone," he said to Jean-Paul and Sgt. Schermerhorn, who sat on the porch. "Thank you for all your help." Joe lowered himself heavily onto a porch step and looked out at the leaves falling in the forest. He heard a soft scuffling as John-Paul went inside and Schermerhorn settled himself on the step next to Joe.

"I'm sorry, Joe," the trooper said. "I 've seen how devoted you've been to her." They sat for a time with just the sound of the brook working its way around the smooth stones. "Jean-Paul said you plan to take your wife back to New York for burial."

Joe nodded.

The trooper moved the brim of his Stetson through his hands. He cleared his throat. "Joe, the thing is, there's something that needs clearing up before you leave the north country. I wish I could let this go till a better time. When I met Jean-Paul's trained wolf, it brought to mind a lot of accusations made by Earl Tierney."

"You know about Bruce?" Joe sat up straight and looked at the trooper.

"Yes. Finding a trained wolf and knowing Jean-Paul is a friend of yours helped me finally put it together. Jean-Paul told me everything while we were waiting for you."

"Are you going to arrest me?"

"Why don't you tell me what happened?"

Joe stared out at the forest. Soon he was picturing the heavy snow cover when Jean-Paul first brought him to the cabin. He smiled briefly when he recalled his first attempts at snowshoeing and Louie barking when he fell headlong in the deep snow.

Then he began to talk softly; he told of finding Earl and Bruce at the trapper's lean-to and the skirmish that followed. "Bruce had a pistol aimed at me when I fired the rifle," he explained.

When he was finished, Joe was surprised at how satisfying it felt to have confessed the whole mess. For a moment he considered telling Schermerhorn that he also carried booze. But he didn't know how to do that without involving Armand. He wasn't ready to do that. Without Armand he never could have paid all Alice's bills.

"Well, Joe," Schermerhorn said, "I believe you had a right to defend yourself. Your life was in danger." The trooper stood up and walked down the steps. He turned to look Joe in the eye. "There are several options. If I take you in, you'd probably spend months in jail waiting for trial. Even if they found you guilty, you'd never be executed. It was clearly self-defense. And you have Jean-Paul for a witness." Schermerhorn set his Stetson on his head and straightened the brim.

"I believe justice will be served and we'll save the county the expense of a jury trial if I close the investigation right here." He reached out to shake Joe's hand. "My condolences on your loss. I have a lot of admiration for the way you've stood by your wife."

"I appreciate your understanding," Joe said. "And your help today."

Schermerhorn turned to go. Halfway to the Ford, he turned back.

"Joe?"

Joe raised his head.

"I have some pretty strong suspicions about a pea green Cadillac."

"You have my word. No rum running," Joe said, watching Schermerhorn get into the Ford and drive slowly back along the rutted path. He mentally added the trooper to the list of good Adirondack people he had met this past year.

These mountains have a way of bringing out the very best or the very worst in people, he thought. He quickly ran through the list of those he had dealt with this past year. The kindnesses of Jean-Paul and Marie. And Kate. And Ursula's devotion to Alice.

Of course, if he lived to be a hundred he'd never understand the bitterness of men like Tom Madden or those who treated tuberculars like they weren't human.

"Well, God," Joe prayed, "Alice is in your hands now. Please take care of her."

The raucous cry of crows reached him from the tops of the evergreens, and from the forest floor the small brook spoke its simple message as it carried the last of the golden leaves past the trapper's log cabin. Joe watched the wolf move through the deep shadows and lower his head to drink the cold black water.